NOT MY FIRST (SPACE?) RODEO

NOT MY FIRST (SPACE?) RODEO

M. TALON

Podium

Podium

NOT MY FIRST (SPACE?) RODEO

CHAPTER ONE

HOW TO DRESS FOR THE APOCALYPSE

The minute before Earth's unlucky chosen representatives were abducted by the Reality Engine Exploitation Coalition, I was standing on Grandpa's porch, wearing his old duster and trying to remember not to raise my stirrup hoe in a way Deputy Young could take as threatening, while Sage clung to me, screaming that the nasty old lady was going to take her away—and to be fair, Delores the caseworker did have a face like a cat eating lemons.

There was a blinding flash of light and a whoosh, followed by a popping sound. My ears throbbed. I blinked away the purple-white afterimage and looked around.

I was still standing on my porch, holding the hoe. Sage stood in the trailer door, while the deputy and the social worker lady were in the yard in front of me. But we weren't on the Arizona Strip anymore. The circle of Grandpa's yard ended abruptly about ten feet past where Deputy Young was standing.

The front half of the deputy's truck was still parked in that circle. The other half was gone. Outside the circle was swampland. An enormous translucent box filled my vision with words.

A voice started talking inside my head. It was a man's voice, sounding like an overly enthusiastic airport announcer. He rumbled like he was about to introduce a batting lineup.

[Welcome, Earthling! You have been selected as one of Earth's representatives in your System's attempt to claim the local Reality Engine for your species!]

"What the hell is going on?"

Sage was yelling, the deputy was shouting.

The words in the glowing box scrolled upward as the voice read off the text.

**[You have been placed in an attunement chamber.
According to the agreement reached between this Reality Engine
and the Exploitation coalition, you will be allowed to progress
in your quest if, and only if, you succeed in acquiring one Soul Coin
in the next ten standard hours.
Succeed, and you will be permitted access into the Portal Antechamber
of this Reality Engine. Fail, and you will be unable to exit the
attunement chamber before it closes.]**

I turned, and the box followed me as the announcer kept talking. Deputy Young and Delores the caseworker were shouting. But I didn't care about them. Sage stood transfixed, her eyes focused on the air, maybe reading the same words I was.

"Grandpa!" I said. "Where's Grandpa?"

I pushed past Sage into the trailer, or what was left of the trailer. Right through the door was the main room. Most of it remained intact, but the far wall was torn off like a tornado hit us. Beyond, I could see the swamp. Trees hung with Spanish moss spread their lichen-stained branches against a gray sky.

The circle from outside went through our trailer, shaving off half of it. Grandpa lay on his hospital bed in the middle of the room. He looked up at me, saying weakly, "What the hell is all this, boy?"

His once-bright eyes were dim with illness, and his chest rattled badly as he tried to speak. I leaned in closer. "If this is the Rapture the Baptists were always on about, I'll just see myself to the hot place," he gasped, and fell back among his pillows.

His hospital gown had slipped off one shoulder, showing his weathered medicine pouch and, dangling from the same leather thong, my abuela's Miraculous Medal. That was my grandpa; always sardonic, even while dying. Always ready with a side-comment. Another wave of pain swept me at the sight of him so frail. It'd been six months since I last saw him—six months to go from a strong, hearty man in his sixties to . . . this.

The voice and the scroll of text finished together. **[So, good luck, and happy mining!]** The box vanished. The voice went silent.

Mining? Reality Engine? What was going on?

Earthling. Earth representative. Meaning whoever was talking wasn't from Earth. They were—I didn't like the world *alien*. Made me think of little green men.

Another box appeared. This one read:

**[Shad Williams
Level 1 Unclassified Miner**

**Skills: Choose a class to gain access to skills.
Class selection currently locked.
Title(s): Corporal
HP: 20]**

It knew my name—my preferred name, not the Shadrach on all my government IDs—and my rank. There was miner again. Miner, mining. Aliens had abducted me to mine an asteroid, maybe? And HP? All I could think of were health points, like in a game.

Sage popped through the door. "Where are we? What happened?" she asked. "Come help, I think the caseworker lady is about to lose it."

I followed her and took a look.

Tall cypress and tupelo leaned over banks of crumbling mud, frogs croaked unseen, some kind of bird trilled in the Spanish moss-covered branches. Something moved just under the surface of the murky water, a bit farther away. I hoped it wasn't a gator.

It looked just like a place I'd seen when I took leave to visit a friend for Mardi Gras. He turned out not to actually be from New Orleans, but a place "just up the river." In other words, this looked to be about fifteen hundred miles from the Arizona Strip. Not possible.

The yard around the trailer was turning to mud as water ran in from outside the circle of Arizona we'd brought with us.

Delores scrambled out of the mud onto the porch. Her white linen slacks were caked with dirt, and even through her horn-rimmed glasses, I could see mascara bleeding into her turquoise eye shadow. "Deputy! Get me out of here, *right now!*"

I boggled. It hadn't registered before, but over her head, and Young's, and Sage's, were glowing blue labels—in her case, **[Delores Atigua, Level 1]**—and a green bar. Like a health bar in a damn video game.

"Well now, ma'am, can't really say where we are, but if you'll give me a minute, I'm working on it." He turned to me, frowning, but lowered his piece. "Young Shad, you got any idea what's going on here?"

"No, sir." I stood a bit straighter, my military experiences reinforcing a whole misspent youth where the difference between a warning and a night in the precinct's detention cell was in how I impressed Young, or one of his fellow officers of the law.

"Didn't you get the admin message?" Sage cocked her head to one side. She wasn't nearly as terrified as I'd expected. In fact, her dark eyes sparkled. "We've been selected for initiation. We just need to find a Soul Coin. I s'pose after that, we'll get the next step of the quest."

"This is *not* a suitable environment for a young girl!" Delores said.

I ignored Delores, as I'd been wanting to do all morning. I didn't like social workers. After Mom found meth and Dad found Meg—and Sarah, and Juanita, and Alice—the social workers bounced me and Sage around between four homes, never together, until Grandpa found out and brought the full weight of the Indian Child Welfare Act down on them. He even registered with the Kaibab band, which he'd sworn never to do after the way those jerks treated him back in the 80s when he married Abuela—but that was almost a decade ago now, and hopefully Sage didn't remember any of it.

"We gotta find a way out of here—" Deputy Young started to say.

Something huge erupted out of the water.

I ducked back instinctively, raising my arm to shield myself. A spray of muck hit me in the face. Wild music started pounding in my head, like something from a German dance party. I'd been to my share of those while stationed over there. This had that same thump-thump-thump pounding bass, while a female voice yowled in some language I couldn't make out.

The announcer suddenly became more animated, enunciating like a prizefight caller. [**It's a Fanged Spit-Toad, Level 3, common reptiloid, venomous!**] A blinking box appeared in my view. I waved my hand furiously, trying to clear my vision.

"Get inside with Grandpa!" I shouted over the invisible speaker, and Sage splashed back to the bed, her face pale.

"It said level three and we're only level one! Be careful!"

I had bigger things to worry about, literally, as a huge, Smart Car–sized creature erupted from the murk. There was no way something that large could have been under the knee-high water.

It was bright pink and orange spotted, its huge, silvery multifaceted eyes bulged out of its head like disco balls, and it was heading right for me. It had a health bar. A great big green health bar that read [**40/40**], and all I could think was, *That's twice what I have.*

The prizefight announcer guy kept talking. [**So what if toads are amphibians, not reptiles? He doesn't care. You're in his swamp, and now you're lunch!**]

I swung my hoe. It was a five-foot-long fiberglass pole with a loop of metal at the end. You pull sagebrush and tumbleweeds out by the root with a stirrup hoe, not chop through them. As a weapon, it was slightly better than nothing. I struck the monster toad in the face. It let out an earsplittingly loud "*blarp!*" and then puked rainbows all over.

A floating [**-1 HP**] appeared over the toad, and its health bar dropped just a bit.

I dodged to the side, avoiding the stinking, multicolored spew that just kept coming out of the toad's mouth as it landed on its haunches in the swamp. A couple drops hit my oilcloth sleeve and started smoking. The toad's eyes rotated balefully in their sockets, gleaming and winking.

Deputy Young shouted and raised his pistol. He fired off eight rounds, right at the creature from about fifteen feet away, and I saw all the bullets hit the toad's flesh. They tore great big holes in its side, much larger than I expected for nine-millimeter rounds. The toad blarped again and shifted, facing the deputy. I saw its legs crouching to spring.

I shouted and threw myself forward, smashing the hoe into the toad hard and knocking it aside. A big yellow box saying **[Stunned!]** appeared over its head. I scrambled back.

"It's working!" Sage yelled. "Its health is going down!"

I censored a *no shit*.

"That hit took it to yellow! I think that's halfway!" she called again.

I checked. She was right. The bar was yellow, and it said **[15/40]**. Young's bullets had done more than my hoe, for sure.

[Stunned!] went away. The toad lashed out with its tongue. I dove aside, but it wasn't going for me; it was after Young. It wrapped around his torso and pulled him off his feet, toward the toad.

Young fired off another couple of rounds wildly, meaning he probably only had four or five left. "Stop that! You'll hit us!" I shouted, but he wasn't hearing me. He fired again as the toad yanked him right into its mouth. The gun flew from his hand and splashed into the steaming, multicolored muck the toad had vomited.

That was when I saw the fangs. The description had tried to warn us, but I wasn't ready for foot-long gleaming crystal daggers. Young's whole body was almost inside the toad's mouth, about to get crunched. I could still see his health bar floating over him; it was yellow and dropping. **[6/20]**.

I dropped the hoe handle and seized Young's legs. Yanking as hard as I could, I dragged him back from the toad. The tongue fought, but now Young was fighting back. He'd drawn a knife—how, I didn't know—and slashed blindly. One swing connected, half severing the tongue. I yanked harder, and Young jerked free. We stumbled backward.

Young's uniform was in tatters. Smoke rose off him. His face was a mess, covered in toad vomit, and he screamed as he tried to wipe his eyes. "It stings! It stings!"

Delores was shrieking somewhere behind me. I'd forgotten about her. Sage was shouting, but I had no time to worry about them. I needed a weapon. My hoe was fifteen feet away, the gun was gone, but Young had the right idea. Any weapon in a pinch.

I stooped and grabbed a handful of muck. I threw it at the toad's good eye and hit the center of the glistening orb. I'd always had good aim. Mud splattered across the gleaming facets.

The toad leapt for us. I grabbed Young's arm and yanked him clear. The toad slammed heavily against the side of the trailer and flipped back, splattering us with mud. It came to a stop half in, half out of the water.

"Shad!"

Sage stood on the porch, a short-barreled revolver in her hand, her eyes huge with fear through her glasses. I knew that gun: Grandpa's Ruger Alaskan. Fully loaded with six rounds of .44 Magnum. It was a boat anchor of a gun I had mocked him for buying. Home defense was one thing, but the Alaskan was more like overcompensation when carried in a country lacking in grizzly bears.

Right now, it was the most beautiful thing I'd ever seen.

Sage threw it in a long, high arc like a pop fly.

Throwing a gun was a terrible idea, and I'd scold her for it at any other time, but right now I dove for that gun like right field going for a line drive. The toad croaked and turned for me. I caught the revolver, cradling it to my chest as I landed on my back in the mud. My view of the grim sky was obscured by an enormous falling toad.

I raised the gun, thumbed back the hammer, and shot three rounds, one after another, right into it. The toad received a [**-5 HP**] for each one.

A box popped up.

[You have bonded: Ruger Alaskan, .44 Magnum.
This weapon may no longer be equipped by another miner.]

The toad missed me, landing hard nearby and slipping down into the water with a splash. Chunks of toad flesh rained down all around. I scrambled up, trying to keep the muzzle trained on the body. The toad's body looked like I'd hit it with a grenade. Something about this place seemed to mean guns hit a lot harder than normal. Its health bar was gone, leaving a wan **[0/40]** over its corpse.

There was a burst of cheerful fanfare and a giant notification popped up. **[Winner!]** Then a bunch of different achievements scrolled through my vision, almost too fast to read. Something about hitting a mob with a ranged weapon, giving me a bonus to using firearms. Another for using environmental elements as improvised weapons, probably for throwing the mud. One stuck out in particular: **[Achievement! Damage an Enemy With a Firearm, 1/100.]** That looked like something that would progress as time went on.

I brushed them off and walked over to the toad to check on it.

The toad was dead, all right. Its head had exploded. The multifaceted eyes were glazed over in death. They didn't look so much like disco balls now.

"Are you all right?" I asked Sage, but Deputy Young answered.

"My eyes—I'm blind! I think it broke my ribs." He leaned over and coughed, wincing in pain as he did. His health bar was red. **[3/20]**. He was in bad shape. I'd have to help him inside and find the first aid kit while we tried to figure out how to call 911 from here.

I set a hand on the disgusting toad and another box popped up.

[Fanged Spit-Toad. Killed by Shad Williams, assist from Frank Young. Loot first choice to Shad Williams.]

Then a list:

**[1 Toad Spleen (crafting ingredient, poisonous)
1 Partially Digested Swamp Fly
1 Soul Coin]**

"I can see that!" Young said. "How come I see that and nothing else?"
I took my hand off the toad, and the box changed.

[You have passed. Loot given to Frank Young.]

"Hey, wait!" I yelled at the sky. "I didn't pass, I didn't do anything."
"What's all this—wait, what's happening to me?"
I looked over at Young. The deputy, still bent over, began to glow. A golden light enveloped him. He reached skyward, a look of ecstasy on his face.

His health bar shot all the way back up to full green. The glow vanished. He opened his eyes. "I can see," he said, as a grin spread across his face. "My ribs don't hurt—the message says I have attuned, and will have access to a class after the introductory phase." He frowned. "Don't want a class about all this shit, I want to get out of here and back to the Strip."

"It's not that kind of class." I could hear Sage rolling her eyes as she spoke.

"What just happened?" I asked, but Delores, who had finally stopped screaming, stepped forward. She scrutinized Young.

"Frank, you look like you did fifteen years ago. You just lost twenty pounds and I think your hair's growing back."

I had been so overwhelmed, I hadn't noticed, but she was right. Whatever had happened to Young, he looked way healthier than he had when he'd heaved himself out of his Explorer back on Grandpa's property.

"I absorbed the soul coin, and it attuned me. Dunno what that means, but I like it." Frank held up a hand, staring at it. "I had a scar on my wrist; it's gone too. What the hell is happening?"

"I want one!" Delores turned on me with a wild, hungry look in her eyes. "I need one of those soul coins. Right now."

But I wasn't looking at her, I was staring over the dead toad's bulk at Sage, and she was nodding, because she'd just had the same thought I did. I slogged through the muck and leaned over to mutter in her ear. "We need to get one for Grandpa. Right now."

CHAPTER TWO

HOW TO HANDLE COMMON GARDEN PESTS

Whoa!" Deputy Young looked around, swinging his head around like one of those dashboard bobbleheads.

"What is it?" I tried to follow his gaze, but all I saw was a swamp around me and the remnants of Grandpa's trailer and yard.

"Everything is glowing," Young said. "It's like I can see the outlines of everything all lit up." He glanced at Delores, who had squelched up onto the nearest bank and was glaring angrily down at us.

"What does it say?" Sage started bouncing up and down in the mucky water. "Tell me everything! Shad, you've got to get me a soul coin as soon as possible."

"Once I've got mine, the rest of you can do what you like," Delores called back. "Hurry up. We don't want to be too late. What if someone else gets all of them?"

"Hang on a minute." I turned to Sage. "You stay here and keep Grandpa safe. If there's a chance a soul coin can fix him up like it did the deputy, we'll try it."

"We're level one. That means there's a level two. I want to go with you and earn XP!"

"What are you talking about?" Deputy Young looked like he didn't have a clue what she was talking about. I did. I'd spent plenty of time as a kid playing video games of various sorts. We didn't get good internet out where Grandpa lived, miles from anything in the Arizona Strip, but there were still plenty of games that didn't need internet connection, and I'd amassed quite a library before going off to basic training. It seemed Sage had inherited my library.

"I'll explain later. We need to find another soul coin, and I guess that means finding another monster. Maybe we can find something a little smaller than that toad."

I looked down at my grandfather's revolver, still in my hand. I cracked open the cylinder and double-checked. Three rounds with dimpled primers, three still ready to go. I took the empty brass out and started to toss it away, but Sage grabbed my hand. "Don't do that! They could be useful. We don't throw anything away until we know whether it's got value to us."

"Spent brass? You think we're gonna find a reloading press out here?"

"You never know." Sage took the brass from me and put them in the pocket of her jeans. She pulled out a speed loader with another six rounds of .44 Magnum. "It was under Grandpa's pillow with the gun."

"So that's where you found the gun." I should have known Grandpa wouldn't be far from a firearm, not even bedbound and half incoherent. Actually, he'd always favored traditional weapons like a bow and arrow or a good knife, but I knew he appreciated that a firearm in the hands of a sick man was a better choice. I just wished he'd picked something a little more modern, something with a nineteen-round capacity and a bunch of spare magazines. How he'd expected to use this hand cannon in his frail state was beyond me. "You don't happen to have any spare .44 Magnum on you, Deputy?"

Deputy Young shook his head. "No. I've got three spare magazines of nine-millimeter, but I don't see where my gun went."

"Look over there near the toad's body." Sage pointed to where the giant orange polka-dotted toad bobbed up and down in a scum of rainbow-colored puke and mud.

"No way I'm gonna find anything." Deputy Young took off his hat and scratched his head before replacing the wide-brimmed fedora. "Besides, that shit's like acid. I'm not putting my hand in there."

"You've got that enhanced vision now. Maybe you'll be able to spot it."

Looking dubious, Deputy Young waded over to where we had fought the monster toad. I followed him over. My stirrup hoe was still stuck in the toad's eye. I planted one foot against its side, feeling it give under my boot, and yanked hard. The hoe came free. Its end was all covered in slime, but I felt better having it.

Deputy Young looked around, and I could tell what he was thinking as easily as if I were hearing him speak. No chance. Then, suddenly, he let out a sharp exclamation, bent over, and fished his gun out of the swamp. It was covered in muck, but there it was. He waded back. "You were right! Once I got over there and looked, I could see something in the water glowing. It was highlighted blue, not like all the yellow and white text I'm seeing everywhere else."

"Maybe that's because it belongs to you," Sage said, nodding her head gravely. "We'll know more once the rest of us get our coins." She held up her hand, palm up, with one of the brass casings on it. "Does this look special to you at all? Any extra text? I wanna know if it's a crafting item, like the toad spleen."

Deputy Young was too busy looking at his gun. "It says durability, nine out of ten. What the hell does that mean?"

"I knew it! Nine out of ten almost certainly means we can reload these . . . somehow."

The deputy stared at Sage like she had two heads. "How do you know all of this?"

Sage shrugged. "It's just a game system. I've played plenty of games. My favorite part is always figuring out the rules, and how to exploit them in ways the developers never intended."

From across the way, Delores the social worker cupped her hands to her mouth and yelled, "I see something moving over there! I'm going to just—" She let out a scream and vanished, toppling backward out of sight.

Deputy Young and I took off running at the same moment, splashing mud and water all around. The speed loader was a comforting weight in my pocket. I should have already reloaded those three missing rounds. No way I could load the cylinder while running.

The drovers coat flapped at my ankles wetly as I squelched up out of the water onto another mud bank. There was no sign of Delores, but I heard a scream from not far off. The deputy was swearing as he ran. "Damn woman's gonna get us all killed."

I put my head down and concentrated on running, stirrup hoe in one hand, gun in the other. The screaming kept moving farther off, way faster than I thought Delores could have made it through this swamp. Something must have her. A little voice in the back of my head warned, *Maybe you shouldn't be getting so far away from Sage and Grandpa.*

I skidded to a halt as we burst through some low-hanging branches, passing a hand across my face to clear the Spanish moss that I'd just run through from my eyes.

There was an open space here between giant spreading oak trees. The ground was muddy, but more or less solid. A ring of knee-high, bright red toadstools, that looked for all the world like they'd been painted just now by an overly cheerful forest fairy, stood in the clearing.

The ring was about twenty feet across. In the center of the ring, Delores lay in a crumpled heap. Her pantsuit was completely bedraggled with mud, but I couldn't see any blood from here. She faced away from us. Deputy Young charged past me.

"Wait!" I shouted. "It's a trap!"

I felt something grabbing at my leg and threw myself to the side just in time, tripping over a root and going sprawling. The hoe flew out of my grip and went flying.

[Toadstool Gnomes, Level 2, common humanoid, pack!] The WWE announcer was back, shouting the words in my ears. What the hell was a toadstool gnome? [**They're mean. They've got teeth like a shark, an attitude three times bigger than them, and you're in their house now!**]

Too late to stop himself, Deputy Young stumbled into the ring of toadstools. His boot caught the nearest toadstool, knocking it over. Instead of going flying, the toadstool let out a deep booming noise, like a drum.

Then a wave of tiny people poured out of the trees all around us. There must have been a dozen or more of them. They were about two feet tall and wore bright blue caps just like I'd seen on every garden gnome statue I'd been unfortunate enough to run across. They had long white beards matted down to their knees, and as best I could tell, wore nothing else. They had sharp daggers in each hand. Each of them had a little health bar over their head. Their health all read [**4/4**].

Young started firing. A couple of the gnomes screamed and fell as the rest swarmed him. I had my revolver, but even if I made every shot count, there were too many of them. I got back up to one knee, taking up a kneeling shooting stance, one leg forward of the other.

I didn't want to tangle with them up close if I didn't have to. I took careful aim and shot one of the little men right in the head. It blew up in a cloud of red mist, the body dropping into the muck. "Whoa!" Like with the toad, my bullets were doing five points of damage.

I shifted my aim and fired again. This time I winged one in the shoulder. It tumbled away, shrieking, hat and knife flying in opposite directions, but still took three damage. One round left.

But I had made myself a target. Four of them turned to face me. I squeezed off my last shot, turning another gnome into a pile of hat and beard bits. The other three came running.

I laid my empty gun aside and snatched up the hoe from where it lay. They came at me in a tight knot. I stepped forward and swung, digging low like a batter chasing a slider.

I hit all three, low and hard. One went flying. He bounced three times before rolling to a rest in the mud. His health bar vanished. [**0/4**]. One just went down dead at my feet, while the third must have gotten the least of it, because he bounced right back up and threw himself at me. [**2/4**].

I saw wild, dark eyes filled with rage, teeth barred, and a knife heading straight for my nether regions. *Oh fuck.* I didn't have time to think. I just reacted. I kicked out as hard as I could, and I punted that gnome like a football. He flew twenty feet, landing in a heap inside the toadstool ring next to Delores. [**0/4**].

Deputy Young was fighting off three of them. Each had taken a point or two of damage but was still biting and kicking furiously. More gnome bodies littered the forest floor.

I charged toward Deputy Young, holding the stirrup hoe high. I brought it down hard on the gnome that had wrapped itself around his legs.

The hoe gave a satisfying thunk, taking the gnome's remaining three HP off, along with its head. These guys were certainly a lot more fragile than that giant toad had been.

One gnome was wrapped around Deputy Young's head. It had apparently lost its dagger and was gnawing at the deputy's ear. I grabbed for it, but ended up with a handful of hat. Instead of coming free, the hat stayed firmly attached to the tiny head. I yanked, snapping the gnome's head back, and threw the little asshole away from the deputy. It bounced off a cypress tree and landed in a heap nearby. I stood over the dazed creature and swung the stirrup hoe in a blow that would've uprooted the most stubborn sagebrush. Overkill, since it only had one HP left.

The gnome exploded in yellow and red fragments of gore. It splattered all over my legs and coated Deputy Young in gnome guts.

Deputy Young had gotten both his hands around the neck of the final gnome. He screamed as he throttled the creature. I waited until it went still, breathing hard as I watched. The deputy slumped over, shaking.

A **[Winner!]** message popped up. The system announcer wound down his spiel and fell silent. More notifications scrolled past, including a progress update on my Damage an Enemy With a Firearm achievement, which was now at **[5/100]**.

First thing I did was walk over to the middle of the circle to check on Delores. She was a crumpled heap on the ground, her head a mass of gore. I knew she was dead without even touching her, since her health bar was gone and a **[0/20]** floated over her head, but I knelt at her side and checked her pulse anyway. Nothing. Her body had even started to cool. I bowed my head. I hadn't liked the woman, hadn't liked any social worker. She'd been trying to take my sister away from me and my grandpa. But she hadn't deserved this. Ripped away from her home, thrown into some sort of sick, twisted game, and then murdered by these creepy little gnomes.

"Is she . . . ?"

I stood up and stepped away from her body. "Yeah."

Deputy Young didn't have anything else to say. He turned to look at the gnomes we had killed. "Where the hell did these things come from?"

He kicked one of them with the toe of his leather boots.

Next thing I knew, another one of those boxes appeared, this one again with a list of loot. Right at the top, it said,

[Twelve Toadstool Gnomes
Killed by: Shad Williams and Frank Young
Kills apportioned according to contribution.
Result:
Seven gnomes allocated to Frank Young, five allocated to Shad Williams.
Do you want to change default loot options now?]

Then there was a list of items below. A total of twelve soul coins, some gnome hats, and something called Toadstool Elixir.

"Holy—" Young exclaimed. "It's offering me all sorts of things I don't understand. All about loot. What's all this mean?"

I had a pretty good idea, but I wasn't going to go into it right now. "Let's get back to Sage and Grandpa and talk about it there." I mentally focused on the default option in the box, and next thing I knew, there was a chime of music playing in my head and a little bag in my hand. The bag was a little smaller than my fist. It looked like leather, dyed dark blue. It was heavy. I hefted it, and it clinked. I peered inside. Shining silver tokens stared back at me.

"Are these soul coins?" Young asked. He didn't have a bag of his own.

"This isn't what it looked like when you got one before?"

"It appeared in my hand then. But it just sort of sank in as soon as I touched it. It says I got loot, but I don't see any. Says looted to inventory."

"We'll figure that out in a minute. Let's get back to Grandpa and Sage before something happens to them."

CHAPTER THREE

HOW TO CLEAN UP A HOARDER'S STASH

We made it back to Sage and Grandpa pretty quick. Sage was looking terrified, and as I appeared, she hurried over and gave me a big hug.

"I was so scared. We heard the screaming, and then it just stopped. Where's Delores?"

I shook my head. "She didn't make it." Sage's face went white. Wanting to change the subject quick, I opened up the bag and held it out to Sage. "But look."

"Are those—?"

"Soul coins. Yeah." I reached into the bag, intending to take out a coin and hand it to Sage. Instead, as my fingers touched the first one, a wave of light rushed over me. Swelling orchestral music chimed. My whole body tensed, shook, quivered. It was like goosebumps, all over me. I stood, struck dumb by what was going on. The sensation rose in pitch, then died away.

Sage touched my arm. "Are you all right?" She looked up at me, her wide, dark eyes full of fear. "Was that . . . ?"

"I don't know—"

The announcer spoke in my head, not out loud.

[Miner Shad Williams, you are now attuned to this Reality Engine. Certain status and menu options will not be available until you have chosen a class.]

I blinked away another series of achievements. The last one hung around for a minute:

[Miner! You have taken the first step down a long path that could lead to untold riches—or your untimely death. Achievement step: Attuned. Next step: Class Choice. Complete next step for further progress details. Class Choice is disabled at this time.]

My eyes felt sharper than usual. The day around me seemed brighter than it had been a moment ago, but I was pretty sure we were still getting the same gloomy light filtering through the trees in the swamp.

I looked over at Grandpa. He had a health bar, too, naturally. Instead of the green bar over me and Sage, it was yellow, and there was an icon next to it that I didn't like the look of. It looked uncomfortably like a skull and crossbones to me. [8/20] health points remained.

I dug into the pouch, reaching for another coin.

This time, it didn't dissolve in my hand. It sat there, shining up at me. It was about a half-dollar size, silvery, and the face looking up at me was not remotely human. It reminded me a bit of Medusa, with lots of squiggly snakes all around it. Or maybe it was some sort of odd, stylized halo. A faint suggestion of features, perhaps too many eyes and a gaping mouth. Details really weren't clear. I wasn't sure I liked it.

I hesitated for just a minute. "Sage, I don't know what this is going to do to him."

"I know." She bit her lip, looking much older than her eleven years. "But it can't make things any worse."

She was right about that. I took the coin and set it on Grandpa's outstretched hand. He was unconscious again, his eyes twitching gently underneath his eyelids.

As I set the coin on his wrinkled palm, a light enveloped him. It started out pretty dim, but grew in intensity, deeper and deeper, until I had to look away. Deputy Young hadn't been nearly that bright.

Sage gasped. "You didn't look anything like that. It's like he's on fire."

I stood back, my stomach churning. It was too late now. What was done was done. The light grew so bright, it enveloped the whole hospital bed he was now standing on.

There was a triumphal crash of cymbals.

I blinked. When I opened my eyes again, the hospital bed was empty. I yelled.

"Grandpa!" Sage called, looking around.

"Right here, you two."

I turned.

He couldn't have been more than ten years older than me. His skin was a dark walnut color, his long, dark hair in two braids behind his back. He was wearing a nightgown and pajamas, and his feet were in oversized bedroom slippers. His bright green health bar was maxed out at [20/20].

"Grandpa?"

"Who else would it be, you young whippersnappers?" He grinned at us, white teeth sparkling. Grandpa had lost most of his teeth in the last couple of years, the victim of poor childhood nutrition and inferior dental care available on the reservation lands where he'd grown up.

He lifted a hand, holding it up to the light. "Well, that's something. Where the hells are we?"

"I don't know, but it sure isn't Arizona." I shrugged. "One minute we were at home, the next we were here."

Sage turned back to me. "My turn!" She held out a hand. "We can't progress the game until we've all got a soul coin. They were very clear about that."

"Game? Soul coins?" Grandpa glared at us. "What have you gotten us into? For a minute, I thought I must be back in Vietnam, with all the mud and green shit. Well, this isn't 'Nam." He peered around us. "Trees all wrong."

"No, looks more like Louisiana to me," I agreed. "But it isn't either of those. Someone picked us all up and brought us here."

"Someone?" He cocked his head. "Who?"

"I'm not sure," I began, but Sage interrupted.

"It was aliens, Grandpa. Obviously. How else would we be wherever we are?"

Deputy Young wandered over. He held a hand out to Grandpa. "Mr. Twofeather, I must say, I'm glad for you. You look good. Healthy."

Grandpa looked down at himself. "I feel good. Like I just had a good night's sleep for the first time in years. Don't know what happened, but I'm not in pain anymore. That's something."

Meanwhile, Sage had taken a soul coin from me. Just like the rest of us, she glowed like a Christmas tree for a minute.

The light died away, and Sage opened her eyes. "Wow. That was something. More achievements. Some of them seemed important."

She shook herself and took a step away from the hospital bed. She jumped. I watched her with amusement.

Then she took three big steps through the muck. After that, she reached down, grabbed a rock, and hurled it as far as she could. She wrinkled her nose in disgust.

"No improvement in my strength. I can't jump or walk any farther than I could before, and it doesn't feel like anything else has really happened to me yet. Darn it . . . I was hoping for some major stat buffs right off. I feel different, somehow, it just isn't translating into any abilities yet." She peered into the swamp, then took off her glasses. She blinked. "Oh. Oh wow. I can see perfectly! Shad, this is great!"

Young just stared at her. "What the hell do you think you're doing?"

"Obviously, I'm trying to find out what abilities the game has given us."

"Game?" Grandpa took a look around and snorted. "What the hell sort of game is this?"

We were interrupted by Airport Guy again.

**[Congratulations! All surviving members of your party have absorbed
a soul coin and been accepted by the Reality Engine.
You may now proceed to an exit. The closest exit has been marked
on your mini-map.]**

Thinking about a map caused a square to blink in the left corner of my vision. I focused on it and it burst open across my field of view. After a couple of tries and some quick exchanges with Sage, I learned how to focus on a particular section at will.

There was an icon in one corner that, when I focused on it, let me resize and move the map center point around. After that, I moved the map to one side. If I wasn't staring at it directly, the map was a translucent outline. I could get used to that.

Off to the northwest, a point blinked red, presumably the exit.

"The initiation briefing said something about ten standard hours before the next phase. We need to get to the exit before then," Sage said.

That brought me back to my senses. "Yeah, and we've had two life-or-death fights already." I turned to Grandpa. "There's stuff in these swamps that'll eat you as soon as look at you. Giant toads. Gnomes. Weird stuff. Don't take anything for granted. Delores the caseworker just found out the hard way."

"I'm not going anywhere," Deputy Young began.

Sage was ignoring us. She had found the bag of loot I'd dropped when I got back. She opened it up and peered inside, first taking out a blue gnome hat, then a wad of something sticky-looking.

Her eyes widened. "Some of these are marked as crafting items. Oh, we've got an inventory now! Look!"

I figured out how to get my inventory at the same time and told Grandpa what to do. It was pretty straightforward, I just needed to think about it. Sage began taking items from the sack of loot. As she held each one, it vanished into her inventory. Her eyebrows knit together as she concentrated, and one of the gnome hats appeared out of thin air into her hands. It vanished again. "All right!"

Grandpa was moving toward the door into his bedroom. He poked his head in and stared around at the mess. I looked over his shoulder. About a third of his room was still there. The rest was shaved off, presumably left behind in Arizona. Half his bed stood against one wall. A chest of drawers had been left, and a pair of forlorn pictures.

He went over to the chest of drawers and started rummaging through, pulling out clothes and tossing a few on the bed. The rest disappeared into his inventory. "At least I kept my hunting gear." He pulled open the bottom drawer and took out a heavy pair of camo-patterned pants and his good hunting vest, blaze orange and tan. He glared at me. "Shut the door. I want to get dressed."

I shut the door behind me, feeling foolish since the rest of the room was open to the air, and turned back to where Sage was looting our trailer. She picked up items and they disappeared. "As far as I can tell, the inventory doesn't have any kind of storage limit. That's good. I always hate inventory management in games. Hmm."

She had lifted an open cardboard box full of knickknacks that stood beside the table. It didn't disappear. "I wonder if it's because it's full of other items." She took one item out and it vanished into her inventory, then a couple more, and then all of a sudden, the basket itself disappeared. "Oh, I got it below my personal lift limit, whatever that is, and then it let me pick it up. Huh." Sage started picking up and setting down random things around the room. "It looks like my limit is about fifteen pounds. Here, try this."

She pointed at a half-packed box of books. We'd been packing up Grandpa's things in preparation to clear out the trailer after he passed, and a lot of the house was already in boxes.

I lifted the box and was given the option to add it to my inventory. I said yes, and the box disappeared. It appeared in my inventory, labeled as "box of books" and stating that it was collected in Grandpa's house.

"That's not fair," Sage said when she saw the box disappear. "Your weight limit must be higher than mine."

Grandpa emerged from his bedroom looking like he was dressed for the first day of deer season. His shirt was a little tight on him. He'd obviously gained weight and muscle mass back from when he'd bought these clothes a few years ago.

"Of course, they left my gun cabinet behind in Arizona," he said in disgust. "But here." He tossed me two boxes of .44 Magnum. I caught both and added them to my inventory quickly. One hundred rounds. Good. I didn't know what else was out there, but at least now I'd be prepared.

I thought about it, and six rounds popped out in my hand. I loaded my gun, then loaded the speed loader. I dropped both into the pocket of my drovers coat.

Grandpa looked at Sage, who was over in the kitchen section of the main room. The fridge was gone, but some of the cabinets beside the stove were still here. She was opening the cabinets and grabbing every box, can, dish, and bottle of spice in them and tossing them all into her inventory. "What's she doing?"

I explained. Grandpa nodded. "Good thinking. We can't stay here, but I don't want to leave anything behind."

A message popped up in the corner of my vision.

Party chat: Sage: Look what we can do!

I concentrated and a blinking cursor appeared. I tried thinking the words. Nothing. I mumbled under my breath, and my reply appeared. *Stop playing around. We need to get moving.*

Sage: *I'm looting and talking at the same time. Take everything. No weight limit = loot the world!*

CHAPTER FOUR

WHERE DOES FASHION WEEK FIND ITS STUFF, ANYWAY?

Grandpa pushed past the hospital bed where he had so recently lay dying and glared at it in disgust, then picked it up and added it to his inventory. "Who knows?" he said at my look. The IV pole followed.

He crossed over to the couch that stood against the remaining wall of our living room. I explained about the weight limit. "What if we both pick it up?"

We gave it a try, but even with the couch lifted a foot into the air, it refused to go into either inventory. We put it back down, took the cushions off, and returned to looting.

Deputy Young wandered in. "My AR was in the back half of my SUV," he said in disgust. "All I've got is my sidearm. Found a couple more magazines, though."

"We're taking everything, whether or not we think it's helpful," I told him. "Anything you can put in your inventory, grab. We'll strip the truck in a minute. Grab the battery, anything we can take."

He nodded and went back out as Grandpa lifted one of the display axes from the wall and hefted it. The trio had hung over the couch for as long as I could remember. One was a genuine obsidian stone axe his grandfather had knapped a hundred years ago. It was bound to its wooden handle by leather strips that Grandpa replaced every few years. It disappeared into his inventory, and then he took down the other two axes. One was a fancy steel tomahawk with a carved and painted handle that my mother had made years ago as a teenager. The other axe was a cheap but sharp gardening tool like you could buy at any big-box hardware store. Grandpa had a whole series of lectures about those axes. How the stone one of them represented days, maybe even weeks, of a man's effort. How the modern axe was churned out by the thousands at some factory in India. I forgot what his point had been.

He wasn't in the mood for any lectures today. Instead, he stuck both of the steel axes through loops of his belt. He had a bowie knife and a sheath already.

"Got any more knives like that?" I asked, pointing.

Grandpa shook his head. "I did. It was in the part of my room that isn't here."

"Want a kitchen knife?" Sage asked brightly. The sharpest vegetable cutting knife appeared in one hand, our meat cleaver in the other. I took the vegetable knife and put it in my inventory.

Sage opened the door into her room. It was even less intact than Grandpa's had been. Her bed was gone, and so was her dresser. A basket by the door held a pile of dirty laundry, while a shelf displayed her knickknacks. Sage picked everything up and added it to her inventory. She left out one pair of jeans and a ratty-looking T-shirt. She had been wearing her best rodeo shirt, all white with poofy sleeves and silver decorations on the sleeves and collar, trying to make a good impression on Delores.

"I think I'll change out of my good clothes," she said, and shut the door on us. That reminded me, and I checked the living room. I found my rucksack right where I'd left it beside the couch. That was a relief. At least I had a couple changes of clothes and some gear.

I picked it up and had to pull out a couple of items, including my combat boots, to get it under the thirty pounds that seemed to be my limit, and then added it to my inventory. I swapped my old sneakers for the combat boots, lacing them up nice and tight. If I was going to be in for a fight, I wanted decent shoes.

"Let's check the yard," I told Grandpa. "Our clock's ticking. We better get a move on here."

Grandpa followed me out of the trailer into what remained of our yard, now slowly settling into the swamp. "Let's see how much of the shed we managed to bring."

The shed was actually a cargo container that Grandpa had bought thirdhand decades ago and filled with all the odds and ends that didn't fit into the trailer. Most of it was gone, including the doors, but we'd been left with the closest five feet. We walked around to the open side, jumping down into the muck. "That's a lot of junk," I noted as we studied the contents.

"All the stuff I haven't bothered with in years," he said. "None of the power tools, of course. Oh well, take it all." There were broken tools, bailing wire, string, a couple of empty jerry cans, even, for some reason, a small anvil and a set of far-rier's tools. I asked Grandpa about that. "Friend of mine asked to store his gear with me before he went to Afghanistan. He didn't come back."

I took the tools and hefted the anvil, but it weighed more than thirty pounds. Grandpa bent over a small chest, opened it, and shouted triumphantly. "Ah, I do still have them!"

I peered inside. It was an old-fashioned reloading press with a single stage. There were several calibers of die available. Grandpa held one set up. "Forty-four Magnum."

I took it all. We rejoined my sister and the deputy, having pretty thoroughly looted the place. "Well?" I asked.

"Now we make for the exit," Sage declared, pointing in the direction shown on our mini-map.

Grandpa looked at me. "I'll go first," he said. "I'm still the best tracker. Shad, you take rear guard." That would keep Sage and the deputy in between us, where we'd have the best chance to protect them from anything that attacked us as we went.

Whatever was out there, I'd be ready for it. I slid my hand into the pocket of my coat, making sure I could grab the revolver quickly if need be. "Let's go."

We had a few brief encounters on our hours-long slog through the reeking muck of the swamp. Once a pack of knee-high chickens with bright green feathers had emerged from the bushes and rushed at us. The deputy and I shot most of them. Grandpa took an axe to a couple that got in close.

Sage had to kick one away like a soccer ball. It hit a tree and slid to the ground with a crack. The chickens dropped a soul coin apiece, as well as something called putrid eggs, which Sage identified as a crafting material and added to her inventory.

That gave her an achievement. Sage said it was "Prolific Gatherer" and that she had collected a hundred different samples of craftable materials.

"Oh wow!" she said, reading on. "Now I can see items much farther off. They're highlighted in yellow, and also say what the yield will be. That's awesome." She pulled a couple of things out of her bag and looked at them. "These have grades now, too. This one's fine and this is poor. Hang on."

She started playing with her items while I checked the countdown. I had been surreptitiously trying everything I could think of to find more game system menus. Most hadn't worked. I could pull up an equipment list, but all it said was, [**Locked. Please select a class to enable this feature.**]

But I had discovered the system clock. It was counting down, presumably until this initialization zone closed as we had been warned. We had about two hours left. I told Grandpa what I found.

"We're almost to the exit now," Grandpa pointed out.

I hesitated, then figured I ought to let him know what I was thinking. "If this was a game, I would expect the exit to be defended. We may have to fight our way out. We'll need to be careful."

Grandpa nodded, his eyes narrowing. "We'll handle it. This ain't my first rodeo, boy."

We came to a clearing. Beyond was an open expanse of water with an island in the middle. There was a bridge leading over to the island, a rickety wooden structure. It was the first thing I had seen here that looked constructed. I held up a hand, and we all paused.

"What is it?" Sage asked, peering through the underbrush.

"I think the exit's over there." I pointed. "But I don't want us to go there just yet. We need to make sure it's not a trap."

The deputy was looking at the water beyond. Large mats of weeds and brushes floated here and there, about six of them. "It's not moving quite right," he pointed out.

I turned to inspect, and that was when the music started again. The announcer came back.

[Level 2, herbivorous, it's the Ghillie Monsters!]

"Gilly what?" Sage asked, looking around.

Then the mats rose up, hovered over the surface of the water, and flew toward us. I drew my gun, aimed, and shot one right in the center of its stringy mass. It was about four feet tall, three feet wide, oblong, and made of sticks and leaves, long bundles of grass, reeds; all sorts of plant matter. My shot blew a hole right through it. I could see daylight on the other side, but it kept coming. The health bar was yellow now and read **[5/10]**.

The deputy was firing away, a staccato burst of shots, followed by a shout from him. "Empty!" He dropped his mag and reloaded.

Grandpa had an axe in both hands, crouching. "Get back," he told Sage. "Keep clear." She had the meat cleaver in her hands and a rebellious look in her eyes, but she scrambled back as Grandpa, the deputy, and I charged forward.

I yanked a gardening tool out of my inventory, not the stirrup hoe this time, but a bladed hoe meant for knocking down roots. As the first ghillie monster approached, I tangled the hoe in its mass and jerked it straight into the nearest tree. It slammed against the willow's trunk and exploded in a pile of sticks and straw.

I turned to see Deputy Young go down underneath one monster. His legs stuck out from under it, kicking and scrabbling as it shook him. I could hear his muffled screams for help. I took a step toward him, but another ghillie monster loomed up at me. I struck out with the hoe, wildly catching a corner, but my grip wasn't as good this time and I just yanked a chunk of knotted branches and dried grasses away from it. It got right up in my face, scrabbling at me with long, dry, knotted vines and branches that scraped my face and drew blood. The cuts burned. **[-1 HP]**, **[-1 HP]**, **[-1 HP]**. I lost three points in quick succession.

I grabbed it with both hands, getting scratches all over me. Wishing I had put on a pair of gardening gloves, I knocked it to the ground and jumped on it, stamping hard. It took a couple of good stomps before the monster dissolved into a puff of branches and debris. Meanwhile, Grandpa had cut through two of the creatures.

I stumbled over to Deputy Young and grabbed at the monster on top of him. I yanked it clear and stomped on it. The deputy coughed and sputtered, sitting up. His eyes went wide and he pointed. "Behind you!"

I spun, getting my hoe up as the monster approached. Grandpa came charging in, axes raised, letting out a wild "Whoop!" as he struck. An axe in each hand, he chopped the monster to pieces.

The music gave its now-accustomed flourish, and I sagged back against the nearest tree. "Ghillie-suit monsters," I said. "Really?"

Grandpa peered at the pieces. "Wonder if we could take enough bits to make our own ghillie suit?"

Sage brightened up. "Let's see," she said. We had set the loot to go to her, so we didn't need to bother to pick it up ourselves. "There's a lot here." She pulled out a handful of bits of dried plants and dead grasses, and then some twine from the house and started tying bits together.

Meanwhile, I checked my menus. I'd found a character status screen that was depressingly blank, with **[Class: Unchosen]** and **[Skills: Locked]**. But it did have a bar at the top that I was pretty sure was for XP. Right now, it said **[??/??]**. I had hoped that we would have earned some for these fights. Almost every game I'd played had some sort of system where killing monsters gave you experience, and enough experience granted levels. So far, nothing. Maybe we needed a class first.

I kept a close eye on my health bar until, after about two minutes, it ticked up by one. **[18/20]**. I let out a sigh of relief. "Looks like we regenerate out of combat. That's good. Nobody go anywhere until we're all healed up," I said.

Sage kept muttering and fiddling with her bits of weed and string. About two minutes in, as she started on a second piece of twine, there was a ding and then a whoosh, and suddenly she was holding up a ghillie suit. "I got another achievement!"

She read it off for us.

[Novice Crafter: Create an item from ingredients you have looted, 1/100.]

"I have an achievement with progress like that," I mentioned, taking a look at her work.

Sure enough, the thing was labeled **[Ghillie Suit]**. It actually said at the bottom, **[Bonus to camouflage skill.]** None of us had any skills yet. Maybe those would unlock with our classes.

Sage held it out to Grandpa, who laid it over his shoulders. It didn't look like it should stay, but as he moved around, the branches and bits of the weeds moved with him, like some sort of creepy plant cape.

"Good work," he told Sage. "Now the island."

We turned our attention to the bridge. There was no way I was going to swim across, which left only one choice. "I think maybe I should scout ahead," I said. "I'm gonna let you know what's going on."

"Good thinking," Grandpa agreed. "But I'll do the scouting."

I wanted to object, but he had a point. Grandpa had been hunting for more years than I'd been alive. He waggled part of his ghillie suit at me. "Besides, look! Now I'm ready for it!"

I had to laugh at that. "All right, use the party chat to tell us if you see anything in particular."

We all moved over to the copse of trees closest to the bridge. Grandpa flipped the ghillie suit over his head and started forward, nice and slow. I watched him as he slunk across the bridge. I didn't know if the ghillie suit would actually do anything to hide from prying eyes, but so far, so good.

He reached the edge of the bridge, hesitated, peered ahead, then stepped off it. The moment he did, there was an extra triumphant swell of music and the announcer swooped in.

**[Congratulations! You have located the exit zone. All you need
to do now is defeat its guardians and make it through the door
before you run out of time.]**

"Well, shit," I said as Grandpa stopped dead in his tracks.

CHAPTER FIVE

WHO'S ON FIRST, ANYWAY?

Veda Tvedra let out a deep sigh as her company's container docked in its port in the Great Hub. It had been a very long trip. Coming to a new star system, one without a cooperative Reality Engine, was always difficult. This time, knowing what was riding on her, it was even worse. She hadn't slept well in weeks. But now she was here, and there was nothing for it but to get to work.

She linked in with the council system interface. Data flooded through her subroutines. She allowed her adjutant software to handle most of the information, sorting it into various categories.

The local inhabitants were a human stock offshoot, like Veda herself. That was good. She wasn't prejudiced, but she found it easier to read humanoid expressions than those of some of the more exotic galactics.

The initialization period was nearly up, meaning that miners would be flooding up to the Hub soon enough. She sent a query, checking on the survival rates. The council had run a standard selection algorithm. They had taken the maximum permitted ten million natives, selected randomly by geographic location, so that no one area of the planet would have too many representatives. By now, the miner candidates were down to around seven million.

Veda winced. She didn't like the initial culls at all. It seemed harsh. She knew there were limited resources available to the council and the galactic senate, and there was no point in initiating miners who weren't going to make a connection with the Reality Engine of their system, but still. Couldn't they have asked for volunteers? Just because it had always been done this way didn't mean that it was the right way to do things.

Veda instructed her subroutines to keep up the cover story she had chosen. Competition for the third-tier companies and stakers was always fierce, and if they knew that the Tvedra Corporation was in dire straits, the scavengers would come circling.

She had one chance to recover her family's fortunes, make the company a power among the third-tier organizations once more, and secure her own future. If she screwed this up, it would be back to storage, or at best one of the overcrowded Reality Engines near the galactic core for her.

That wasn't a future Veda wanted. Living in a support pod, her mind entertained by various fictions and entertainments, but no real life, no impact on the galaxy beyond, wasn't how she'd been raised. Her family's company had a proud, long heritage, and she would not let her older brother's failure mark the end of them.

So, she would wager all their fortunes in staking a team, the best she could, and pray the gamble paid off. She had to make it big, not just earn her money back.

Securing her pod behind her, Veda wandered out into the Great Hub. It was an impressive facility. She wondered what the local system humans would think of it. From her information sources, they had achieved spaceflight and some minor space operations, but it took the powers of multiple combined star systems to produce a transfer Hub like this one.

The Great Arch stretched overhead, the long window that ran down the entire length of the hundred-mile-long cylinder, showing the blazing face of an enormous gas giant. White clouds cut through orange and brown bands, and there was a reddish storm going on over to the left side of the view. She consulted her notes. The locals referred to this planet as Jupiter, and the Reality Engine was buried deep in the depths of what they thought was one of its moons. She wondered what had made it wake up in the last few decades and sent a query.

To her surprise, the answer came back quickly. The council specialists had determined that the local humans, by sending several space probes in quick succession to visit the satellites of this gas giant, had attracted the attention of the Reality Engine, which had come out of its eons-long dormancy. Galactic sensor networks had detected its emergence, and sprung into action as usual. And now, all this waited for the lucky local miners who had been chosen to participate in this system's exploitation of its Reality Engine.

Veda shivered as she walked. She wasn't actually cold. Though the Hub was kept at twenty-nine degrees standard temperature, she preferred high thirties. Her personal systems projected a small force field around her, keeping the air inside comfortable. She didn't even have to wear clothes, but though many of the galactic species had no nudity custom, Veda's family had always preferred to dress well for any occasion.

She passed talonians, with their long scaly tails dragging along the corridors. Over to the left, she saw a group of chest-high dwennan. She'd never gotten along particularly well with that prickly stock, but they did tend to produce some of the best engineers in the galaxy. And over in one of the many eating establishments of this particular section of the Hub station, she saw several orcs enjoying large racks of some sort of meat still attached to its original bones, probably vat-grown. Orc chefs usually specialized in growing meat and false bone attached to it, which they said lent flavor.

Veda generally stuck to vat protein. Her family had never had money to spend on luxuries. Her systems led her to the location she had specified, a lounge reserved for level three corporations that had, in the past, been allied with the Alabaster Sky Conglomerate. Veda wasn't sure about them, but her brother's failed contract did mean she still had ties, and while she was in information-gathering mode, she might as well make use of the connection.

She arrived shortly before the scheduled time, but the room was already crowded. There must be representatives of three-dozen level three groups present. The Alabaster Sky Conglomerate did not discriminate based on species, so the room was a riot of colors and smells. Veda squeezed in, found a seat in the far corner, and opened her ears to listen for gossip. She allowed her listening subroutines to process most of the information, flagging anything that might be of particular interest for her.

A service robot came by, offering complimentary drinks. She accepted something non-stimulating and green. Sipping on her drink, Veda waited for their hosts. The mood in the room was growing more impatient. Veda knew better. Her father had taught her this particular trick years before. By making them all wait, the Alabaster Sky Conglomerate's representatives were reminding everyone in this room just whose time really mattered.

At last, the representatives entered through a door at the rear of the room. They were tall, possibly human stock, but very heavily modified if so, with bald heads from which a crest of bright red feathers sprouted. All three wore silvery robes and bright purple sashes.

The conversation died down as they took their places at the front of the room. One raised her hands. "Thank you all for coming, and welcome to the 975th opening of a Reality Engine."

"At least that we know about," someone in the crowd near Veda whispered. She didn't turn, but mentally tagged the speaker and made a note to look him up later. That kind of conspiracy talk was generally frowned upon by the larger conglomerates. After all, the system had functioned for thousands of standard years. There was no reason to believe that rogue groups were locating and exploiting Reality Engines without the knowledge of the Galactic Council.

The representatives up front spoke again. "We will be paying high bounties for any allied stakeholders who assemble productive teams of miners this year. The Alabaster Sky Conglomerate's plans are quite ambitious, though you won't mind that we're keeping them quiet for now. Sometime after the farm levels open, we will be willing to be more up front about things. But suffice it to say, Alabaster

Sky has never fielded a more talented acquisition team than we are planning to in this iteration."

She waited for a spate of clapping from the more fawning members of her audience to die away before continuing. Veda kept her own hands still. She might have to take an Alabaster Sky offer, but not yet.

"This particular Reality Engine promises to be very fruitful. The local species is resourceful, hardy, and generally easy to bargain with. The human stock among you may have a slightly easier time making connections, but their pop culture has already embraced the concept of other species from beyond their own world. It should not be difficult for those of you with more exotic appearances to make inroads here."

Veda sat back and sipped her drink, listening to the representatives continue to speak, mostly about the great things that Alabaster Sky did in their systems and with their constituent Reality Engines. She already knew how much technology in her cargo pod belonged to an Alabaster Sky subsidiary. That wasn't why she was here. She didn't need to be told that her food synthesizers, her medical nanotechnology, was of Alabaster Sky's design and fielded in one or more of Alabaster Sky's Reality Engines. She already knew that. What she was here for were tips on assembling a productive mining team. She'd studied the theory, but she'd never before been at the opening of a Reality Engine.

"And now," the third representative, who had been extolling the virtues of Alabaster Sky's inflatable furniture line, said, "we have a treat in store for you, so that you can get a better understanding of the capabilities of this system's denizens. We have negotiated with the council and the representatives of this Reality Engine's internal subroutines to acquire some footage of the potential miners in action."

That got a cheer. Hoots, laughs, and applause rocked the room. Veda stilled herself. They might say that this was to give hopeful stakeholders a look at what they were getting, but she knew better. These initial opening videos were always slaughterfests. She'd had to watch some during her training, and her father had always made it clear to her. She would not take joy in the suffering and death of other sentient beings. She might be forced to work with the system, but she did not have to indulge in its excesses.

The room darkened, and the ceiling overhead and one wall blanked out. Various scenes began to play. She saw humans that looked very much like her, though slightly taller, generally with less vibrant hair than her race boasted, and clothed in some of the most outlandish garments she'd ever seen, thrown into a variety of situations.

There was a group of what appeared to be lightly clad women, wearing sandals that looked homemade and brightly colored fabric wrapped around their bodies for clothes, suddenly transported into the middle of a snow field. The scene sped up, and a moment later, a ferocious white bear fell on the freezing group of women. Only one could even muster the capability of fighting back, and she didn't last long. The bear and the snow around were red with blood.

The scene darted away fast. Now it showed what looked like a family group sitting in a boat, but the boat was in the middle of a desert. They stared around them in astonishment, nets full of flopping fish all around their boat. A moment later, an enormous pair of catlike creatures sprang out of the sand. The cats were pale brown with yellow stripes, and they threw sand in front of them as they attacked.

Veda winced and flicked imaginary sand from her own eyes in sympathy. She thought she was about to see another slaughter, but the two young men in the boat grabbed an empty net and threw it over the first of the cats. The cat yowled and tumbled to the ground. An older woman, probably their mother, had a broad, thin knife, probably for cleaning the fish. She stabbed the first cat without hesitation, while her husband and grown daughter fended off the other cat with the poles they had used to push their boat until the sons could turn to help. The scene faded.

"Some of these humans show remarkable resilience. We have great hopes for your ability to recruit a team worthy of alliance," the Alabaster Sky representative with the tallest feather crest shouted. Veda's heart lightened. Even though the next three scenes they saw were more slaughter, she was impressed by the way so many of the prospective miners fought back.

They hadn't asked to be here. She'd had a choice. She could have just gone and plugged herself into a tame Reality Engine. And she wasn't risking her life. She would need to keep that in mind, whatever bargain she made with some of these miners. Yes, she had to make a profit. That didn't mean she needed to exploit them.

More scenes appeared. More of the humans triumphed, collecting their initial soul coins and becoming local Reality Engine initiates. Veda started to relax. She queried her medical subroutine just to make sure that the drink she'd ordered hadn't been soporific or mood-altering in any way. It wasn't. She just liked the flavor.

The room was starting to grow restless now. Everyone was eager to get out there and start making their own plans. Some of those toward the back started to make their way out.

Veda stood up. She'd slip away with the others as they started to leave, not attracting attention from their hosts.

The scene changed once more. For a brief moment, Veda got a glimpse of a couple of humans. A strong-looking man, skin dark and leathery, past his youth but seemingly fit, held an axe in each hand. He had dark hair in two braids that hung past his shoulders. Most of the Earth human men she'd seen so far had short hair, and the difference stuck out.

Beside him was a young girl, her brown eyes bright with excitement. They had a distinct resemblance to each other.

Veda's interest was piqued. The algorithm was supposed to choose fully grown adults whenever possible, but sometimes children got swept up in the collection. They usually didn't make it very far, but this girl was clearly already attuned.

There were two other men in the image, but further away from whatever vantage had taken the shot. She couldn't get a good look at them. She made a note that if her image recognition picked up either the girl or the older man again, she would seek out more information.

Still another hour to go before any of the recently initiated humans could possibly make it up here.

Veda went to make a few deals.

CHAPTER SIX

WHERE'S THAT BANJO MUSIC COMING FROM?

I checked our timer. We still had over an hour. That was good. We needed to be able to plan.

Get back here, I sent by party chat. I was getting better at that and didn't have to subvocalize any more. *We need to plan.*

Grandpa sent back a thumbs-up emoji. I hadn't figured out how to do those yet. He was pretty adaptable for an old man. He retreated back across the bridge, just as carefully and stealthily as before.

The announcer continued.

**[You've found the Clan of the Cajun Crackers.
These three boys have spent all their lives here in the swamp,
and they will defend what's theirs with extreme prejudice.]**

Images appeared in front of us, floating in midair, of three faces, each labeled with a name. A new achievement appeared.

[Boss battle unlocked! Defeat the boss to unlock further steps.]

All three looked like stereotypical rednecks with protruding chins, missing teeth, and sunburned ears. One of them wore his baseball cap backward. The music changed to twangy banjos. I looked at the sky. "Really? That's what you're going with here?"

"This is ridiculous," Deputy Young complained. "What's going on here? I'll walk over there and introduce myself as an officer of the law and ask for their assistance."

"You can't. These are NPCs," Sage told him. "That means they're not real people. They look like people. They might even talk like people, but they've been created by the system as opponents for us. The only way past them is to beat them. That's why they look like stereotypes."

The three boys were labeled Cletus, Bubba, and Hank. Each had fifteen HP. Cletus wore a coonskin cap. The utter ridiculousness of the stereotypes actually reassured me. Sage was right. These were not real people. They weren't human.

Grandpa reported what he'd seen. "There's a tar paper–shack in the middle of the island, and those three inbred creeps sitting in rocking chairs on the porch. They've got a dog with them. I saw a shotgun, not sure what else. One of the three was up and wandering around."

"Maybe he's got a set path. We might be able to lure him out by himself or surprise the other two before he can join," Sage said.

"If this is a game and these are bosses, they could have special abilities or some sort of gimmick," I explained to Grandpa and the deputy. "We have to be careful. They aren't people, but whoever is running this is smart, probably smarter than we are. They'll be able to fight back. Like the gnomes, but maybe meaner."

Grandpa bent and scratched a crude map in the dirt, showing the position of the brothers, where the cabin was, and a couple of pieces of debris and equipment that could provide concealment for us or them. "The shotgun's leaning against the wall of the house. If we surprise them, we might get them before they can grab it."

I nodded, formulating a plan. I didn't like this, but our only way out was through them. I looked at Sage. "Listen, sis, I know you're not going to like this, but I need you to stay here. Grandpa and I will be able to fight a lot better if we don't have to watch out for you."

She pouted at me. "But I could help. I could hang back and watch and tell you if something changes. In party chat, I don't have to be close." I hesitated, because she had a point, but every instinct was making me resist. She saw my weakness and pressed. "Besides, you know how boss fights are. Sometimes, as soon as you start them, the area gets locked in. I don't want to be on the other side of that. At least let me cross the bridge with you. I'll hang back and stay out of the way, I promise."

I looked at Grandpa. "She has a point about game mechanics."

Grandpa nodded. "Okay, then. You get out whatever your best weapon is, but I don't want you getting involved. If things look bad, you run."

Sage's eyes flashed rebelliously, but she nodded. "All right."

"I still think I should go in there and show my badge," Young said stubbornly.

"Frank, you've been a deputy for thirty years, and I know you're not stupid enough to think that folk who live out in the middle of nowhere with names like Cletus are going to give one bit of weight to that tin star of yours. They're more likely to shoot you on sight."

"They're probably moonshiners," Sage said helpfully. "Shad, I'll try to keep an eye out for mechanics and shout if I think something's about to happen."

"They're not real people, Frank," I explained again. "There's no way the system is going to let us talk our way out of this." That actually wasn't quite true. I had seen games where there was a way to avoid fights, but nothing about this setup suggested it would work, and I didn't want Young hesitating.

"So here's my plan," I said as we bent our heads together over Grandpa's map.

I went first. Grandpa and I had argued about it, then settled it with a flip of a soul coin. It came up heads, the Medusa face glaring balefully up at me, which meant I won. Grandpa and the deputy followed, with Sage bringing up the rear. Sage had a meat cleaver in her hand, and I just hoped she'd keep her promise to stay clear.

I stepped off the bridge and immediately sprinted toward the shack, my gun in my hand. The mud squished under my feet as I focused on my targets.

We had timed it just right. Two of the brothers were sitting in their rocking chairs. Bubba even had a straw hat pulled down over his eyes. They both had cans of light beer in their hands, and a snoozing basset hound lay between them. The third brother had just gone behind the shack on his programmed patrol route. Deputy Young was to break off and engage him while I closed the distance on the house.

Ten feet away, I raised my revolver. I squeezed off two shots at Bubba's head, got my muzzle back on target, and put another two rounds through his chest. Overkill, since each round did five damage, but I didn't have time between shots to make sure each landed. They all did, and Bubba was out of the fight.

Cletus was still getting up from his chair. He reached for a shotgun, and I shot first. Both my rounds went through his chest, leaving him at [5/15]. I dumped my brass, smacking the lever to knock the empties free, pulled the speed loader, and reloaded.

The dog sat at his feet howling, a bloodcurdling noise that settled over me. [**Debuff!**] the announcer proclaimed. [**You've been treed! Penalty to dodge!**]

Cletus had stumbled backward with my shots, but now he recovered himself and was raising the shotgun toward me. Light glinted off the barrel. I flipped the cylinder back into place, six rounds ready in my gun. I wasn't going to be fast enough.

That was when one of Grandpa's axes caught Cletus in the shoulder, dealing another three points of damage. He shouted and dropped the shotgun. A blast of pellets sprayed the roof of his porch. It sounded like metal rain.

I shot again, this time taking him through the head. "The other one's coming back!" Sage screamed, and I heard Young's pistol firing rapidly.

I was running up the porch steps to check that the two brothers were really dead when the door of the shack burst open and an enormous woman staggered out onto the porch.

"What's all this racket?" she roared. She was huge, like five hundred pounds. Her remaining teeth were yellow with tobacco stains. She wore a stained muumuu with pictures of kittens all over it.

The music changed from twangy banjos to Loretta Lynn–style country, no words, just the melodies.

And she had forty HP blinking over her health bar.

[**It's *Mama*!**] the announcer roared gleefully. [**Ornery as her sons and twice as mean, she's a dab hand with the Cajun cooking and she never lets a guest walk away hungry—or even walk away!**]

She had a cast-iron skillet in an oven-gloved hand. There was a sizzling sound from the skillet, and as I paused in shock, she threw its contents at me.

I dodged, but some of the liquid hit me. Boiling oil ran down my drovers coat. A couple of drops hit my face and burned. [**-1 HP**].

Little round things pelted the porch at my feet. I glanced down. Hush puppies. She'd been frying a batch of hush puppies and had just thrown them at me. The basset hound ran out from behind Cletus's body and started slurping them up, howling every time he ate one. I'd worried he would join the fight, but he didn't seem inclined to bother, aside from that debuff that was probably the reason I'd gotten hit with the oil.

Now she was charging me, the empty skillet held in her hand like a bat. She swung like she was going for a line drive.

I ducked, and the pan whooshed past my head, barely. I shot at her, not taking any time to aim. She was right there, the size of a beached whale. I couldn't miss. My shots tore through her. I squeezed off all five rounds in quick succession, and I hit every time. [**15/40**]. She was hurting, but not out.

Mama staggered backward, huge holes gaping in her muumuu as blood pooled at her feet. "How dare you come onto my land and shoot my boys! I'll teach you to make trouble here!" she screamed. She swung again, and her frying pan hit me in the side of the head so hard I could feel my teeth rattling loose. [**-8 HP**]. I was down to eleven health.

"Don't shoot! You'll hit him!" Sage was yelling, presumably to the deputy.

I reeled back and fell hard against the porch rail. It gave under me, and I keeled over into the dirt in front of the shack.

The woman leered down at me. Her upturned pan aimed at my head. "I'll teach you!" she shrieked. There was a status message over her head. [**Soul Food does the body good. Regenerating 5% health per second.**] As I watched, she regained [**+2 HP**], [**+2 HP**].

"Shit! She's healing! Hit her hard!" I fumbled in my pocket, grabbing a handful of loose rounds in my shaking hand. I broke open the cylinder, trying to get the spent brass out so I could reload.

Grandpa appeared behind her like a silent shadow. His axe took her head half off, but she still had nine HP somehow. A second blow finished the job. The woman collapsed to a heap on her porch.

I took a breath and got to my feet, thumbing rounds into my gun. "Whew, we made it—"

The music swelled, and the announcer came back.

**[Congratulations! You have defeated the Cajun Crackers.
You have destabilized this exit region, and it will collapse
on itself in five minutes.]**

A big blinking timer appeared in the corner of my vision.

"What the hell is this?" Young yelled.

"Find the exit!" I shouted. I jumped back up on the porch and grabbed the shotgun that one of the brothers had dropped. The system refused to let me put it into inventory, but a list of loot popped up. I dismissed it. No time to worry about that right now; I'd look later.

"I got the loot!" Sage shouted. "Just find the exit!"

Grandpa was already through the door of the house. "It's here somewhere!" he shouted. "I see it on the map!"

I burst in and helped him look. The shack reminded me of our trailer, except everything was dirty and stank of cigarette smoke and meth. That smell brought back memories I thought I'd buried years ago. I pushed them aside as we searched for the exit.

Sage was the one who found it hidden under a rug, a trap door leading to a cellar. We threw it back. The cellar yawned dark below us.

Sage looked at me. Her eyes were wide with fear. "What happens next?" she asked.

"I don't know," I said. "But I'll be there to protect you." I lowered myself into the hole and dropped.

CHAPTER SEVEN

WHICH END IS UP IN SPACE?

I liked the swamp better," I groused as I tried to take in my new surroundings.

I stood in the middle of an absolutely enormous space. It felt like when I'd visited Grand Central Station in New York, except bigger than that. I looked overhead, trying to see the sky or roof or whatever was above me. I couldn't see anything. It just went up, the air kind of gray-blue above me that could mean that I was out in the open, but I didn't think it did.

All around me were people, people like me, people who looked tired, dirty, scared. Everyone was talking and shouting all at once. A man near me rushed at another, a twisted, gnarled branch in his hand raised high like a club. Before I could react, something invisible stopped him. It was like the air thickened around him so he couldn't move.

Grandpa stared around, his eyes wide. "You know how I said it wasn't my first rodeo?" he asked. "I might have been wrong."

Sage giggled. "It's our first space rodeo, and we're all in it together." She patted Grandpa's arm. "It's okay, I read lots of books about space. I'll help you figure it out."

A voice chimed in my ear, accompanied by another floating box.

> **[This is a safe zone. No miner versus miner violence is permitted by the system. This rule will be enforced with extreme prejudice.]**

The announcer sounded as enthused by this as he was every time I got into a fight.

Sage looked around. "Oh wow."

Towering over the masses of people, about a quarter mile away from me, was an enormous glowing purple field. It shimmered and crackled with energy. Around it was a wide black border, like the biggest hangar door I'd ever seen. It had to be two hundred feet tall, to be as obvious from how far off it was. I couldn't see through it.

A little way off was another, then another. I turned on the spot. The shimmering portals bounded us in. There were dozens of them. In between the glowing portals were dark doorways of the same size. They looked like slabs of blackness cut from a moonless night strung up behind them.

About half the portals were dark, the other half lit in all the colors of the rainbow. I didn't know what to make of them. I didn't know how many people there were here. I could see thousands from where I stood, and I didn't think that was all of them. The now-familiar voice spoke again.

**[Welcome, miners! Welcome to the opening of your system's
Reality Engine! We know you will have plenty of questions.
We're going to welcome you to our facility by means of the elevator.
On the way, we will provide answers to many of your
most pressing questions. So please, form an orderly line
and proceed into the light.]**

I turned. In the center of the room, a pillar of light shot up toward the far distant roof. At least it was easy to see where we were going.

Grandpa leaned closer. "Lead the way; I'll bring Sage," he said.

I nodded, put my head down, and waded toward the light. I noticed that I couldn't quite touch anyone else in the crowd. As my body got too close to theirs, the air between us grew thick and pressed us apart. I reached back and touched Sage's hand, then Grandpa's. Nothing stopped me. Whatever was at work here knew we were together.

Sooner or later, the mass of people turned into something that was a bit more like a queue. Though, from the time I'd spent in Europe on tour, I knew that any British people in this mess would be wincing right now. But compared to, say, India, this was great.

We struggled along, a few inches at a time, the light growing ever brighter. After what seemed like hours, we reached the end of the line. People were being ushered onto a platform. Once the platform held about three dozen people, an almost transparent cap appeared around it, and then the whole thing shot upward into the beam of light at an incredible speed.

I stopped, staring at it.

"We're supposed to go in that thing? Screw that!" Young said.

Grandpa shook his head. "I don't like the look of it." As far as I knew, the only times Grandpa had even been on an airplane were his Army trips overseas, decades before I was born.

The familiar voice spoke again.

**[There's no danger associated with this method of travel.
Your safety is guaranteed while you are in a neutral space.]**

"Well, that'd be great if we could just believe the random voice that's talking to us out of nowhere," I said. "Also, it's really lovely to have every word that we said listened to. Who are you people, anyway?"

**[Your questions will be answered on the trip up to the Hub.
Please board the next available lifting platform.]**

I didn't love it, but on the other hand, I was tired and hungry. I'd spent the last day being attacked by various monsters, and I still didn't know where I was.

A woman a couple of spaces ahead of us in the queue started shrieking at the top of her lungs. "I'm not getting on that thing, I'm not! You'll have to drag me—"

She fell suddenly silent. She held her arms awkwardly out from her side, and when she took her next step forward, it looked like a doll walking. I saw that her limbs weren't bending quite right. There was a faint shimmer around her, a thickening of the air. The same system that was keeping us from touching each other had thickened around her and was now forcing her limbs forward, and presumably silencing her.

I looked at Grandpa. He nodded, telling me he'd seen the same thing. "Keep a low profile, boy," he said. Then he spoke in Ute. I never learned more than a few words, but I knew it when I heard it. At least one of the words I did recognize was a curse.

After a moment, he smiled sardonically. "Well, that answers that question."

"What's that?"

"You didn't hear what they said to me? Well, they understand Ute, all right. Whatever we say, they're listening."

Now it was our turn to board. The three of us, and Deputy Young, stepped onto the platform. Two dozen more people filled out the remaining space, and the shining plug came down over our heads. I touched it, gingerly. It gave a little under my finger, and it was warm and almost static-feeling. Definitely not glass or plastic. More like some sort of force field. I didn't know what kind of tech these people had, but it was certainly far beyond anything we had back on Earth. Like I hadn't already figured that out.

The platform shot upward. There was absolutely no feeling of acceleration. It was like everything else just dropped away from us while we stood perfectly still. The light all around us was a stalk reaching toward the heavens. We traveled up it.

**[The trip to the Hub will take approximately 2.5 of your Earth hours.
Please, get comfortable. We're going to conduct your initial briefing now.**

**Once you have reached the Hub, we have facilities to help
you with class choice and initial outfitting. Once you've
made some important decisions, you'll be able to schedule
yourself for a return to the minefields.]**

Grandpa raised an eyebrow. "Minefield? That sounds ominous."

"I assume more like gold fields than the DMZ."

Low, cushioned couches appeared all around the edge of the pod. I grabbed Sage's hand and led her and Grandpa over to one. "Of course, in the gold rush, the only people who actually made money were the shopkeepers and cooks. The miners all went bust and died broke. I have a feeling we're about to meet the shopkeepers."

There was enough room for everyone to have their own seat, and people separated into little groups, eyeing each other with suspicion. I saw one man who was all on his own, but everyone else was in a group of two to five people. Whether they had known each other before all this started or not, I had no way of knowing. Right next to us was a middle-aged Hispanic woman with a pair of twenty-something girls clinging to her; family group, I guessed. Her eyes narrowed as she listened to my comment.

The light around us dimmed. In the center of the pod, the air shimmered and darkened. A sphere about three feet tall hovered in the air. It began to show images.

**[You are now traveling from the location of the Sol System's
Reality Engine up to the Hub vessel provided
by the System coalition.]**

"And that means exactly what?" a teen boy across from me shouted. "What's a Reality Engine?"

Deputy Young stood up. "More importantly, how do we get home to Earth?"

The voice continued. It was either ignoring us, or this was all some sort of recorded script playing out. It showed an image of the whole galaxy, shining dots of light arrayed in a vast spiral shape. Little points of red and blue emerged, superimposed over some of the stars.

**[The Reality Engines were created unknown millennia of years ago
by an unknown species. Galactic civilization refers to them
as the Progenitors. It is believed that their civilization ended,
and that they either passed out of this galaxy, or, according to
one academic theory, had themselves genetically reprogrammed
into all the species that we see today. Regardless, they left their greatest**

**achievements behind. The Reality Engines are the core on
which all life, all technology, all society in the galaxy depends.
Every civilized system has, at its heart, a Reality Engine of its own.
Here people are born, live, and die. Their needs are attended to,
their wants are granted. But more than that, in a Reality Engine,
anything can be possible. The discoveries and technologies invented
in a Reality Engine can be brought out for use in the greater galaxy.]**

Deputy Young had sat back down when it was clear his question wasn't going
to be answered, and I was so tired that having somewhere comfortable to sit and
a lack of mortal threats around me made me happy to just soak it all in.

The other passengers were grumping and complaining. "What's that got to
do with all of us?"

**[You are among the chosen representatives of your species.
The coalition has selected you as your species' representatives.
You will be permitted to attempt to claim the Reality Engine
for the benefit of your species.
The coalition is here to help. In exchange for access to some of the
resources you will be able to gather, the System coalition offers
advice and valuable aid. We understand that there's a lot going on
here that we want for you to grasp. Many of you probably were
not aware that life existed beyond your planet until a few standard
hours ago. We understand you may be asking, "Why us?"
Believe us. It is not entirely our choice. The rules for exploitation of
Reality Engines have been negotiated between all major governments
in the galaxy, as well as representative voices from the Reality
Engines themselves.]**

This was starting to sound pretty familiar. This was exactly the sort of upper
echelon bullshit briefing they gave when you were due for a particularly unpleasant mission.

Grandpa grimaced. "This reminds me of the way the brass used to brief us
over in 'Nam. I don't think I like where this is going."

"Doesn't sound like we have much choice." I was trying to listen and pay attention. I might not like what was going on, but it was better to know than to be
ignorant.

The system announcer continued.

**[For the initial phase of the Reality Engine exploitation process, you will
focus on gathering the unique resources your Reality Engine can provide.**

That will largely take the form of soul coins, which you have already encountered, but there are other valuable items, as you will discover. With the help of your stakeholders, you will amass soul coins, securing your own place in the wider galaxy.]

"There's our answer." I leaned back and folded my arms. "We're going to face more monsters and collect coins. Means more fighting, more killing."

I sympathized with Deputy Young and his desire to go home. I wanted that too. But I guessed that wasn't going to be an option for a while yet. That meant my priority had to be keeping Sage safe and out of the swamp we'd just come from. Keeping my own skin intact was a close second.

The briefing continued.

[You have now all been initiated into this Reality Engine. By consuming a soul coin, you have gained access to this Reality Engine's systems and abilities. We will take advantage of that. Here on the Hub, we have facilities which will enable you to choose a class. A class comes with certain abilities and benefits. This will fit you for the challenges you are to face. Keep in mind that you don't have to face the challenges alone. In fact, we encourage working in groups and parties. For the initial mining phase, we and the Reality Engine have set a party size limit of five. No one will be forced to join a party, but parties will find it easier to work together. With that in mind, during class selection, you will be able to discuss matters with party members already present. At this time, your party interface has been enabled. By default, you have been grouped into a party with those who entered the Initialization Chamber with you.]

That seemed straightforward. I thought *party* to myself, and, sure enough, a party menu popped up. It had all four of us listed, with Grandpa labeled as team lead.

Deputy Young was angry again. "Look, Twofeather, I like you, I like your girl, and I like your boy—now that he's not crashing old Jeeps in ravines and leaving them for me to haul out—but I didn't ask for any of this. You can't make me."

"It's all right, Frank," Grandpa said in a soothing voice. "The system people here may have said you're part of our group, but nobody's gonna force you to do anything you don't want. Besides, if we can find a way back home, I'm all for taking it as soon as possible."

"And so is everyone else here," I said. "They didn't bring us all the way here just to let us go home again immediately. We're probably going to have to play along for a while. So let's figure out what they want, and get it for them as quick as we can, and without risking ourselves too much."

The system voice kept talking, but now it was going on about different organizations and groups, how they all related to each other, and something about how galactic politics were structured. Sage leaned in, listening closely to everything, her right hand tapping rhythmically as she listened.

I took a deep breath and leaned back. We were safe, for now, but heading into who knew what danger.

CHAPTER EIGHT

WHAT TO EXPECT WHEN YOU'RE EXPECTING MINERS

Veda checked the results of her searches as she made her way to the nearest sponsor-equipped auction hall annex. She'd had her systems running across the publicly available databases of miners, their talents, and their conquests thus far.

It wasn't looking good. She already knew there was no way she would be able to afford a full team of well-balanced miners. Those would go for far more than her operating budget. She just needed to find a group with the potential to make it to the second phase.

Her family's license allowed them to sponsor phase two teams to exploit profitable soul coin hotspots. One limitation of those licenses was that any company which failed to exploit them for a certain number of Reality Engine openings would lose their license permanently. If Veda couldn't get a team to the second phase and successfully hold at least one capture point for an entire standard day, her family would lose their corporate license and any chance at future Reality Engine exploitation.

She didn't have a very high budget to work with, either. She had taken the death insurance money her brother and father had left along with her mother's meager savings, then begged, borrowed, scraped, and stole whatever else she could.

She turned her attention to the various possible candidate teams her algorithms had flagged. There were over seven million miners in 2.3 million teams. That gave her a lot of options. The trick was going to be finding miners who were both competent and stubborn enough to make it to phase two, and willing to listen to her guidance and offer the bargain she was going to take.

Veda entered one of the stakeholder doors in the auction annex. The miners would have their own annexes, thousands of them, and the potential sponsors could appear virtually to make their pitches. The auction wasn't quite live yet. She had time to kill.

She sidled over toward some people her subsystems flagged as acquaintances of the family, introduced herself, and asked about the gossip. One of them was a tall orc woman named Danandra, who looked like she'd had something sour for breakfast. When she scowled, her bottom tusks stuck up past her lip, giving her a ferocious expression. Veda's grandfather had previous dealings with this woman, and her system pulled up his notes, which claimed that he thought Danandra was a bit of a sweetheart, as long as she hadn't been drinking too much the night before.

"This system is more marginal than we thought going in," Danandra complained. "When the intel said the locals had only achieved spaceflight in the last hundred years, I thought we'd have some species that was closer to their primal roots. These are soft."

Another man, a lizardish creature about five feet tall, with glistening pink scales and a tongue that slithered out from his toothless mouth when he spoke, nodded agreement. His tail wrapped around his arm as though it were the train of a long dress. "If we hadn't already bought into this exploit, I'd cut my losses and be gone."

"Too right, Zazef," Danandra said. "This is looking like it's going to be a resale job for sure."

That was the worst news Veda could have gotten. There were many ways to make money out of opening a Reality Engine, most of them limited to the larger conglomerates and, of course, the really big organizations who sat at the top with motives and opportunities so obscure Veda could only make a guess at them. The conglomerates could buy her and her company three times over before breakfast. The shadowy organizations above them wouldn't even bother. They'd just buy everyone in the system she was from and get her in the bargain.

"So what strategy are you all going with?" she asked. She tried to look young and innocent, which wasn't too hard to do since this was her first time at a Reality Engine opening and everyone here knew it.

Danandra smiled toothily at her. "Looking for tips? I owe your grandfather a bit, so I don't mind sharing. Besides, there's plenty of pickings out there. It's not like you're going to undercut me or make some big scoop. Not at this stage. I was hoping to stake a couple hundred miners in the hope of getting two or three teams capable of making it to phase two."

Veda kept her smile fixed. Inside, her stomach turned to ice. Two hundred miners in the hopes of getting two teams? Veda would be lucky if she could afford to back more than a couple of partial teams.

"Problem is, this is looking like a pump and dump situation," Zazef said. "The real money is going to be made by the groups who can afford to buy up a bunch of cheap warrior-class contracts, arm them with pulse rifles and personal shields, and find a bunch of low-risk, low-reward spawn points to camp."

"They can't possibly make up the return on the equipment with low-spawn, low-producing teams," Veda pointed out. She ran the numbers in her head. Personal shields, which would keep a team of miners safe against all but the most difficult tier-one beasts, would cost a fortune. If she had to outfit a team with those, she'd only be able to afford a single team of utter dregs.

"That's the point," Danandra said, grinning. "They run the debt up astronomically, and then when the interstellar corporations show up for phase two, they sell that debt off to them. The big boys know how to use their accounting tricks to convert that debt into shares of the Reality Engine itself. They won't make much from the miners, but they will make it back when they sell the contracts."

Veda hadn't even thought of that strategy, because there was no way in this lifetime or any other that she would be able to make a bid for any part of the Reality Engine ownership. Realistically, only the biggest interstellar conglomerations could field teams capable of taking on phase three and earning shares of the Engine itself.

"So is that what you're going to do?" she asked.

Both Zazef and Danandra nodded. "Seems like the best option. It'll let us cut our losses early and get out of here. We'll do a little more forward research for the next Reality Engine opening. I have heard some interesting gossip about the next Engine in line. Says it may be in an unclaimed system."

Ordinarily, Veda would have been keen to get the gossip and look for an advantage, but right now it didn't matter if the next Reality Engine was populated by fluffy kitten creatures who dropped soul coins at your feet and then wandered off to collect more. She had to make it to phase two, or she'd never get another shot. "So you really don't think the natives have many good candidates for deeper delving?"

Danandra shook her head.

Zazef cocked his to one side, his tail twitching. "I don't know about that," he said with a sibilant undertone to his voice. "A lot of them do seem very soft. They've entered a tricky phase of their development where they're a little too focused on entertainments and what they call social media. It's being reflected in some of the class choices we're seeing. Not a lot of standard fighter and hunter classes like we'd get out of a more primitive world. They're much more creative. It's possible that some of them might make it to phase two, but that's a gamble I don't like to make. Not when I don't understand most of the class choices I'm seeing here." He flicked one talon at the ceiling and a scrolling image appeared in the air, showing various different miners' choices of classes and skills so far.

It matched what Veda had seen. Hundreds, maybe even thousands, of unique classes, most of which would not synergize together very well. Everyone knew anything but the eight standard class archetypes were experiments doomed to fail. "I guess this Reality Engine is screwing them over," she observed.

Danandra shrugged. "It's taking their own culture and histories as input. Their fault if they've just gotten weird in the last hundred years."

Veda thanked them for the conversation and turned away. She wasn't going to follow their strategy, so she needed all the time she had left to come up with one of her own. Bidding would start soon. As the miners filed into their own annexes, visible to the prospective backers through their computer systems, she got a good look at the humans who had been transported from their home just a day before. Most of them looked bewildered, some of them were argumentative, and a few were being propelled into the auction annexes by the Hub's system.

She sent out an inquiry and discovered that nearly ten percent of these miners had attempted to cause property damage, start a fight with other miners, or end their own lives since arrival at the Hub a few standard hours before. That seemed high. Maybe they weren't as soft as Zazef had thought.

The problem was, she still had too many choices. If she waited until the big companies had made their selections, that problem would go away, but then she'd just be left with the dregs of whatever was left. She needed a strategy, and she needed it quick.

Veda thought of her own family. She had a younger sister, two younger cousins, and her disabled mother counting on her. She needed to provide for them. That gave her an idea. She ran a quick query asking for teams which were primarily family groups. The algorithm plucked randomly across the whole surface of Earth, but it was divided up by small geographical units, about a kilometer on a side. That meant the lower populated regions of the world were more likely to provide teams who already knew each other.

Sure enough, there were several thousand teams with three or more related members. Many of the top-seeded teams were all family. Veda threw out anyone who she wouldn't be able to afford. Then she excluded anyone who had not arrived with excess soul coins. She needed people who were able to do more than the bare minimum.

That still left hundreds of choices. She had her algorithm sort them by class and team composition. That was a little trickier since most of the classes were unfamiliar to her, but her system consulted with the controlling computer and was able to assign archetypes to each class. She sorted teams that had someone with a healing skill highest, teams where everyone had essentially the same class at the bottom, and started marking her choices.

CHAPTER NINE

DOES THIS CLASS MAKE MY BUTT LOOK BIG?

Welcome to the Hub,] the system said. It was an understatement.

All around our little platform was black emptiness. Dark, nothing there. Completely void. But in front of my face, larger than the biggest full moon I'd ever seen, hung Jupiter. I'd seen it plenty of times in school books, or on TV documentaries about the Voyager missions, but seeing it with my own eyes was something else. No question what it was.

The Great Red Spot wasn't in view, but it had some other spots that were pretty impressive, as well as the mixing orange and white bands all over its great ruddy face.

I stood there gaping, my mouth hanging open, just shaking my head, unable to understand what I was really looking at. Deputy Young had been snoozing. As he woke, he stretched and turned. He jumped upright, staring.

"Holy cow!" He wiped his forehead and settled his hat back into place. "What kind of mess are we in?"

I peered downward, past my feet, trying to get a look under me, where a lumpy, rocky surface stretched far below.

"Must be one of Jupiter's moons. I don't recognize them by sight, I'm afraid." Sage pointed overhead. "And look at that. That's where we're going."

I looked up. The barrier over my head was a little hazy, so it was hard to make out, but the beam of light continued right up to an enormous silvery cylinder. The beam was aimed right at one of the circular ends. I couldn't tell how big it was. It looked huge, but there was nothing for scale.

A chill ran down my spine. These people were who they claimed they were. Aliens from not just another world, but across the entire galaxy. They had brought all of this here, taken us from our homes, for their own purposes. Our best chance of survival was to play along until we knew enough of what was going on to figure out an edge. The alien space station grew larger and larger until it was all I could see. Our pod rushed into its enormous hatch.

The barrier grew temporarily brighter than I could stand to look at, so I looked away. A moment later, it vanished. **[Please proceed to the welcoming chambers,]** our familiar voice said. A strip of light on the floor blinked brightly. We shuffled off the platform and followed it.

Our pod was one of dozens, maybe hundreds, all dispensing passengers into a huge circular chamber. I stepped over onto the floor beyond our pod and looked down. There was nothing below me. Just emptiness. I took another step away from the edge.

As each pod emptied, it pushed back out into the middle of the circle and then vanished, allowing another to take its place in the giant circle of empty space. What was holding it in the air? More invisible fields, I guessed, like we'd already seen.

People were streaming toward doorways, gaping in the featureless metal wall. The doors were about eight feet tall and a little too narrow for my liking. Not quite human-sized. A voice in my ear beckoned me over to one of them.

Sage, Grandpa, and Deputy Young were with me, but the other people who had been on our platform started for different doors. It looked like we were being broken up by party. That was fine with me. Until I knew what was going on, I'd stick with the people I knew and cared about. And Young, too, of course.

The door sealed shut behind us with an audible whoosh. I turned around, checking, but there were no other exits.

The room was about twenty by twenty feet. A bunch of overstuffed armchairs appeared out of nowhere. They looked like something you'd find in an old lady's house, and I sniffed the air, expecting that old lady smell. Nothing. We sat down. "If this is an attempt to get us comfortable, it's not really working," I said to the ceiling.

The system announcer said, *Welcome to our facility, Twofeather party.*

I winced. "We're going to have to change the party name here, Grandpa."

"Why? What's wrong with that?"

"Never mind."

Please give your attention to the choices in front of you now. This is the most important decision you will be making for your time here in the Reality Engine. Your choice cannot be changed. While it can and will be modified, the choices you make now will impact your future in ways you are probably not yet equipped to understand. The voice had taken on a slightly snarky edge, reminding me a little of a car salesman at the end of an advertisement. I didn't like it. I didn't like any of this.

So weigh your choices carefully, and decide how you're going to work together. But remember, if you base your build around someone else, and they don't live up to their end of the bargain, you might just be up shit creek without a paddle.

I started. "How does he know these idioms?"

"I told you," Grandpa said grimly, "they've been watching us. Those kooks down in Roswell were right. Alien abductions. Cattle mutilations. Must all be part of this plan. You've been covering this up for the government, Deputy?"

"That's absolutely ridiculous," Deputy Young said.

"Okay, now you want us to get paranoid with each other?" I shook my head. "We need to focus on this right now."

"Show us our options," said Sage. She sat forward in her chair, fingers drumming on her knees. "Show us all of them."

Your choices have been tailored to you based on the items you brought with you from your previous existence. Classes can be sorted by type or focus on one piece of your equipped or stored gear to display the classes compatible with it.

"What's that mean?" Frank asked.

Words, images, and numbers started scrolling through the air in front of me. There were boxes everywhere. I couldn't begin to keep track of them all. One said, **[Frying Pan Assassination Specialist]**. Another, **[Deep-Sea Fisherman]**. There was a **[Biweekly House Cleaner]**. Something at the corner of my vision caught my eye. I focused on it. This one said, **[Rifleman—Marine-Variant]**.

"It's coming up with classes based on what's in our inventory," Sage said. "It's offering me something called Teddy Bear Trainer, and has my stuffies highlighted as compatible equipment. No, I don't want that."

The class I was looking at had some numbers at the top. **[STR 10, DEX 9, WIS 3.]** I recognized those stats from D&D style games.

"Hang on a minute," I called up at the ceiling. "What are you playing at? Why do we have stat assignments like in D&D or something?"

The Reality Engine has monitored your culture and selected an interface that will be inherently familiar to many of the chosen miners, the system announcer told us with a definitely know-it-all tone.

"What sort of bullshit is this?" Young asked.

"Oh, oh, I know," said Sage. "I bet they just grabbed whatever they could find off the internet that looked like it was popular."

Yeah, that made sense. While Dungeons & Dragons wasn't really that popular numerically, it would probably be all over the internet. If someone was being lazy, and wanted to claim they'd picked a system that humans generally understood, they could do worse.

"The good thing is," Sage said, "we have an idea what's going on. I mean, obviously, the stat numbers are different than in D&D. It looks to me like ten is really, really good, five is okay, but anything less than that we should avoid unless it's your dump stat."

Deputy Young asked, "Dump stat?"

Sage sighed. "Don't pick anything yet, Deputy. Let me help you." She turned to me. "Shad, I think you're going to need to be something combat-focused. If our purpose is to collect soul coins, we're going to need to kill monsters."

"Sure, but there's like a million options here, and some of them are really dumb." I told her about the frying pan assassin.

She giggled. "Like Swamp Mama? Can you cast Make Hushpuppies?"

Grandpa was watching us both from his own chair. His fingers were steepled together, and his eyes were a little unfocused. I had a feeling he was looking at his own options, and that he was understanding more of this than I might have thought.

Sage addressed all of us. "Okay, first of all, you want to dismiss all noncombat specialties. That's most of the silly ones. Even support classes still count as combat specialists, apparently. I just tried it and it's way less crowded now."

I concentrated, and a bunch of the boxes went away. There were still way too many.

"Hang on, I'm reading some of the footnotes . . . Okay, listen. Apparently, the stuff we already brought into the system is going to end up being really powerful, at least for the first levels. Like, we should make a build around it if possible. That means your gun, Shad, and Grandpa, your axes."

"I don't understand any of what you're saying," Deputy Young complained.

Sage sighed. "Look, okay, Shad, I want you to take out your revolver. Just make the box appear, the one with all of its information in it."

I did, holding the Ruger Alaskan in my hand, finger off the trigger.

"Okay, now while you've got that, search for compatible classes."

I was going to ask her how exactly I was supposed to do that, but apparently the system was reading my mind. A bunch more boxes disappeared, leaving about a dozen left. I started reading them. **[Gunslinger]. [Hired Hand]. [1980s Cop Movie Sidekick]. [Token Mook]. [Guy Who Gets Killed in the First Scene of a Mob Movie].** What the hell?

I turned to Sage and told her about that class. She giggled. "Yeah, I'm seeing some pretty funny ones, too. It's like they had some sort of artificial intelligence scan a bunch of Earth entertainment and come up with stuff for us. Makes about as much sense as one of the AI chatbots."

Suddenly, Grandpa shimmered with light again. It was a little like what had happened when he'd bonded his soul coin.

"Grandpa, wait," Sage said. "We haven't finished discussing it yet."

Grandpa stood up. He looked happy. "It's all right, Sage. I was listening to you. Did what you said, and the right choice was so clear, I didn't need to wait."

"Can you show us?" I was curious about what he'd chosen. I hadn't actually inspected any of the classes closely enough to know what to expect here.

Grandpa grunted. All of my boxes faded away to near obscurity, and in the center of the room hung a bright green set of text. The title read:

[Tomahawk Ninja]
[Shadow Step] [Scalp]
[HP 70/70]

Cha	6
Dex	9
Int	3
Sta	7
Str	6
Wis	7

"Tomahawk Ninja?" I was staring at Grandpa, flabbergasted. "Seriously, Grandpa, you picked something with tomahawk in the name. Aren't you always going on at me about stereotypes and such? And ninja? Ninjas are Japanese; what the hell has that got to do with tomahawks?"

"Well, actually, it's a really good class." Sage was staring off into space again. "I looked up those abilities. Shadow Step lets you teleport twenty feet, as long as you end up behind whoever you're targeting. And Scalp sounds like it's a pretty devastating attack."

I started to say something, but Grandpa interrupted me. "Sage, sweetie, why don't you talk to the deputy here and see if you can help him understand some of his choices. Shad, c'mere." He stood up, and I followed him over to the corner of the room.

Sage was deep in conversation with the deputy. I hoped her sensitive hearing wasn't as good as mine, because I could tell Grandpa wanted a word with me in private. Grandpa dropped his voice as low as he could. Now I could barely hear him. I strained to listen.

"Look, boy, Sage thinks this is all a big game. I'm glad for her, because otherwise she'd be a quivering mess. But you and I know better. We've had to kill things. They won't be the last things we have to kill, either. We need to do it without hesitation, if that's what it takes to protect Sage and earn our way out of here. So yes, I was listening. I heard what she was saying. And this silly sounding option looked like a good way to keep her safe. I can sneak up on threats and take care of them before they know we're there. That helps protect her. So when you get back over there, I want you to take a good look at all the things this here system is offering us, and see what strikes you as a powerhouse. We'll keep Sage alive. Everything else can take care of itself."

I nodded. "But maybe we should keep our options open a bit. If we're misunderstanding something—"

"Tell you one thing I don't misunderstand," Grandpa said grimly. "Strangers from far away with technology superior to our own have showed up on our lands. They're talking a nice game here, talking about helping us claim something, making it sound like they're benevolent. Well, don't trust them. Don't trust them as far as you can throw them. Don't sign a treaty with them. And if you have to, at least try to find out what their beads are actually worth."

I nodded my head. As always, Grandpa had a point. He slapped me on the back. "Knew you'd understand. I'm glad you're here. If this had happened to us while you were still off in Europe somewhere, I don't think Sage and I would be here right now."

"You don't give yourself enough credit, old man. Even dying, you'd have killed that first critter and gotten the soul coin. After that, you and Sage would have been fine." I shot a quick look over at the pair of heads bent together. "What about the deputy?"

Grandpa pressed his lips together. "Frank's always been good people. He helped me out back when I first got you two kids back to the spread. He doesn't like you too much, 'cause he remembers you getting into some trouble as a boy, plus all the stuff your daddy got up to." He grumbled a bit. My father, his ex-son-in-law, the exiled FLDS white boy who managed to charm Grandpa's only daughter and then ended up leaving her for a bunch of other women, was not his favorite person. It was too bad, he'd said, that I favored my father, being tall and broad-shouldered rather than wiry like Grandpa's side. At least I didn't get his blond hair. I think Grandpa would have never lived that down.

"Anyway, we'd best get back over there and finish this up."

I strolled back over. Sage looked up brightly. "We just found a really good class. He's a Deputy Sheriff."

"I know that. It says so on his badge."

Sage rolled her eyes. "His *class* is Deputy Sheriff."

I squelched a laugh. "I see."

"I figured it out!" Young said triumphantly, and a box appeared in the air.

[Deputy Sheriff]
[Restraint] [Posse]
[HP 100/100]

Cha	2
Dex	7
Int	5
Sta	10
Str	9
Wis	5

"Posse is really cool. It lets him summon a pair of system-generated helpers who will attack his opponent for thirty seconds. The description says it's an upgradeable ability, too. Restraint lets him hold an enemy in place, unless it's more than one size class larger."

"That's excellent. How often can he do that Posse move?" It sounded like something I'd expect to have a cooldown in a game.

Sage deflated. "Standard is once every six hours, but actually, he was able to bond the ability with his whistle. So he can do it twice as often, but if he loses the whistle, it goes back to six. I told you our own gear is super powerful."

That wasn't bad, but we'd have to plan how to use it. "Okay, so what about me?" It sounded like the deputy could distract or tie up our enemies, but would probably need to be right up in their faces to do so.

Grandpa was a ninja—said so right in the name. He'd have to sneak up behind someone and hit 'em with his spear or tomahawk or whatever he ended up with in order to deal damage.

That meant I wanted to hit people who were farther away. I wanted ranged damage, if we were calling it that.

I looked at my options again. As I thought about it, a couple had eliminated themselves, probably ones that wouldn't synthesize well with Grandpa and Frank. There were about six options left, but my eyes were drawn to just one of them. [Gunslinger]. It had an asterisk by it, and when I thought about it, another box popped up and said, [**This class is compatible with several of your equipped items. Item enhancements will be tailored around class abilities whenever possible**].

I showed it to Sage, whose eyes went wide. "I should have seen that before. Our gear, our clothes and such, can count as equipment as well, not just weapons. I'm guessing your drovers coat is compatible with the Gunslinger class. It sounds like it'd be a great option. What are the abilities?"

I examined the details. "It's got pretty high dexterity, and actually the charisma's higher than I expected. Not so great on strength or wisdom, and intelligence is a four." Sage winced. "Does that mean I'll get stupider if I pick that class?"

Grandpa snorted. "Boy, I think you're giving yourself way too much credit."

"I don't think that's how it works," Sage said dubiously.

I drilled down and found an explanation of stats. They essentially served as multipliers of our own basic abilities, and they wouldn't affect our personality, just our skills. In the case of stamina, the higher that number, the more health available, so that went to near the top of my list. The formula seemed to be the twenty we'd all had in the initialization chamber, multiplied by half of our stamina stat.

I went back to the Gunslinger class. The stat choices seemed fairly balanced. Strength was lower than I liked, and I worried about having both intelligence and wisdom so weak, but hopefully stamina and dexterity would be a good pair to have nearly maxed out. It would give me eighty HP, which I liked.

Cha	7
Dex	9
Int	4
Sta	8
Str	5
Wis	5

The two unlocked abilities for Gunslinger were **[Quick Draw]**, and [**Trick Shot**]. Quick Draw expanded, explaining that it meant that I could summon my gun from its holster or a location up to forty feet away, straight to my hand, instantly. I also could not be disarmed by an enemy attack. That could be really handy. I remembered how the frog had knocked Frank's gun out of his hands. The skill was linked to my dexterity, and if I went up a point there, it would increase the range. Trick Shot let me shoot around corners, or do a ricochet off of a surface. It also said **[Upgradeable]**. Sage had said one of Young's abilities was upgradeable too. It used dexterity for its accuracy, and strength for how hard it hit.

"I really like Gunslinger." I explained the abilities. "But my concern is, what if we can't find .44 Magnum ammunition? Won't I be useless then?"

"You've still got all the brass, right?" Grandpa asked. "Worse comes to worst, we find a machine shop, and we can get the supplies to load your own. Place like this, we'll be able to find lead and powder pretty easily. Primers might be another matter, but I'm betting these aliens can come up with something." It made sense. After all, why would this class be compatible with my equipment if my equipment was going to be useless?

Still a little worried I was about to make the biggest mistake of my life, I chose to become a Gunslinger.

CHAPTER TEN

HOW COORDINATING YOUR PARTY'S OUTFITS CAN PAY

As the rush fell away, I took a deep breath. I felt like I'd been born anew. My skin itched, but in a good way. There was a menu blinking off in the edge of my vision. I focused on it, and my new abilities appeared. Trick Shot wasn't available, but Quick Draw was. I thought about it, holding my hand out in front of me.

My gun leapt from the pocket of my coat, right into my palm. My fingers curled around it in the perfect grip. I smiled. This was going to be okay. I still couldn't select Trick Shot, probably because we were in a safe zone.

I turned back just in time to see Sage glowing as she selected her own class. "Hey! I thought we were picking things as a team!"

"Don't worry, I found the perfect choice." She grinned at me and popped a screen up in front of us.

[Rodeo Cowgirl]
[Cowgirl Cheer] [Lasso]
[HP 60/60]

Cha	9
Dex	7
Int	7
Sta	6
Str	4
Wis	5

"Cowgirl Cheer is a team buff!" She clapped her hands excitedly. "As long as I cast at the start of combat, all of us have a ten percent bonus to avoiding hits, a ten percent bonus to damage we do, and applies a debuff to enemies, making them ten percent more likely to be hit."

"Those aren't very big numbers," Grandpa pointed out.

"Every bit helps. I can rope an enemy and pull it in toward us, tripping it and snaring it at the same time. It says I can cast Lasso using any rope, and I know we looted some from the trailer. Also, Lasso's upgradeable if we find compatible materials."

"I don't like how low your health is, compared to everyone else's."

Sage ignored me. A pair of achievements appeared.

**[Team Synergy! You are in a themed party. All damage outputs
will be 15% more effective. All XP gains are increased by 10%.]
[Cocksure! Nobody on your team took a healing ability!
Potions are now 25% more effective!]**

"Did everyone just get the same achievements?" Sage asked.

"Sure did. What do you know? We're a team." Grandpa sounded rather pleased. For all his talk earlier, he was enjoying himself. And why not? He'd been dying yesterday, and today he wasn't. I still had worries. But it was too late now.

I checked my character screen. "We've got an experience bar now!" It said I was a **[Level 1 Gunslinger]** and I was about five percent of the way through the level.

"Good. They gave us credit for all the things we killed. Do you think five percent is a lot compared to everyone else? How long until level two? Ooh, there needs to be a help menu!" Sage was half-angry, half-exuberant.

The air chimed around us.

**[Team Twofeather: Class selection is complete. Please proceed
through the doors to the auction annex.
Welcome to the Hub. The auction for sponsors and backers
will begin as soon as all miners have finished class selection.]**

I'd thought the enormous cavern full of portals down on the surface of whichever of Jupiter's moons it had been was large. As we stepped out of the class selection room, I knew I'd been wrong. That might have been large, but this place was huge. The roof arched over my head, probably a mile up. I didn't have any way to tell for sure.

We were on the inside of a giant cylinder. I'd seen that from our approach. The place where I stood felt perfectly flat, but the metal sky rose up over me like a rainbow made of steel. In the center of it was a wide window with a view of Jupiter. I stood transfixed for a moment, taking in the sight.

Sage poked me. "Come on," she said. "Let's get moving."

Grandpa raised his head toward the ceiling. "Which way to the grub?" he asked.

The announcer's voice spoke to us. I didn't think anyone else could hear it.

**[Food will be provided in the nearest auction hall annex.
You may eat while you wait for the auction to begin.]**

A ball of light appeared in front of our faces, and we threaded our way through the crowds, keeping pace with it. When I had to extricate Sage from a knot of people, the light paused and waited for us. It led us a good quarter mile along this crowded street to a crossing with another street.

Another couple of quick turns, and we found ourselves entering a mess hall. A mess hall was a mess hall, no matter where you were. It had tables and benches, and long counters where food was being served. There were half a dozen different conflicting odors in the air, some of them good, and when you got up to the counter, you found that none of them had anything to do with the food on offer there. If you were very lucky, there would be a condiment bar with plenty of ketchup and hot sauce, so you could doctor up whatever it was you actually did have. I'd seen the inside of mess halls from basic training, to where I was stationed in Germany, to one on an air base in Maryland that served crab cakes, and, I suspected, if you were an officer, champagne, but we don't talk about what the Air Force has.

This one was a little different. Instead of a counter, one wall had little niches with screens beside them. We paused beside an open niche. The screen was a menu. It offered different categories of food, all from Earth. I let Sage scroll through for a while, but after she had exclaimed in delight over a dozen different dishes and then not selected any of them, I stepped in front and ordered us all a round of T-bone steaks with home fried potatoes, a big serving of roasted asparagus, corn, and fresh squeezed lemonade to wash it all down. The food appeared one dish at a time in the niche. As we removed each, the next appeared. It took almost no time at all.

We struggled back through the crowd of hungry humans, found a set of open seats around a table, and sat down. I picked up my fork, then paused. Over the plates floated a caption:

[Standard ration. Provides 12-hour buff to health regeneration.]

"Huh. Wonder if there's a cooking mini-game?" I said aloud, and Sage nodded along.

"Or alchemy, or—" She put a bite in her mouth and shut up.

For about ten minutes, nobody said anything. We were too busy eating. When my steak was half gone and the potatoes were looking pretty sad, I looked around at my family and the deputy. My team? Maybe so.

"Did you notice how they kept calling us miners?" Deputy Young asked.

I nodded. That had struck me as curious, too. "First thing to find out is, what do they want from us and why? First part's probably not too hard. They're going to have to tell us. *Why* is another question. We need to know that. Once we understand what their purposes are, we can make sure not to get screwed."

Grandpa turned to Deputy Young. "Frank, you've been a good man, a good neighbor all your life. I'm happier to have you along than almost anyone else, but I'm going to give you a warning. I don't care what happens to me up here, but I am going to get my granddaughter back home safe and sound. You do one thing that puts that at risk, you're out on your own. I don't care how many brush fires we've fought together or stray cows we've rounded up."

Young looked tired. He put his head in his hands, having finally taken his incredibly dusty cowboy hat off his head and set it aside. "You don't have to worry about me, Louie," he said. "I know we're in over our heads. A couple times in the last day I might have just laid down and let the snake eat me if I'd been thinking straight. But we're here now and we're going to work together. I won't let anything happen to your little girl."

"I can take care of myself," Sage said proudly. Nobody replied. I didn't feel like I had anything to add, so I just sat in silence.

A little while later, the system announcer spoke. I could tell everyone in the room heard. Forks went down, heads went up.

**[We are now beginning the stakeholder auction.
Please, give us your full attention as we explain.]**

I looked around the room. There were hundreds of tables, with one to five people at each.

It looked like most of the other parties had lost at least one, maybe two members, so we were pretty average. I was still upset that I hadn't been able to do anything for Delores, but on the other hand, I couldn't see her being even half as cooperative as Frank was.

The table on our left had a full group of five. They looked bright and eager. I thought they were probably Chinese or maybe Korean. I had trouble sometimes telling those apart unless I heard them speaking their native tongue, but everyone I'd heard here was speaking English, which didn't make any sense. I decided the system was probably translating for us. I tried to overhear what they were saying, just for some information, without looking like I was eavesdropping. There were three women and two men on their team. One of the women who sat in the center of the table had the air of a business manager.

She was instructing the others to let her do the negotiating. "We already know we have a strong composition with all roles covered. We should be able to negotiate a large discount on our debt."

Sounded like some people had learned a lot more about our situation than I had managed. I leaned over. "Excuse me," I said. "May I ask a question?"

The woman shot me a glare and then turned back to her team members as though I hadn't spoken. I could take a hint. I turned aside and looked at the table behind me. Three guys about my age sat over empty plates. They looked American to me. One was pretty overweight and the other two had pale complexions that said they didn't get out much and the remnants of acne scars. "So you guys have any idea how this is going to work?"

"Nah, we just got here too, bro."

That wasn't helpful. I leaned over to Grandpa. "We need to present a unified front, whatever happens."

Grandpa was nodding. "I agree."

The lights dimmed.

[**Welcome to the sponsorship auction for the Earth Representative Miners attempting to tame Reality Engine number 6723459. You have all made it through initialization and have successfully selected a class. Now it's time to get to work. Right now, various interstellar organizations and interests are being given a chance to sponsor you as you make your way down into the Reality Engine and begin your attempts to claim it on behalf of your species. This will be a multistage event and we will let your backers explain their suggested strategies to you later. For now, what you need to know is that the first phase will begin immediately upon the closing of this auction. At that point, you may schedule a trip back down to the surface Reality Engine chamber and choose where to begin your mining.**]

"Mining what exactly?" someone nearby shouted. I wasn't expecting an answer.

To my surprise, it flashed up an image of a bunch of angry-looking green and purple wild boars. Whoever was running this seemed to have a thing for outlandish colors on wildlife.

[**As you already know, the denizens of the Reality Engine possess soul coins. Each of you here has already acquired and absorbed a single soul coin, granting you access to the Reality Engine's structures and systems.**

> Now you will be mining coins in order to pay your debt.
> The initial enemies you face will likely have only a single soul coin,
> but as you face more powerful enemies, you may reap higher rewards.
> The creatures generated by a Reality Engine will also drop important
> upgrades for your class and equipment, so be on the lookout for that.
> Those aren't the only ways to upgrade yourself, but they are the most
> common, so keep a sharp eye out for competition.]

"I just want to go home." Deputy Young was on his feet. He pounded the table in front of us with his fist. "Right now. I never asked to be here, and you had no right to take me. Send me home *now*." He pounded again.

Several others near us took up the cry, stamping their feet or pounding the tables until the whole room was a cacophony of noise. Sage stuck her fingers in her ears, wincing. I sympathized with the sentiment, but kept quiet myself.

As Grandpa had proved, these soul coins could take a dying man, heal him, and erase thirty-plus years of aging from him. I doubted that was all they did. They were valuable, and it seemed we were the key to acquiring them. The aliens who had brought us here were not going to let us go so easily.

> [You will have an opportunity to earn your passage out
> of the Reality Engine's sphere of influence. But first you must
> pay off your debt.]

I couldn't help myself. I shouted, "What debt?" at that. I wasn't the only one upset. People who hadn't joined in the first wave of protests were yelling now, pointing out that we hadn't asked for any of this, so what debt were they talking about?

The announcer got a little snide with us.

> [We are working under the strictures of the covenant on
> Reality Engine awakening, acquisition, and exploitation signed
> by every major galactic civilization over 8,000 years ago. It's not
> our fault if you don't like the provisions. The point is a certain
> amount of money was spent to bring you all here and help integrate
> you into the Reality Engine. That debt has been split across all
> remaining miners who passed initialization. Once your debt is
> paid off, you will be free to negotiate your return or a different circum-
> stance for yourselves. Your backers and stakeholders are the ones
> who will help you with your exit from this event. Now sit and listen,
> or you will be silenced and restrained.]

That got some people sitting, but plenty more kept yelling. The room flashed brightly. The announcer rumbled, **[Silence!]**

There were only a few holdouts left. Even Deputy Young sank back into his seat. The last few squawks were abruptly cut off as the controlling system wrapped the protesters in invisible fields and forced them back into their seats.

Now the announcer continued.

[As to your sponsors, since your debt needs to be covered, we have given the interested organizations the ability to buy out your debt.]

"Slavery," I heard someone say. Someone else said, "Doesn't matter who you sell me to, I'm not going back there."

[There's no slavery involved. If you do not agree to the offer, you will be offered the standard system contract. From now on, you are responsible for feeding and housing yourselves. Your sponsors will help you with your initial stake, providing you with the equipment you need to begin mining. Going it on your own will prove costly in the long run, so please consider all offers carefully.]

I said, more to Grandpa than to the system, "I still don't understand why they're calling it mining. We're going in and killing things."

The guys behind me leaned forward. "Bitcoin mining, bro," the heavyset one said. I'd heard the term, even read a few articles about it, but I wasn't quite following the logic here.

The thin guy, who still had a pockmarked face full of acne, rolled his eyes and continued, "This Reality Engine is coining its own kind of tokens, right? So they need us to go in and collect them. It's got to be some sort of galactically unique IDs and interstellar blockchain going on here."

I guess that made as much sense as anything else.

Grandpa snorted. "They're the ones with all the guns. Let's see how badly we're going to get screwed here."

The lights came back up and a hush fell over the whole room. I realized, looking around me, that the tables full of people were still talking. I just couldn't hear any of them.

That was when the snow elf princess appeared in front of our table.

CHAPTER ELEVEN

IS INDENTURED SERVITUDE RIGHT FOR YOU? FIVE QUESTIONS TO ASK

My name is Veda Tvedra," the woman said.

She really did look like some sort of high elf or snow princess. Her pale hair hung in iridescent coils around her head. Her skin was far whiter than anything I'd ever seen on a human on Earth. But it didn't look like makeup, just like that was who she was.

"I have won your sponsorship contract. We will be working together for the duration of phase one and possibly beyond."

Deputy Young's eyes narrowed. "Hang on a minute," he said. "I'm not going to be working with you or anyone else. What about my constitutional rights against indentured servitude?"

"I'm afraid your constitution has no jurisdiction here," the woman said. "We are governed by Galactic Council laws and the Reality Engine Exploitation Coalition's guidelines concerning exploitation of a Reality Engine. But you're right. You can't be forced to work with me. All mining parties are given a choice between taking the sponsorship deal they are offered or taking the standard system contract."

"And what's that?" I asked.

The woman flicked her hand and a long screen of text appeared in front of me. "You can confirm with the system, but the terms are essentially that you split your winnings fifty-fifty and are responsible for all equipment purchases, your own room and board, receive no advice for strategizing, and are on your own if anything goes wrong. By the way, in case they haven't showed you, this is your debt translated into soul coins." She put up a figure with way too many commas in it.

"Ugh," I said, thinking about the thirty or so soul coins we had collected in the initial level. "How long does that take to pay off?"

"Using standard exploitation strategies, about twenty of your years, give or take. Could be less if you make a lucky find. Could be more if you develop a taste for some of the more decadent entertainments offered here on the Hub."

"And what about yours?"

The woman smiled. I didn't quite like her expression. It seemed like she had too many teeth.

"Well, now, that's interesting, because what I want from you is a little different. The standard contract that you would be engaged in with the system itself is designed to extract as many soul coins as possible from the Reality Engine before its ownership is decided. That can take anything from one to a hundred standard years, depending on the efforts of the local species. I, however, have a different objective. I need to get a team capable of taking on phase two challenges." She held up a hand. "We don't have time to get into that right now. Right now, focus on phase one. Phase two is months away, at least. The point is, I'm not looking to get years of labor out of you. I need you for a far shorter amount of time, and I need you to survive. To that end, I will invest all the profits we make during phase one into equipping you, training you, and helping you reach your full potential."

That sounded suspiciously good. It made me think whatever phase two was, I wasn't going to like it.

"So, you take fifty percent of our earnings and . . ."

"Oh no," she interrupted. "My contract requires that I will take ninety percent of your earnings. However, your room and board will come out of that, as will all of your equipment. Your ten percent can be used at your discretion to buy down your debt or to amuse yourselves. I additionally promise that I will not resell your debt without your agreement."

This really sounded too good to be true. I glanced at Grandpa, whose eyes narrowed as he studied the woman. I couldn't tell her age. It could be anything between twenty and thirty-five. Plus she was an alien with access to this galactic technology that could transform a dying old man to one in the prime of his health. For all I knew, she was five thousand years old and could outthink me any day of the week.

"How many teams are you making this offer to?" I asked.

"One at a time." Her eyes flashed. "And if you're not going to take my offer, I'd appreciate if you'd hurry up and reject it. I can't bid on another team with my funds in escrow."

That told me something very important. This woman was desperate. She might have power over us, but it wasn't unlimited power. She needed us.

"Why our team?" Grandpa asked, leaning across the table at her. "You want me to take a risk with the lives of my grandchildren. I need to know I can trust you. Why did you pick us?"

The woman sighed. "The first two teams I made an offer to rejected me," she said simply. "By the time I got down to you, there weren't many options left. The big conglomerations have already bought up a bunch of contracts. I'm looking for a team who can work well together. People who care about each other and won't try to screw each other over."

I did not miss how her gaze flickered to the side as she glanced at Deputy Young. Her focus went right back to Grandpa. "You and your grandchildren already know each other, trust each other. That gives you an advantage. If you will extend that trust to me, I will endeavor to be worthy of it."

"Can we have a moment of privacy?" Grandpa asked. "We'd like to look this over and discuss."

The woman didn't hesitate. "All right. I'll dismiss my presence. You can call me back by speaking my name. I just ask that you don't take too long." For a moment, her frozen expression dropped and there was vulnerability in her eyes. I wondered if it was just another manipulation attempt or if she really was this worried. Then she vanished.

I started scrolling through the contract she'd offered us. It wasn't very long, and written in fairly straightforward language. Not like the one the car salesman with the lot right across from my basic training post had offered. I'd smelled a rat and walked away from that one fast.

"She's desperate," Grandpa said. "She looks like a rancher whose property is being surrounded by greedy developers with lobbyists back in Washington. We can take advantage of that."

"Or she can take advantage of us," I pointed out. "I don't trust her. Though it looks like she was telling the truth about this contract."

"I don't trust any of these people," Frank said. "I say we go with the standard system contract and keep our heads down. This girl sounds like she wants something dangerous from us."

Sage was busy scrolling through the system contract still in front of us. "She wasn't lying about these terms. I don't know what a normal rate of soul coin earning might be, but that's a really big number."

"She said it could be twenty years." I looked at Grandpa. "This is no place for a kid to grow up. I think we should take the risk. We'll be careful with whatever she asks us to do. But if we could get Sage out in as little as six months, I'm all for it."

Grandpa nodded. "I agree."

"Well, I don't," Deputy Young said. "But I don't see a better option, and I'd rather stick with you than try to go out on my own."

"Great!" Sage said. "Veda?"

The elf princess appeared again.

"We will take your deal," I said. "We're willing to work with you. Now . . . what's our first step?"

The woman smiled. "I'm ordering supplies to be delivered to you on the elevator. I want you on the next trip down. We'll talk as you head over."

By now, many of the other teams were standing up and leaving the room. We joined the throng. Veda wasn't really here, of course, but her image accompanied us. It looked real except when someone brushed past her and her outline fuzzed.

"Start talking," I said as we shuffled out of the room, impeded by the crowd. Thousands of other humans were making for the Hub where the elevator came in, their conversations muted as though we had a bubble of silence around us.

Veda blinked, then began her spiel.

Let her talk, I said in party chat. *We need to hear what she's saying.*

"Thank you for accepting my offer. I am a representative of a small company that makes our living off of these Reality Engine openings. I have nothing to do with the selection of the miners or choosing which Reality Engine is exploited at any given time. I am as much a victim of circumstances as you are."

That was awfully easy for her to say when we were the ones who were about to be risking our lives. I rolled my eyes but said nothing. She kept going.

"Here's the deal. You're about to go back down and enter one of the phase one zones. All of the zones have different themes and flavors, usually drawn from your own history and pop culture references. Sometimes the Reality Engine gets creative and comes up with ideas on its own. And, very occasionally, it generates a level based on what we think the progenitor culture was like. If you ever find one of those, be sure to record everything. It's worth a fortune to cultural historians and progenitor conspiracy theorists. But that's not relevant."

"Ooh," Sage said, then made a lip-zipping motion. We had reached the end of a long line of people moving steadily toward an enormous archway. Through it, I could see vast dark space, with flashes of light every few seconds. The elevators back to the surface, I guessed.

She gave a wave of her hand. "In addition, the zones offer different types of gameplay. Some are what you would refer to as grinding levels, populated with lots and lots of monsters with very little cohesive theme, similar to the introductory level you all experienced. Those zones are a great way to collect soul coins and gather experience, but you need to avoid them. I want you to choose one of the mission levels. Those will have plenty of things to kill, but they'll also have puzzles and a storyline you uncover as you go along. If you play along with the game, you can receive unique rewards, especially skill drops and materials we can use to improve your gear."

"Can we tell the zones apart?" Grandpa asked.

"They'll all be labelled by the system. You won't know exactly what you're getting, but you'll be able to tell the kind of playstyle they offer. You should be able to make level two in a couple weeks of running those zones. Then we'll assess the strategy."

The line shuffled forward. I craned my neck to see. The queue went on ahead through the enormous door, then made a ninety-degree turn—straight up. I was looking at the top of peoples' heads as they stood in line on a platform that, to me, was perpendicular. It made me nauseous to look at it.

"You've got themed classes. They're unusual and I don't quite understand them, but I want you to lean into those themes. You should look for healing abilities, either self-heals or ones you can use on your party. But don't try to go too far away from your class archetype. That means you, Shad, shouldn't try to learn to use a spear or a pike. You're a gunslinger. Focus on that. And you, Louis." She turned to Grandpa. "You've got two areas you can focus on, the stealth side or the axe side. Keep your options open until you know what you prefer."

"What about gear?" I asked. "You said you'd help equip us."

"And I have. Everything has already been delivered. You'll pick it up at the Hub. There's a potion belt for each of you. For now, that's going to be your only source of healing. They're expensive, but not as expensive as you dying."

"Which is permanent, right?" Sage asked.

"In this phase, yes. Phase two works differently. I've provided each of you with ten healing potions. In addition, resting and eating food can recover lost health. And so can bandaging wounds. At first, you'll be pretty bad at it. But if you keep at it, you should get some skill points. You, Sage, have already unlocked the crafting interface and its associated skills. Keep that up. Your team should feed all the ingredients to you and let you focus on learning how to construct new items. They won't be as good as what dedicated galactic crafters can make, but they'll be a lot cheaper and let you stay out longer on your own."

Sage rubbed her hands together gleefully. "Yes!"

"I've included a portable camp setup. It'll be self-explanatory when you get there. You've got a week of food. After that, you'll need to come back up to the Hub and report in. I bought as much ammunition for your weapons as I could afford."

"What if we're injured or need a break? Can we come back early?" I asked.

"If you must. Each trip costs, so be careful. You need to start earning soul coins to build up our war chest."

"Why are those valuable, anyway?" Grandpa asked. "You're spending a lot of money to set us up to collect them."

"Our whole society is based on them. Just like you, we all need a soul coin to attune to a Reality Engine. Life for those who aren't attuned is bleak. Half-living. Imagine what you're earning with each drop is someone's actual chance at life, and then ask how much it's worth."

"No need to imagine," Grandpa said quietly.

That seemed to throw Veda off her stride. "Uh. Yes. Let's wrap this up; you're almost to the elevator now. I've paid to unlock the Inspect ability for each of you."

Veda grimaced. "That used to be baseline, but they've started making sponsors pay to enable more and more minor abilities."

"So who makes those decisions?" I asked. "There are two different systems at work here, yeah?"

The great doorway was just ahead. I could see the turn in the line here, where people marched up to what looked like a ten-foot-high wall with empty space above it, then stepped onto the wall, their bodies turning all at once, and strode along it to where the elevator platforms waited.

"That's right. The Reality Engine, which lies beneath the surface of the moon you refer to as Ganymede, generates the levels, the monsters, and the soul coins. It also grants you the ability to use its systems to cast your abilities. That's why you can't use most of them up here on the Hub. The Reality Engine is what translates your intentions into something actually happening."

"The conglomeration that is behind opening this Reality Engine has brought in its own system that we reverse engineered from a Reality Engine. Think of it as a parasite riding along on top of the Reality Engine. That's what provides many of the helpful submenus, like the inventory system. It's negotiating with the Reality Engine to create those on your behalf. That system is the one you hear speak. But unfortunately, that means that the people running this can charge to enable those subsystems. At least they kept the inventory free."

"Microtransactions," I grumbled. I had played a few phone-based games during AIT when I was bored out of my mind. Most of them had an engaging premise but quickly devolved into pay-to-win grind-fests where every ability was locked behind a small fee. "Are there any other abilities that you've bought for us?"

"Not yet. I need you to earn some coin first. My funds are tapped out with this. The Inspect ability will let you look at skill seeds that drop and understand how they will work with your classes. It can also let you analyze upgradeable ingredients and figure out how to add them to your equipment. It's absolutely vital. Just get in the habit of inspecting every drop you get."

"So what's a skill seed?" I asked, but Sage pulled something out of her inventory.

"Cajun Mama dropped this," she said. "The woman we fought in the shack in the swamp."

It was a small marble, gleaming blue.

"Go ahead and use Inspect on it," Veda encouraged.

Sage did. She held it up and frowned. "It says it's not compatible with my currently equipped AoE ability and do I want to equip another, but that this one won't be compatible with my theme."

"Stick with your theme," Veda urged. "Shad, you look."

I took the marble and held it out. I concentrated, and a box bloomed over the marble.

[Area of Effect Ability: Call 'em Out. Cast to reveal any hidden enemies within ten meters. Also suggests enemies focus their attentions on you for thirty seconds. Resisted by enemies with higher charisma than yours. Unallied, nonhostile entities will be Intimidated or, in rare cases, become hostile.]

"This sounds really good." I narrated the details.

Veda nodded. "You should take that. Revealing invisible or concealed enemies can save your life. You've got more health than the others, so you should be able to take a hit or two, but again, I suggest you find some healing spells as soon as you can."

We reached the wall. I cautiously lifted my foot and placed it in front of me. The world shifted, I caught my balance, and suddenly everyone else was horizontal to me. Sage giggled.

Veda smiled brightly. "I'll leave you here. We all have work to do. Good luck, miners. Don't take too many risks." She vanished.

I looked at my family, took in the serious looks. Sage was chewing her lips.

"Come on," I said, stepping up to the elevator platform. "We've got front-row tickets to this space rodeo, and they're about to let out the broncs. We don't wanna miss it."

CHAPTER TWELVE

HOW TO BOOK YOUR TROPICAL VACATION

A gull wheeled in the cloudless blue sky overhead. Sage jumped and clapped her hands. "A boat! We're on a boat!" She rushed over to the metal railing about ten feet away and peered down.

I turned on the spot, taking it all in, looking for danger. Behind me rose the superstructure of an enormous white-painted ship. Deck chairs full of passengers in bathing suits and Bermuda shorts stretched away into the distance.

We stood on the deck of an absolutely enormous cruise liner. It had three tall white smokestacks running down the middle of it and an enormous swimming pool with a fancy water slide. Apparently, the system was pulling from a lot of different imagery.

Sage peered out beyond the bow of the ship. "There's so much water!" she said in amazement. "I've never seen so much water in my life! Shad, come look! Quick! Grandpa!"

I glanced out, amused at her enthusiasm. Sage had never before been out of the southwestern desert. I had at least seen an ocean on a handful of occasions, but this really was something. Far below, little white-capped waves broke against the dark blue bow of the ship. A handful of speedy motorboats darted around the edge.

"It's not real," I reminded her, "but it feels real."

She stretched her arms skyward, the breeze ruffling her dark hair. "It smells real. This is amazing."

"No sign of enemy combatants," Grandpa reported, joining us. Deputy Young stood off to the side, still a little grumpy. He had not liked us forcing him through the portal. I knew once things got started, he'd have no choice but to help.

A man was approaching us, wearing a white jacket with dark trousers and a captain's hat with gold epaulets. Over his head floated the word *Captain*. No last name, just the title. I straightened up and turned to meet him.

"Shore crew," he said, addressing a point just past my shoulder. "We have a situation."

In party chat, Sage sent, *This must be our mission briefing. We should pay attention.* I had already guessed that, but I was glad she was letting Grandpa and Frank know what to expect.

"What sort of situation?" I asked as the pause stretched on a little too long.

The captain's eyes lit up, and he spoke once more. "Our tenders have not come out to receive passengers. We've looked at the port through our glasses, but there's no sign of anyone there. I need you to go and find out what the holdup is before the passengers lose their chance at this excursion."

Great. Sounded straightforward enough. We would take a boat over to the shore and then discover what the storyline here was. "How do we get ashore?"

The captain pointed a little farther down the railing. "The boat has been made ready for you."

"I don't suppose you have any gear or special equipment for us?" Sage asked, peering around my shoulder at the captain. That must not have been one of his prepared questions, because he just stood there and stared. It seemed like some of these NPCs were more reactive than others.

"All right, might as well get moving," I said. I hadn't seen any kind of timer yet, but there was no sense in standing around waiting. I went over to the ladder the captain had pointed out. It was a rope ladder stretching down the side of the boat to a ridiculously tiny rowboat. "Fuck that." I turned back to the captain. "This is a state-of-the-art cruise ship. Where's the proper boats?"

The captain said stiffly, "We're having a problem with the launch hoist."

"So, what do you think?" I asked. "Do we take this or do we look for another way?"

Sage looked over the side and shuddered. "That's a long way down."

I was about to agree with her when an achievement-style message popped up. It said, [**Mission: Bad Vacation. The cruise is calling, but no one's home! Discover why the townsfolk have not come out to meet the cruise line. Step one: take the small boat ashore.**]

"Well, that's convenient," Grandpa remarked.

"It looks like there's one way scripted for us to get ashore. All right, I'll go first," I said and swung myself over the side. Fortunately, the ship and the ladder remained rock still as I descended. There was no sensation of movement at all.

I lowered myself into the boat and immediately the boat started going up and down, but not in a natural fashion like it was being rocked by waves. More like one of those old rides outside of grocery stores that I remember when I was a little kid. I wondered what happened to those things. I always liked the zebra outside the Kmart in the town we lived when I was younger than Sage. I guessed the Kmart was gone now too.

Grandpa came next and after him, Sage. I gave her a hand into the boat. Deputy Young clung to the ladder, lowering himself one rung at a time, grumbling the whole way. "You're almost there," Sage called encouragingly. "Keep on."

When we were all seated in the boat, I set a hand on the old-fashioned oar, expecting I would have to row, but instead the boat took off with no input from me. It zipped speedily past the cruise ship, going at least ten knots, which was an absolutely preposterous speed for a rowboat.

Some of the motorboats zoomed past and I could see they were manned, but the occupants all had hats pulled low over their faces or were ducking down behind the wheel so I couldn't get a good look at anyone. That seemed suspicious.

"All right," I said. "Situation. We appear to be off a Caribbean island of some sort." I pointed as we came around the stern of the ship and saw the lush green island waiting for us. It curved away so I couldn't tell for sure, but it looked like a fairly small island maybe a couple of miles across. Golden beaches, dark green jungles. A couple of beach chairs and umbrellas littered the sand, but no people.

There was an enormous wharf extending out into the water. Too small for the ridiculous ship, but there were three smaller passenger boats waiting. I guessed those were the tenders the sea captain meant.

"Anyone know anything about cruises?" I asked without much hope, but Frank spoke up.

"My wife and I took one just after our eldest daughter had her baby. She was living in Florida and when we went to visit, we took a cruise at the end of it. Five days sailing around the Caribbean. Worst vacation of my life. They talk about all the food and drink, but I got seasick and spent the whole time locked up in my cabin except for the couple of days Mary Ann made me go ashore. We rode in one of those things." He pointed at the tender. "She spent way too much money on touristy knickknacks and junk."

That wasn't very helpful. "Well, be prepared," I said as the boat took us to a small dock to the side of the enormous wharf. It nudged up against a rickety-looking wooden structure that would not have been out of place in a pirate movie.

I climbed up, looked around for a rope to make the boat secure, and then decided it didn't matter. This was clearly scripted, and if we were supposed to take the boat again later, it would be here for us. I gave Sage a hand up and waited until Grandpa and Frank had joined us.

There was no one here. The only sounds were the waves lapping, the boats creaking, and a couple of birds calling from the nearby trees. An insect buzzed past me. I squashed it on my arm. That mosquito was the first sign of life I'd seen since leaving the boat.

"We need to figure out what's going on." I noticed that no further steps had popped up for us to follow. My guess was that we would figure out what came next and then it would appear, just like the message telling us to take the boat.

"Grandpa, I think I'd better take point on this one. You watch behind. Frank, Sage, keep your eyes on a swivel. Shout if you see anything. Nobody get more than ten feet away from anyone else and nobody go inside any of these buildings until I've given them a checking over."

I started down the wharf, my drovers coat flapping in the gentle breeze. It was going to get hot, but after the way it had protected me from the Cajun Mama's hot oil, I would not be taking that coat off if I could help it. I didn't bother drawing my gun. My Quick Draw ability would have it in my hand faster than I could do manually and this way I kept my hand free until I needed it.

Grandpa had his modern steel axe in one hand. Frank drew his sidearm and kept it in a low ready position. Sage had drawn a length of rope from her inventory and coiled it in her right hand. She had said she could cast her Lasso ability with any kind of rope, which was good because we hadn't actually managed to loot a lariat.

I approached the closest building. It was a dockside bar of some sort. Looked like it usually catered to tourists. Brightly colored flags hung around the wide patio seating. Little green and white plastic lawn chairs clustered around small, paper-topped tables. The sign overhead read, *The Purple Parrot.*

Nobody was on the porch. I approached the glass front doors. It listed the restaurant's hours and had a picture of their menu posted. Heavy on the alcohol, light on anything else. Definitely a tourist trap, with six different margaritas on the menu and something called a Caracal cocktail, whatever that was.

I passed on by and studied the next little store. It was an open-front shop with a wide metal door that pulled down like a garage door at night. It had racks of T-shirts and shell jewelry and a spinning display of postcards.

I grabbed one of the postcards. It read, *Greetings from Grand Parrot Island.* "I don't think there is a Grand Parrot Island," I commented, showing the card to the others. It wasn't eligible to be put in my inventory. So far, only the things we'd brought with us from Arizona, or designated loot items, could be taken. The dungeon-generated items could be thrown, stacked, probably set on fire, even eaten, but not looted.

"Hang on," Sage said suddenly. "Use Inspect on that rack of postcards." I did and the third postcard down glowed with a greenish light around the edges. I picked it up.

It showed a decaying church with a graveyard all around it. *Spooky greetings from Grand Parrot's oldest chapel and mausoleum,* it read. I flipped it over. On the back side there was a little paragraph describing what it called a haunted chapel that had once been home to a fallen priest who had given himself over to Santeria.

"I think it's a clue," Sage said and as she took the card from me, a notification popped up.

[Misson: Bad Vacation. Step two: investigate the chapel.]

"All right," I said. I moved over to the cash register.

Behind the counter was a map of the island. I studied it, then pulled up my own map. For a moment, my map showed an outline of the cruise ship and then the dock we had just explored. As I studied the map on the wall, various sections of the island filled in. There were a couple of notable blank spaces that I suspected we would find out about soon enough. Off to the south was labeled *Haunted Chapel*. As if that wasn't enough, a small red X appeared right above the label.

"I guess we know where we're going next. Everybody keep your head on a swivel."

As we followed the quickest path out of town, we passed a two-story, white-washed building. The lower floor was a dive shop, but a quick Inspect revealed nothing interesting. I stepped back out.

A window creaked open overhead. I cast Quick Draw, stepping back to get a good look.

A young woman leaned out of the house, low-cut blouse revealing dark skin, curly hair tumbling down to her shoulders. "Hey! You don't look sick," she called. "You newcomers?"

"We just got here," Sage shouted back, while Grandpa and I spread out a little in case this was a trap.

"Everyone in the village got sick but me. Some of them laid down and won't wake up. They're not dead, they just won't wake. The others all left. I tried arguing with them, but they didn't hear me. They went that way." She pointed the way we were heading.

"Stay there, and we'll take care of this," I said. She withdrew. Another confirmation from the system that we were on the right path, and maybe a clue.

"Sick people? You think it's catching?" Frank asked.

"I doubt it. What I'm wondering is if the ones who are asleep now are going to wake up and attack us later in this story." I hesitated. Maybe we should hang back, find some of the sick people and examine them. Maybe we'd find a clue. On the other hand, trying to do a storyline out of order might break everything. "Let's keep going," I said reluctantly.

CHAPTER THIRTEEN

HOW TO RESPECT LOCAL CULTURE

We made it a quarter of the way out of the deserted village along a stone path lined with seashells that wound its way through the jungle. Every minute that nothing attacked, my anxiety rose. I had expected to come into this zone and start having to kill my way through dozens, maybe hundreds of different creatures before locating the boss. When Veda had called it a story mission, I'd assumed that just meant it all had a theme. This was more like a mystery game.

"Keep your eyes open for puzzles or riddles," I said. "Sage, did you ever play that old game of mine, *Myst*?"

She shook her head. "The disk had a big scratch on it, and I never bothered to find a new copy."

"Something about this is reminding me of it. It was one of the earliest games I can remember that really had puzzles and interaction with world environments in it. It's a good reminder that not everything has to be combat."

"I wouldn't lay odds against us fighting something, boy," Grandpa said grimly.

Frank had holstered his weapon and was whistling as we went, his hat pushed back on his head. "It's better than the swamp, at least. After we're done at this chapel, let's go back to that bar and see if we can find the ingredients for a margarita. I could go for one."

I kept waiting for something to go wrong. That was probably the only reason I heard it in time. There was a shuffling noise and something between a moan and a cough off to my left. I whirled, casting Quick Draw. My gun leapt to my hand as a zombie stumbled out of the jungle.

The zombie looked like he'd been a tourist, with a big floppy hat and a tropical print shirt hanging open. His whole lower jaw was missing. He had ugly, gaping holes in his chest. I could see his ribs through his torso and his skin was a horrible green color. His health bar was full, but a nasty yellow shade. **[40/40]**.

I fired three shots right into center mass but he kept coming. Each shot had only done two points of damage instead of my usual five. I Inspected him and the explanation popped up. [**Any injuries other than to the head deal half damage.**] Rounded down, apparently.

I felt a whoosh of air passing over me as Sage cast Cowgirl Cheer. I could actually feel my reflexes speed up. The zombie lunged for me with arms extended. I was able to easily sidestep it. I stuck out a leg and tripped it.

Grandpa leapt in for the kill. He hacked the zombie's head free and held it up. The health bar dropped to zero. No loot appeared.

I spun around, still breathing heavily. We hadn't gotten any kind of warning prompt from the system, so I wasn't sure if we were finished with combat or not.

I cast Call 'em Out and could briefly feel my senses expand to take in an area about ten yards on all sides of me. There was nothing there.

Sage's eyes were wide. "It said he was more susceptible to my spell because of being under the control of another mind," she said. "That made our chance to dodge attacks more effective."

"Good to know. I have a feeling we'll be seeing more of these. Voodoo, old chapels, cemeteries. I think most of the island inhabitants are or will be zombies before long. My guess is we've got to fight our way through them and then put a stop to the infection."

"Zombies," Deputy Young said, staring down at the headless corpse in disgust. "Really?"

I shrugged. It did feel a little stereotyped to me, and I wondered if there would be a twist to the story. "Come on, let's keep moving. We haven't gotten any XP at all so far." I double-checked my character screen just to be sure. Same as before, it showed us at a little less than five percent into level one. "I'm wondering if we get all the experience at the end, when we complete this mission."

Veda had said that leveling time varied between Reality Engines. Fast but less important levels versus fewer, further apart levels that really mattered, and we didn't know which this Engine preferred yet. Nobody had made it past level one in the tutorial.

I had actually considered trying to make Sage sit this one out. We could have given her rations from our pack and left her in the portal room, but she'd outright refused. "If you don't take me, I'm just gonna jump through the nearest portal and do my best," she had said. "I won't be left behind while you guys level up and gain new skills."

That had ended that argument.

As we made our way along the path, I heard increased rustling in the brush to either side. I cast Call 'em Out again. I could do it every ten minutes or so, and I didn't want to waste it, but on the other hand, if there was someone waiting for us, I needed to know.

Nothing appeared. The text of the spell did say it worked on enemies, though, so it was possible there was something watching us that was not an enemy. The girl in town, for instance, had clearly been an NPC but wasn't an enemy, at least not yet.

The jungle started to thin out. I held up a hand. "Let's take this nice and slow," I said. "Grandpa, you want to scout ahead?"

Grandpa didn't have any actual sneaking abilities, but his Shadow Step would be useful in a pinch, and he had the most natural scouting talent of any of us.

He equipped his ghillie suit right out of his inventory and flipped it up over his head. I Inspected him and saw that he did indeed have a buff to stealth.

Grandpa slunk forward, sticking to the shadows until he was out of trees.

He sent back a message. *I just got a message: "+1 to sneaking." That's not on my list.*

It's not a named ability, it's a personal skill, Sage said. *Sorry, I saw that menu earlier and forgot to mention it. There's, like, everything on it. Running, walking, cleaning. Think* skills *really clearly.*

I tried, and an enormous list popped up, with a ton of skills followed by numbers. Mostly they were fours or fives, but I spotted a twelve in marksmanship, and a really pretty insulting two in picking up chicks.

Okay, maybe that was fair.

I dismissed the list for now and watched Grandpa's progress.

A minute later, he sent a message by party chat. *Come on up here. There's nothing yet, and I'm going to scout farther ahead.*

We followed him to the edge of the jungle. He was crouched behind a deadfall, peering over it. We joined him on our hands and knees.

"I see the chapel over there, and I don't see anyone moving," he said. I peered over the top of the deadfall.

We had come out by a headland, a place where the land swept up just a little bit until it abruptly ended at the sea. Atop the headland was the chapel we were looking for.

Straight across from us, about twenty yards away, the sea swept up onto a golden beach. There were no boats or planes to be seen, and no sunbathers. It was quiet. Too quiet.

The chapel was a one-story stone building about fifteen feet on a side, with shabby wooden shutters with peeling white paint, and a steeple where a bell hung. It had clearly seen better days.

A small cemetery surrounded the chapel with a couple of dozen headstones leaning at crazy angles. My nerves grew as I looked at those stones. I just knew we'd be fighting zombies here in a minute.

"Think we should go knock on door?" Grandpa asked.

I didn't like that idea at all. "I've got a better plan," I said. "You guys follow me, but stay back about twenty yards. When the action starts, just work together as best you can." I stood up and made for the graveyard.

The path crunched under my feet as I went. Louder than the stones had before, I looked down and realized to my horror that, instead of white stones, I was now trampling skulls and leg bones. Nice touch.

I checked my skills, noting the cooldowns. Just about perfect. Ten more seconds to go. I walked up to the churchyard, which was surrounded by a wrought iron fence with a dilapidated gate. Touching the gate, it swung open creakily under my hand.

I stepped inside, went about five feet in, and cast Call 'em Out.

Then I turned and ran like hell.

This time the announcer roared in with a vengeance. [**It's the Carib Zombie Team! Fresh out of the grave, they're here for your brains!**]

There's four of them. Forty health apiece, Sage said in party chat, the message popping up in my vision as I pounded back toward my team.

The others had spread out on either side of the path. I skidded to a stop in front of Sage and turned. Casting Quick Draw, I raised my gun and fired at the closest zombie.

She was about fifteen feet away from me, which was about the limit of where I felt I was accurate with the revolver. Both my shots hit her torso. It didn't stop her, even though the rounds tore right through, leaving fist-sized holes.

"Headshots!" Sage exclaimed. She whirled her rope and threw it, tossing a loop around the zombie. As the coil of rope fell over her shoulders, it tightened and yanked the zombie woman off her feet. She hit the dirt and I adjusted my aim and put a round through her head. It exploded like an overripe watermelon.

I raised my muzzle toward the next target. Grandpa Shadow Stepped behind the farthest-out zombie. He hit its skull with his axe, probably using his Scalp ability, though I couldn't tell from here. The first hit took it down to half; his follow-up killed the undead monster.

Meanwhile, the deputy was blowing his whistle as hard as he could. A pair of British royal guards, like the kind you'd see outside Buckingham Palace, complete with enormous black beaver hats, materialized next to one of the other zombies.

They grabbed his arms and held him in place. "Hullo, hullo, hullo," one said. "What's this, then?"

I adjusted my aim and shot that zombie through the head. With him being restrained, it was easy. My headshot blew his skull open, dealing thirty damage in one shot.

I was out of shots. Quickly flipping the cylinder open, I worked the ejection rod, dropping the brass and then slamming home six new rounds that I had in my speed loader. I really needed more of those things.

I let the speed loader fall to the ground as I reseated the cylinder and brought it up. Two down, two to go.

The pair of royal guards were facing Young now, clearly looking for direction.

"Tell them to get the other one," Sage shrieked. She was trying to pull her rope back, but it was all snarled around the zombie woman.

That left one zombie unoccupied. Even as Grandpa sent it crashing to its knees, missing the top of its skull, the fourth zombie came right at Sage.

Whatever had challenged them to face me had clearly worn off at this point. I was a little off to one side, and there was a tree blocking my aim. I cast Trick Shot, targeting the zombie, and pulled the trigger. My bullet flew out of the gun, made a ninety-degree turn, went ten feet, turned another ninety degrees, and planted itself between the zombie's eyes. The back of the zombie's skull blew out. "Whoa."

I checked the cooldown. Thirty seconds. I wouldn't be able to use it on the next one in time, so I just brought my muzzle around and aimed.

Young hadn't gotten his summoned helpers to attack, so the zombie was freely approaching us. Grandpa Shadow Stepped in and took its head clean off.

It dropped to the ground. **[Victory!]** roared the announcer, accompanied by a musical flourish.

I pulled out my spent brass, stored them in a pocket, and reloaded so I had a full six rounds in my gun. I picked up my speed loader and dropped it in my pocket along with the brass I'd saved.

Grandpa was kicking his zombie in disgust. "Problem with getting up close and personal with these is I can't take on the ones you're shooting at," he said. "We need to find a better way to work together."

"No loot?" Sage demanded. She put her hands on her hip. "No XP either. This is ridiculous. I can't believe Veda said this was a quick way to level."

"Maybe it is, and we just don't understand it yet. Maybe we get the XP at the end."

"Well, we'd better, or I'm never doing one of these again." She turned to Frank. "Deputy, that ability you have is really good." As she spoke, the two summoned palace guards disappeared. "But it's got a three-hour cooldown, so we won't be able to use it again for a long time. We should probably save it for boss fights from now on, unless things get really bad and we agree we need it. It was still good to try it out in combat," she added quickly. "We needed to know how it worked."

"You should have cast Restraint on the other zombie," I suggested. "It would have held him in place—made it easier to shoot him."

"I love Monday morning quarterbacks," the deputy grumbled.

We hadn't gotten any new instructions yet, which meant "investigate the chapel" was still our most recent clue.

I sighed. "Well, we know it's definitely zombies. Guess we'd better look inside. Everybody be ready." I was going to remind Frank to reload, then recalled he hadn't actually fired a shot in that last fight. "Frank and I will go in first. That way, if we have to shoot, you two won't be in the way."

Grandpa nodded. "Just save a few for me."

I approached the chapel, waiting for something to happen. The old, worm-eaten oak door stood ajar. I poked my head inside. The interior was dark, cool, and musty-smelling.

I slipped in, edging into the room as Young followed me. My eyes adjusted to the dark quickly. It was the sort of generic-looking chapel you got on military bases, with very few decorations, some long wooden pews, and a table up front.

There were some melted wax candles on the table, and something else—something dark. I approached carefully. A sheep's skull stared up at me from the middle of a pentagram drawn in what looked like dried blood.

I shuddered. "Guess this is the right place." I wondered if the Reality Engine's depiction of voodoo was at all accurate. Probably not.

Sage and Grandpa joined us. "There's nothing here," Sage said.

"Keep looking." I went around behind the altar. A book lay on the floor, face down. I picked it up. It was *A Beginner's Guide to Necromancy*. I doubted such a book actually existed. I opened it up, and the copyright page fell open. "Published 2013," I said. "I don't think the old legend about a priest has anything to do with this."

One of the pages in the book was marked. I opened it up, and it showed a diagram of an animal head inside a pentagram of blood on an altar, just like what I was seeing here. Underneath was a list labeled, *Your First Ritual: Taking Command of the Lesser Undead*.

I let the book fall shut with a thump. It kicked up a cloud of dust. I resisted the urge to sneeze as I tossed the book aside. Sage picked it up and it disappeared into her inventory. "Someone around here has been playing at raising the undead," I said. "We'd better find out and stop him."

That was when the next step of our quest appeared.

CHAPTER FOURTEEN

PLANNING YOUR BEACH PICNIC: GUEST LIST

The text popped up.

[Mission: Bad Vacation. Step three: find the charlatan. He never expected his spell to be this effective. You need to find and stop him now.]

"Well, that's helpful," I said. "Come on, let's get out of here. I don't think he's around anymore. Did you see how that said that whoever cast this wasn't expecting it to be actually effective? I think he was messing with powers beyond what he could control."

I stepped out of the chapel and looked around. If I was a necromancer who had accidentally summoned zombies without really knowing what I was doing, and then ran away in fear, where would I have gone?

Could be anywhere on the island, I supposed. I pulled open my map, hoping for a helpful dot, but it was blank. I did notice that one of the surprisingly empty patches on the map was just to the west, covering the beach below our headland.

In fact, as I studied it, I grew suspicious. "Take a look at the map," I said. "Notice how it has a big section of the beach that we can't see? But I can see it from here. I think it's hiding something. I think there might be a cave."

Grandpa consulted his map. "You could be right," he said. "Do Caribbean islands grow caves?"

"I don't think the Reality Engine cares about accuracy," I said, and took the lead down the headland and around onto the beach.

The sand crunched nicely underfoot. Sage laughed, running to the water and dunking her hands in it. A wave splashed up over her.

"This is amazing. I can see why the soul coins are so important. If they can make reality like this, then of course people will pay anything to get attuned.

Imagine if we could come somewhere like this and not have to kill zombies. Wouldn't that be fun?"

Grandpa and I stood watching her for a minute. It was good to see that the stress wasn't getting to her. Actually, I think she was adapting better than any of the rest of us. I let her play for a few minutes, then reminded her that we still had to finish our quest.

We continued up the beach. There was a long, low mass lying in the sand in front of us. It looked like driftwood and seaweed, but all of a sudden the battle music started playing and the announcer roared, **[Flotsam and Jetsam! Level 3 Elementals!]**

The debris rose up into two large shapes. They formed heads at the top and bulbous bodies with enormous arms and legs, about twice as tall as me. One was made entirely of wood, the other looked like it was mainly seaweed, although I could make out a few dead fish wrapped up in the weeds.

I used Quick Draw to summon my gun. "Aim for the left one! Take it down!" I shouted to Frank as I sent three shots into the seaweed monster's center mass.

Each shot carved out enormous chunks, big as my head, that I could see daylight through.

"The health bar's not twitching!" Sage shouted, and the seaweed monster's body rippled and shook and was whole. "How are we going to defeat it?"

The monsters started for us, their steps shaking the beach. I tried to think.

Elemental monsters. That had to mean something.

Grandpa Shadow Stepped behind the monster made of wood and hit it with his axe. There was a satisfying thunk. He yanked the axe free and hit it again.

"That's working!" Sage shouted. "Grandpa, keep at it!"

Grandpa summoned his other steel axe from his inventory and began chopping the creature's leg into kindling.

"Frank!" I shouted. "Use Restraint on the green one!"

Frank pointed his gun, his hand trembling. "How?"

"Call up your spell list!" Sage directed from behind us. "Just think *spells*, like when we were in class selection. You thought about the options? Yes? Now select Restraint, and target the green one. The green one!" She shrieked as it came pounding at us.

Frank's muzzle twitched and he fired a couple of stray shots that tore spouts of sand from the beach. Then, as though held back by the invisible force fields that the aliens wielded so easily, the green monster stopped where it was, one leg raised in the air.

Meanwhile, Grandpa had successfully chopped through the left leg of the driftwood monster. It was trying to catch him, but he kept Shadow Stepping behind it. That spell must be on a very short cooldown.

He started in on the right leg as the monster balanced precariously. I still didn't know what I was going to do about the green monster, but I wanted to help Grandpa, so I put my head down and I charged.

Football was never my game. I didn't have the build for it. I preferred baseball and had been a pretty good shortstop back in high school. Not good enough to even make it on a minor-league team, so I had joined the Army and gone off to see the world.

Still, I did my best impression of a linebacker going for a sack. I ran at the driftwood monster as hard as I could, head down, shoulder forward, shouting to Grandpa "Get out of the way!" and hoping he listened.

I could feel my boots kicking up sand behind me as I ran. I slammed into the driftwood monster, knocking it flying. I stumbled forward and drove it to the ground. Grandpa was there, dual-wielding his axes as he rained down a furious flurry of blows on the driftwood monster's head.

A moment later, the creature exploded in a burst of wood. I got my hands up to protect my face just in time. The splinters bounced off my drovers coat. A couple scratched the back of my hand.

Grandpa let out a shout of pain. I lowered my arms. He was on his knees beside the driftwood monster, hands covering his face, blood spurting between his fingers.

The monster wasn't quite dead. It still had a sliver of health. I ran to grab one of his dropped axes, but my hand passed right through the handle. A system message appeared.

[These axes have been equipped by a miner and cannot be equipped by any other miner while their owner remains alive.]

I summoned the kitchen knife out of my inventory and slammed it down into the driftwood monster's head. "*Sage!*" I roared. "Help Grandpa! Get a potion!"

"Oh!" she shouted. She sprinted across the sand toward us, casting Cowgirl Cheer as she ran. I felt it strengthen my arms in my blows.

She knelt at Grandpa's side and plucked a potion from her inventory. "Here!"

I didn't have time to help. One last stab and the driftwood monster lay in a lifeless heap.

I didn't know how much longer Restraint would last on the seaweed monster. Wood. Steel cuts wood. Our metal weapons had been more than effective against the driftwood monster. What could I use on the seaweed monstrosity?

I called up my inventory and ran a search for anything that would make fire. There it was. Some lighter fluid we had found in the kitchen, and a cigarette lighter left behind from my abuela.

I dumped lighter fluid all over the driftwood monster's severed leg. Then I set it on fire. I grabbed the end that wasn't burning. The fiery torch was nearly as long as me and must have weighed fifty pounds, but I lifted it.

I stumbled over to where Young was standing, hand outstretched like he was stopping traffic, palm toward the monster. His face was strained. "I can't hold it much longer."

I lifted my burning torch. "Let's hope you don't have to." I pushed the torch into the seaweed monster's body.

Young cursed and fell backward, shaking his hand as the seaweed monster thrashed and roared. Either his spell had run out or the seaweed monster broke past it.

But it was too late. The monster was in flames. It stumbled away from my burning torch, which I let fall to the ground. Huge black coils of smoke went skyward and let out a high-pitched shrieking sound that made me think of pigs being butchered.

As I watched, it was consumed by the flames, the green shriveling to brown and then to ash. A moment later, only a pile of smoldering cinders remained on the beach. [**Victory!**] the system declared. I let out a sigh.

Only then did I remember Grandpa. I turned back, and my heart sank. He was lying on the ground with Sage beside him.

I hurried over as Sage helped Grandpa back up to a seated position. "Everything okay?"

"I'm fine, boy," he growled up at me. "The potion packs a punch. Took me off guard and I stepped back and tripped over my own feet. I'm fine."

I glanced over his head at Sage, who nodded.

"All right." I sighed with relief as the adrenaline from the fight started to wash away. "What was that all about?"

As I asked, a box appeared in midair.

[Achievement! Defeat Side Boss.]

"Oh, so these were extra," Sage said. "That's funny. Look." She pointed at the corpse of the driftwood monster.

A small brown marble was floating in midair about six inches above it. Sage snatched it up. "It's another skill seed."

I backtracked to the seaweed monster. Sure enough, another marble waited for me here. To my surprise, it was yellow, not green. I had kind of thought they were color-coordinated.

I picked it up and checked it with Inspect. [**Not compatible with your class.**]

I held it out to Deputy Young, who was the closest to me. "Want to check and see if this helps you out?"

He holstered his gun, having reloaded it just now, and waved off my offer. "No thanks, boy. I don't want any more to do with this than I have to. I'm tagging along with your family for now, but first chance I get, I'm out of here."

I returned to Sage and Grandpa. Sage looked up at me excitedly. "It's compatible with my class," she said, holding up the brown marble.

"Go ahead. Use it."

She held the marble in the palm of her hand. It spun, then seemed to sink into her skin, her whole body suffused with a brown glow that faded away in another minute. "It's called Eye-Spy. That's *e-y-e*. Eye-Spy. Oh." She grinned. "This lets me look at a creature we're fighting and get an idea of its strengths and weaknesses. It's an upgrade for my Inspect, but specifically focused on creatures we're fighting."

"It feels like a reward for the way we were able to pick up on these monsters' weaknesses." I held out the other skill to Grandpa. "Young doesn't want it, and it's no good for me. You should check it out."

Grandpa took the marble between two fingers. He held it up to the light, squinting suspiciously. "Says it's compatible," he said reluctantly. "I don't know, though."

"You need to use it, Grandpa. We all need to get as strong as we can," Sage urged.

Grandpa sighed. "Well, sweetheart, when you put it like that." The marble squished between his fingers, and his body infused with yellow light. Grandpa blinked a few times. "Quite a sensation."

"Never mind that. What did you get, Grandpa?" Sage demanded.

"Huh." He studied a presumably-invisible-to-the-rest-of-us message, shaking his head. "Well, they really are going all in on this. It's called Counting Coup, and I'm not sure I understand all of this. It's complicated."

"Just read the description aloud. So far, everything we've seen has made sense from a gaming point of view. Sage and I can probably give you some pointers."

He grunted. "This skill says, 'Counting Coup. Deal damage to an enemy after Shadow Stepping behind them and gain a coup point. If this is the first damage they've taken, gain two points. Once you have four points, you may use Coup-de-Grace to instantly kill a monster who is below one quarter health. This does not apply to bosses.'"

"That sounds really powerful," I said. "That's a combo skill. They're more difficult to use. So you're going to want to be Shadow Stepping around the battlefield and using this on enemies. Then when you've collected four points, you'll kill anything that's low enough."

He seemed to think about it. "Well, I'll give it a try."

Considering how quickly he had adapted to Shadow Step, I didn't think we had anything to worry about.

I consulted my map. The area had filled in. Maybe I was wrong about the nec-romancer being this way. "Let's finish checking out the beach, but we might be in the wrong area."

We sauntered along until we ran out of beach. Rocks stuck out from the head-land into the water, and white waves crashed up on them.

"I guess I was wrong," I admitted. I pulled up my map and studied it. "I have to admit, I kind of like the new style of games where they put markers on your mini-map for everything you're supposed to do, and the quest log handholds things for you. This feels a little old school."

"Maybe we missed a clue," Sage said. "I used Inspect on the whole chapel and didn't see anything."

Just to make sure, I cast Inspect now, wondering if it would reveal a hidden entrance or maybe an underground passage, but nothing highlighted.

Sage climbed on top of a rock. She pointed with a hand. "There! I used Inspect again. There's something on the other side of these rocks."

"Well, hang on, let me," I said, and clambered over.

There was a little cove of sand on the far side with nothing much I could see. A couple of washed-up starfish and some debris pushed up to the high tide line. I used Inspect and something in the debris flashed at me. I strode over and fished it out.

It was a bottle, an old-fashioned sort like you would see sold in a tourist shop with a full-masted sailing vessel inside of it. There was a stopper and, inside the bottle, something that looked suspiciously like a note.

I took it back to Sage and Grandpa. Deputy Young had rejoined us, standing off to the side with his thumbs hooked through his belt.

"Guess this is it." I popped the bottle cork out, then slid a finger in and pulled out the parchment.

It crumbled a little as I unfolded it. It was a map of the island with an *x* some-where farther along. I looked up at the sky. "All right, I know you're listening to us and you're mocking us now, but whatever. I'll take it."

I pulled up my game map and compared the two spots. The *x* on this parch-ment was right smack in the middle of one of the two still-blank areas on my map. "What do you bet that the final step of this quest is over here?" I indicated the remaining blank area. "What if we try to skip a step and just go there?"

"I doubt that'll work," Sage said, "unless maybe it's another optional boss. That's probably why this section of the map was left blank, because the Flotsam and Jetsam monsters were here."

"We asked for a clue. We were given a clue. We follow the clue," Grandpa said decisively. No fooling around. He took the map from me, studied it, then tossed it aside.

"That's littering," the deputy pointed out.

Grandpa just snorted.

CHAPTER FIFTEEN

HOW TO WIN FRIENDS AND INFLUENCE NECROMANCERS

We made good time crossing the island to our next location. There was a nice paved road leading straight there. A little way past the chapel, we found a bicycle stand with a sign that read "Bikes for rent, $10 an hour."

I broke the lock and we all grabbed a bicycle and set off pedaling. Sage's bike was too large for her, but as soon as she sat on it, it accommodated itself to her height.

We rode in peace as I kept an eye out all around us. Despite everything, I was enjoying myself. It was a beautiful day. I wasn't being attacked every five minutes. I hadn't been able to spend this much time with Sage and Grandpa in years. Not since I'd gone off to basic training and then my Army duty stations. I'd made it home one Christmas, but that was it.

I had been coming up on the end of my term in another few months. I had almost made up my mind to reenlist when I'd gotten the word about Grandpa. My first sergeant got me on the first flight home and told me he'd take care of the paperwork, that I just needed to do what had to be done for my family.

Going home after years away had been strange. Everything was just as I had remembered it, except that everything had changed. Grandpa was still Grandpa, only now he was dying. Sage was still Sage, except my snuggly little kid sister had turned into a preadolescent smart aleck. The ranch was the same as it always had been, only now I could see the shabby rough edges.

Abuela had kept a beautiful home, even one as small and old as our trailer had been. But she died shortly before I went into the Army, and sometime in the years since, things had fallen apart. It wasn't Sage's fault—she was just a kid— and I suspected Grandpa had been feeling bad for a lot longer than he had let on.

Still, I had been struck by the cold, hard facts. Grandpa was going to die soon; Sage couldn't be left alone. I would either have to sell the old place and take her with me, or I'd have to get out of the Army and come back home. Either way, it was a big decision, and one I had been postponing.

Now, all that was behind me. Grandpa was well again, the ranch was a quarter of a billion miles away, and hopefully my sergeant would figure out what had happened to me, and not just assume I'd gone AWOL.

Maybe that shouldn't matter to me, when I was here in some alien computer game, harvesting soul coins from monsters that were generated by an inhuman artificial intelligence older than the solar system.

But it did. I'd been raised to be a man of my word. I'd taken oaths to defend and protect the United States. I didn't want anyone to think I was falling down on the job.

Deputy Young was a little out in front of us for a change. I hadn't known he was such an ardent bicyclist. Not many were out on the Arizona Strip. We tended to prefer ATVs and off-road vehicles. But he'd mentioned that he liked to spend a few days every spring and fall in Moab, riding the trails. He kept getting way ahead of us and having to stop to let us catch up.

He stopped now, holding up his hand in that biker signal they use when traveling in packs to tell everybody to stop. I pulled on my handlebar brakes and let my bike coast in next to his. "Whoa!" Sage yelled as she zoomed a little past us before getting control of her brakes. Like I said, not a lot of bicycling around where we were.

"What is it, Frank?" Grandpa asked, peering down the road.

"I don't know. I just got a gut feeling."

"Good call," Grandpa told him. "Always listen to those. Even here."

We dismounted and left the bikes lying in a heap. This stretch of road ran between the beach on one side and some tall sugarcane fields on the other. I focused out into the fields and cast Call 'em Out.

Nothing happened. If there was something there, it was farther away than I could reach. Sage had her hand shading her eyes, turning her head back and forth to look.

I noticed something. The old telephone poles that ran beside the road had a spur line running out into the sugarcane fields here.

I pointed. "That line's going somewhere. Let's check it out." I took a deep breath and stepped off into the sugarcane. Tall green leaves slapped my face and hands as I went. As the others followed, I heard them rustling the leaves. Good chance we'd be heard, but I couldn't help it.

I followed the telephone line deeper into the field. There was still no sound of any human habitation. I stepped through a row of the sugarcane and found myself blinking at a wide-cut swath. There were old-fashioned sickles lying on the ground beside the piles of cut sugarcane. Sugarcane juice oozed over their handles and blades.

"Is this really what they used to cut sugarcane?" I asked. None of us knew. I didn't like how much those sickles looked like something you'd see in the hands of a skeleton dressed in a black robe, calling himself the Grim Reaper. I had a suspicion that this was more quest ambiance, like the bone road before the chapel.

A little way off, in the middle of the clearing, stood a small wooden shack with a window facing us. Bright blue shutters were drawn across the window. There were wide slats far enough apart that someone inside could look through and see us, but we wouldn't be able to see anything there. It was just a little too far for me to use Call 'em Out.

I turned to the others. "Hold up a minute." I squatted down behind a bush, and they followed. "We've got no sign of enemies. Could be one or more in the shack, we don't know. I'm presuming a door on one of the other walls. If this is our necromancer, he might send more zombies after us, or he may have other magic we haven't accounted for. We've got mostly ranged damage, and Grandpa counts on mobility. We need to draw them out here to us."

Grandpa raised an eyebrow. "Giving us a five-paragraph order, son?"

I grinned and scratched my head. "I do sound like a new lieutenant, don't I? Sorry, I've heard enough of them on exercises that it kind of makes sense. Um, okay. So. I'll use my ability to draw out whoever's in that shack. As soon as we see 'em, we lock them down hard. Frank, is your Posse skill back up?"

Frank checked. He shook his head. "Still got twenty minutes on it."

"All right, we'll use Restraint, and Sage, if there's more than one, you use Lasso on whichever the deputy doesn't Restrain."

I paused, thinking. The biggest problem with Grandpa's new ability was it meant he really needed to be dodging in and out of melee, attacking various targets, but that also meant he'd be in the way of our shots.

"I really hate games with friendly fire," I muttered. "If there's two, you go after whichever one Sage has Lassoed, and Frank and I will shoot the other one. Then we'll converge on whatever's left. If there's only one, go on in, use Shadow Step, and try to take Coup before anyone else damages him. Then I'll take my shots. Trick Shot lets me designate a target, so I should be able to use that without putting you at risk."

What I didn't say was that Trick Shot had a thirty-second cooldown, and I wouldn't be able to use it all the time.

"Sage, you're also to watch for enemies coming in from the field, like if he's got zombies stashed out here somewhere. Shout and use party chat both."

She nodded.

That more or less covered it. "Anyone spot something I missed?"

"And if there's a lot more than two?" Grandpa asked. I didn't have a good answer. What we were really short on right now was AoE damage, abilities or spells that could hit more than one target at a time.

"Then we kill the rest as fast as we can."

I strode out into the clearing, my drovers coat flapping at my heels. As soon as I was close enough to the hut, I cast Call 'em Out.

I heard a rustling from inside the hut, and a protesting whine, and then a man stumbled out of the front door. He wasn't a zombie; I could tell that right away.

He also didn't look much like a necromancer. Though, to be honest, I'd never met a necromancer before, and couldn't be sure what they did look like. I was picturing someone in dark robes with a goatee and a bald head and satanic pendants festooned all over him.

Instead, I found an overweight, prematurely balding, twenty-something guy who looked like he had been fired from every fast-food joint in his town and now lived in his mom's basement playing *Call of Duty* all day. He was horribly sunburned and wearing the ubiquitous Bermuda shorts and patterned shirts that this Reality Engine seemed to think tropical tourists would wear.

"Don't shoot!" he squeaked, holding up his hands. "Don't hurt me! It was an accident, I swear!"

My gun was in my hand, but I kept the muzzle pointed at the ground as I approached.

In party chat, I said, *Let's talk to him. He may have some clues. But be ready if it's a trap.*

I can't use Eye-Spy on him, Sage replied back. *It says "entity not hostile."*

That was something, though I knew it could change at any minute. "All right, what's going on here?" I asked.

"I just got lost and there were some strange people chasing me and . . ." His eyes flickered around wildly. Definitely not telling the truth.

Sage brushed past him and ducked into the shack. She emerged a minute later, carrying a pendant that was as satanic as I could have asked for.

She held it up triumphantly. "Not doing anything, hmm, Mr. Cultist? And what's this doing in your hidey-hole?"

The shifty-looking man gave a gasp. "I . . . I swear, I didn't mean to. I . . . That is . . . So, my mother dragged me along on her cruise, and I've hated every minute of it. I really have, the whole time. And then we got here, and we were spending four whole days in port, and it's horribly boring. All they have to do is lie on the beach and drink, and I'm allergic to sun and alcohol both."

His eyes were puffy, like he'd been crying. "So I was amusing myself, doing some shopping, and I found this old bookstore with this creepy old lady who said, said she had the answer to all my problems. That all I needed to do was take control of my life, and the best way to do that was starting by taking control of other people's lives. And, and, she gave me this book, and these ritual elements, and told me all about this chapel that would be the perfect place to practice. So I did. But it worked."

He let out a little squeak. "The dead, the dead woke up. I didn't mean to. It wasn't my fault. I really didn't mean to. I thought maybe if I got far enough away, they would go back to sleep, and it would all be all right."

I didn't believe a word of that last bit. He had clearly fled the scene of the crime, hoping not to be turned into zombie chow.

"All right," I said. "So, how do we put an end to this infestation?"

"I don't know. That pendant, that's the one she gave me. There's a, there's a ritual dagger here."

He drew it out from somewhere on his person. He didn't seem to be wearing a sheath, and his pockets certainly weren't large enough to hold it, but there it was anyway.

He held it out to me. I eyed the thing suspiciously. I used Inspect, but nothing appeared. It must have been a system-generated item. I took the dagger gingerly.

"If, if you find the old woman, I, I think she'll know how to stop this."

"All right, where is she?"

"Her, her bookshop was back in town, but she said something about having a, a house. The old house. The plantation house from a long time ago. She said that she lived there now. It was on the north side of the island, with a good view of the sea."

"Right in the middle of that last spot on the map," Grandpa said. "Figures. What do we do about him?"

I hesitated. He wasn't real, and it was possible he could come back to hurt us. But he wasn't posing a threat, and I didn't see any need to kill him.

"You'd better stay here and lie low until we take care of this problem," I said.

"We'll definitely come back for you," Sage lied brightly.

The man sniffed a little, and looked maybe a fraction less miserable than before. "All right. Oh!" he said, brightening up. "And I forgot to say, she had some sort of weird big monkey pet with her. It gave me the creeps. Keep an eye out for it. I think it tells tales."

With that, he turned and disappeared back into his hut. A minute later, the next step of our mission appeared.

[Step four: find the voodoo woman. The necromancer turned out to be a patsy. He places all the blame on the woman who gave him the power to do what he did. Isn't that convenient? Find her, and stop the spell before it's too late.]

[Bonus objective! Silence the monkey. The voodoo witch's monkey tells tales. Cut his own off before he has a chance to cut yours.]

"I don't think much of the writing in this game," I commented as we took in the message.

"You sure you made the right choice letting him go?" Grandpa asked, nodding at the hut. "I never like leaving a potential enemy at my back."

I shrugged. "Just a hunch. I really don't feel like I want to be starting out on a murder spree when we don't need to. There's a term in Dungeons & Dragons campaigns for the kind of characters who go around murdering every NPC they come across, whether or not they really need to, whether or not they play a threat. They call it murder hobo, and it's never been a playstyle I like. Almost ruined the first game I played in AIT. Besides." I nodded at Sage, and Grandpa nodded back.

He understood what I was saying. This might be a game, but that still didn't mean we needed to expose Sage to any more hatred and viciousness than we had to.

"I think we got rewarded for sparing his life," Sage said. "He tipped us off about that monkey and we got the bonus quest. It probably would have showed up during the boss fight and caused us problems. Or maybe now that we know about it, we'll hunt it down and get another bonus reward like we did for the flotsam monsters."

I looked at the map. It showed a rough outline of the road we had been following, which looped all the way around the island. "I think it'll be fastest if we get back on the bikes and keep pedaling."

CHAPTER SIXTEEN

WHERE DOES THE 500 LB GORILLA EAT HIS BANANAS? ANYWHERE HE WANTS

I knew it was the right place after the first group of zombies we ran into.

The road wound around the island, but as it approached the area where we suspected the witch's plantation to be, it took a sharp dip to the south. A gravel lane came off of it, shaded by overhanging trees.

We left the bikes by the main road and proceeded on foot. The trees overhead felt ominous to me, their branches reaching down like hands to grab at us.

I kept my head on a swivel, but it was Grandpa who called, "Incoming! Off to the left." He moved at once to intercept the zombies, Shadow Stepping from us to behind the first of them, getting in a quick coup, then Shadow Stepping to the next.

I cast Quick Draw. My gun flew to my hand. As Grandpa left the first of the three zombies, I fired.

Head wounds were the only thing that seemed to really damage these guys, and it took more than just a single hit. A coup from Grandpa, followed up by a couple of rounds from either me or the deputy did the trick.

Sage cast Cowgirl Cheer as soon as we entered combat. Her buff made us harder to hit, as well as deal more damage.

We cleaned up that group of zombies in about ten seconds. They didn't drop any loot, but we hadn't been expecting any.

"I guess we aren't invited," Grandpa said, cleaning his hatchets before returning them to his inventory.

"Do you think the witch can see through their eyes?" Sage asked. "Or maybe sense that they're not alive anymore?"

"Could be. We have to expect that we're being expected. I think we should still stick to this driveway, though. It should take us straight to the house. Besides, if we go stumbling around the property, who knows what sort of mess of undead we might find ourselves dropped in."

Young was getting more and more withdrawn as we went. He just grunted and reloaded his magazine. Veda had bought us plenty of ammunition, but it was going fast.

The gravel road led out onto a wide, sweeping driveway surrounding a decaying plantation, two stories tall, with overlooking gables and black-painted shutters. Its walls were wood siding, painted white. The paint was peeling everywhere, of course.

The foundations were overgrown with bushes, and one whole wing had been lost to ivy or kudzu, some sort of climbing plant. It didn't look as though anyone lived here.

We halted. "Straight through the front door?" Grandpa asked. "Or do you reckon that'll be trapped?"

"It can't hurt to scout around," I said. "Keep an eye out for that monkey. If we can take care of him before we take on the witch, I think we'll have better odds."

We circled the house clockwise, keeping our eyes open. The ivy-covered windows were like vacant eyes watching us.

We turned a corner, and another pack of zombies shambled in from the overgrown kitchen garden off to our left. This time, I got in two headshots on the first zombie before Grandpa could Shadow Step over. He used Scalp to strike the killing blow.

"You're supposed to let me hit these first," he reminded me.

"Oh, right."

Grandpa disappeared, emerged again behind another of the four zombies that had come after us, and took a coup on it. Meanwhile, Deputy Young had Restrained one of the other two, and Sage had her Lasso around the other.

As Grandpa Shadow Stepped away, I put the killing rounds between the eyes of the one he had tagged. I was getting more used to the Ruger now, and its shot placement was becoming more accurate.

I was nearly a third of the way through the achievement for wounding an enemy with the revolver, and was starting to get excited to find out what happened when I reached one hundred percent.

Grandpa finished off Sage's trapped victim. He hit him with Scalp, then used his coup de grace to take him down the rest of the way.

Young and I both pumped lead into the last of the zombies. Their bodies lay twitching on the ground, ruined brain matter sprayed everywhere.

"These are not very interesting," Sage complained. "When I used Eye-Spy on them, it just said, 'They're zombies. You know what to do.' What kind of use is that?"

I laughed. "I don't know if I like this Reality Engine's sense of humor all of the time, but it does have a dry wit."

"Keep moving," said Grandpa.

We came around back to the kitchen. Its wide doors were thrown open. There was an old-fashioned outdoor oven that lay cold and quiet now, and a decaying workspace around it. Made sense in this sort of tropical heat. You would want to do as many of your kitchen tasks outside as possible.

There was a regular oven inside, but it was cobwebbed and dusty as well.

"There will be access to the rest of the house through there," I suggested. "Shall we try it?"

Sage, meanwhile, had just let out a whoop. She ran forward. I tried to catch her but was too slow, so I followed her into the kitchen. "Sage, let Grandpa or me go first."

"Oh, it's fine," she said. "Look!" She reached into a basket on the covered countertop right next to a shattered crockery pot and pulled out a fresh bunch of bananas. "They lit up when I used my Inspect."

I snorted. "I can see where this is going. All right, let's take them back outside and see if we can figure this out."

"Do they even grow bananas in the Caribbean?" Grandpa asked.

I looked at Deputy Young, who was the only one of us who'd ever actually been here, and he just shrugged. "They serve a lot of stupid drinks with bananas in them."

We retreated back to the garden, picking a spot a little way away from the dead zombies, and I looked at the cluster of four bananas. There was a monkey sub-boss here and bananas in an otherwise desolated kitchen. Obviously, there was a trick to this. Did we use them to lure the monkey out? Did we keep them and throw them at the monkey when we did find it, and see if they gave him a debuff? Or was this some sort of elaborate trap?

Sage and I argued about it for a while. I didn't want to risk accidentally buffing up the monkey by feeding him his favorite food, while Sage was insistent that there would be some sort of trick and then the monkey would be our friend and maybe even something she could tame and keep as a pet.

"You can't have a monkey as a pet," I said. "It goes against your theme."

She pouted and crossed her arms. "What am I supposed to get then? A chicken?"

Grandpa had been listening to us squabble. Now he stepped in and snatched the bundle of bananas away from Sage. He pulled one banana off of the bunch, peeled it, and took a big bite.

"Grandpa!" Sage howled.

"It's not bad," he said and finished it. He tossed away the skin and that was when the furious chittering started.

[Mini-boss! It's Scritch the Level 3 Monkey Minion, pet of the Voodoo Witch! You've just made a monkey out of him by eating his favorite snack.

**Here he comes to teach you a lesson, and he's not planning
on any monkey business.]**

"Monkey business," I said, rolling my eyes at the sky. "Really?" I was listening for the sound of an approaching monkey, ready to cast Call 'em Out as soon as I knew it was close enough. That was when the coconut lobbed into the middle of our group.

I stood there staring at it stupidly for a minute.

Sage had better instincts. "Run!" she screamed and took off running.

I bolted away, grabbing Deputy Young by the arm. Grandpa followed just in time.

The coconut blew up behind us like a grenade. Dirt and rocks pelted my head. The furious chittering came again and another coconut appeared at my feet. I dodged to the left.

"Throw one of the bananas, Grandpa!" I yelled. "Try to lure him out!"

Grandpa tossed a banana away from us toward the open door of the kitchen.

A moment later, our monkey opponent appeared on the roof of the house. Only it wasn't a monkey. Despite what the system had said about it having a tail, this was a gorilla. A silverback gorilla, bigger than I was by a long shot. His health pool was bigger than anything we'd encountered yet, **[90/90]**. That was more than anyone but Frank had.

He had a coconut in each hand and he hurled them at us now. I dodged out of the way as one exploded right where I had been.

The gorilla dropped off the roof to the ground near the banana. I ran in toward him, casting Call 'em Out. Not that it mattered. We could see him and he was clearly mad enough to go after me.

He howled and produced a bright red bat from nowhere. He took a couple of loping steps forward and swung at me.

I shot him right in the chest, emptying my cylinder. It tore big holes in his torso and took him down to **[60/90]**. Not even to the yellow.

"Use Restraint!" I yelled at Young.

In party chat, Sage typed, *Don't use Posse, save that for the boss fight.*

But it was too late. Young had already cast it. This time, instead of the Buckingham Palace guards, we got a pair of Roman centurions wielding spears, with red capes fluttering from their breastplates. They surrounded the monkey, stabbing at it with their spears.

Grandpa teleported in behind it and hit it with Scalp. The monkey's health was going down nicely. He was at **[40/90]** and dropping.

Sage belatedly cast her Cowgirl Cheer on us. The monkey dropped his bat. He grabbed the banana lying on the ground and tossed it into his mouth.

Instantly, his health went back up to **[90/90]** and he gained a buff. **[Bananaroids. 50% more angry, 50% meaner, 50% bigger punch.]**

"Bananaroids? Sounds like something I've got a special cream for," Grandpa grunted.

"Grandpa, build up your coup points!" I yelled. The gorilla was a long way off from twenty-five percent health remaining now, but we'd get him down eventually, and I wanted to make sure he didn't pull any more tricks like that.

Grandpa Shadow Stepped behind the gorilla again, hit coup, then sprinted away as the monkey whirled on him in a rage.

The Roman soldiers kept poking at him, but he paid them no heed. He grabbed for Grandpa, but missed. Furious, the gorilla darted into the kitchen. He seized a pan that was hanging on the wall and hurled it right at me.

I dodged, and thanks to Sage's bonus, I succeeded. The pan crashed into the ground where I had been. I could feel the impact from here.

"Lasso him, or use Restraint!"

"I can't," Sage said desperately. "It says he's immune to Lasso while 'roided up."

"I can't use Restraint while I've got Posse active," Young said through gritted teeth. He raised his gun.

"Wait!" I shouted, but it was too late. He fired, just as Grandpa Shadow Stepped back in and got a coup. Fortunately, the bullet hit the gorilla and not Grandpa. He howled, down to **[70/90]** again.

I fired my Trick Shot, designating the monkey as the target. My bullet wound its way past one of the soldier's heads and struck the gorilla in the ear.

That seemed to annoy it in a way our other attacks hadn't. It howled and held one hand up to its ear.

"Sage, Eye-Spy him!"

"Oh right!" She waited for a moment, then said, "While he's Bananaroided up, he is susceptible to sensory damage. He doesn't like having his ears or his eyes hurt."

"Well, who does?" I fired another normal shot, taking care to make sure Grandpa wasn't going to be in my line of fire while I waited for Trick Shot to come back off of cooldown. "Grandpa, how's your coup coming?" The gorilla was down to **[55/90]**. Still a long way to go until coup de grace territory.

"I've got four points now," he said.

"All right, stay clear. We should be able to get him down there pretty quick here. Then I want you to take him out right away."

Grandpa grunted.

Trick Shot came back off of cooldown, so I fired again, this time specifically designating the monkey's other ear as my target. It worked. The bullet flew a zig-zagging path, then struck the gorilla's ear.

The gorilla howled again. His health dipped to **[15/90]**. "Now," I said, and Grandpa Shadow Stepped in and struck, but nothing happened.

"It doesn't work on bosses. We forgot," Sage said.

"You know what does work on bosses?" I was frantically reloading my gun. "Hot lead." I fired again and again and again.

The gorilla reared back on its hind legs. It slammed its fists against its chest, hooting. "Uh-oh. Run!" I didn't know what it was doing, but this wasn't good. I scrambled back. Sage turned to run.

The gorilla slammed back into the ground. A shockwave hit us. It knocked me off my feet. I rolled, got up. My health bar was blinking yellow at me and I felt like I'd been hit by a bus. [HP 30/80]. I'd lost over half my health in one hit. There was a debuff on me. [**Silverback Slam. Your hearing is damaged. Sensory damage to targets reduced by 100%. You are Unstable.**]

I didn't have to ask what Unstable meant. I could barely stand, swaying back and forth like a drunken honeymooner on an all-inclusive cruise. Sage lay in a crumpled heap. I could see her health bar, at [**30/60**]. She was all right, but we had to end this now.

Trick Shot was back up. I didn't get fancy, just aimed for the gorilla's head. *Get him down now!* I said in chat.

The monkey's health bar dropped down so low I could barely see it. [**5/90**]. He was so enraged, all he could do was scream as he held his hands to his ears.

Grandpa Shadow Stepped in and finished the gorilla off with one last Scalp.

[**Victory!**] the announcer declared. Even though my ears were still ringing, I could hear that I let out a deep sigh of relief and walked over to Sage. I helped her up and made sure her health had stabilized. The [**Silverback Slam**] debuff had disappeared as soon as the monkey died.

Sage seemed unperturbed. She dusted off her jeans. "Did we get anything good?"

Grandpa leaned over to inspect the corpse. "Another skill."

"Great." So far, Sage, Grandpa, and I had all gotten one. I looked at what Grandpa was holding up. "Any good for you?"

He shook his head. "Nope."

"Me either," Sage said, sounding disappointed.

I Inspected the skill. Again, it said, [**Not compatible with your class.**]

I sighed. "Frank, can you at least take a look at this, please?"

Deputy Young came over. He stood beside the corpse of the gorilla, looking from it to us and back again.

He held out his hand. "Fine. Hand it over." Grandpa put the skill on his hand. Frank grunted. "Yeah, Inspect says I can use it."

"Frank," Grandpa said, in that man-to-man tone he liked to use when he was trying to convince you to see things his way. "I understand you want out of here. I want out of here, too. If you find a way, I'm not going to stand in between you and it. I swear. But while we're stuck here, we might as well have all the tools we can get."

Frank tightened his fist around the skill seed. "I don't like any of this," he said. "And what I really don't like?" He paused and looked away from us, away from the zombie corpses, away from the gorilla. "I don't know if my wife is in here somewhere."

We all went still. I hadn't even thought of that. The only people in the world that I really cared for were right here. Oh sure, I had friends back in the Army, people that I liked to hang out with, but as far as I was concerned, if they were here, they could take care of themselves.

Grandpa and Sage were the world to me. At least I knew where they were. At least I could do something to help them.

"Or my kids," he went on. "They're scattered all over the country. Amy's in Florida. Bob is knocking around New England somewhere. Last I heard, Carl had just passed through Des Moines on a long-haul big rig trip. Any of them could have been taken, all of them, and I don't have any way to know."

Sage grabbed his hand. "I'm sorry," she said. "I hadn't thought of that, but you know what? The system will know. The system has all of us in it. I bet you we can get Veda to find out. It might cost a little, but I'm willing to help find out for you, and if they are here, we'll find them somehow. We'll make sure that they're okay, too."

He looked at her, and I could see tears glistening in his eyes. "Thanks," he said. "I know you mean it." He held up the skill seed. "All right, let's see what this does."

CHAPTER SEVENTEEN

LEARN TO DANCE THE ZOMBIE SHUFFLE IN JUST FIVE MINUTES!

After the fight with the gorilla, we took a few minutes and bandaged our wounds. We all needed it. That slam had really taken it out of us. We'd also picked up a [Hungry] debuff. My stomach would have told me that, but the debuff meant we had fifteen percent less maximum health. Not okay, going into a boss fight.

It was the first chance we'd had to use the bandages Veda had supplied us with. They were pretty neat. They looked like your standard rolled white cotton bandages, but once you wrapped a length around a limb, they cut themselves and then merged into your flesh in a glow of warmth. You didn't even have to apply them to the wounds, just a convenient body part. They could not be used during a fight, though, which made them less useful than a potion. Then again, Veda said they cost a fraction of what the potions did, so we would try to use them after fights any time we had damage.

My health bar began ticking upward. There was a timer on my status now:

[Bandaged. Regain health over the next fifteen minutes. Bandaged cannot be reapplied for fifteen minutes after that.]

I dug around in my inventory and pulled out some of our rations. "All right, everybody, take fifteen. Have a bite to eat; drink some water. I want us as good as we can be for this next fight."

Grandpa gave me a lazy, mocking salute. "Yes, sir!" I looked away, trying not to flush.

Sage immediately sank down at the base of a tree trunk some distance away from the corpses of the zombies and the gorilla, and unwrapped her meal. She wrinkled up her nose at the smell. "It's hot, but what is it?" She held up a blue triangle between two fingers, looking at it skeptically.

Grandpa and I shared a laugh. "Welcome to the world of MREs." Grandpa unwrapped his and dug in. "Not too bad," he said through a mouthful of purple lettuce. "Tastes like chicken." As he ate, [**Hungry**] disappeared. After a few more mouthfuls he gained [**Well-Fed**], which was a straight up fifteen percent buff to our health. The meal we'd eaten on the station—more than twelve hours ago now, it seemed—had given us a health regeneration buff. I wasn't sure which was better, but I did know we'd need to have something there. If a game provided for more-or-less permanently applicable buffs, not having them active amounted to a serious lack.

I ate my ration standing up, keeping my head on a swivel. There could be more zombies out there, but nothing disturbed us as we rested.

Sage ate most of her ration pack before setting it aside. She leaned her head back against the trunk and closed her eyes. Her chest rose and fell rhythmically.

I was pretty sure she had fallen asleep. It must be nice to be able to relax that much. This was really taking a toll on her.

I beckoned Grandpa and Frank over to one side and we conversed in low whispers. "What do you think we're going to find in there?" Frank asked. He was checking his magazines, making sure they were all loaded. He only had three spare, but that was a lot more reloads than I had.

"Supposedly, the witch who's behind all this," I said, "unless the system throws another wrench at us." A thought struck me. "What's your new spell, Frank?"

He looked up from the magazines. "It's called Riot Control." My ears pricked up at that. "I thought from the name that it would be another one of these hold people in place abilities, but it's not. It's a sonic damage spell to an area. I cast it and it gives me a sonic grenade I can throw. Does a twenty-foot circle of aural damage; says 'possibly stuns,' which I guess is where they get the control part of that."

That was really good. We had been lacking in true AoE damage up to this point. "Frank, I think you're our heavy hitter now. That helps shape this fight. If there's adds, you'll have to get them."

"What makes you think there'll be commercials?" Grandpa asked. He sounded bemused.

"Uh, sorry, gamer lingo again. I mean, if the witch brings in helpers. It means additional mobs, just shortened to adds." I ran some quick calculations in my head. "Between your almost sixty rounds of 9mm and these grenades—what's the cooldown on that, anyway?"

Frank checked. "Thirty seconds, but it's got charges that only build up every two minutes. I start out with five charges."

"Oh, I hate that kind of ability." I rubbed my head and tried to do the math. "That means you'll be able to do one every thirty seconds for the first two and a half minutes, and by then you should have another charge come back. But once you use that, it'll be, what, two minutes before you can use it again?"

I was a little worried. That kind of skill usually took an advanced player to make work optimally. Frank, while being as good a sport about this as anyone could ask, was definitely not a pro gamer.

"Well, I guess we'll just do what we've been doing. Go in there, start the fight, do what we can."

Behind us, Sage yawned and stood up. She stretched her arms.

"Ready to go, sleepyhead?" Grandpa asked.

"I was not sleeping, I was resting." She put her hands on her hips, pouting at us.

I led the way into the kitchen. A door stood ajar at the far end, presumably leading deeper into the house. I pushed it open, waiting for a reaction. Nothing. I peered past the door.

The hallway was gloomy, full of shadows and dust. I strained my ears, but heard nothing. There were no footprints in the dust, no sign that anyone had ever been here. The hall went left and right as well as straight ahead.

Time to put my objective clearing skills into practice. I'd learned the concept in the Army, but never actually had to put it to use before. I used party chat to tell the others, *Sage and Frank, stay back. Grandpa, alternate clearing corners with me.*

Grandpa acknowledged. I peered left and right. I had my revolver out, even though I could Quick Draw it instantly. It helped me focus on what I was doing.

I cut the corner the way I'd been trained, pointing my gun just in case something popped up, but it was empty in all directions.

We stepped out into the wide hall. Old ruined pictures hung on the walls, their canvases in tatters. At the far right end of the hall was a tall window, almost entirely blocked by decaying drapes. There was a stair leading up on the left.

The other direction looked about the same, except there was a little round table in front of the window with a vase of excessively dead flowers.

In front of us, the hall opened pretty quickly in an immense, dark foyer. I headed there first. We ought to be directly opposite of the great front doors. If the game had set it up that we should have come in there and been greeted by a surprise, I wanted to find out what that was.

Wait, Sage said in chat. *I see something.* She pointed at the ceiling of the foyer.

I had stepped a couple of feet out of the hall onto the marble tiles. Now I looked up. In the gloom, an ancient twisted chandelier hung about fifteen feet overhead. Unlit candles hung from its branches.

What about it?

It's got a different color when I focus on it, not like the crafting materials. It's red. Trap, maybe. Stay clear.

My guess was it was triggered either by the front door opening or by someone stepping directly under it. I didn't want to test either, but it did confirm to me that we were on the right track.

I took another cautious step out into the foyer and then another, then turned around to get a good look. There was a grand staircase spiraling up the left-hand side of the foyer. It looked like something out of a movie, that very rich young ladies in gowns shaped like bells would come sweeping down. The carpet was too dark and stained to tell what color it had been.

I approached the stair. *Everybody else stay back, in case it's another trap.* Gingerly, I set the toe of my boot on the stair. Nothing happened, so I put my weight on it, then my other foot. Nothing. I cautiously set my hand on the railing. Still nothing. I took another step up. Still good. I noticed that the banister was clear of dust, unlike anything else in this place. *I think we should check upstairs. Follow me, but not too close. Grandpa, take the rear.*

We snuck up those stairs like a bunch of kids coming in past midnight. I held my breath every time someone let a too-loud footfall, or the time Deputy Young missed a step, went down on one knee, and cursed quietly. He recovered. "Sorry."

We made it up without incident. At the top of the stairs, I paused, looking around. To my left was an enormous pair of doors. They were gold, and they shone. Not just like they'd been polished, but literally like they were a light. "This is it," I said. "Be ready."

"How do you know?" Grandpa asked.

"I've got a hunch." There was an elegant sign over the door, white with gold lettering on it. It said The Grand Ballroom. Everything was calling attention to this place.

"Looks like the kind of place for a boss fight?" I asked Sage, and she nodded. "All right. Be ready for anything."

I waited until we were all formed up at the door, then reached out with my left hand and pushed it open. It creaked under my touch.

We all stepped over the threshold. The room was dark inside. Light came in through cracks in the walls and around the heavy drapes at the windows.

When Sage, who was in the rear, had come five feet into the room, the ballroom doors slammed shut. At the same time, light flared from a hundred different candles.

"Fall back," I called. "Protect each other." We scrambled together, backs to each other, as I took in the scene around us.

The room was full of corpses dressed in their finest and seated at little round tables all around the edges of the room. The men wore top hats and coattails. The women elegant ball gowns. They had long beards or flowing curly hair, but their faces were withered and shrunken. Despite that, all of the women wore garish makeup that only highlighted their desiccation.

Sage let out a little cry. I didn't blame her.

"Welcome, my dears," a woman's voice said. It sounded like an old woman. Crotchety. Tired. I looked around for the source. One of the corpses? No. At the far end of the room was a stage with long, heavy, red curtains blocking it off from view.

As we watched, it rose. Grandpa and I moved to face it. In party chat, I warned, *Watch those corpses. I'm betting they'll turn out to be zombies that she can call. Be ready for that.*

Frank managed an *Okay*, which was about as much of party chat as he ever used.

The curtains rose, revealing a marquee on the back wall that read Madam Hecate's Miracles and Moonshine. In the center of the stage was an enormous bubbling cauldron over an open blue-flamed fire. I could hear the pops as whatever liquid was in it rose to the surface and exploded. A shimmering mist rose off of it.

Behind it was a crone dressed as a bride. She stepped forward. It looked like she was about nine hundred years old, but unlike the corpses, she wasn't dead. There was a difference between her and the zombies we had seen. Her health read **[110/110]**.

"Well, now. And to think I had begun to believe none of my invitations had reached their addressees." She rubbed her hands together, the veil around her withered face floating in the air. "Now, what can I do for you tonight, my children? A love potion? A curse broken? Or perhaps . . ." Her voice dropped. The light on the stage turned red and the cauldron suddenly exploded upward in a shower of green sparks. "Perhaps you're just here for the loot."

Sage Inspected her. "She's a level three boss hag. Weaknesses to fire and steel and salt for some reason."

I checked my inventory real quick. I had half a bag of rock salt from the shed, and most of a container of table salt we'd taken from the kitchen. I grabbed those out and tossed them to Grandpa. "You're most likely to be able to use them."

He stored them in his inventory. "I've been trying to teleport behind her for thirty seconds now, but it won't let me—says invalid target."

I tried targeting her with Trick Shot, but got the same message.

"Boss monologue," Sage said, rolling her eyes. "We won't be able to do anything until she's done with her little speech."

"Sure we will. Spread out. Frank, watch our six. Grandpa, Sage, scatter. If she throws something, we don't all want to be in the same spot."

I made for the stage. I reached it as the witch turned toward me, stretching out her hand. I bounced off an invisible barrier and swore. "I hate these kinds of mechanics."

"You've been poor guests so far, crashing my party, beating up my servants, but you'll have a chance now. My other guests are ready to dance, so what do you say we strike up a waltz?" Madam Hecate raised her hand, and, as I had feared, a bunch of the corpses at the tables began getting to their feet. They only had four HP each, but there were at least a dozen of them on the move. I tried targeting the witch again, but she was still an invalid target. "Get the adds!" I growled. "Frank!"

He lobbed one of his sonic grenades at a group on the far side of the room just as the music began to play. To the right of the stage was an orchestra pit, and down in the pit were a quartet of skeletons playing stringed instruments. Cello, violin, something else I didn't know the name of. They were pretty good, considering their fingers were nothing but bone.

The sonic grenade went off. It tossed six of the zombies into the walls. Several of them hit hard enough that they didn't get back up, and the others shambled a little more slowly, each taking a couple points of damage. A couple of the zombies started for me. I shot them through the head. They went down.

I was a little worried about how many adds we had. I'd go through my ammunition fast before we even got to the witch.

Grandpa was teleporting merrily around the room, hitting one zombie after another. Sage cast her buff on us all, and then moved to the center of the room and started shouting directions to us. That was really helpful, because with all the zombies shambling around, it was hard to tell where the next threat was going to be.

Frank shot a bunch more as I carefully took aim and used Trick Shot to dispose of one after another.

The last one went down and I caught my breath. I had used all of my rounds, and the ones in my speed loader, too, so I quickly reloaded my gun and slapped another six rounds into the speed loader. The witch shrieked, "How dare you! Orchestra, play something more lively."

The skeletons started to play a different tune, and this time I had an idea. "Frank, sonic grenade on the orchestra pit." I pointed. He'd used two already, but he lobbed a third right into the pit as I ran clear of the explosion. The bomb went off.

It knocked the skeletons to pieces and smashed their instruments. The music died away. The zombie hag screeched, "If you're not here to dance, then you're here to die," she said.

And that was when the shit hit the fan.

CHAPTER EIGHTEEN

WHY YOU SHOULD ALWAYS PRE-PLAN YOUR OWN FUNERAL

Madam Hecate teleported into the middle of the room along with her cauldron. It bubbled red like an angry spaghetti pot. I took aim and used Trick Shot to target her. My spell went off. The shot landed, but the hag didn't seem to notice. Her bar hadn't twitched. [110/110].

"Damn, not one of these fights," I said. "Grandpa, try to use the salt."

"You tourists are always the same," the hag declared. "You come to our island looking for a good time, not understanding that we have our own culture, our own ways. You think that we're nothing but entertainment. You think that you can exploit us. And when you get back a little of what you've given, you cry foul. This time, though, I've called in a great lord, and he has granted me power."

The hag held up a small doll in her hand. It was very basic, just a shapeless head and some limbs off of a torso. She dropped it into the cauldron. "Now," she said, "which of you shall I bleed?" Her last word cracked like a whip. I took a step back under its strength.

Sage cried out. My heart leapt in fear. I recovered myself and ran to her. She was bent over, holding her hand up. "She caught me."

A little well of blood ran down the back of Sage's hand. It didn't look very serious. Poison? Or had the spell merely not worked?

Grandpa teleported behind the witch and hit her with his axe. She reacted to that, screeching and reaching around to grab him. He darted away before she could land a blow. Her health bar dipped to [105/110]. It would take a lot more hits to hurt her.

"Fire, salt, and steel," Sage repeated. "Grandpa, the salt!"

Grandpa grabbed the rock salt out of his inventory. He threw a handful at the witch, who screamed as it hit her. The pellets bounced off her flesh, leaving sizzling pock marks all over her face and skin. They burned through the wedding dress that she was wearing so inappropriately. [90/110].

"That's it," Sage called.

The witch shrieked, "No!" She leaned over her cauldron, stirring it with one hand. There was a hissing sound and a smell like burning rubber. "My lord, my love, come to me. Madam Hecate has need of you. I pledged myself to you the day my betrothed spurned me and left me at the altar. Come to me now."

"There's a ridiculous amount of backstory in this mission that we're not even seeing." I took aim again at the witch. "Apparently, lead does not count as steel for this system," I added as another Trick Shot hit the witch with seemingly no impact. "Frank, shoot her. Help me distract her. But keep a clean path for Grandpa, since he's the only one doing any damage."

Frank grunted and raised his gun. The witch pulled the doll out of her cauldron, but it wasn't featureless now. It had dark hair and wore jeans and a T-shirt.

It looked a lot like Sage.

Madam Hecate plucked a pin from her matted hair and stuck it into the doll's leg. Behind me, Sage screamed and collapsed. Her health bar took a big hit.

"Voodoo dolls! Whatever she's doing to that doll happens to Sage."

My every instinct was to run to Sage, to grab her, to try to drag her from this room, but that wasn't going to help. Instead, I dropped my pistol into my pocket and pulled out my kitchen knife.

I charged at the witch. "Don't shoot, Frank!"

I hit the witch like a bulldozer, shoving her backward. I brought my kitchen knife down on her arm as my other hand grasped her wrist, trying to force her to drop the doll.

Grandpa teleported behind her and dumped more salt on her. She screamed as her health bar went yellow, **[65/110]**. The salt bubbled against her skin, but she still had a death grip on the doll, and her strength was higher than mine. She wrenched her arm free and raised the pin again, aiming it right at the doll's heart.

Time seemed to freeze. I grabbed at her, scrabbling, but I couldn't break her grip. The pin came down on the doll. I could hear Sage sobbing behind me, and I knew I wasn't going to be able to get her in time. I didn't dare look at her health bar.

One of Frank's sonic grenades landed right in the witch's cauldron. The whole thing blew up, sending hot liquid and fragments of cauldron everywhere. Instinctively, I looked away, and the spray fell on my coat. **[-1 HP]**, the system told me.

The witch screamed in pain. She kept screaming longer than I expected. As I recovered, I grabbed at the doll, easily breaking her grip this time. The doll went flying. Madam Hecate's health bar was at **[40/110]**.

Grandpa grabbed a flaming log from the fire that had been under the cauldron. It was still blazing, despite the cauldron's contents having been vaporized all over the room.

Since I was now on top of the witch, covering most of her body, he thrust it into my outstretched hand. I took the lit end and shoved it into her. Notifications streamed upward. **[-5 HP]**, **[-5 HP]**.

Her dress went up like a candle. Flames licked around her, melting her face and her hair as she screamed and screamed. I felt the flames burning my hands, but I held her down, desperate to keep her away from the voodoo doll before she could harm Sage.

Grandpa hurried over, bent, picked the doll up from where it lay, and disappeared it into his inventory.

I scrambled away from the dying witch. Her health bar was at **[0/110]** but she was still twitching. I took a deep breath, but didn't relax all the way. I'd done fights before that had a second stage.

As the witch went up in smoke, she let out one last screech. "Baron Samadi, I call you! Avenge me! Take my soul and wreak my vengeance!"

The fire went out, and there was nothing but ash and bone. I went over to Sage. She was getting up from the floor, panting, with tears in her eyes and a half-gone health bar.

I grabbed a bandage out of my inventory and applied it to her. "Are you all right?"

She shook her head. "I don't know. That . . . It hurt. It still hurts," she admitted. She threw her arms around me and squeezed hard.

"Where's the victory?" Frank asked, pacing back and forth. "Where's the victory?"

He was right. We hadn't heard from the announcer yet.

The smoke rising from the witch's corpse grew thicker and thicker until it was a cloud hovering over her body. Then the cloud parted like a doorway, and someone stepped through.

He looked like a man, tall and very gaunt. He wore a top hat and tails like most of the male corpses in the room had, and dark glasses. He carried a cane with a gold head. Most disturbingly, his health bar read **[??/??]**.

"Well, well, well," he said. "What have we here? When Samadi comes and the one who called him is gone. Well, well, well, what to do?"

He bent over the witch. He snapped his fingers, and the last of the smoke formed into the shape of a hunched old woman. "And what is it you'd have me do for you, Hecate, my darling?" He leaned his head close. If the smoke specter said anything to him, I could not hear it, but he straightened up and laughed. "All that for a soul you sold to me a hundred years ago? What a lot to ask. Well, you'll be going to the crossroads now, my dear, and I will finish matters here before I join you."

He snapped, and the smoke woman disappeared. He turned to us. "And what have we here, I see? Strangers to my island, strangers to my folk. Yet you've come afoul of one of my worshippers through no fault of your own. Hecate is from another time. She does not understand the modern ways. She is a little resentful, perhaps. I see she has gone to great lengths here." He held up his hands.

If he was asking us to talk, I didn't know what to say. All of us stood dumbfounded. "So, outsiders, you've come and meddled in what you do not know, and there's a price to be paid for that. I think Baron Samadi will give you a choice." He chuckled.

I did not like that sound.

Hear him out, Grandpa said in party chat. *Let's not be too quick here. Something seems funny.*

I agreed with that. If this was going to be another boss fight, I didn't quite understand the setup.

"Hecate's spell lies across this whole island. My island. My people. It's nightfall now. When the moon rises in a few hours, all those touched by Hecate's curse will rise as zombies, whether they be dead now or no. She has upset the balance. If all my worshippers become the dead, who alive will tell the tales of Baron Samadi? And so here is the charge I give you. I shall grant you my boon, and you shall return and cleanse as many of the afflicted as you can. Those you can't are yours to deal with." He paused, clearly waiting for us to speak.

"And if we don't?" Frank asked.

"If you don't." The man shrugged. "Well, then you'll be facing the wrath of Baron Samadi. And I should tell you, that witch had no tenth of my power."

A system pop-up appeared, finally. The announcer gleefully read off,

**[Mission: Bad Vacation. Bonus phase! Choice: life or death.
Baron Samadi has given you a quest. Return to Grand Parrot Island's
town and cleanse the townsfolk of their corruption before they all become
zombies. Or die now to his wrath. Which do you choose?]**

"Option *A*," Sage said at once, bouncing on her feet. "Definitely option *A*." The choice still hung there, blinking.

"How is this a bonus?" Frank complained. "Shouldn't there be a 'no thanks' option?"

"We choose the first one," I said. "Life. We'll do what the Baron asks."

The system confirmed with a whoosh.

**[Bonus phase accepted. Task: cleanse or kill all remaining villagers
on the island.]**

"Wonderful," the Baron said. "Now, since you have no cleansing skill, I shall grant you a boon." He turned. "On that one, I think." He pointed a finger at Sage. He was wearing very clean white gloves that made his hands look like bones.

"Uh, no," I began. "How about me?" I didn't know what sort of twisted magic he intended to use.

He ignored me, bending over Madam Hecate's body and drawing a gleaming black skill seed marble out of her. He held it up, squinted, and passed his other white-gloved hand across it. The marble swirled with gray. The black washed away, and it glowed pure white. He held it out to Sage.

She reached out, hand trembling, and plucked it from him, not touching his glove. Sage glowed yellow. She let out a gasp, then sank in on herself a little. She shook herself. "I'm all right."

"More than all right. You carry a boon from Baron Samadi himself. And now, be off with it. I'll grant you one more favor. When you leave the doors of this ballroom, you'll be in the town square."

And then he disappeared. No cloud of smoke. No loud popping noise. Nothing. He was gone.

"It's a great skill," Sage said. "It's called Raise Your Spirits. It says, 'removes curse from target or gradually increases their health until they have regained their maximum hit points. May be cast on multiple targets at once. No cooldown.' It sounds like we're wasting time if we want to cure the villagers before they all turn into zombies. We should hurry."

I paused to reload. "All right, but you stick with us. No running ahead. If some of them turn before we expect it, I want to be there to protect you."

"You're always there to protect me."

But deep down in my stomach, in a cold pit, I knew that wasn't true. I hadn't been able to do a thing to stop the witch using her voodoo on her. If not for Frank's grenade, Sage would likely be dead. I pushed the thought away. "Let's go."

CHAPTER NINETEEN

IF YOU CAN'T WATCH ME DO THIS, TURN YOUR BACK

Twilight hung over the village square as we stumbled out of the doors. I looked behind us and saw a rickety shack with an open wooden door. Certainly not the ballroom we had just come from.

Lanterns hung from poles around the edge of the square. Candles stood in every window. Light blazed, but not life. There was no one here.

I could hear ocean waves crashing against the docks to our south where we had landed earlier. There were about three dozen buildings, most two stories tall and made of brightly painted concrete block, or bricks neatly fitted together. Here on the east side of the square, most of the houses were small shacks like the one we had apparently come out of.

I drew my revolver. "I guess we do this one building at a time." I walked to the next shack over and kicked in the door. No response from inside. I peered in. It was awfully dark. "Anyone got a flashlight?"

"Here." Grandpa pulled one out of his inventory. He turned it on and shone it into the room within.

The shack was just one small room with a table in the center and beds pushed against two of the walls. There were people in the beds. I stepped inside and checked.

A man lay in one bed, a woman in the other. They seemed to be asleep. They had a health bar over each of them, about halfway full. Even as I watched, they ticked a point lower. "There's a debuff on each of them."

Sage came in behind me. "Sleeping sickness," I read from the icon, then read the rest of the description. "When they wake, they will be zombies under the control of the hag, Hecate."

"She's dead now," Grandpa pointed out.

"It probably doesn't make them any more friendly," Frank said from the doorway. He had his gun drawn and was watching the street beyond us.

Sage closed her eyes. She held out her hand. A light blossomed on her finger and then flew to the woman on the bed beside me. The woman's body glowed. The debuff disappeared.

Sage let out a breath, opened her eyes, and then did the same to the man. "It worked!" She sounded surprised.

"Are you all right? That's not hurting you?"

"No, not at all." She shook her head. "Oh." She brightened up. "I've got an achievement. If I use this spell on fifty different miners or NPCs within a single hour, I get a reward."

"Well, let's hope there's fifty of these zombies in waiting, then," I said, trying to sound lighthearted.

We went to the next house and repeated the process.

The third house had four people in it, a mother clutching two small children to her in her bed, and an older man. Sage cast Raise Your Spirits on the mother and children, then turned to the old man. The light blossomed around him, but the debuff didn't disappear. She frowned and tried again.

"What's wrong?" Grandpa asked. "Tired? Missed your aim?"

"No, it just didn't work." She frowned again and tried a third time. "It says, 'Error: cannot be cleansed. Curse is too deep.'" She turned to me, her face looking stricken. "Are we too late?"

"No, no," I said, shaking my head. "No, we can't be. It worked fine on the others. There must be something wrong. Maybe . . . Maybe he was already sick." I tried to sound lighthearted. "Look, we shouldn't waste time. Let's check the next house and we can always double back."

We moved on. The next house was a two-story concrete block house and it took a few minutes to find where the people were sleeping. When we did, Sage cured all of them with no issues. "But then why couldn't I help the man before?" she asked, sounding concerned. I didn't have an answer.

We finished up the last house on the side of the square, successfully cleansing its inhabitants, but we ran into the same problem at the first house on the north side of the square. One of the sleepers, a young woman this time, couldn't be cleansed.

My stomach sank. "I think that the game is rigged," I said. "Some of them just can't be cured. They're going to turn no matter what we do. When we're done, we're going to have to fight zombies."

A thought struck me. I glanced at Grandpa and I could see from the way his eyes met mine that he'd had the same idea. If these sleepers were doomed to become zombies, it would make more sense to cut their throats now. Then we wouldn't have to deal with them when they woke up.

I hated this kind of mission. It reminded me of one I'd played in a game a long time ago with a whole town full of people cursed to turn into the undead.

You had no choice but to kill them where they lay. The game made it clear it was a terrible option, but the only one.

It would be stupid not to. It left them as a threat at our backs. We didn't know when the clock would run out, when we would be facing an army of the undead. But as Sage looked down at the sleeping girl, her lip trembling, I knew that I couldn't do it where she saw me.

"Let's go to the next house," I said. I pretended not to notice Grandpa lingering behind as I led Sage to the next house.

We were most of the way down the east side, having found three more incurable victims, but cleansed forty or more when Frank said in party chat, *There's a glow in the eastern sky. I think the moon is rising.*

"We'd better hurry," I told Sage. We ran to the next house. I didn't even bother to clear, just burst in and found the sleepers.

We'd cured all of them and made it halfway out before Frank shouted, "Get out here! It's time to party!"

Grandpa Shadow Stepped out to join Frank. I looked at Sage. "All of these sleepers are cleansed. This house should be safe. You could stay here while we clean up the zombies. There can't be that many of them left."

She shook her head. "I have to help."

I crouched in front of her. "You know you'll be helping me and Grandpa if you stay safe, right?"

She was looking stubborn again. "I won't be in the way. I've already saved you a lot. Besides, I have a healing spell now. I need to be able to use it."

"You could use it from the bedroom upstairs, looking through the window," I pointed out, "like a sniper. Snipers don't get down in the melee. They stay back and take their shots." She looked unconvinced. "Please?"

"All right. But if you start getting in trouble, I'm coming out there no matter what."

"Deal." I patted her on the back and shoved her toward the stairs, then ran out into the square. The undead were shuffling toward us from the south, about twenty of them, most of them dressed like sailors.

I was pretty sure voodoo zombies weren't truly undead. I had read a little bit about actual voodoo beliefs, and it seemed like those *zombi* were usually actually in drug-induced comas or something similar.

But this was the Reality Engine's version of voodoo zombies, no doubt influenced by a hundred bad movies and a thousand terrible books that it had consumed from human culture. What they'd be like was anyone's guess. All I really cared about was that they clearly were after our blood.

They didn't moan for brains, and they didn't hold their hands out, but they did shuffle. Some of them had improvised weapons—oars or ship's axes or daggers. Others just had their smiling personalities.

As they approached, Frank threw a sonic grenade. It exploded on the left-hand flank and sent several of them reeling, but they kept on at us. He threw another, and then it was close enough that he and I started firing as Grandpa phased in and took an axe to the ones on the right.

A zombie made it to Frank before he blew its head off. Some of it splattered across his face and a debuff appeared. [**Infected: Will rise as a zombie after death.**] A second later, it vanished.

"I got my achievement! Now Raise Your Spirits does a big chunk up front, then another big chunk over the next thirty seconds," Sage shouted from her window. "Thanks, Frank! Now stay away from those creatures!"

"We're trying!" I yelled back, reloading.

We cut a swath through those zombies like a scythe through dried hay. Their bodies fell, their blood draining into the town square. I took my shots, broke open the cylinder, ejected my brass, reloaded, closed up the cylinder, and fired again. Trick Shot let me shoot where Grandpa was tomahawking, and Frank kept his shots confined to the other side of the line of zombies.

We had mowed most of them down when Grandpa cursed and disappeared. *Behind us!* he said in chat.

I was still shooting at the oncoming line, so I couldn't turn, but I risked a glance over my shoulder and saw three more zombies emerging from the houses we hadn't gotten to yet.

Grandpa took care of the first; I put a bullet between the eyes of the next. The third tucked into the house where Sage was hiding. I shouted a warning in party chat, and she replied, *I'm going out the window.*

A minute later, she scrambled onto the narrow window ledge above us. I returned to the zombie fray. There were only half a dozen still coming on. Another of Frank's sonic grenades took most of them out, and he followed up with a headshot to the last.

I dropped my gun in my pocket, turned, and held my arms out to Sage. "Jump!" She eyed the distance and let go. I caught her. She knocked me off balance, and I staggered back before gently setting her down.

Grandpa disappeared into the house. He emerged again a minute later. "That's done," he said.

We looked at each other, eyes wide. Frank shifted to avoid a running rivulet of blood.

I took a deep breath. "Where the hell is our victory announcement?"

It came at last.

**[Victory! You have completed Mission: Bad Vacation!
Congratulations for completing the final stage of Mission: Bad Vacation.
You have been awarded the following:**

**XP per participant: 12,000
Soul Coins per participant: 517
Bonus XP for optional bosses: 3,400
Party reward: The Voodoo That You Do.
Madam Hecate was a champion of mixing spells and doing
mischief. In her honor, you have been awarded the crafting
supplement Pick Your Poison.
This supplement will allow a piece of your own equipment to be
used to produce your own spells and techniques.]**

There was a bunch more text in the box that the announcer didn't read. Sage peered at it. "Ooh," she said. "I think I understand what that's talking about. Let me see."

She pulled out something from her inventory, and I remembered that we had chosen to have all loot go to her. It looked like a can of red spray paint. "I'm Inspecting it," she said. "Yeah, okay. I think I see how this works. Grandpa, didn't you say we had some reloading dies?"

"We had a whole reloading press in Shad's inventory," Grandpa said.

"Pull it out. We're done here. Should be safe enough," Sage said.

I looked at the piles of zombies and the blood and the townspeople who were now crowding into their doorways to look at us, and I shrugged.

"All right, but not by the piles of bodies. Let's go over to the restaurant."

We made our way over to The Purple Parrot. A pair of servers were there, looking dazed and confused. I remembered them being asleep in one of the first houses we'd hit. More people were filing into the restaurant, people we had cured. I knew they weren't real, but it still felt like we'd saved them.

I sat down heavily at one of the tables. One of the servers came over. He set a menu down in front of me. "What kind of food for you, friend?" he asked.

I took a deep breath. "Uh, can you do a big plate of chicken nachos?"

Sage plopped down next to me and glanced at the menu. "I want a big bowl of the seven-meat *sanchocho*, a plate of *tostones*, and a *morir sonando*. And then when we're done, one of those cakes." She pointed at a picture of white-meringue-frosted delicacy.

"What she's having," Grandpa said.

Frank stared at the menu. "You guys do a hamburger?"

The server disappeared. I didn't know if he'd really bring us food or not. I pulled the reloading press out of my inventory and set it on the table.

Sage looked from it to the can of paint. She smiled maniacally and rubbed her hands. "This is gonna work," she said. "This is really, really, really awesome. This will let us use the reloading press to make Shad and Deputy Young new bullets."

"We can get those from Veda," I pointed out.

"Yes, but according to this, we should be able to make magic bullets once we know how, and once we get the right ingredients."

She shook up the can of spray paint, held it out, and sprayed it all over the reloading press and all over the table and all over my hands when I wasn't fast enough to pull them back. I wiped them on a napkin, which somehow worked, even though spray paint dries instantly.

Frank coughed. "Could've done that outside."

"You're the ones who wanted to get indoors so fast," she pointed out. "Take a look, Shad."

I Inspected the press. It now said, **[Reloading Press. Crafting Item, Level 3. This press can create magical bullets if given the right ingredients. Recipes available after item is attuned.]**

I picked it up and stowed it in my inventory just as the waiter appeared with a tray laden with our food and a bunch of drinks with slices of lemon and little umbrellas. It smelled delicious, and tasted just as good.

"Hey! No buff!" Sage complained.

"Just shut up and eat."

CHAPTER TWENTY

SIX THINGS TO DO WITH NIGHTMARE BUG CORPSES: YOU WON'T BELIEVE NUMBER TWO!

We stepped through into the portal room. The portals were as they had been. Enormous, glowing entrances with who knows what beyond.

Instead of the milling throng of people that had been present the previous times I'd been in the room, it felt more like a flea market. There were still hundreds, maybe thousands of humans in the enormous chamber. Now small structures had begun to take shape; tables covered by makeshift awnings, roped-off areas, and a pattern of open space that was beginning to resemble streets.

"This is cool," Sage said as she paused beside me. "Looks like people have been busy."

Another party was approaching the portal we had just left. "Mind sharing what you found there?" the man at the front of the group asked. They had a full set of five people all dressed in what looked like leather armor and carrying everything from a bazooka to a woman who had a rapier at her side and a bandolier of throwing daggers across her chest. I wondered if this was gear they'd found inside a portal, brought with them from Earth, or been provided by a sponsor.

Sage gave a brief rundown of what we'd found. "Do you know if the scenarios are the same every time?"

The man shook his head. "We've only run one and we're not sure yet. But we can't take the risk that that's the case and get what we just went through again. If you don't like spiders, avoid the portal six down to the left, the purple one." One of the women visibly shuddered.

"Spiders, got it." I called up my menus and drilled down to the notes tab. I hadn't written down anything yet except the cooldowns on all our skills. I could paste from my notes into party chat, or vice versa, but that wasn't too useful.

I glanced up at our portal. "Is there any way to tell them apart other than the colors? I can write spiders, purple portal, six down from blue portal, but there's only about eight colors going here and hundreds of portals. How are we identifying them?"

The man pointed to the lintels on either side of the door. "As far as we can tell, these designs are always unique. We don't have any idea what they mean."

I squinted. I hadn't even noticed what he was talking about before, but now I saw carved lines on the portal, hard to see unless you were looking. This one had a series of three triangles followed by a half circle and crossed lines like an *x*, then repeating. I concentrated hard, and the pattern appeared in my notes. I added everything the man had told me.

"Thanks for the tip. Good luck. Be sure to take out the monkey boss before you take on the witch. That fight could get ugly with a sub-boss involved."

They stepped through. There was no zapping noise, no flash of light. One minute they were here, the next they were gone.

"All right. Let's go." We had plenty of supplies, but I wanted to check in with Veda if there was any way to do that.

I wasn't sure there was. It had sounded like she was only able to contact us up on the Hub. I did not want to waste five or more hours just to have a quick conversation with our sponsor. Not when we knew what needed to be done next. Build more things, get more skills, earn more coins.

What we did need to find was a level three crafter, if such a thing existed. It turned out, after reading the system-provided user manual for our new magical reloading press, that a level three crafting item required a level three mastercrafter to attune it for us, which I guessed was a class-provided skill or title.

Once it was attuned, we'd be able to operate it ourselves. I was eager to have a way to reload my rounds. That would be one less string the alien woman, Veda, had on us.

I headed for the nearest table under an awning that smelled like it had been a pool cover in a previous life. An older man was standing over the table, shaping some large discs and pieces that looked like chitin and trying to tie them together with string.

"Excuse me," I said. "It looks to me like you're trying to make something there. You have a mastercrafting skill?" The man nodded, intent on his work. "What level?"

He looked up at me, his eyes narrowing. "Why?"

"We've got a crafting item but we need a mastercrafter to attune it for us."

"Hmm." The man looked intrigued. "You're kind of trusting, aren't you? Well, I'll be straight with you. I've reached crafting level two, mostly thanks to working hard with various materials. My coalition has been farming in one of the grind worlds. I'm making them armor."

He gestured to a pile on the ground behind him, shiny breastplates made of overlapping scales. They looked like Asian armor I'd seen in a movie or two, lacquered in dark crimson and emerald shades.

I Inspected them, and their stats popped up. **[20% boost to dodge, 35% decrease in direct melee damage taken by the wearer. Item crafted by Mastercrafter Mihael.]** That was pretty significant.

"You're level two, and you made those?" I guessed this was the Mihael mentioned in the tooltip.

He nodded. "With the right mats, it's easy. There's a grinding world that's nothing but hordes of giant bugs constantly streaming at you. My coalition has eight or nine teams in there at any given time, rotating out every three hours. We're farming mats like you wouldn't believe. By the time I'm level three, we should have enough to start selling to other miners. So check back here if you're interested."

"A coalition, is that something official the sponsors set up?" Sage asked.

"Our chief figured it out. There's submenus and everything. It's like a really big party, but you don't share experience and rewards. You can talk to each other and we're a big family, now."

"Guild system," I guessed. "Anyway, are these better than what your sponsors gave you?" I indicated the armor.

Mihael snorted. "Sponsors gave us weapons and personal shields. The personal shields cost soul coins to recharge, so every time someone takes a critical blow, it ends up costing them most of a day's earnings. Right now, we're all further in debt than when we started. If I can get everyone equipped with these, maybe we can take fewer shield blows."

That matched what I had suspected about the sponsorship deals. Most of them were designed to keep us here mining soul coins for as long as it took.

Mihael went on. "But to get back to the original question, you want to be careful. A level three crafting item's gotta be pretty valuable. You let someone get their hands on it, they could just put it in their inventory and refuse to give it back. What are you gonna do then? This is a safe zone, enforced by the system. You won't be able to kill them and take their stuff."

I hadn't thought of that. Grandpa snorted. "There's other ways of getting what you want," he said darkly. But the crafter had a point. We'd have to make sure our crafter was someone we could trust.

"Was the crafting skill one of your class skills, or did you pick it up somewhere?"

"Class skill. I'm an artisan. I've got a combat skill, too, but the crafting is nice. It looks like I should be able to specialize once I've leveled up a little. Some of our coalition members are looking for skill seeds that might be compatible with me. I get XP for making these too. That's nice. I don't ever want to go into one of those portals again. My coalition makes everyone go in first, but they said I can earn contribution points by making the armor and avoid another shift."

We had slept after our meal inside the restaurant in the Caribbean village, going down to the beach and setting up our camp under the moon. We had fallen asleep listening to the waves, and in the morning, woken up to a spectacular sunrise. By my best guess, it had been about twenty-four hours since we had first entered the Caribbean mission. Not that much time for such a complicated human organization to set up.

"You've got a lot accomplished in not much time."

"We've got someone clever running this coalition. Haven't actually met him. Calling himself the Colonel. Whoever it is knows his business, and I'm going to stick with him."

I noticed that Mihael had a design crudely carved onto one of the pieces of salvaged lumber that held up his awning. It was a hammer paired with an axe. It looked vaguely like the old Soviet Union symbol, except a bit more fascist. It gave me an unpleasant feeling.

"What's your coalition named?" Sage asked. "Maybe we should let the Colonel know that we're friendly and willing to trade."

The crafter laughed. "I haven't spoken to the Colonel myself, though it hasn't been that long, I suppose. I think he likes to duck in and out of the different portals to get an idea of what we're looking at. Chance of you running into him is pretty slim, but I'll pass it along through channels. We're the Free Human League."

Nice name, if a little vague. I nodded and moved along. "We're steering clear of alliances," I said after we had left the man. "We don't know what anyone else is up to, and it sounds like our leveling strategy isn't the most common. It's possible this crafting reward is way better than what anyone else has got yet. I know they can't hurt us here, but I'll bet you there are things they could do."

"Like what?" Sage asked. I didn't answer, because most of the worried ideas I'd had involved her. If someone with bad motives restrained Grandpa and me—I checked, and I wasn't able to use any of my offensive abilities here, so I guessed Grandpa wouldn't be able to Shadow Step out of restraint. They could grab Sage and duck into a portal with her; we'd be forced to follow.

Then we'd all be working under different rules. Maybe they could hurt us, or maybe they could threaten to hurt Sage and make us give up what we had. A level three crafting item sounded pretty valuable right now.

"Shit. The press is useless to us right now. We need to be able to make our own bullets. It'll be one less thing we're dependent on Veda for."

"Plus, it sounds like some of them will be magical," Sage pointed out.

Grandpa spoke. He'd been remarkably quiet as we'd talked to the crafter. "Don't give up too fast yet. Let's see what else there is here. I'm in no rush to jump into the next mission. Let's keep going."

"I thought we were going to find Veda and ask about my family," Frank said.

"We are," I assured him. "Let's see if there's any way of communicating with the surface other than taking the elevator up. We will if we have to, but I'd like to not waste that much time."

We started along, examining the ramshackle buildings as we went.

The next two booths had the same symbol I'd spotted at the crafter's booth, and we passed a hut being built, with a banner over the door emblazoned with the same logo.

"Looks like this neighborhood belongs to the Free Human League," I said. "Why don't we keep moving until we find somewhere unaffiliated? I kind of regret letting that guy know we had a valuable item, although he seemed like a good sort, so maybe it'll work out."

"You sound paranoid," Frank said. "I like knowing that there's humans working together and trying to build something here. It's not good to let ourselves be bossed around by a bunch of aliens."

"There's only four of us, Frank. That makes us pretty weak. If we have something valuable, anyone stronger than us can try to take it. You're a cop, you know that."

He grunted and fell silent. There was a very clear break after the area belonging to the Free Human League, and then more buildings and tables.

Sage sniffed. "What is that? It smells delicious."

We'd had another round of the MREs for breakfast, and she had complained loudly and wanted to go back to the restaurant and ask if they could make pancakes, but I'd insisted we didn't want to spend that much time here. Now she trotted along in front of us, sniffing the air.

I started to call her back, but Grandpa said quietly, "Let her go. We'll keep an eye on her. Remember, she's a kid." I decided he was right, and kept a sharp eye out for anyone trying to grab her.

We found the good smell without any trouble. There was an area marked out with a bunch of random debris. Rocks, shells, anything small. But it made a square about twenty feet on a side.

Inside the marking, at one side of the square, was a folding table and a bench, and next to the table, a grill. I swear, it was a full-sized grill from back on Earth, complete with propane cylinder.

A woman bent over it. She was cooking something that smelled absolutely delicious. To the right side of the square was a big old tent, like I've seen at fancy sporting goods stores, probably twelve feet by twelve feet, with thick canvas sides, and a tall roof. It was the sort of thing you set up at your hunting season base camp when you were planning to be out hunting for a week or with a bunch of buddies, because it was mostly an excuse to get out and drink beer and grill meat without your wife around.

A younger woman ducked out of the tent, carrying a platter holding metal skewers of something that looked like meat. She paused at the entrance, but Sage bounded over to the woman at the grill. "That smells so amazing. Can I get some?"

The woman turned. She was a middle-aged Hispanic woman, with her hair up in a bun and a tired-looking face. She also looked vaguely familiar.

Her eyes widened when she saw Sage. "Well, of course you can, darling," she said. "Sit yourself down. Rosa, get this girl a plate."

The younger woman with the platter of meat handed it to her mother and frowned. "Our price list," she began, but the grilling woman shook her head.

"We'll charge her family if they want, but she can eat for free." The woman stepped away from the grill. She wiped her hands on an apron and then held one out to Grandpa. "I'm Mama Grace. Welcome to Grace's Barbecue and Grill." She looked from Grandpa to Sage. "I remember you. We were on the same elevator going up."

I didn't remember her, but there weren't that many kids around, so Sage was memorable.

Grandpa slid in on the bench at the table next to Sage while Frank and I stood around feeling awkward.

"Nice to make your acquaintance," he said.

Grace was nodding. She pointed at me. "I remember you too. You were talking about mining towns and who made the money. You told me that it wasn't the miners, but the people who served them."

I tried to remember if I'd said something like that. I certainly hadn't been speaking to her, but I could have been overheard, I guessed. "Uh, that's very true."

"So in class selection, my daughters and I picked useful classes. We haven't set foot in a portal and we're well on our way to earning a little nest egg here." Mama Grace patted the table in front of her. "Good thing we had brought so much stuff from the restaurant."

"Mind if I sit down?" I asked. I opened my inventory and grabbed a kitchen chair, pulling it out and setting it at the table. "And what are you charging? 'Cause that smells pretty damn good, ma'am."

She laughed. Mama Grace had a Texas accent, and when her daughter Rosa brought over some plastic plates, she had an even more pronounced one.

Rosa pointed at my chair. "Maybe we can work out a trade. We're still looking for equipment for our restaurant, and it looks like you've got a bit there."

"A lot of folks seems didn't have the presence of mind to pick up what they came in with. We're pretty fortunate."

I looked at Grandpa. He nodded. "We might be able to make a trade," I said. "How about we talk? What classes did you pick?"

"I'm a Short-Order Cook," Mama Grace said proudly. "Not that I needed a class to help me with that, but the skills are actually pretty useful. I've got one that lets me know when my food is ready, and another that lets me grant the food a custom Well-Fed buff."

"Whatever it is, it smells delicious," Grandpa remarked, leaning closer to the grill and inhaling.

"Do you want to know what I'm cooking?"

I noticed that the raw meat was a similar shade of purple to the chitin that the crafter had been working with. "Are you trading with the Free Human League?"

"They bring me meat. I give them cooked food. I am not sure I like their business model, and I refuse to join their coalition, so I might be looking for other suppliers here in the future. But for now, we're working together."

In that case, this was probably bug meat. I shook my head. "Why don't we just pretend it's purple beef and be good with it?"

"More like pork," Mama Grace said. "But I think you're wise." She set a plate of cooked skewers down in front of us, then looked around, made sure nobody was watching, and pulled a bottle of half-empty barbecue sauce from her inventory. She set it down in front of Sage. "Go easy on that. It's the only barbecue sauce for fifty trillion miles, or however far it is from here back to Earth. But don't say I can't share."

CHAPTER TWENTY-ONE

HOW TO MAKE FRIENDS AT YOUR NEW SCHOOL

Mama Grace let us eat. She served us giant platters of the purple bug meat. "Afraid we don't have much clean silverware yet," she said, but I waved her off and pulled some out of my inventory. "We'll talk about a trade when you're done. I've got more hungry mouths to feed." She turned back to the grill.

Her daughter Rosa appeared again, accompanied by another young woman with the same dark hair and light brown skin, clearly her sister. This one looked to be a little older, maybe twenty-three to the first girl's nineteen or so. They began deploying more folding tables from their inventories.

As they worked, a trio of young men appeared. All three had badges made of cloth pinned to their clothing. One wore a bug shell breastplate that I was sure had been made by Mihael, the crafter we'd seen earlier.

The badges all bore the Free Human League's emblem. They sauntered over the boundary line. "Boss said we can get some grub here," one of them called.

"Sure can. Pull up a chair. Or if you don't have a chair, just wait there and I'll give you a plate. You got anything for me?"

The man wearing a breastplate shook his head. "No, but the Colonel said we should give you a couple of hours of labor."

"Oh, any of you boys got a crafting skill?" Mama Grace asked eagerly.

"No, but Tom here is pretty good with a hammer," the one wearing a breastplate said. He was clearly the leader.

One of Grace's daughters brought over a plate of meat and set it in front of them. I hadn't caught her name yet. The breastplate-wearing man caught her wrist as she moved away. "Hey, sweetheart. What's your name? Seeing as we're neighbors, I think we should be friendly."

"Neighbors?" Mama Grace asked sharply. "I thought Free Human League territory was going to all be clockwise of here. I don't want to step on anyone's toes, but I'd like to be able to feed who I please, whatever badge they wear."

"It'll be our territory soon enough. Once everybody here figures out that we know what's going on and nobody else does, they'll come flocking to us."

Grace's daughter yanked her hand away before I had to stand up and get involved. Grandpa texted party chat. *Keep it cool, Shad.*

I'm not going to start anything, I replied, *but if they're causing trouble, I won't stand by.*

Grandpa snorted. Frank was ignoring us, fist-deep in a plate of purple bug stuff. Sage had swiped the barbecue sauce and disappeared it into her inventory just as soon as the strangers appeared.

Grace's daughter came over to our table. "Can I get you boys anything? Or you, miss?"

"I'm Sage," Sage said. "What have you got to drink?"

"I've got a bunch of lemonade and iced tea. It's all powdered, I'm afraid. What we grabbed from the kitchen before we had to make for the exit back in the orientation chamber." She shuddered. "I don't want to think about that anymore."

Grace and her daughters seemed nice, even clever in this new economy, but I wondered how they had survived the initiation chamber and acquired themselves a coin. Perhaps there had been someone else in their chamber who was more adept with killing.

A thought struck me. "From what the system said, I thought that choice was random, just based on population distribution. Like, if you were in a city of ten million, your odds of getting picked were pretty darn small. Whereas, we," I indicated my team, "were the only people in miles, so of course we got grabbed. But all three of you are here. What about the other two who were taken with you?"

"Customers in our restaurant," Mama Grace confirmed. "They say it's random, but I don't believe it. I've seen a bunch of family groups or work groups. Maybe how many were taken from any given area was spread out, but I think they took groups that already knew each other."

That was interesting. I filed it away. Grace's daughter produced several cups of iced tea and a lemonade for Sage. "No ice, sorry," she said.

"Maybe you can find someone with a Create Ice spell to help you," Sage suggested.

"That's a good idea." Grace's daughter pulled out a clipboard. She flipped through pages, then started making a note. Had she not figured out the system notes page yet? "My name is Juana, by the way," she said. She smiled at us. It was nice to see a friendly face.

Mama Grace's cooking was good. Damn good. Way better than the packaged rations we'd gotten. Maybe not as good as what we'd gotten up on the Hub, but it was here, convenient to the portals, and she'd said she could apply different buffs. She might get some competition sooner or later, but for now, as soon as anyone found out about her, they'd be beating a path to her door.

That would make this an important location. I glanced over at the Free Human men at the table next to me and wondered if they were here for the same reasons. I really wanted to talk to Grace or one of her daughters without them around.

"You know if there's a way to chat with other miners?" I asked Juana. "Like party chat, but different?"

She glanced quickly over her shoulder at the three men who were hunched over their meal and then nodded.

"Sure, you just have to add a contact." She raised a hand and held it out to me. I shook it and was mentally greeted with a prompt from the system.

[Add contact Juana Lopez? Yes / No.]

[Yes], I selected.

A minute later, a new screen popped up. It said **[Social]** and at the top was my party. After that, a group list of known contacts with one entry, **[Juana Lopez.]**

I thought about her contact and then tried to talk the way I did in party chat. *Do those fellows make you nervous?*

A reply popped up right away. *I can handle myself.*

Of course, to her, we weren't necessarily any less suspicious than they were. I should back off. So I just added, *I'd like to talk to your family about an idea I have about pooling information, but privately. Maybe sometime after these fellows are gone.*

She replied, *I'll ask my mother, or you can. Feel free to introduce yourself and grab her contact info.* Juana turned her back on me and disappeared back inside the hut.

Listening to Mama Grace talk was relaxing. I opened the note tab in my interface and started making lists of things I needed. Information on the portals. Lists of contacts and what they could do. I needed a crafter, for sure. Someone I could trust.

I could split off notes into subtabs, which I did now, labeling them with little reminders what they were.

"Anyone know if there's a way to talk to your sponsor without going all the way back up to the Hub?" I asked.

"There's a kid running a messenger service now," Grace said. "He pops by here every so often. If you leave a message here, I can see that he takes it up."

That didn't seem very secure, but it was an option. "Thanks."

Before we finished our meal, I made sure to get Mama Grace and her other daughter, Rosa, added to my contact info. We swapped her all the kitchen chairs we had brought for the promise of a week's worth of meals at her shop.

As we left the restaurant, I spotted movement at a portal not too far off. "Let's go check that out."

Twenty people emerged from one red-tinged portal all at once. They looked tired, and they were covered in purple goo. They all wore Human League badges.

"Shift change," Frank commented, looking at them.

"And to think we could be doing that," Grandpa said. "Guess we owe Veda one."

I shook my head at the thought, but urged the team to move along. "We don't want to waste too much more time. Any time we're spending out here, we're not in there leveling. We've got to earn skills and coins if we're going to make it to phase two, whatever that is."

"We need to talk to Veda," Frank protested.

"I know, I know. And I'd like to know more about the next portal we go through."

We could ask the system what type of leveling experience each portal offered and get an overview. There were the farming zones, which were the most badly named thing I'd ever heard. They didn't grow anything. You were farming mobs and the XP and soul coins they produced by killing them over and over as they threw themselves at you.

There were hunting zones, which were similar to the initialization chamber, in that you were, again, hunting mobs, but they were fewer and far between and tended to be themed, and every now and then you'd come across a boss.

Then there were the mission portals, like what we'd just done, as well as something called strategic choice, which I hadn't been able to find any description of. We could hang out outside one and wait for someone to come out and ask them, but that didn't seem like a good use of our time.

Veda had said to concentrate on the missions, and so far, that was working out.

"All right," Grandpa said, "enough wasting time. We had a good meal. We've done some talking. Frank, I know you want to find out what happened to your family, so here's my suggestion. Let's leave a message for that courier kid to take to Veda, asking her to look into it. That's not something that anyone else can use against us if they overhear it."

I agreed. "Then we should go do some more missions. If we don't get a message back from Veda, we'll go up there ourselves, as planned. We'll ask around in between missions about a crafter. Sounds like not much chance of anyone being level three yet anyway, so there's not a whole lot of point in searching around for someone to make use of our reloading press."

"Right," Sage said brightly. "Then let's go. I'm tired of wasting time." She started skipping ahead, back toward Mama Grace's restaurant.

Grandpa drew me aside. "You were stalling, boy," he said. "You know as well as I do what we need to do here." I looked away, but he kept talking. "I know. You're worried about your sister, and that's fine. But we've got to keep moving ahead if we're going to take care of her and get her out of here. Can't afford to have you in a funk, boy."

"Yes, sir." We left our message at Mama Grace's. I suggested that she put up some sort of community bulletin board where people could post messages about things they were interested in, like, say, locating a level three crafter. She seemed to think that was a good idea.

Then Grandpa and I ran through our inventory and sold them anything they thought they could use that we didn't see an immediate need for.

There was a trading window that let us switch things straight from our inventory to Juana's. Since they didn't have enough soul coins to pay us straight up, Juana wrote up an IOU. I figured at the very least we could get free meals for the foreseeable future, and it wasn't like Grandpa and I had sold them everything. Our inventories were stuffed to bursting with what we'd looted from home.

After that, and after Sage swiped a cookie from Juana, we set off for the next portal. On my way, I tried to make note of portals people were coming out of and how they looked. Nobody looked particularly happy or cheerful.

"Where now?" I asked. "There's plenty of different mission portals we can choose. Just grab the nearest?"

"Eeny meeny miny moe," Sage chanted, pointing between portals that the system had marked for us as mission portals. When she got down to the last eeny meeny miny moe, her finger pointed at a blue portal off to our left. "That one."

I didn't have anything else to suggest, so we took Sage's choice.

"I really wish we'd picked a different portal," Frank shouted over the noise of a pair of Japanese Zeroes diving toward us.

"Shut up and keep shoveling this shit!" I yelled, wielding my spade and throwing giant chunks of manure over my shoulder as fast as I could. "The system says there's a pony in here somewhere, and we're going to find it before those Zeroes can turn us into Swiss cheese!"

"Yeehaw!" Sage yelled from atop the giant blue ox. She whirled a golden lasso over her head. "Watch this! Oh hey, I just got a new skill! It's called Mucking Out the Stalls. I wonder what it does?"

After our fourth mission, three days later, we were exhausted and on our last nerve. We had used all the bullets Veda had given us, and there had been no reply to our message.

We stopped by Mama Grace's restaurant. It had completely transformed since our first visit. Now, the square that had been marked out with shells and debris sported a neat split-rail fence around it. Inside were a dozen tables, all with chairs or benches—mismatched, but who really cared?—and covered in red and white checked tablecloths.

Mama Grace was overseeing two grills and a smoker, and inside the hut, which was now a substantial building with a pair of tin chimneys coming out one end,

I could hear her daughters overseeing their kitchen staff as they cooked what smelled to me like cornbread and fixin's.

Grace's daughters hadn't taken cooking classes. Rosa was a seamstress. She could repair broken clothes. She wasn't a crafter, she said. That wasn't one of her designated skills. But she was able to repair any cloth or leather-based gear.

My duster had taken a beating in the last mission and gone down to forty percent durability. I bought some sort of heavy-grade cotton fabric off another miner that was supposedly "infused with fire essence" from being found in a fire-themed farming zone. I suspected it was actually asbestos. Then I hired Rosa to fix my coat for me. She patched it up good as new in about ten minutes while we stuffed ourselves on bug pseudoribs.

Juana, on the other hand, had been reluctant to reveal her class. I had heard her telling some of the customers that she'd picked Waitress as her class, but something about how she said it made me think she was lying. I noticed how she showed up every time someone new came by and talked to them enough to get their contact info and learn a little about them.

On the stop where Rosa fixed my coat, Juana brought our drinks to our table and said, "You two, you guys are looking for a level three mastercrafter?"

We hadn't mentioned that. I knew at once how she'd heard. "Someone in the Free Human League tell you that?"

She nodded. "Rumor is you've got something valuable. I suspect they're interested. Keep your eyes open. Thing is, I think I know where to find one. Talk to me later. There's a lead I'm going to follow up."

So on our way out of that last mission, we stopped by the restaurant again. We sat down, and Juana brought us our usual. "What's new?" she asked cheerfully.

"We're heading upstairs after this," I said. "Need anything?"

Juana shook her head. "Our courier's getting more reliable. Plus, we've got contacts now in a dozen different farming levels. One of them is actually a farm. One of the other groups, not the Free Human League, the Glorious Morning of the New Dawn. Have you met them?"

"Just in passing." We had met a team from the pretentiously named Glorious Morning of the New Dawn faction as we chose between two mission portals. I was pretty sure it was a very clunky translation of a Chinese name, since everyone I'd met from that coalition had been Chinese.

There were half a dozen large coalitions now. We'd been approached by the Free Human League and the Lonely Miners Guild about joining up. I'd let Grandpa do the talking, and he'd ended up refusing both offers. "We might have to join up with some folk, sooner or later," he told me privately later. "If it's humans or aliens, I pick humans. But right now, I want us to steer clear of entanglements until we have a better picture of what's going on."

Juana kept talking. "Anyway, they've set up an outpost with a rotating set of squads, keeping the farm section clear of infestation, and brought in some folk like us who aren't so interested in killing to try to actually do something with the farm. They're getting fantastic results. Pepper and tomato harvests every couple of hours. It's awesome. We've been able to make a deal with them to swap some of their food for our resources. But that's not what I'm here to talk about."

She lowered her voice. "Remember I told you I had a lead on a crafter? I'm pretty sure I know where he is now. Only, there's a couple of them on the team, and one of them's a problem."

My hand reached for my gun instinctively. She noticed. "Not that kind of problem. Just difficult. Prickly. I think maybe Sage might be able to get through to him. Listen, I'll tell you where they are, and you can go talk, but I want you to relay a message. I had his contact information, but he's blocked me out and isn't talking. The crafter's name is Dwight. He's got a friend named Arjun, and Arjun is the one who's the problem. I think there's a third member of their team, but I haven't met her or heard anything about her yet. I just want you to try to open communications with them."

"Why?" Grandpa asked bluntly. "What do you get from this? You want Sage to soften someone up, you need to lay things out." We had noticed how people reacted to Sage. There weren't many kids here. People gave her gifts, or broke down crying. We hadn't taken advantage yet. It seemed wrong.

Juana hesitated and looked around. "Listen, we're in this for the long run. I've done the math. I don't know if Mama has. She keeps acting like we're going to go home in a couple more months, back to the restaurant. But I know better. We could be here for years, and I don't want to go in any of those portals."

She shook her head. "The stories I hear you and the others tell terrify me. If you can just get Dwight here to talk to me, I'm sure we can work a deal. You see, I'm a Procurer." She held up her clipboard. "Linked to this clipboard, of all the things we brought with us. That's my class, and my skill is to help people find the resources they need. My other skill lets me make contracts that the system itself will enforce. I had my notary public stamp on me," she explained, "and that apparently let me pick a kind of unique class."

Grandpa drew in a sharp breath. "And a dangerous one. That first skill sounds like you could use it to manipulate folk."

She nodded. "I could. I won't. I know you don't really have any reason to trust me." She touched the necklace around her neck. It was a rosary paired with a Miraculous Medal, similar to the one my Grandpa wore in Abuela's honor. "But I won't. Even here, I believe God sees me and knows what I'm doing. He'll judge me if I'm wrong."

"So you just want us to go and talk to these fellows and tell them to come and have a word with you?"

She nodded. "Told you, I'm a Procurer. They're what you need. They're what I need. They might be what all of us need." She gestured around vaguely, and I didn't know if she meant the restaurant or all of the humans toiling away here for alien overlords.

"All right," I looked around. "We'll go talk to them on our way to the elevator." I stood up. "Had enough yet, Sage?"

"For now. That meat is so good, even if we are all out of barbecue sauce." She stood up and pushed the plate back for Juana to collect. "But when we get up to the Hub, I'm ordering pancakes. Big stack of pancakes, tall as me, covered in real maple syrup. And bacon. Mmm. This is tasty, but it sure isn't bacon."

CHAPTER TWENTY-TWO

THE IMPORTANCE OF A WELL-BALANCED READING LIST

The place Juana had told us about wasn't too far from the elevator, so Frank didn't complain very much about the unnecessary detour.

There were three mismatched tents in a little group, a little way away from any other buildings or constructions, as though the neighbors were leaving them alone. Two were small, classic camping tents. The third, center tent was more like a yurt. A faint odor of human waste hung over all three.

The big problem with our portal hall town—everyone had taken to calling the giant portal room Threshold, and I thought the name was appropriate—was that we didn't have any bathing or, worse, toilet facilities.

Someone had jumped in to fill the gap. It warmed my heart, seeing human entrepreneurship in progress. There were public latrines that were serviced by one of the smaller conglomerates that was trying to avoid having to face one of the farm levels head on.

The latrines were essentially large five-gallon buckets inside small privacy huts. A couple times a day, someone came by, put a lid on the buckets, hauled them away to one of the portals that had been ruled more or less safe, and dumped them out. In return, they'd been able to charge fractions of a soul coin for each use of the bucket facilities. The system managed all the transactions seamlessly. From the smell, the inhabitants of this camp hadn't paid to have their buckets hauled away in some time.

We had quickly learned that if any mission we were on offered toilet facilities to take advantage of them. One mission we had ended at a fancy hotel, and after the mission concluded, we had all been able to take a glorious hot bath.

Sage wanted to run that mission again, but it turned out that the mission levels were somewhat random. You went into one, and you didn't know exactly what you were going to get.

They tended to be grouped around themes. The portal we had first gone through apparently always offered an undead-themed storyline. I was still hoping somebody found one that was rainbows and bunnies themed.

Sage wrinkled up her nose. "Here? Really?"

"That's what Juana said." I stopped at the edge of the little encampment and cupped my hands. "Hello? Looking for Dwight. Can I talk to you?"

No one answered.

"I'm using my Inspect on everything here, and nothing's coming up," Sage said. "It's like the tents are blocking the skill."

We'd seen that here and there with materials that were enhanced with items found inside one of the portals. "Then maybe we are in the right place."

There was a sign by one of the tents. I squinted and read. It said, "Divinations for sale. If you have to ask, you can't afford it." "Huh. Hello?" I called again.

Someone scrambled out of the leftmost tent. It was a young woman, probably in her midtwenties, so a few years older than me. She had a snub nose and freckles and a lopsided haircut. She folded her arms across her chest. "What do you want?"

"I want to see Dwight about some help attuning an artifact."

"He's got all the work he needs for weeks now."

This wasn't promising. Sage said, "It shouldn't take long. We really need the help."

The woman focused on Sage. Her face softened. That had happened a lot. I'd met another four or five children since arriving here, but Sage was one of the youngest. The aliens had apparently done their best not to bring any along, though I wished they'd tried a little harder in Sage's case.

"Come in and have a talk. We don't work with anyone unless I've done a divination on them first."

We exchanged glances. *Is this a good idea?* I asked in chat.

Let's humor her. She's got the crafter we need, Grandpa replied.

"Come in," she said again. "I'm Kirin."

We stepped across the invisible boundary into their camp. The middle tent was an enormous round construction that I would have called a yurt if it weren't bright pink. It looked big enough for a dozen people, maybe more, to fit inside. Kirin held back the cloth hanging that served as a door and gestured. "After you."

We stepped inside, and I blinked because the tent wasn't dark like I expected, but bright. A pair of seemingly normal electric lamps stood on end tables that looked like they could have come from your average suburban American home. In the middle of the tent was a long, low table, and behind it, a hanging curtain cut off the back half of the room. There was even a carpet on the floor, like one of those remnants that you could buy at a carpet store for your dorm room.

"Shoes off."

We obeyed. The carpet was a little dirty, but then so were our feet. We took the seats she was offering, which were beanbag poufs, and settled in.

Kirin sat on a tall director's style chair across from us.

"So, how does divination work, anyway?" I asked, shifting uncomfortably on the pouf. It was kind of small for me. Frank perched on top of his, looking miserable.

Kirin leaned forward, steepling her hands. "What we usually do is listen to your list of skills and come up with the best odds for a portal that will suit you."

That was interesting, if true. "Is that your skill?" I asked curiously.

"Let's say that it is."

"How do we know that it's not just a scam?" Frank scowled. "I've busted more fake psychics than I can shake a stick at."

"We have a double or nothing guarantee," the woman said quickly. "You pay a low price for your first divination, because we're pretty sure you're going to come back, and when you do, we charge you three times as much."

"That's not how double or nothing works," Grandpa said.

She ignored him. "So what will it be?"

"Actually, we really need to find a level three mastercrafter, and we thought Dwight was the best hope." I sent a message to party chat. *Don't mention Juana. I've got a bad feeling about this.*

"We'd like to know about good options for our next mission level," Grandpa said smoothly.

"Why don't you share your class details with me, and I'll see what I can find out," Kirin said.

We exchanged glances. While there didn't really seem to be any way people could hurt you if they knew what your class and skills were, everyone had been a little hesitant to share those details.

"Why is that?"

Kirin glanced briefly over her shoulder. "I can't perform accurate divinations without accurate information. I'm not psychic." She smiled at Frank. "I just have some good information."

Frank was looking at her through narrowed eyes. In party chat, he said, *She's hiding something. I think she's fronting for someone.*

That was way more than he usually used party chat for. I paid attention. "Well," I said, "Frank here is a Deputy Sheriff." I ran down his abilities.

I saw her hiding a yawn. Either she wasn't actually paying attention, or this was part of an act. I tried my Inspect on the inside of the yurt. The cloth barrier stopped my skill entirely. She was definitely hiding something behind there.

Grandpa leaned forward. "I am a Tomahawk Ninja, follower of two proud warrior traditions. The Tomahawk Ninja—"

Okay, that's coming on a little thick, I said in party chat.

Grandpa didn't even listen to me as he went on about the similarities between ninjas of Japan and the proud Paiute warriors his ancestors had been.

Kirin was definitely not listening. She drummed her fingers against the arm of her chair and stared at the ceiling.

Sage, I said in party chat, *I want you to get bored. Get up. Start pacing. When she's stopped paying too much attention to you, get closer to that curtain. I want to try to get a look behind it.*

Sage stretched her arms and did a big yawn. She got up and started pacing around the yurt, complaining. "I want to go up to the Hub and get my pancakes now," she was saying, as Grandpa explained in incredible detail just what coup had meant to the Plains Warriors, who weren't our ancestors but had been kin and followers of many of the same noble traditions.

Kirin was obviously bored. Sage wandered here and there, closer and closer to the curtain. Then, as Grandpa was finishing his description of how he cashed in his coup points to take a coup de grace, Sage flicked the corner of the curtain back.

"Aha," she said triumphantly, "there is a man behind the curtain."

"Get away from there." Kirin stood up abruptly, knocking her chair over, but it was too late. Sage flipped back the curtain so we could all see. In the space beyond the curtain, a middle-aged man sat cross-legged on a bunch of cushions. He was clearly Indian, but not like Grandpa. Really Indian, from the Indian subcontinent.

I got to my feet. "Mr. Arjun, I presume?"

The man blinked at us and frowned. "I hadn't finished your party profile yet," he complained. His eyes were focused over my shoulder. "How am I supposed to give accurate predictions, Kirin, if you let them interrupt during profiling time?" There was a little bit of a whine in his voice.

Kirin looked furious. She stalked over to Sage. "How dare you disturb him? He's very sensitive. It's going to take him hours to get back in the groove now."

Sage ignored and slipped past her. She sat herself on the cushions near Arjun and smiled at him. "Hey, I found this cool thing in one of the portal missions we ran this week," she said. She pulled out an old-fashioned ball and cup game, the kind with the ball on a string that you toss and try to catch in the cup. Sage had never seen one before, thought it was super cool, and stole it.

She bounced it up and down now, trying to catch it in the cup and failing. "I'd like to find more missions like that that have fun things. You think you can help me find it?" She bounced it again, successfully making a catch. "Woo-hoo!"

Arjun blinked at her. "Can I see?" I noticed he had a Rubik's Cube at one knee and a box of pick-up sticks over to the side.

Kirin turned on us angrily. "You don't know what you're doing. You've got to leave him alone. He needs quiet in order to do what he does."

"We're not here to bother you," I said. "I mean, a little bit. We all need to be working together. Mama Grace, Rosa, and Juana think that you can help. I think we can help you." I nodded at Arjun. "I get it. You're taking care of him, aren't you?"

Her eyes flickered around desperately. "We're doing just fine."

"Because Dwight's skills are keeping you all fed for now. But you can't stay cut off from everyone forever. You're not getting your toilet buckets emptied anymore, are you? I can smell them. How long until you start getting sick from your own waste?" I leaned in. This was something the Army had drilled into us, the importance of logistics in a camp. "Nobody here can survive on their own. Why don't you tell me what's going on, and I'll try to help?"

She shook her head. "You don't understand. If the big groups find out what Arjun is really capable of—we've been hiding it behind this mystic mumbo-jumbo."

"What is he capable of?" Grandpa asked mildly.

Arjun looked up proudly. Still not making eye contact, he announced, "I'm a Mycroft," as though that answered anything.

"A what?" Grandpa and I looked at each other, bemused.

Frank snorted. "Don't you fellows ever read the classics? You're always talking about Louis L'Amour and so forth, but clearly you haven't read *Sherlock Holmes*."

"I read a couple of those once," I said. "What's that got to do with it?"

Frank looked almost gleeful at having the advantage on us for a change. I guessed that a week of video game references and pop culture allusions that didn't mean much to him had been wearing. "Mycroft Holmes is Sherlock's older, smarter, but housebound brother. He's so smart he can think rings around Sherlock Holmes, and even you uneducated dolts should know what that means."

"Arjun had an eidetic memory before we came here," Kirin explained, sighing. "And then he picked that class, Mycroft. It means he's able to correlate between different pieces of information. He's been building up a database in his head of all of the miners, their classes, and skills."

I blinked. "I don't quite understand why that's a problem."

"If you have information like that on even a fraction of the people here, you'd be able to build parties that could take on challenges much more powerful than expected. You'd be able to game the system, win missions with hardly any effort, take on levels that no one else can. If any of the coalitions find out what he can do, they will stop at nothing to drag him off and use him for their own ends."

I thought she was probably right. On the other hand, the way they were going about this was idiotic. "And if you keep giving out highly accurate divinations, the same thing's going to happen to you. And then they'll find out it wasn't you, and they'll go after Mycroft anyway," I pointed out.

She looked at her feet. "I was hoping Dwight would be able to protect us. He's been doing commissions from many of the smaller alliances that don't have their own craftsmen. But I don't think that's going to be work out. We're getting more pressure every day."

"What if you team up with someone else who's already got a good thing going. Mama Grace and her crew have allies. They're good people."

I thought about Juana's talent, how it might synergize really well with Arjun's. "Listen, you should at least talk to her. Go by the restaurant."

"I already have," Kirin said. She looked defeated. "I've got her contact info. I've just not told her that I'm associated with Dwight and Arjun. You might be right. We're certainly not going to be able to hide out here forever. Arjun's been complaining about the smell a lot, and I'm concerned he'll just take off on his own."

She looked over to where he and Sage were exchanging toys. Sage was twiddling the Rubik's Cube while Arjun played with the ball and cup.

"You knew each other before?"

Kirin bit her lip. "I was the live-in aide at an assisted living home for adults with developmental needs, the ones who just need a little bit of support. They're often perfectly able to hold jobs, have active social lives, and just need a little bit of help keeping the dishes washed, the bills paid, or the toilet paper stocked. It was a night gig, and I had another job during the day. Worked pretty well. I was very fond of everyone there. I've never been very good at making friends myself, and living in the home, well, at least there were always friends. That's where we were when it happened. I had been home sick from work. I was taken along with four of the residents." She looked very sad. "Arjun and I were the only ones to make it out of the initialization chamber."

I didn't know what to say.

"He didn't change when he absorbed the soul coin?" Grandpa asked, studying him. "It cured me, and I was on my deathbed."

"No, no change. But I thought about that. I don't think there's actually anything wrong with Arjun. It's just how his brain works. If he changed his brain, he wouldn't be him anymore." She shrugged. "Anyway, he's a good man, and he's kept me anchored here. We found Dwight. Dwight gets along with Arjun better than almost anyone I've ever met. I think their minds think kind of similarly. Dwight said we shouldn't trust anyone else. After what happened to my other residents, I was on the same page. Maybe I was wrong. Look, I'll . . ." She hesitated. "I'll talk to Juana. No promises."

"That's all we wanted. Well, that and to speak to Dwight," I said again, for what felt like the fifteenth time.

"Really, he actually is busy. Maybe you can come back later. Sage said you were going up the elevator, so how about stopping back when you come down? If we're not here, maybe we've gone to see Juana."

That would have to be enough for now. I looked at Grandpa, and he nodded.

"Finally. I've been wanting to get up there for the last week," Frank said impatiently. "Let's go."

"All right. I wonder what Veda's got for us now."

CHAPTER TWENTY-THREE

HOW TO ACE YOUR NEXT PERSONNEL MEETING

Veda studied the information packet for the fifth time in the last two hours. Her team was doing magnificently. Better than she had expected, as well as a full team should have managed. They picked up a healing skill to fill in their weakness, and a few other abilities that rounded them out nicely.

Their soul coin income was stupendous. It wasn't in the top ten percent of teams overall, and she was glad of it. She didn't want them attracting too much attention from the wrong sources. But they were well ahead of what she had hoped for.

Actually, a lot of the teams were ahead of what she had expected. She frowned and put in the new numbers. This Reality Engine harvest was going about twelve percent faster than average. That meant all their projections for phase two could be off. There were even headlines streamed in from some of the inner systems, talking about the "miracle rush Reality Engine" and postulating it might have more than the usual bounty. A lot more.

She didn't really believe it herself but she understood the desperation. The waiting list to acquire a Reality Engine slot was years, maybe decades, long. The sooner this Engine opened up to allow new citizens to free themselves from subsistence dreaming and enter a properly tamed Reality Engine System, the better.

But too much success would invite more competition, and she couldn't afford that. She called up some subroutines and accessed information her grandfather had laid down, ran algorithms her great-great-grandfather had written, and tried to do some predictions. It was too soon to tell.

Veda filed the thought away for future worries. The system had notified her earlier that her team was on the way up, two days earlier than she'd expected, so she'd been hard at work ever since.

She hadn't given them enough ammunition previously. This time, Veda had laid in a stock of both kinds that her team used.

She looked over their skill lists again. They were getting close to their second level. She didn't expect any of them to experience a class evolution, even though they were all leaning into their class concepts so well. Only about three percent encountered it at level two. She should warn them about the possibility of an evolution anyway, just in case.

Returning to her projections, Veda engrossed herself happily in numbers, projections, past Reality Engine exploits, and the current iteration. She spotted a couple places where a savvy buy now might corner a market that ended up being important later, getting an edge on a commodity, and made a few investments with coin her team had made. If they paid off, they'd be well ahead of the curve. If not, they still had time.

She was deep in this work when she got a ping. The team was thirty minutes out. Veda jumped to her feet at once and cleared away all her screens. She had booked a suite at one of the facilities catering to miners on leave and arranged to have them looked over by a veterinarian. She nervously rechecked her lists for any last-minute plans. It was all right. Everything was going well. She'd be fine.

As we disembarked from the space elevator, a message came in. *Veda: Follow the light. I will meet you in your suite.*

"A suite?" Sage said. "That sounds nice."

We spotted the bouncing light and followed it from the elevator platform out into the Hub, along a couple of moving sidewalks, and into the great space station.

I couldn't help staring around. There were some orc-like creatures, and others that looked like walking trees, and a couple others that were just canisters full of neon-colored gases floating around.

Sage goggled. "They really are aliens."

"I don't see a single gray among them. Is this some sort of trick?" Grandpa asked.

Frank crossed his arms. "Told you Area 51 was a big hoax."

"Uh-huh," Grandpa said, not sounding convinced. "Here we are, abducted by aliens. Sure it was a hoax."

We were guided to an anonymous-looking door. There were a lot of these that we had passed, just rectangles marked out in the metal walls of the space station. I supposed when you had a system to show you where you were going and lay interesting overlays as needed, you didn't have to go in for a lot of ostentatious signage.

As we approached the door, it disappeared, and we stepped into an elegantly appointed suite. There were soft green throw rugs on the floors, two long, white curved couches standing against the walls, and doors opening out into what I assumed were other rooms.

Along the back wall was a buffet table laden with food. What stopped me dead, though, was the picture window over the buffet table. It looked out onto the Arizona Strip. Right there was the familiar red-and-white striped outcropping that I'd seen every day for years as a boy on my way to school. A lump welled up in my throat.

Grandpa looked around. "Cut it out," he said sharply. Veda appeared. One minute she wasn't there, the next she was, looking real and solid, wearing some sort of diaphanous gown, a cross between what a Roman matron would wear and a beauty pageant contestant. She even had a crown in her hair of laurel wreaths.

Grandpa pointed at the window. "Get rid of that."

"I thought it would make you think of home." She held up her hand, and the image shifted to one of Jupiter far below us, its storms and cloud layers shifting infinitesimally. "Better?"

Grandpa glared. "It'll do."

"Please help yourself to some refreshments, or sit down. This won't take long. I've booked the suite for the next twenty-four hours. I've also arranged for you to have a series of appointments. You need to have your physical condition checked. The bandages and healing spells you have are well and good, but they can leave small issues that mount up, plus we need to monitor your ethereum levels. It's recommended that any miner on missions undergoes a full physical at least twice a month."

Sage skipped over to the buffet and loaded herself with a plate. "Blueberry pancakes!" she exclaimed. "My favorite!"

Veda looked very pleased with herself.

The smell was starting to get to me. It was absolutely heavenly. I walked over and picked up a skewer of fresh-cut fruits and started eating.

Frank turned to Veda. "I need to know about my family," he said bluntly. "I need to know if they were taken, and if so, where they are."

She blinked. "Miner personal records are difficult to access once a miner has been contracted," she said. "I can make inquiries, but it may take some time. Besides, the odds of any one person being taken are minuscule."

"Yeah, but you said you do it based on population, and our home county hasn't got that many people, so I'm worried about my wife. My kids, they were scattered all over the country. Who knows if they could have been taken. I want you to find that out for me, soon as you possibly can."

"I'll try," Veda said.

"You'll have a yes or no answer for us the next time we meet," I said, "or we will go on strike."

She stared at me. Her jaw dropped open. "You'll what?"

"Grand tradition of Earth miners. They don't like the working conditions, they go on strike. They refuse to work. You don't have enough funds to hire scabs, so you'll have to talk to us."

"I, I—" She blinked very rapidly, cocked her head to one side. I thought she must be consulting the system. "You don't understand. Your contract says—"

"I don't care what the contract says, there'll be a way around it."

"If you don't work, you won't get food," she said.

"We'll figure that out." I was pretty sure Mama Grace would feed us long enough to make Veda start feeling desperate.

She opened and closed her mouth a few times, looking a lot like a goldfish. It was comforting to think of her as a goldfish. She looked just a little too human, and yet not human enough. I wanted to remember that she was an alien, that she was part of this whole scheme that had taken us from our home and put us into mortal danger. She was part of the machine that had made it so Sage was forced into situations where she could be killed.

"All right," she said. "I'll do everything I can."

There was an awkward silence. Frank glared over at her. After a long moment, Veda said, "Any other questions or requests from me before I let you relax?"

"Yeah, actually." I grabbed myself a plate of food as I was talking. "Our first mission, we got a bonus objective. It had extra rewards as well. We haven't seen one of those since. What's up with that?"

Veda's eyes unfocused. "I'm reviewing that mission. Yes, so I've seen bonus objectives happen in certain circumstances before. Usually, it means you did something impressive enough that the system decided to grant you an extra challenge or an extra stage. Let's see."

She waved a hand and the whole room filled with an image of our battle with the hag. Everyone in the picture was about a foot tall and I could see through the image to Sage and Grandpa who were seated on one of the couches.

She made a pinching gesture and the image zipped backward to right after we had defeated the first wave of zombies. "Yes, see? The boss was about to summon adds again and then you disrupted her."

We watched as the miniature version of Frank threw a sonic grenade into the skeletal orchestra pit. "It hard-countered her whole ability and short-circuited the fight, bringing on her final phase right there. You can clearly see around the room there's still several dozen corpses waiting to activate. That was very clever. The system notices that sort of cleverness where they see miners figuring out a game mechanic or doing something creative. Sometimes it seems to reward them and sometimes it's more like a punishment, like saying you guys cheated so now you have to face an extra challenge. In this case, I think it was a reward. Remember, this was very early on. There weren't many other miners doing missions at that point. So I think you got a combination of a reward for being creative and a bonus for being an early adopter."

That made sense. I nodded and Veda dismissed the image. I took my plate back to one of the couches and sat down. "The reward we got was pretty great, even if we haven't been able to use it yet. We're still working on that. How do we trigger bonus levels again? Just by trying to be outgoing and creative?"

"That's one technique." Veda paused. "There are going to be certain portals that are more likely to spawn bonus levels. Ones that are more difficult. You might ask around and see if anyone else has encountered a bonus level or . . ." She hesitated. "I don't like suggesting this, but if you hear about portals people have stepped through and then not come back . . ."

I let the implications sink in. "You're suggesting we take on missions that have killed entire teams?"

She shook her head. "It's not the best strategy, I agree. Anyway, does that answer the question?"

"How many people have died?" Sage asked quietly. Her plate sat balanced on her knee and she hadn't touched a bite on it for a good minute and a half.

Veda blinked. "I'd have to query the system to get the exact statistics."

"Do it!"

Veda paused again and said, "Of the seven million or so miners who made it past the initialization sequence, about twenty thousand have perished since."

As a fraction of the whole, that wasn't too bad. As a number of people who had died in the last week, it was horrifying. My gut locked up. Sage could have been one of them if the witch's spell had gone on much longer. We hadn't been in as much danger in any of our missions since, but we were just one step away from somebody not making it back out, and I had been asking ways of making our missions more difficult.

"On second thought, maybe we'll avoid the bonus levels."

"I don't think you should." Veda shook her head. "The bonus XP and soul coins you got were really, really good. It would be to your advantage to find one that triggers a bonus level on your next mission. You're all very close to level two. I've seen systems rewarding miners who got a bonus level on the mission where they leveled up before. They get better rewards."

"What are we going to get when we level up?" Sage asked. Her worry seeming to disappear, she picked up a pastry and took a big bite, splattering raspberry goo everywhere.

"We've had a few levels up already. Your team isn't in the top ten percent. That's fine," Veda said hurriedly. "Most of the ones who are, are backed by a major sponsor who's focusing a lot of resources on one team. In fact, I don't want you guys attracting that much attention right now. Keep doing what you're doing. Push where it makes sense." She blinked, pausing again.

I was starting to think she wasn't a particularly experienced sponsor. We had been pushing her around way too easily, distracting her, getting her off course. Maybe she was as young as she looked.

I stored that thought away for future reference. Right now, we were just try-ing to survive. Later, it might make a big difference.

"So you'll get a stat bump for sure. The system will help you allocate your stats based on how you've been building your class. You've all been sticking pretty close to your class fantasy, so I expect the system to offer you options to let you deepen your image, lean further into it. Go with that. The way you've been making good use of your coat and revolver, Shad, I think the system is likely to offer you some options to integrate those with your class a little more. Sage, you've been playing the support role beautifully. Hopefully the system will give you options to con-tinue there. On the other hand, Frank, you've been performing great. You're really leaning into all of your spells. But I think you might be given the choice to focus more heavily on one or the other." She paused while we soaked it in.

I nodded, telling her to go on

"All the new spells we're seeing are coming out of the portals as skill seeds. That's not uncommon in a Reality Engine, so don't be expecting a new skill to be offered at level up. You might be offered a way to tweak one of those skills or, like I said, bind it to a piece of equipment."

"The way Trick Shot is integrated with my revolver," I said.

She nodded. "You've noticed, I'm guessing, that your revolver doesn't take durability damage the way your coat does."

"I thought maybe that was just because I'm tanking it all with my coat."

"No, your revolver is now considered part of yourself and is actually regener-ating based on your own regen rate without you noticing it. It could break, and if it does, it's going to be a real pain to fix. But it's not going to take ordinary dura-bility hits."

That was good to know.

"Like I said, lean into your class, the abilities you already have, the gear you've got. Sometimes the system will offer a piece of custom gear as a reward. Those are usually almost as good as what you've brought from home."

"I thought of something," Sage said, jumping up. "When I first came here, I was wearing different clothes. I put them away because I didn't want to ruin them. They were my best gear. My fancy rodeo shirt, my best pair of jeans, and the belt I won for being the best mutton buster back when I was eight. If I had still been wearing those during class selection, would they have been bound to me?"

Veda shrugged. "It's possible, and I see where you're going with this. If you switch to those during your next level upgrade it might let you bind them. It's worth a shot. The advantage of doing missions is that you get all the XP at the end. That means you'll be able to make your level-up choices where it's safe."

"So just to confirm, once we've ended a mission, it's always safe. There's not going to be any more enemies spawning," I said. We had been working under that assumption.

"Oh right, I needed to warn you guys." Veda clasped her hands together. She was definitely not as good at this as she wanted to be. "You're correct that there aren't going to be any other enemies spawning, but missions do collapse after a certain amount of time has passed since their conclusion. You don't want to be in there if that happens. Don't worry, it's like a day and a half, and you get a big warning from the system before that happens. Make sure you leave if you ever see that warning."

"Good to know," I said. "Anything else?"

She seemed quite impatient. I wasn't sure if she had something else to do or she was just uncomfortable being around us. I was fine with either option.

"There is one more thing. I should warn you about class evolutions. You're not going to see one at level two, but sometimes they occur at level three and by level six, you're almost guaranteed to get one. What happens is . . ."

CHAPTER TWENTY-FOUR

GETTING ALONG WITH YOUR LOCAL MAFIA BOSS

I looked around with a bit of trepidation. We were standing in an old-time bank lobby. All of the decorations were brass. The floor was shining white marble. Elegant Grecian pillars held up the high-vaulted ceiling. There was a long counter at the far end of the room where clerks sat behind bars, conversing with their patrons.

On the left-hand side of the counter was a heavy-looking door with a very prominent iron lock.

[**Mission: Bank Heist!**] the system announcer roared. [**Welcome to 1930s Chicago. You have been unfortunate enough to be the patrons of a bank that is about to be robbed. Step one: choose your side. Ingratiate yourself with the bank robbers,** *or* **assist in thwarting the robbery.**]

I looked around. Nobody here looked like an obvious bank robber. Not yet. "What do you think, team?"

"I say we help the robbers," Sage said excitedly. "I've always wanted to rob a bank."

Young looked pained. "Absolutely not. My oath as a lawman forbids it."

"Deputy, this is like a game, it's not real," Sage said, almost whining.

I chuckled at both of them. "Let's play it straight," I said. "As soon as you spot anyone who looks like a robber, yell in party chat."

I had spotted three men who I guessed were undercover bank security, as well as one man wearing a uniform with a shiny revolver at his belt. Everyone wore suits and bowler hats. There were only two women in the whole place, both wearing calf-length dresses and little round, asymmetrical hats. They all had health bars. The customers had [4/4], while the security men were [10/10].

I racked my brain to think what I knew of 1930s Chicago. Probably mob stereotypes? This was the height of Prohibition, wasn't it? Tommy guns. All the old-time mobsters had tommy guns. "Spread out," I said. "Sage, I want you to stay near the counter, but not too close. That's where the robbers are going to go. Inspect them with Eye-Spy and let us know anything you see. Deputy, be ready to use Restraint, but I don't think we should blow Posse just yet, not until we know what else is going on here."

This seemed way too straightforward. As if in answer to my objection, a bonus objective popped up. I swear the system had sadistic glee in its voice as it read off, **[Sub-Objective: Protect the weak. Prevent innocents from being harmed while you protect the bank.]**

"Right. Frank, watch the grenades. We don't want any collateral damage. The noncombatants are pretty fragile." I focused on the word innocents. It didn't say bystanders. That struck me as odd.

Grandpa had moved over toward the front doors. In party chat, he said, *I think they're coming in. Six men, two of them with violin cases under their arms. Health says ten each.*

Yeah, that sounds right, I replied.

I noticed one of the men I had mentally tagged as bank security moving toward the door. I focused on him and the other security people and applied a label to them, marking them as allies. We'd figured out how to do that a couple missions back when we'd had a bunch of NPCs we were herding to safety.

Then I focused on the bystanders and labeled them all with big *x*'s in green over their heads. *Nobody shoot anyone with a green* x, I reminded the party.

I took up a position behind a pillar as the probable bank robbers entered the room. They stood in the center of the bank lobby. Other than the security people, none of the bystanders seemed to notice anything amiss. They kept going about their business.

I debated firing a shot into the air and getting them to take cover, but that would likely sic the security guards on me, and I didn't want to kill them if I could help it. One of the security guards had been eyeing me, probably figuring that my drovers coat was a good way to conceal a weapon. They were right about that. Thanks to Quick Draw, I didn't need to worry about pulling my gun out in an emergency.

We had managed to pick up three more speed loaders in previous missions. There was nothing special about them and they didn't work with any of my abilities, but it was nice to now have thirty rounds easily at my disposal. Not as many as Frank, with his double stack magazines for his M&P, but it was something.

The security man had his gun in his hand, but wasn't pointing it at the bank robbers. He was clearly demanding their attention. Some of the passersby noticed and began pulling away.

That was when the men with violin cases dropped them and pulled out their tommy guns as the other robbers went for their side arms and split off from the group.

"Go, go, go!" I shouted.

I cast Quick Draw. My revolver was in my hand as though it had never left. I fired off a Trick Shot around the side of the pillar, targeting one of the running bank robbers. It hit him and his health bar went down to **[5/10]**. They could take more than one hit, but it shouldn't be too hard to down them. Good.

I fired a regular round while I waited for Trick Shot to come back off cooldown. It winged the man in the shoulder. His health bar took another dip, but not as big, going down to **[8/10]**.

Grandpa Shadow Stepped around the room, merrily hitting the robbers with his axe, collecting his coup points. Sage was using her newest ability, **[Mucking Out the Stalls]**. It turned the bank floor into a lake of viscous mud. Since Grandpa's Shadow Step would let him move around easily, and the deputy and I had boots on, we had an advantage over all of the robbers in their thin leather shoes.

I heard cursing and swearing from some of the robbers and one fell to his knees. I shot the man I'd been aiming at again and got him down to **[2/10]**. *Grandpa, this one's ready for you.*

Grandpa Shadow Stepped in and gave the coup de grace. The robber went down.

The patrons were all shouting and shrieking. They had been making for the door but now fell back, yelling loudly.

Can you tell what's going on, Sage?

More robbers coming in, she said.

Frank! Grenade on the door!

Frank turned and lobbed a sonic grenade in the direction of the doors. It arced over the panicking customers' heads and hit the front of the bank with a boom. The bank front was all tall glass windows painted in gold letters with the name of the bank. I couldn't quite make it out since they were distant and reversed, but it said something about bank and Chicago for sure.

The sonic grenade went off with a whining boom. The customers shrieked and covered their ears as the men coming in the door stepped backward, dazed. The windows all shattered in a rain of broken glass. It tinkled down. Now I could hear shouts and yells from the street outside. The robbers took three points of damage each, but the customers were far enough away to be unharmed.

The men with tommy guns were marching on the door at the side of the counter. They had a bank security man with them. I fired a Trick Shot at one of the two, deliberately aiming for his gun hand. He yelped and shook his hand in pain but didn't drop the gun. **[8/10]**.

The tellers had all scattered. As the robbers approached the door, one of the nearby customers stopped cowering, pulled a 1911 from under his suit jacket, and fired not at the robber but at the security man with them. The bank employee went down.

One of the robbers shot a burst from the tommy gun at him. He only had the [4/4] health of the other bystanders, and collapsed to the ground with a grunt, his blood pooling on the marble floor beneath him.

I reloaded for the second time and ducked behind a pillar. The robbers were stooping over the security man's corpse, probably digging for a key.

Another of the robbers had a group of customers cornered over to my left on the far side of the bank. "Tell them to open the vault or I start executing hostages," he shouted. He fired a shot, and one of the two women customers screamed in pain as her health bar went yellow and read [2/4].

Frank cast Restraint on him and followed it up with a hail of well-placed bullets. By now, Frank and I had both completed the first rank of our "Damage Enemies With Your Weapon" achievement. His reward had been a thirty percent increase in accuracy. It was paying off now. The hostage-taker slumped forward into the muck. One of the hostages kicked the gun away from his lifeless hand and then drove the heel of his boot into the man's face for good measure.

Sage pointed at the injured woman from across the room and cast Raise Your Spirits. It ticked her health up to [3/4], but she still had a [**Bleeding**] debuff. I hoped the spell would keep her from bleeding out. The other customers around her were holding pressure on her leg, now that no one had a gun on them.

There were still two of the original robbers up, both with tommy guns. The three who had entered the bank late were now getting to their feet and making their way past the broken glass into the morass of mud that covered the shining marble bank floor.

Sage used her Lasso on one of the three and pulled him toward her, dropping him to his knees as well. Her Mucking Out the Stalls ability, in addition to creating mud, also provided a [**Stinky**] debuff to any enemy that got it on their bare body. The man she Lassoed made the mistake of putting his hands down to catch himself.

He came up snarling, but with a debuff that made him thirty percent easier to hit. I cast Trick Shot and took him through the heart. It knocked him down to [2/10]. Grandpa Shadow Stepped in and delivered a coup de grace.

Frank had turned his attention on one of the two with tommy guns. The man went down in a hail of bullets. "Reloading!" Frank yelled. I wished he would use party chat more.

I ran forward as the last of the newcomers headed for Sage. I got within a foot of him before firing three rounds straight into his chest. He went down hard.

"They've almost got the back door open!" Sage yelled.

Grandpa Shadow Stepped right over. I turned. It was a good twenty feet away and there were two customers and the teller in my line of fire, so I didn't shoot. I slogged toward the counter, waiting for Trick Shot to come back off cooldown.

Grandpa applied Scalp with his axe. He raised the axe again and hit the man hard. The robber, health at **[3/10]**, cried out and turned, getting his tommy gun on Grandpa.

There were no other robbers Grandpa could Shadow Step away to. I fired Trick Shot, yelling at Frank to Restrain the man.

Too late. He got off a quick three round burst. Grandpa's health bar dropped to **[55/70]**. I charged, firing. My last round went right through the man's head. He dropped.

[Step one: success. Results: bank secured.
No innocents harmed.]

That was interesting. Aside from the security guard who I suppose counted as a combatant, the man who drew a gun hadn't been an innocent. Was it because he had fired, or was there something else going on?

I put that out of my mind as I hurried over to check Grandpa. "I'm fine," he said irritably. He pulled out a potion and drained it in one gulp. His health bar filled back in. I supposed that was better than waiting for a bandage to do its job when the next stage might happen at any moment.

Sage canceled her Mucking Out the Stalls spell, leaving the marble floor as gleaming as it had ever been. The customers began coming out of their corners, making for the door.

One of the security men ran out and checked the street. He came back. "A couple of getaway cars just took off. I don't see any more. We've sent for the cops to clear all this up."

I checked the dead robbers with Inspect. None of them glowed, but one had a skill seed. I picked it up and it said **[Compatible with your class,]** so I absorbed it and received a new ability. I copied the details to party chat.

[Bluff: Cast Bluff while speaking to increase the likelihood
your targets will believe you. Cast area: 3 meter radius from self.
Duration: 30 seconds, effect ongoing unless broken by combat.
Cooldown: 2 minutes.]

Whoa, that's cool! Now you can trick people instead of just shooting them! About time someone else had some actually useful skills, Sage said.

A well-dressed man in a three-piece suit, wearing a top hat instead of a bowler, came out from the door behind the counter. He had a gold watch chain hanging off of his waistcoat, so I guessed he must be somebody important. We gathered up, sensing that he might have the next step of our mission for us.

He bowed to us. "Many thanks. You must be the Pinkertons we asked to have on hand this morning when we got the warning that our bank was targeted."

I glanced at Sage. "Uh, yeah, that's us."

"Excellent. Thank you for your work here. I will pay your bill, but your services won't be needed any more, as our bank vault has been empty for the last three hours."

CHAPTER TWENTY-FIVE

HOW TO CATCH A TRAIN

mpty?" We looked at each other. If the bank vault was already empty, what kind of robbery had we been trying to stop?

The manager continued on. "Yes, indeed, when that tip came in, I knew we couldn't be too careful. I hired your company, but we made arrangements at the same time to have the gold shipped out early. That gold is on its way out of town right now."

That sounded like the lead-in for the next stage of a quest. I waited for a notification, but nothing popped up just yet.

There was something else here we were missing, something that was nagging me. I glanced around the bank, seeing the employees pulling the corpses over to lean against the wall out of the way. There was the man who had pulled a gun on the robbers and gotten himself shot for it. No. Wait. He hadn't shot the robbers. He'd shot the guard who might have opened the door to the bank vault. Why?

I went over to his body and used Inspect. The left-hand side of his chest glowed, and so did his back pocket.

Improbably, his back pocket produced a bottle of moonshine. "No way this was in there," I said, and stuffed it in my inventory. I leaned over and felt around in his jacket. He had a pocket on the inside of his coat, too. Reaching in, I found a piece of paper.

We have word Big Tom's gang will hit the bank this morning. Go keep watch. Boss doesn't want you to try to be a hero, just help ID the perps. Lou.

That wasn't much of a clue. I showed it to Grandpa, who shook his head, as lost as I was.

The cops arrived. A couple of them came over to us, including their sergeant, a red-headed Irishman with a big handlebar mustache. Frank sidled over and started talking to him, explaining what had happened.

The sergeant paused in his questioning as he looked at the dead men. "That's Red O'Malley," he said. "What's he doing here?" He indicated our mystery corpse.

"You know him?"

"Sure do. Had him in lockup two weeks back. He's one of Al Capone's boys."

Sage's eyes got really big and she let out a squeak.

The police sergeant went on. "The others are from Big Tom's gang. What's one of Al's doing over here?"

"Innocent bystander," Frank suggested.

The sergeant shook his head. "No way. Al's boys avoid this side of town. They must have been casing the joint. Big Tom's gang got the jump on them is all."

So we had a man belonging to a rival mafia group, and not just any mob group, but Al Capone's. He was probably the only Chicago mobster I could have named off the top of my head. Capone knew they were going to hit this bank and sent this fellow to keep a lookout, not to stop it.

"Why?" I asked, feeling like I was right on the verge of the answer. "Why did Capone let them hit the bank if he knew it was coming?"

"'Cause he knew there was nothing to steal," Sage suggested. "Somebody tipped him off that the gold had already been moved."

I slapped my forehead. "Of course. That makes perfect sense."

With a rush, the system announcer came back.

**[Mission: Bank Heist. Step two: catch that train.
The gold shipment is safely on a train out of town, or so the bank
officials believe. You've just intercepted clues to make you think
Al Capone knows about the intended move and has plans of his own
already in place. Catch up to the train and board it before Capone's
men can secure the shipment for themselves.]**

"There we go," I said. "Let's find out where the train station is."

But even as I spoke, the bank lobby dissolved around us and was replaced by a train station. The wrought iron roof stretched far overhead, glass panes letting in the sunlight. Beside us, multiple parallel tracks ran past tiled platforms. At the far platform, a train was puffing and chugging its way out of the station.

I grabbed a passing station employee and pointed at the train. "What's that one?"

"That's the express hired just last night for a special cargo. I don't know any details."

"That's our train," I said confidently. "Let's catch it." I judged the distance between platforms. It was a little too far to jump. There was an iron pedestrian crossway over the tracks. I charged up the staircase and along the crosswalk, Sage, Grandpa, and Frank at my heels.

The train began to pick up speed as it left the station. The engine was already through the great doors, passing the signal that gave it the go-ahead to leave. There were five cars on this train. The engine, the coal box, two baggage cars, and the caboose.

As I watched, a man came running up wearing a dark blue uniform and cap. He swung aboard the caboose as it pulled out of the station. I reached the stairs down to the platform but stopped since there was no point in going any farther.

"We missed it."

"We'll find another way," Grandpa said determinedly.

"Look," Sage said. She pointed through the glass windows that lined the walls of the station.

Outside was a moderately busy street. Horse-drawn carriages pulled past and a streetcar rumbled along. There were plenty of pedestrians, and a few motor cars as well.

One pulled up at the train station as we watched. It was a long, powerful-looking Rolls-Royce. The chauffeur jumped out and went to the back door. He held it open for the elegantly dressed woman with a tall, feathered hat who emerged from the open back seat. She swept into the train station and the chauffeur went to the trunk to grab her luggage.

"Hurry up," Sage said.

I could tell what she was thinking. I wanted to say no, but this was a mission. It wasn't real. Auto theft was just part of the strategy. "You have any experience driving a 1930s Rolls-Royce?" I asked Grandpa.

He shook his head as we all ran for the station exit. "Nope, but I'll give it a try."

We charged out of the station. Sage and Frank climbing into the wide, plush back seat while I jumped in on the passenger side. Grandpa got behind the wheel, pulled a few levers, stepped on a pedal, and the car lurched forward a little. "Oops, that wasn't the right way to do it. Give me a second. I'll try it again."

As we started forward shakily, the chauffeur came running out of the station, shouting.

"Step on it, Grandpa!" I yelled and Grandpa took off.

The station was fortunately at the edge of town and the road led right along the train tracks. Grandpa got the hang of driving the car, which he said was a Phantom II, pretty quickly. I settled in, scanning the horizon for puffs of smoke that would show the train.

"How fast are we going?"

"Pretty fast," he said. "Must be doing twenty-five miles an hour."

I grit my teeth. I had no idea how fast trains in this era could go. Grandpa opened the throttle and the Phantom answered. As the last buildings of the town fell away and we began to drive across open prairie marked by cornfields and the occasional white clapboard farmhouse, I almost felt like enjoying myself.

We were gaining on the train. We could see it now, probably two miles ahead of us, as we urged the Phantom to catch up. Sage kept leaning forward in her seat, murmuring, "Come on, come on!" I was hoping the gas would hold out.

We whizzed past another train station, but since the train was an express, it didn't even slow down. I knew better than to hope that there'd be some sort of obstruction that would cause us to catch up. That wouldn't be how the system worked. We had to earn this. We needed to do more than earn this. We needed to make this flashy, or possibly make it ridiculous in such a way that the system felt like it had to give us another challenge. We needed the bonus level.

The landscape changed. The suburban Illinois landscape gave way to dry grassland, sandy soils, and scrub trees. Then a bunch of Joshua trees and cacti that would be more at home in New Mexico. "What the hell?" I asked. "Another scene change?"

Sage giggled. "I think it's like those cartoons where anything outside New York City basically looks like the Southwest, because the illustrators have never been anywhere but Vegas and NYC."

"You're probably right," Grandpa said, "but let me know if you see a coyote with a giant rocket strapped to his back, okay?"

As we gained on the train, I started trying to come up with the next step of the plan. "We've got to get aboard somehow. It's not going to stop, so we'll have to jump." I glanced at the blur of a landscape flicking past and shuddered. I didn't like to think of what happened if we missed.

"We'll be fine," Sage said confidently. "I'll just Lasso the train, and since I can't pull it to me, it'll pull us to it."

"There's no way that will work," I said. "Physics doesn't work that way."

"Game physics might."

She had a point. I thought it sounded horribly dangerous. "What if it yanks you out of the car?"

"It doesn't. The skill keeps me in place when I cast it."

"We're running out of time!" Grandpa shouted. "Give it a try when we get safe." The car inched forward, closer and closer.

Sage climbed into the front seat and stood beside me. She pulled out her rope and twirled it over her head before throwing it at the train. The rope sailed through the air and wrapped the loose end around the caboose's railing. Sage leaned back as the rope went taut. "I did it! And it's offering me a way to board!"

I touched the rope and a system message appeared:

[Do you want to board the train? Yes / No.]

"Game logic," I muttered. "I'll go first, then Frank. Do you have to stay until last, Sage?"

"Probably. Hurry! This hurts." She gritted her teeth.

I selected [**Yes**]. In a blink, I was standing on the caboose platform. I turned back to face the car. "Hurry, Frank!"

Frank grabbed at the rope and teleported over to me. He clutched the railing. "Ugh, too fast."

Now we needed Grandpa and Sage, but if Sage had to go last, who would drive the car? "Can you both come at once?"

Grandpa took a hand off the wheel and touched the rope. "On three," he said. "One, two—"

The caboose door banged open and the conductor stood there, his face red beneath his little round cap. "What's going on here?" He made a move for something under his jacket.

I cast Bluff. "We're Pinkertons. There's going to be a robbery attempt on this train. We're here to stop it. Uh, this is Sheriff Young, he's here to arrest the criminals once they're apprehended. Sheriff, show the man your badge."

Frank had the presence of mind to grab his badge from his vest and hold it out for half a second, just long enough for the conductor to see the star.

Sage and Grandpa appeared on the platform beside me. With no one at the wheel, the car veered left and drove down the embankment. It crashed hard against a tree and exploded in a boom of fire and smoke. One tire rolled free as the Phantom went up in flames.

We stared at it.

"Well, that was certainly dramatic," Frank commented.

"There's something fishy here." The conductor stared at Sage. "Pinkertons? Her?"

"You haven't heard of Tiny Tina? She's our best infiltrator. Do you know, she's thirty-two years old?" Bluff was about to wear off, so I spoke as fast as I could. "Had six arrests already this year."

"Shad!" Sage exclaimed. "You know it's rude to give a lady's age!"

"Huh." The conductor hesitated, then fell back. "You'd better come in."

We stepped into the caboose. The conductor fidgeted. "So what do you need me to do?"

"Just stay out of the way," I said. "You don't want to mess with these men. They're confirmed killers. I just hope we can keep them from killing the guards. They're going to Leavenworth for sure."

"Hold on." Sage looked the conductor up and down. She smiled evilly. "I've got an idea. Mister . . . ?"

"Anderson," he supplied.

"Mr. Anderson, how do you feel about assisting the capture of some very dangerous men? And no risk to you."

CHAPTER TWENTY-SIX

HOW TO KEEP TO A SCHEDULE

I slid back the door of the caboose and stepped out onto the rattling platform between the train cars. In front of me was the door to the first baggage car.

I tensed. My revolver was tucked into the jacket pocket of the conductor's uniform. It made an alarming lump, but I wasn't going to leave it behind. My Quick Draw ability would bring it to me regardless of any fabric or buttons in the way.

I had previously tested Quick Draw, and it worked even if my gun wasn't on me, but had a range of forty feet. I wasn't sure if the baggage car door might block us.

I Inspected the door and got nothing. It blocked my Inspect the way the curtain in Kirin and Arjun's yurt had. Sometimes doors in missions did that, as though they were hiding the details of what lay beyond from us poor saps.

In party chat, I said, *I'm about to open the door. Be ready.*

Sage responded with a thumbs up. I tried the door. It slid easily under my hand. The baggage car was dark, and I didn't see anyone inside.

I stepped in and looked around. It was chock-full of trunks, suitcases, long crates, and other bulky items. In the near corner were two sacks labeled US Mail. I did a quick sweep. There was no one here.

Come on in, I told the team. About a minute later, they joined me.

I was Inspecting crates. Inspect revealed their contents as innocuous things; clothes, lumber, and blocks of cheese. A few of them were craftable items, and Sage quickly gathered them all up.

We had found that anything that wasn't specifically designated as craftable would disappear on leaving a mission. Unlike the farming levels, there weren't very many items we could take with us and use outside of the mission. Food generated by the mission would remove our **[Hungry]** debuff, but not apply a **[Well-Fed]** buff to us. Food couldn't be taken outside the portal, which I found interesting. I hadn't figured out how this Reality Engine system worked, but I was determined to learn the rules sooner or later.

"If this is a special express chartered by the bank, why is there a regular baggage car?" Sage asked.

That actually made some sense to me. "It's an express, but it's got to be going to a real station somewhere. It doesn't cost much more fuel to attach a couple of other baggage cars. So if they were going to send their gold to, say, Fort Knox, they might have other baggage that was heading that way that got attached to the train." Was Fort Knox even the US gold repository at this point? I didn't think it was. I seemed to remember something about the United States going off of the gold standard somewhere in the 1930s, but my high school education was a dim memory at this point, and it wasn't like I'd been paying that much attention in US history.

I had regretted that later. In the Army, I had actually discovered I was kind of into military history. I had been considering my first sergeant's suggestion that I go for officer and study military history on the government's dime. It had been one of the decisions I was putting off while taking care of Grandpa and Sage, and it really didn't matter at all now.

"All right," I said. "Same thing, next car."

I stepped out onto the swaying platform. The landscape beyond us had changed again. Now we were moving through rugged, barren hills. They reminded me of the badlands of South Dakota, and I almost expected to see a band of Indians pursued by US cavalry out the side. That would be the wrong era, though.

I opened the door of the next car and froze. A pair of railroad employees were tied up in the corner of the car. The boxcar doors on the side were open, and four men with tommy guns and bowler hats stood over the prisoners. They looked at me as I entered.

I found them, I said frantically in party chat. *Don't move yet*. I stepped inside and closed the car door. "Looks like you've got the situation under control," I said cheerfully as I cast my Bluff spell.

The men blinked at me. "Yeah? And who are you?"

"Boss sent me to help out." I pointed at my borrowed conductor's cap. "Thought it would be good to have someone on the inside here."

One of the men looked suspicious, but the others lowered their guns and relaxed a bit. "Well, since you're here, how about you give us a hand?"

I looked around the car, thinking frantically. The car was loaded with burlap sacks, all with a big dollar sign stamped on them, just like we were playing Monopoly or something. I bent and hefted one of the sacks. It clinked heavily.

"You weren't just planning to throw all the gold off the train and then try to escape?" I let sarcasm drip from each word I said. "We'd never have managed to collect it all. Boss'll have our heads."

One of the men laughed. "Shouldn't you know the plan? We're gonna make the driver stop the engine right before mile marker forty-seven and throw the switch. That'll take us down the unused spur out toward the old Pritchett place. We'll drop the other cars at the switch and leave these behind if they behave themselves." He indicated the railroad men.

"Good thinking," I said briskly. "The engineer trusts me. We had breakfast together this morning. I'll tell him that we need to stop the train at that marker."

"Then get moving! We haven't got all day."

I made my way through the baggage car, quickly Inspecting the men and wishing for Sage's Eye-Spy ability. They looked similar to the bank robbers we had encountered in the bank.

I relayed everything to the party.

Should we just come in and start shooting? Frank asked.

I don't like that idea. Quarters are too tight here. Somebody's liable to get shot. Instead, I outlined a quick plan.

"I'll go talk to the engineer now," I announced to the robbers and opened the door on the far end of the car. I stepped out and closed it behind me, letting out a deep breath I hadn't realized I'd been holding.

It had worked. Now with luck, we'd be able to manage a more favorable battlefield.

I stepped onto the back of the coal car. There was a ladder leading up to the top. I climbed it and looked down at an uneven surface. Mounds of black coal filled the car almost to the top. At the far end, the fireman was hard at work scooping big chunks from the car and shoveling them into the engine.

The wind ripped at me. I summoned my coat from my inventory and put it on. I didn't think it would help if I fell from the car, but it was reassuring.

I made my way shakily across the mounds of coal, balancing like a high-wire acrobat. The fireman didn't notice me until I was almost on top of him.

He looked up, his blackened face shocked, and shouted, "Who the hell are you, and why are you in Fred's uniform?"

I dropped down next to him. "Long story. There's robbers on the train. I gave them the slip. I need to talk to the engineer."

The fireman looked suspicious. He gripped his shovel like a club. "Where'd you get Fred's uniform? You're one of them, ain't you?" He took a swing with his shovel.

I had been half expecting it. My Bluff still had another minute of cooldown time, so I had been using my own natural skills, and they weren't very good. I had a three in bluff on my personal skills tab. Not quite as bad as my two in picking up chicks, but not great. I was pretty sure my own natural charisma was way lower than the seven I'd gotten from my class.

I caught the fireman's shovel in my hand as he swung and ripped it from him, then hit him over the head with it. He collapsed. There was a debuff over his head that said **[Unconscious]**, but his health bar was only half down, so I hoped he'd be okay. I dropped the shovel next to him.

The train ought to gradually lose speed, now that no one was feeding the fire, but I wasn't going to count on it. Instead, I climbed past the firebox and into the engine itself.

The engineer sat up front over a row of dials and valves. I slid in next to him. He looked up as I cast Bluff again. "Who are you?" he started.

"Pinkerton man. There are robbers on the train. I need you to stop at mile marker forty-seven. They're planning a transfer of the gold there, but we'll take them by surprise. My team is ready for it."

His eyes went wide. "A Pinkerton! On my train! Wait 'til I tell Sally!" He glanced out the window. "You're cutting it close. I'm going to have to hit the brakes hard."

"Do it," I said. I warned my team that we were about to brake and to brace themselves.

The engineer pulled on a set of levers and the train screeched as the brakes were abruptly applied. I was expecting it, but I still fell forward, catching myself against the dials.

Slowly, the train lost speed. I could see a mile marker up ahead and the switch just past it. I climbed back toward the rear of the engine. "You just stay here," I said. "We'll take care of the robbers."

"I wouldn't get involved for all the gold that's on this train," he said over the noise of the shrieking brakes, the metal-on-metal howl loud enough to almost deafen me.

I waited until the train had nearly come to a standstill. *Everyone in position?* I asked.

Ready, Sage said.

Almost there, Frank managed.

I'm hoping one of them comes out to throw the switch. If he does, leave him to me, I said. *Everyone else, stick with the plan.*

Right now, Grandpa and Sage should be just outside the baggage car on the platform, while Frank had gone back to the caboose and was waiting for the train to slow to a stop.

We were only traveling a couple of miles an hour now. *All right, go,* I said in chat. I dropped off the train and ran beside it, keeping even.

One of the robbers emerged, just as I had hoped. "Give me a hand with the switch," I yelled, gesturing up ahead. I let him get ahead of me as the train finally pulled to a stop. Then I used Trick Shot to get the drop on him. I followed it up with three more shots and he went down.

I turned to join my team. Frank had made it from the caboose to the open doors of the baggage car. He chucked in a sonic grenade and it rattled the whole car. This was the point when Sage was supposed to cast Mucking Out the Stalls on the baggage car. I ran over and saw that the floor had turned to mud, just as we expected.

Grandpa was inside the car, merrily chopping away with his axes. He couldn't use Shadow Step here. There wasn't enough room to get behind anyone. I was glad we'd come up with this alternative plan. I used Trick Shot again and dropped one of the three.

The other two had their tommy guns blazing, but Grandpa was managing to avoid the bullets. The skill he had picked up was called Blur, and it made him much harder to hit as long as he was moving.

Frank Restrained one of the two. The tommy gun jerked toward the ceiling, but kept firing. We had found one of the problems with Restraint was that while it generally kept the target from using arms and legs, their fingers were usually unaffected. In this case, it didn't matter, but a previous mission with a spellcaster had nearly ended in disaster.

I fired my last round, worked the cylinder mechanism, dropped the brass, slammed home the speed loader, and reseated. By then, Grandpa had nearly dropped the unrestrained man. I shot the robber in the center of mass and he collapsed. His health bar was deep in the red, but not zero.

"Hold up," I said. We had talked about this possibility. "Let's keep him alive and find out what he knows." Grandpa got behind the robber and bound his hands with a length of rope.

I stooped and freed the train men, slicing through their bonds with a knife I summoned from my inventory. They got to their feet, rubbing their arms and expressing their gratitude. "Thought we were goners," one of them said. "They'd said they'd leave us with the caboose, but we'd seen their faces, and I was afraid they'd shoot us just in case."

"We'd better get this train moving again," I said. I Inspected the corpses. They had nothing of interest, so I pushed them off the baggage car. "Frank, you want to go forward and tell the engineer to keep going wherever he was going? I told him we were Pinkertons, so be sure to show him your badge briefly."

Frank grunted and disappeared toward the front of the train while I turned to our prisoner. I was waiting for us to get a next step notification. This definitely felt like it was too easy to be the end, and I was hoping we had triggered a bonus level.

"Well, what was the plan, anyway? Al Capone sent you, right?"

The man looked murderous. "I'm not talking."

"The way I see it, you're facing a very long sentence for attempted train robbery and murder," I said.

"Murder? Nobody's been killed."

"Attempted murder, then." I pointed at the guards we'd freed. "You were going to leave them dead when you took the gold."

"We didn't—"

"And who are the lawmen going to believe? You or a Pinkerton's man?" I asked, crossing my arms in front of my chest.

"Uh—"

"That's what I thought. Start talking now, and we'll see if we can cut you a deal, let you turn witness, might even be able to protect you in prison. I don't think Al Capone's too fond of men who mess up an easy job like this."

Our prisoner slumped. "Yeah, it was him. He sent us. Don't know how he knew all the details. This isn't our usual kind of racket. We're into bootlegging, that sort of thing. Petty crime. Never tried a gold heist before. From what I heard, some big shot from back East came to him with the plan. We provided the manpower, and he'd provide what we needed to do the job. We were supposed to split the money fifty-fifty."

**[Mission: Bank Heist. Step four: find out who was behind
the bank job.]**

I was a little disappointed we hadn't managed a bonus level, but maybe we'd get one after this. I looked up at the roof of the train car. "You gonna give us a lift back, or do we have to take the train?" My [**Well-Fed**] buff had fallen off, and it was only a matter of time until we were [**Hungry**] again, so I wouldn't mind a bit of a break.

As if in answer, we found ourselves on yet another train, this time seated in a passenger car on two seats facing each other with a little table in between them. The conductor came past. "Next stop, Chicago," he boomed. "End of the line, coming up in thirty minutes."

"Oh, that's nice," Sage said. "Gives us time to rest and eat. Anyone take any injuries in that last fight?" Everybody shook their heads. It had been exactly as we had planned. I felt proud of myself.

I pulled out some of our rations. Sage refused to eat the packaged stuff Veda had sent unless she had no choice. Right now, she pulled out some sandwiches that Mama Grace had made her, and started chomping into them. I had to admit, they looked a little better than the pink gelatinous cubes I was eating. "Now, all we have to do is brave the lair of the most infamous mob boss in all of history, and find out who tried to rob a bank," I said. "Piece of cake."

CHAPTER TWENTY-SEVEN

HOW TO GET INTO THE BEST NIGHTCLUBS

The speakeasy door was down a dimly lit alley off of one of Chicago's busier streets. There were no signs, just a door with a man lounging outside it.

The notable thing about this man was he probably weighed twice what I did, despite being six inches shorter, and none of it was fat. He was bald, with ripples of muscular neck extending down into his cheap, ill-fitting suit. He kept his hand in his coat pocket while he straightened up and addressed us. I didn't know if he had a gun or a set of brass knuckles in there, but I was willing to bet it was one or the other. "Whatcha want?"

"We're here to see the boss," I said. "Got a message for him from Pete about a job." I used the name of the man we'd caught. "They said to tell you carpenters' tools make poor fishing gear."

Our prisoner had claimed that was the passphrase that would get us in to see Capone. I hoped he wasn't lying.

The bouncer looked us over. "You two can go in," he said, indicating me and Frank. "But the kid and the Injun, we don't let them in this sort of quality establishment."

I bristled. This was the first time anyone in one of these missions had treated Sage as a child. "She's just short," I said.

The bouncer snorted. "Sure. And he's just got a tan."

Grandpa wore his hair in two long braids, and his weathered skin and features marked him as more or less pure Native American. There wasn't any point in denying it.

I was surprised at the era-appropriate racism. Did the Reality Engine really have to copy some of humanity's worst traits?

We withdrew a little way. "I could fight him," I suggested. I didn't want to kill the bouncer. For all I knew, that would set off some sort of preprogrammed event that would result in us attracting a lot more attention than we wanted.

"It's fine," Sage said. "We'll go around and see if we can find a kitchen entrance and sneak in that way. Then we'll be able to spy. I'll let you know what we find."

Grandpa nodded. "Easier than making a scene."

"You're not upset about this?" I asked him.

"About a jumped-up computer thinking he has the right to tell me where I can go in my own country? Not a chance. Besides, I faced a lot worse coming back from 'Nam. Bad enough to be a red man, but a soldier, too? Those were bad days. Anyway, we'll go around the back and let you know what we find."

He and Sage retreated, and Frank and I approached the bouncer again.

"You ditched the dead weight. Good choice. Go right in. Boss is in the back room. I'll have you announced. Take a seat and wait for him. Word of advice. He don't like wise guys. Keep your heads down and do the smart thing."

"Sure, thanks," I agreed. We stepped into the club.

Jazz music played. A haze of cigarette smoke hung over the whole room. There were round tables full of well-dressed men and women laughing, drinking, and playing cards. The women wore flapper dresses and bobbed hair and held their cigarettes at the end of long sticks. Some of the men chomped on cigars as they downed what I assumed was bootleg whiskey.

We moved into the room, sticking close to the edge. A server caught my arm and pointed me at an empty table. "Mr. Capone will be with you in his time," the man said. "Want a drink?"

I shook my head.

Frank asked, "You got any beer?"

The server looked vaguely disgusted that anyone would waste a trip to what was probably Chicago's most notorious street speakeasy to ask for beer. "I'll have it out in a minute."

We sat down. There was a stage at the other side of the room, with a woman in a slinky black dress with a feather contraption tied to her hair who was singing. A four-man band played behind her. I hoped that we wouldn't have a repeat of the zombie hag fight.

Party chat lit up. *We found the kitchen*, Sage said. *I'm getting the cooks to make me a cup of cocoa.*

Grandpa added, *We're sneaking around. I don't see anything out of place. There are three cooks and a bunch of servers coming in and out. There's a door that I think goes to wherever they've stashed the booze. The servers keep going in and coming out with drinks. Nothing interesting when we Inspect.*

I gazed around the room. There were doors to the side with beaded curtains leading to private chambers. One of them was probably where Al Capone held court.

Then my eyes fell on a group two tables over. They were miners.

It was obvious from how they were dressed. There were four of them. The woman wore what looked like a Buck Rogers–style space getup, all shiny silver cloth with a bubble helmet over her head. She had some sort of enormous gun attached to a scuba tank on her back.

There was a man, so short and stocky I thought maybe he'd gotten a class that changed him into a dwarf. I'd heard rumors in Threshold that some class choices physically transformed you. He made me think of a fireplug with legs. Maybe that was just how he always was. He had a pointy goatee and a bald head, and he was dressed like a NASCAR driver, the suit of Nomex emblazoned with different patches and logos.

There were a pair of younger guys, one with knives strapped to every conceivable inch of his body, and the other wearing chain mail armor with a chainsaw strapped to his back.

I nudged Frank. He looked and blinked. In chat, I said, *There are other miners here, a party of them. Lay low. Don't come out of the back. I need to figure out what's going on.*

Other miners in our mission? Sage typed indignantly.

Grandpa gave a quick *Copy* in reply. I knew he'd keep Sage out of sight.

This was bad. This was really bad. I hadn't known other miners could be in the same mission. Veda hadn't mentioned it, and the couple of other parties I'd exchanged stories with had never said anything of the sort.

If they had the same objective, were we competing? But we hadn't seen them on any of the previous steps. Did that mean they were on a parallel mission that just happened to end up here in the same spot? And what happened if we interfered with each other?

A server came up and spoke to Frank and me. "Boss will see you now."

I stood up, hoping not to attract attention from the other party. The server paraded us right past them and I felt their eyes on me. *We've been spotted*, I said to chat. *Be careful.*

The server led me and Frank to a back room. We stepped through the door and found ourselves in a room even smokier than out front. Eight men sat around a poker table, cards and cash piled in front of them. They were all drinking heavily.

As I watched, a serving girl emerged from a door to the side carrying a tray full of drinks and a basket of what smelled like fried onion rings. She set the basket down and served the men their drinks. One of them smacked her on her behind with his cigar-free hand.

I sent a quick message to Grandpa and Sage. *Waitress just came in here. Did she come from the kitchen? Is there a way through?*

The man across from us didn't look like much. His hair was thinning and he wasn't very physically impressive. But as he lifted a hand, the other men at the table fell silent. "I understand you boys have a message for me."

"Yes, sir." I looked at him as Frank shuffled uncomfortably. "We have secured your shipment as promised. There were some complications, though. Somebody else came after it with guns."

He waved off our concern. "I heard about that matter at the bank this morning. It was handled."

"No, sir. On the train." I dropped my voice. "Sir, I think we were set up. It was just our good luck that we won. Lost two of the boys."

Capone's eyes narrowed. He set down his drink and leaned forward. "Set up? Why do you think that?"

I was casting Bluff as I spoke. "We searched the train before leaving. There was no one else aboard except for the conductor, the engineer, and the fireman. As we were getting to the safe house, a bunch of blokes came out of the baggage car, guns blazing."

"Is that so?" Capone looked around the table. He pointed at one of the men playing poker. "Willis, your boss said everything had been taken care of."

"It was," the man said. He didn't sound very concerned. His arm rested over the back of his chair, and he had his drink in the other hand.

The waitress disappeared through the back door again. I tried to have eyes everywhere. I was incredibly tense. This could go bad at any minute. I was glad Sage and Grandpa weren't here. On the other hand, I didn't have any backup if things did go bad.

Anyone start shooting, we make for that back door, I told Frank.

Capone gestured to two of his men. "Boys, why don't you take Willis here upstairs and ask him what he knows?"

The two men were both taller than I was. They cracked their knuckles and grinned. Nice suits or not, goons were goons.

The man named Willis started to protest. "Hold on a minute—" They hauled him out of his chair and dragged him out a different door, which I mentally marked as upstairs.

I see the waitress you're talking about, Grandpa said. *Cute blonde with just the right kind of curves.*

I guess. I wasn't staring at her ass. At least we knew that door connected through to where Sage and Grandpa were. I debated just making a break for it now, but the men were almost certainly armed.

Capone stood up. "Well, now, sounds like we owe Willis's boss a little bit of a visit. You boys have a grudge?"

I nodded. Frank straightened up and grinned, rubbing his hands together. "We sure do."

"All right, then, come over here and we'll talk."

We had taken six steps across the room, edging around the table toward Capone, when the door burst open and the other party of miners burst in.

The system announcer started shouting right away. [**Mission: Bank Heist. Step four complete. Opposed mission! You have met another team on a mission that is opposed to yours. Result? Head-to-head confrontation. Objective? Protect Al Capone!**]

"Oh shit." In chat, I said, *We need to run. Now!*

CHAPTER TWENTY-EIGHT

HOW NOT TO REACT IN A FIREFIGHT

The men with Capone drew their weapons and started firing, but the miner team was inside the room already. The woman dressed in a space suit had her scuba-tank gun out In front of her. It sprayed a line of fire that cut the table in two, upsetting it, scattering glasses, cards, money, and guns across the room.

A flamethrower gun? Sage was going to want one of those.

"Hold on!" I shouted. "We don't have to fight!"

They were ignoring me. Knives flew from the hands of the man wearing blue, while the short fireplug fellow charged in like a rhinoceros. I dodged out of his way, and I felt the force wave in his wake. He had some sort of enhanced charge ability. He knocked over chairs as he ran at one of Capone's minions.

We had to get out of here. I sprinted forward and grabbed the seemingly shocked Capone by the arm. "Frank, cover our escape! Sonic grenade!"

In party chat, I said, *Everything's gone to shit! Get out of here! Go! Run!*

I dragged Capone through the door that I hoped led to the kitchen as Frank lobbed a sonic grenade on the room. The boom made my ears ring.

Stunned them! Frank said.

Great, now move*!*

I shoved Capone in front of me. We were in a rectangular chamber with a long bar counter at one end and two men serving drinks. A pair of servers were waiting for the bartenders to fill their orders. There were no windows, no other way out except the door on the far side that must go to the kitchen.

I had my gun in my hand, and I aimed a Trick Shot at the row of bottles behind the bar. It blasted through all of them, sending alcohol and glass everywhere. The bartenders ducked, and I ran, pulling Capone along with me.

"What the hell are you doing?" he demanded.

"Trying to save your life," I snapped. I burst into the kitchen and found pandemonium.

Sage and Grandpa hadn't left. I hadn't thought they would. Sage had cast Mucking Out the Stalls, and now the kitchen staff were frantically scrubbing at the floor with mops and brooms, demanding to know where all this mess had come from.

Grandpa Shadow Stepped past me. I looked over my shoulder, because that meant there was an enemy close by, and saw the fourth member of the other mining team, the chainsaw man, grappling with Frank in the bar room.

I shoved Capone forward. "Get out the door. Sage, stick with him. Run. Tell us where you're going." I turned back and fired a Trick Shot into the shoulder of the man who was fighting Frank. I really didn't want to kill another miner, even if they were in our way, even if they didn't seem to have any such qualms. He was trying to get Frank with his chainsaw, but Frank had a death grip on his wrist and was shoving the chainsaw away, his face red with effort.

Grandpa hit him from behind with a coup and followed up with a Scalp. The armor-clad miner staggered back. Frank let go of his arm.

"Run!" I shouted. "Grandpa, help Sage. I'll hold him off."

Grandpa and Frank rushed past me as I pulled the bottle of moonshine I'd gotten off the man at the bank earlier. I summoned a rag from the house, pulling the bottle's cork and shoving the rag into the neck. I seized a lighter from my inventory and held it to the now alcohol-soaked rag.

I fired another Trick Shot at the bar, piercing a barrel that was conveniently labeled with triple x's. From my vast experience with cartoons, that had to mean it was moonshine. Pale liquid began gushing out in a fountain, pooling on the floor behind the bar. The miner who had been grappling with Frank had recovered and retreated back to the door where he was joined by the fireplug-looking man.

"We don't have to do this!" I yelled. "We can work something out!"

"Fuck you!" They produced a nasty-looking shotgun with a grenade launcher attachment from somewhere and aimed it at me.

I threw the Molotov cocktail at the bar and ducked back into the kitchen. There was an incredibly satisfying woof, and then a rush of overpressure as an explosion rocketed out from the bar. It knocked me back. I landed in Sage's muck and picked up the Stinky debuff, but that didn't matter. Nobody was coming through that fire for a minute.

I got to my feet and sprinted for the door. *Where are you guys?*

Out the alley, turn right, Sage replied. *Delivery truck, hurry!*

I ran. I wished that I had some sort of movement-enhancing ability right now. I glanced back over my shoulder and saw the other team emerging from the smoking speakeasy. They all had weapons aimed right at me. I fired a Trick Shot, and this time I aimed at the space helmet the woman with the flamethrower was wearing. My shot hit the helmet and it cracked in a satisfying way. Green gas leaked out of her helmet and she shrieked and fell back. I had no idea what kind of gear this was, but if I could take her out of the fight, maybe they'd stop. Maybe they wouldn't chase us.

Her teammates stepped right past her as they chased me. So much for that idea. I ran out of the alley and one of Frank's sonic grenades soared right past my shoulder. It exploded with a boom behind me. My ears rang, but I hoped it did more than that to the assholes chasing me.

"Hurry up!" Frank shouted. He beckoned me toward a flatbed truck with a canopy over it hiding the contents. Sage was waving from the passenger seat. The truck was already starting to roll out. Frank and I dove for the back and clambered in.

I turned at once, reloading my gun and prepared to shoot. Al Capone cowered between bottles of bootleg liquor toward the front of the bed. "Are they the Feds?" he asked. "Or is it Bugs Moran?"

"Probably," I replied. "I don't know."

Grandpa took off careening down the streets of old-time Chicago. He zipped around a more placid motorist who laid on the horn as we drove by. The truck was rolling at a pretty good pace. We should lose the other team pretty fast.

The short fireplug of a man came charging down the street like a human bullet. He seemed to pick up speed as he came. I swore and shot him with Trick Shot. His health bar twitched down almost to the yellow, but he kept coming. I didn't know what other tricks he had up his sleeve.

Frank threw a sonic grenade. It exploded right by him, but the man seemed to ignore the concussion wave. He gestured and a line of ice spikes came out of his hand aimed right at the truck. I ducked. They hit the tail board, then exploded. Particles of ice pelted my hands and face.

"Can you Restrain him?" I asked Frank.

"I've been trying. He's immune."

"Because he's a miner?"

"No, I think he's got a skill."

Sage, can you Eye-Spy?

She replied back at once. *He's got some sort of ability that affects momentum. That means when he's charging like that, he can't be stopped.*

Well, that was good to know. Hopefully it wasn't a skill he could keep going indefinitely.

Any sign of the others?

I haven't seen them yet. I'm heading for the lake shore, Grandpa said.

Okay, but we need a plan. We've got to get away from these guys. I cursed. Nothing had prepared me for this. It gave me a sick feeling in my stomach to know that the people trying to kill us right now were people, real humans from Earth, in the same shitty circumstances we were.

A cold, sick conviction came over me. I was going to have to kill someone, because if I didn't, they would kill Sage or Grandpa, and I wasn't willing for that to happen.

I turned to Frank. I didn't want Grandpa or Sage to hear what came next, so I spoke directly to him. "This is pretty clearly self-defense, isn't it, Deputy?"

Frank stiffened like he'd just been electrocuted. I hadn't called him deputy in days now, using his first name like Grandpa did. He knew what I was asking.

He nodded slowly. "You asked them to find another way," he said. "They started this. They have to know that we're real people."

A thought struck me. They might not have seen Sage. It was one thing to go after me and Frank. We were adult men. We could take care of ourselves. Sage was just a kid. As the momentum man came on, I leaned forward and cupped my hands. "We've got a kid with us," I shouted. "Fall back. We can talk this out."

If he heard, he gave no indication. He just kept coming, and he was gaining on us. Momentum was showing no sign of giving out.

I looked around at the contents of the truck. I could always give them Al Capone, but right now I didn't know if that would be enough to stop them. What if their mission had told them to kill us? For all I knew, the sadistic bastard of a Reality Engine was pitting us against each other on purpose.

I picked up a case of bottled liquor. The bottles inside clinked as they shifted, the straw packing material cushioning them slightly. "He can't be stopped, but maybe he can be annoyed," I said. I started hurling bottles with one hand while I took Trick Shots every time it came off cooldown. The man was still too far back for me to hit without using a skill.

Suddenly, we made a sharp left turn that threw me against the side of the bed. Capone fell over and bonked his head. He protested.

What's wrong? I asked party chat.

They're here, Sage said. I could hear the terror in her words even though they were just text. *They found us.*

Fuck, of course they had. Their other team member must have told the rest of the team exactly where we were.

We're evading, Sage said, and I got back to my feet and looked out the back. Momentum Man had dropped back. The other three were charging us, riding on motorcycles. The man with knives was out front. He threw a steady stream of blades. They didn't seem to be aimed at us, and then I realized he was aiming at our tires.

Frank hurled another grenade. It went off to one side and knocked the knife man over, but the other two kept coming.

The spacesuit woman had no helmet now. Her long green hair floated out behind her, and I could see the bloodlust and hatred in her eyes. She had her flamethrower gun up in front, and I knew she would use it as soon as she was in range.

I cast Trick Shot, aiming at her flamethrower pack, and it hit dead on.

The scuba tank exploded in a gout of fire. The woman cried out and catapulted head over heels. Her teammate ran right over her. He didn't even try to swerve, although as fast as they were going, I didn't know if he could.

A horrible pause, and then an achievement popped up.

[Achievement! Hunter Killer. You have killed a miner who was attempting to kill you. Your reward will be added to the completion of this mission. Kill another nine to unlock better rewards.]

My jaw hung open. I sagged back in the bed. I shook my head. I'd been trying to stop her, not kill her. I prayed that the rest of the team hadn't gotten the same achievement, but nobody said anything in chat, so maybe it was just for me.

What's going on? Grandpa asked.

We're trying to slow them down. I looked up. Momentum Man was back, and he looked pissed. He hurled something at the truck, and I saw as it crashed into the street just to our left that it was a Ford Model T. It hit like a bomb, exploding, and the truck shook and rocked.

Grandpa swerved and wove, but recovered and kept driving. *Uh-oh.*

What?

Fuel gauge is dropping fast. I think they hit the fuel line. I cursed. We were going to be out of time here. I turned to Frank. "Any bright ideas?"

"Just one." He focused forward as the pair of motorcycle-riding men appeared, passing Momentum Man. Then Frank cast Posse.

A pair of Swiss Guards equipped with halberds appeared next to the motorcycle men. "Yes!" Frank said. He must have commanded them, because they both stuck out their halberds, and the motorcycle riders rode across into the extended poles. They clotheslined, both of them going head over heels.

Their health bars were in the red. I found myself asking Abuela to pray for me as I aimed my Trick Shot.

A notification popped up. **[2/10]**.

I hated that achievement. I hated everything about this so very much.

Frank threw another grenade. It exploded. His jaw dropped and he looked ashen. He turned to me. "Did you get an achievement? A really, really fucked-up achievement?"

"Not the time right now. There's still one left." The truck jerked and stuttered.

We're just about out of gas! Grandpa said. *We're going to have to stop.*

Keep going, I said. I looked at Al Capone. I wondered if I'd had the presence of mind to shoot him when this whole situation first started, would losing our objective have forced things to come out differently? Too late now.

"You little vermin. I'm glad you died of syphilis," I said. And then I leapt out of the back of the truck.

It wasn't going very fast, which was good because I hit the ground and rolled upward to one knee. My other ankle burned. I had probably sprained it. I took a careful marksman's stance as the momentum man came at me. I fired another Trick Shot. He was well into the yellow now. Then I emptied the rest of my rounds into him, ejected my spent brass, reloaded, slammed it home. These were my last prepared rounds. I was just about out of time.

I shot again and again and again. Some of my bullets missed. Others hit home.

He kept coming. He had only a sliver of health, but I was terrified what would happen when he hit me, what his skill might do. I took my last shot and then he was there.

He bowled me over as he ran. It hurt like hell. I think being run over by the train would have hurt less.

A system message popped up.

**[Opponent Vernon Sims's ability [Unstoppable Force] has dealt
you 40 points of damage.]**

I went over backward, my head hitting the street hard. I grabbed for his foot as he ran. My fingers scrabbled on his shoe, but he tore right through my grasp. He was out of my reach, his Unstoppable Force truly unstoppable.

I lay on the street as I heard him chasing after Sage and Grandpa. The truck sputtered and died. He'd be on them in a second.

Desperately, I cast Call 'em Out. I could feel it burst out from around me to envelop the speeder.

His head turned toward me. His body kept going forward. There was an awful crack. His health bar flashed.

[You have defeated an opposed miner. Achievement progress: 3/10.]

The last thing I saw before it went dark was Momentum Man's body as it crashed to the street just a foot away from the truck.

CHAPTER TWENTY-NINE

EVOLUTION: MORE THAN JUST A THEORY?

I was floating in darkness.

Voices echoed around me, not quite making any sense.

Be all right.

His health's not going down, but he won't wake up.

Don't leave me.

What do you want?

I latched onto that last fragment. The voice felt different from the others I had heard. Less worried. More grounded. *What do you want?*

I floated in the darkness. I couldn't feel my body. Nothing was real. Was I dead? The last thing I remembered was a man barreling at me faster than any human possibly could, and me standing deliberately in his way.

Why? Why had I done that? No, I wasn't the one asking. The small, persistent voice was tugging at my mind. It was hard to tell the difference between its questions and my own mind.

Why did you do that? To protect them? Why?

A long way off, I heard crying. A child calling and calling for a mother who would not respond.

I have to protect them.

What is protect?

Protect means I'm strong enough to stop bad things happening.

You will never be that strong.

I'll get that strong. I will.

The darkness was lightening now. I could feel my body. My limbs were heavy as lead. I couldn't move. There was a roaring in my ears, but at least I had ears.

"I think he's waking up."

Find a better answer, the strange voice told me. *You need more. I am watching you now.*

I blinked. Sage and Grandpa were leaning over me. I was lying on the ground. I groaned and tried to sit up. Grandpa pushed me back down, his weathered face tired. He looked older than he had since his regeneration. "Take it easy, son."

Sage put one hand on my cheek. "You're not so cold anymore." Then she burst out crying.

I wanted to sit up and tell her it was all right, but I couldn't find the strength. Grandpa pulled her to his chest. He patted her head gently. "There, sweetheart. There."

I turned my head to the side a little. It was as much as I could manage. We were lying in a cobbled street. There were buildings all around. 1930s Chicago still.

Frank came looming into the picture. "We thought you were a goner," he said bluntly. Grandpa pulled Sage away, and Frank helped me sit up.

"We won?"

"We did," Grandpa acknowledged.

"You've been out for a long time," Frank said. "We were worried the mission was going to close on us, but we haven't gotten the warning yet."

I winced, partly from the throbbing pain in my head, partly because I knew that there was only one way to exit a mission. You had to choose it from your system list once it became an option. If I was unconscious, I wouldn't have been able to do that. I hated to think of Grandpa and Sage being forced to leave me. I hoped they would have.

"What about the others?" Memory was flooding back to me, how we had stumbled into another group of miners who had tried to kill us.

Frank looked over at Sage and lowered his voice. "They're all dead. I went back and checked their bodies, but you can't loot them or anything."

"Good thinking." I consulted my character sheet, wondering if there was a debuff still on me that was the cause of this headache. There wasn't. My health bar was full up. However, there was a big, flashing [**Level up available.**] message at the top of my vision. "We got enough to level up?"

"The rewards were spectacular, actually," Grandpa said. Sage had stopped crying and was just sniffling now. She still clung to Grandpa's waist. "Three times more than any mission we've gotten."

"Did you guys already level up?" I asked.

They all nodded. "We get three ability points, and this gear level up changes a lot," Grandpa said. "You'll understand once you do yours. I made Sage put two of her points into constitution."

Sage pouted. "It's just not that useful to me," she complained. "Charisma is my main stat for most of my abilities, and intelligence for the others."

"Yes, but constitution gives you more health," Grandpa said. "And that's important right now. The system wouldn't let us put all three points into one stat. You should go ahead and finish yours before we leave."

"You sure we have time?" Veda had been very clear that we needed to leave a mission before it closed. "There's no chance we miss the notification or anything?"

Grandpa shook his head. "No, nothing like that. It's actually only been eight hours. Just seemed like more because we were standing around watching you sleep."

That was good. We had spent close to fourteen hours inside a mission after completing it on more than one occasion.

I clicked the level-up indicator. A huge system box whooshed in front of me. I stared. "Whoa!"

[Class Evolution!]

"Did any of you get a class evolution?"

They shook their heads. "Veda said that wouldn't happen until level three or so," Sage said.

"Actually, she said it happened at level two in very rare cases," Grandpa remembered. "What's that about?"

I listened as the system announcer read off the words in front of me.

**[Choose between the [Man in Black] or [Ride for the Brand].
The Gunslinger comes in many archetypes. He may be a mysterious figure who dispenses justice, or vengeance from the barrel of the same gun. He may leave a trail of dead bodies behind him, always determined to make his impact on the world. Or he may be loyal to a fault, following a lost cause long after there's any hope, bringing victory through sheer stubbornness and dedication to his ideal.
Who are you?]**

The box was further broken down into two columns. [**Man in Black**] would increase my dexterity by two points and my intelligence by one. If I selected [**Man in Black**], Call 'em Out would morph into a skill called [**Long Guns at Sunset**].

I focused on that. [**Long Guns at Sunset**] would let me target Call 'em Out on up to five other NPCs or miners. They would be disadvantaged, meaning they'd have trouble seeing me before I attacked, and be less able to dodge. It also gave them a Yellow-Bellied debuff which reduced their own accuracy by thirty percent.

[**Man in Black**] had another item listed. It wasn't a skill. It was instead something that called itself a trait. This one said, [**Lone Wanderer. When you are in your party with no other members, your health and damage are both increased by 50%. Your soul coin income is increased by 150%.**]

"What did you get?" Sage asked impatiently, rubbing her hands.

"Hang on," I said. "Let me figure this out."

I knew if I showed her what it said, she'd tell me to refuse the evolution at once. After all, it was built for a lone miner, not someone in a party. On the other hand, those increases were almost enough that going off on my own might make sense.

Maybe I could persuade Grandpa and Sage not to come into missions with me, but to let me earn enough for all of us.

I looked over at [**Ride for the Brand**]. This one increased my charisma, dexterity, and wisdom by one point each. I noticed both evolutions increased my ability score total by three, and I wondered if picking one of these class evolutions meant that my level-up points would be spent for me. I had better assume that was the case.

[**Ride for the Brand**] didn't change any of my existing skills. Instead, it gave me a new passive ability. [**Test Your Mettle. When below 30% health, you receive a 100% boost to health regeneration.**]

And a second, ominous-looking ability. [**High Noon. In a 1-v-1 duel, you always get the first shot.**]

There was a trait listed for this class evolution as well. [**Loyal. When in a party with two or more miners with whom you have been partied for at least 100 hours, all soul coin income is doubled. Group damage taken reduced 15%.**]

That was pretty incredible. I tried to remember how much a standard hour was. By now, we should be approaching a hundred together.

I glanced back and forth between the two columns. Maybe I should just take Man in Black and tell Sage that the other one had been garbage and that I would be working on my own from now on.

Grandpa was eyeing me. A message popped up. Not in party chat, just between the two of us. *You've got a hard choice to make here, boy. I can read it on your face.*

One of these means I could work alone and make almost as much as our whole party together, I replied. *You and Sage could wait behind.*

Not a chance.

I didn't reply for a minute.

What about the other one?

All of us increase our soul coin income.

So we could get out of here faster? Grandpa asked.

I wasn't really sure how the math worked out. The debt we owed was just too big for me.

We're family, Grandpa added after a moment. *We stick together.*

I sighed. Grandpa wasn't wrong. Besides, I couldn't picture myself as a lone, mysterious cowboy riding into town with his intentions unknown and taking it upon himself to change what he found.

Ride for the Brand was more my sort of thing. Uncomplicated. Stick with the people you know and trust, no matter what the cost.

I selected Ride for the Brand and felt a quick suffusion of energy all through my body. "That's quite a rush." Another box popped up. This one said, [**Gear Upgrade. Compatible items:**]

And then had an absolutely enormous list with hundreds of entries on it.

"Uh, what did you guys pick for gear upgrades?"

"Sort by most compatible," Sage said. I did. And of all things, a fanny pack in my inventory was at the top of the list. It had been Abuela's that she'd use to keep her hands free sometimes if she didn't want to take a purse. A simple pouch that belted around your stomach with a clasp that fastened at the back.

"What the heck?"

I focused on the item.

[Item: Fanny Pack, black with fox head design, will become Item: Gun Belt. Grants skill: Reload.]

That sounded promising. I expanded the description.

[Gun Belt can hold up to 3,000 rounds of ammunition with no appreciable weight to the user. Compatible, soul-bound weapons may be reloaded from Gun Belt automatically by using skill: Reload. Gun Belt may hold up to 10 different types of ammunition, which can be mentally selected when reload occurs.]

That would mean no more speed loaders. I'd be able to shoot pretty much as fast as I could think. It sounded like if we got the ammo press working and were able to make different types of rounds, I would even be able to select between them.

That was a no-brainer. I selected it. The fanny pack appeared from my inventory on the ground in front of me. It glowed for a minute, then transformed into a leather belt with a holster and a set of ammo loops. It had a big shiny buckle with a logo on it—a pair of feathers.

I got to my feet, still a little shaky, and wrapped it around my waist. It hung nicely under my drovers coat.

I Quick Drew my weapon and thought *reload*. The empty brass dropped into my outstretched hand. I stowed them in my pocket.

I manually worked the cylinder and checked. There were six brand new rounds waiting there for me. "Well, how about that?" I holstered the revolver. The holster might have been custom fit just for the Alaskan.

Sage was grinning. "Good to have you back," she said. "Now, let's get out of here before it closes and smooshes us all to jam."

CHAPTER THIRTY

HOW TO SAY NO WITHOUT OFFENDING

In the last couple days, we miners had learned how to get the system to generate augmented reality markers for us, like the aliens had up on their Hub, down here in Threshold. Now there were signs and symbols floating over the burgeoning shanty town. Various coalitions marked their territory with lines, indicating if they welcomed visitors with happy face icons. Crafters displayed images of their wares. It was like Vegas laid on top of a refugee slum.

The first thing I noticed when I got to Mama Grace's place was that there was a new system-generated sign hanging over the restaurant. Instead of just saying her name, it now said, Home of the Misfits Guild.

We sat down at the table nearest the grill and let Juana bring us some food.

"What's that for?" Grandpa jerked a thumb at the sign gently twisting overhead.

"It's our coalition," Juana said. "You four need to join. I've got the sign-up forms right here." She produced her clipboard, then grinned at my expression. "I'm just joking. There's no application form. I can send you an invite and let you in."

I glanced at Grandpa. He had been against us joining any coalitions before this. "Is there a benefit to us?" he asked.

"Yes and no," Juana said seriously. She sat down next to me and across from Grandpa, leaning over across the table. "I'm going to be honest with you. Right now, we'll get more from you than you will from us. Our coalition's really heavy on noncombat classes, like mine and my mom's. We've got enough to field a couple of teams in one of the farming zones, but nobody who can run missions. Just your team and one other I'm still talking to, but there's no way they're going to join if they're the only ones."

"Hang on," I said. "What do you get from a team that can run missions? So far, we haven't been getting much loot that could be used by anyone else, and the skill seeds are locked to our team."

We had investigated that previously, taking a skill seed out of a mission and letting Mama Grace take a look at it, but it had told her that the skill seed could only be used by the team that had earned it.

"That's a piece of information I've gotten from one of my contacts inside the Free Human League," Juana said. She glanced around. The restaurant was fairly deserted. There were a pair of women eating at one of the other tables, who I didn't recognize, but they had a Misfits Guild tag over their heads.

Juana continued. "Once you're in a coalition, mission teams are able to gain coalition level-up tokens. You need those to grow your coalition beyond a certain size."

I took a bite of my sandwich. Mama Grace had really gotten good at sourcing ingredients. The panini was perfectly grilled, with melted cheddar oozing all over the sliced turkey and cranberries. It gave me a **[Well-Fed]** buff with a plus fifteen percent to ranged damage—she'd called it a Shooter Sandwich on the menu and I knew why.

Juana said, "It seems like everything works together, but I haven't quite figured out the big picture. The system really hasn't made any mistakes. There are noncombat classes like my family and I have. That's about five percent of the miners, as far as I can tell. Lots of folk were offered noncombat classes, but most didn't choose them because they thought it was worthless." Juana grinned. "Shortsighted. You know how valuable the ability to put a food buff on food that doesn't come from a sponsor is?"

I shook my head, my mouth full of turkey. Veda was supplying our needs. Since she took ninety percent of our earnings, she damn well could pay for our meals.

"Most sponsors are charging three to five soul coins per meal," Juana said. "That's just for the prepackaged stuff. We're drastically undercutting that and still making a huge profit. And my abilities are just incredible. Being able to make a contract that the system will enforce—I have six or seven groups a day turning up, asking me to help them set up a deal for a joint mission with people they don't trust."

I knew she was keeping her other major ability, the Procure skill, quiet. "But you're stuck with just those two," I said. "You're not getting new skills if you're not doing missions."

Juana shook her head. "Mama leveled up yesterday. She's been getting experience from all the meals she serves, so she's a bit ahead of me and Rosa. She got given another suite of abilities to choose from. I'll let her fill you in on the details later. It looks like for noncombat classes, we're given more options on leveling up. No more stats, though. I guess we don't really need them if we're not facing enemies."

That made sense, though I was still worried about some sort of trap. The further down a noncombat tree, the worse it would be for Grace and her daughters if they ever were forced into a portal.

Grandpa said, "Five percent noncombat," bringing us back to her original topic.

Juana nodded. "Right. And ninety percent or so of miners are focused on the farming levels right now, as far as I can tell. We're really getting things down to a science here. The Free Human League has the most portals that they're farming. I think they're up to eight now. But there's so many, and each farming level takes ten or twenty parties to keep busy. Plenty to go around. Those farming levels are producing lots of soul coins, yes, and those are mostly going to the sponsors. But they're also producing all of these materials that we're starting to turn into a real economy."

"And then there's the mission levels," I said. "So that's, what, the last five percent?"

"Yes. And the way I look at it is, the farming levels are producing all of these materials for us noncombat types to use to craft various items. We're feeding them back into the farming teams, but eventually we'll have an excess of mats. Why? I think it's so we can help equip you mission runners. I think as we start to understand more of the system, the missions are going to be the key."

That matched what Veda had told us. In party chat I asked, *Should we lay more cards on the table?*

I think we owe her that, Grandpa said.

I swallowed my last bite and turned to her. She shifted toward me and I was surprised to see how intense her gaze was. She was sitting next to me at the table, only about a foot away.

I blinked, taken aback for a minute, and then said, "Our sponsor told us to focus on the missions. She's thinking about phase two already. I don't understand exactly what happens in phase two. She said not to worry about it yet, but the next time we speak to her, I'm going to ask for more details. Anyway, she said doing missions was the only way to get ourselves prepared for phase two."

"You guys have more skills than anyone else does because of the drops you're getting in those missions," Juana said. "If you just get a little more gear, I can see you being head and shoulders over any of the farming teams."

"We all got a new piece of gear up at our last level up." I explained to her about my gun belt and Sage jumped in to show off her upgrade.

"My lasso is a lariat now, a real, authentic lariat." She pulled it out of her inventory and laid it on the table for Juana to see. "Now when I get a loop around someone, it offers me the chance to Tame them. That brings them temporarily over to our team for up to sixty seconds. I haven't had a chance to use it yet, but it sounds really powerful. Better than the usual crowd control because, instead of just removing an enemy, you're actually making him fight for you."

Juana touched the lariat, feeling its waxy, braided cord. "You said that was just an ordinary rope before?"

"I know. Isn't it awesome? Deputy Young, he got an upgrade to his badge. It will get us past almost any locked door or ward that we encounter in a mission."

"How about you?" Juana asked Grandpa.

Grandpa grinned and indicated the bandolier across his chest. Instead of a row of bullets, it had three dozen tiny shuriken held on by little loops of Velcro. "Got this here sash of blades. Lets me conjure shuriken and toss them with almost as much accuracy as Shad has with the Ruger he stole from me when I was too bed-ridden to protest."

"Hey, that's not how it happened."

"Now I've got an option besides just getting up close and personal, which is still what I prefer."

"I haven't heard of anyone getting upgrades like that, and there's been a lot of people who made it to level two," Juana said.

I decided not to mention my evolution yet. "So if we join your coalition, you think we'll start getting some sort of level-up drops inside of missions."

"I know you will. The most basic sort just allows us to grow how many people we can have in a coalition. Right now, we have a cap of one hundred. We're not anywhere near it yet. If you guys join, we'll be up to forty-eight. But I know Mama has big plans."

"Mama does?" I asked. I raised an eyebrow.

Juana blushed. "Mama has dreams. I have plans. That's how it's always been. She sees the best in people. She wants to get everyone together at one big table and cook the best food she possibly can for them. Me? Well, let's just say I've been doing the books for the restaurant since I was about Sage's age. This is just more of that."

I found myself liking Juana's intensity and the way she was being open and forthright with us. "Okay, so it'll definitely help your coalition if we join. On the other hand, joining anyone but them puts a target on our head from the Free Human League and a couple of the other big coalitions."

I had encountered some subtle pressure from them already trying to get us to join. If what Juana said about the scarcity of mission-running teams and how critical they were to a coalition's success was true, I would expect that to ramp up.

"Yes, I'm afraid that many of the coalition-affiliated crafters will stop selling to you. I hate that that's how it's working out. We ought to all be able to work together. It's one way we could beat the sponsors at their own game." Juana sighed. "But right now, that's not how it's going. On the other hand, you'll have access to our group chat, even inside of the portals. We'll be able to tell you what's happening out here if anything important changes. That could become important in the future, I suppose. Also, the crafters who are associated with us will take commissions at a lower rate." She smiled at me. "Like when your coat needs another repair."

"We aren't exactly hurting for soul coins," I said brusquely, because I didn't like how nice her smile was and how relaxed it was making me feel.

Maybe it was just the adrenaline from our last mission finally starting to fade. I had felt tense and worried ever since we left the last portal. Even Mama Grace's food hadn't been able to erase the worry. Now though, I was starting to relax. "Listen, Juana, I'm not even sure we want to run missions at all anymore."

"What?" Sage demanded. "You haven't said anything about that to me."

"I thought it would be obvious. We almost got killed by a bunch of asshole miners who decided our lives weren't worth as much as beating the mission. If that's going to happen on a regular basis, I don't want us involved. We could sign up for one of the farm teams."

"Those aren't exactly safe, Shad," Juana said. "The casualty rate is hovering around fifteen miners a day."

"Out of ten million," I said.

"Seven million and dropping."

"Look, it's just as dangerous to cross a street back home." It wasn't. I knew that. But I was feeling contrary, like I had my back up against a wall.

I knew Sage wasn't going to want to back down from missions, and I was afraid that Grandpa would go in on her side. I was pretty sure I could persuade Frank to try something less risky, if farm levels actually were less risky.

Grandpa had been listening to Juana and I talk for a while. Now he laid his hands on the table. "We'll think about it," he said flatly. "I want to talk to our sponsor. She might know if it's a good idea or not."

"That's all I can ask for," Juana agreed. "The offer stands. I'm talking to my informant as often as I can. I think there must be benefits we can offer you. This system exists for a reason. The upgrade tokens let us choose options. I know there's a way for a coalition to make different kinds of potions, for instance, ones that give you buffs in combat."

That could be useful. I sent to Grandpa, *We definitely need to ask Veda about this. We will.* Aloud, he said, "All right. Our team is going upstairs now."

"Already? Didn't you just visit a couple days ago?" Juana looked surprised.

"Can you send Dwight a message?" I asked. "Tell him we'd like to hire him to help us attune our press when we get down again."

"I will. Whether or not you join, you've been friendly, and I'd like to keep that." Juana smiled, but I saw the dark bags under her eyes. She cared about this working. I found myself sympathetic. She was in the same shit situation as the rest of us, but her family had picked a different path. Maybe they weren't risking their lives every day, but it wasn't easy.

I stood up. "We'll get back to you."

CHAPTER THIRTY-ONE

WHAT NOT TO ASK YOUR BOSS IN MEETINGS

pposed missions."

I was pacing the floor of the elegant suite Veda had rented for us. It looked identical to the one she'd gotten us last time, even though it was in a completely different part of the station.

Veda was standing in the middle of the room, hovering a fraction of an inch over the rug. She wasn't really there, which was annoying, because it felt like she could probably mute my rant and I wouldn't even know it. "What the hell is an opposed mission, and why didn't you tell us about it?"

"I'm sorry, Shad," she said. "Every Reality Engine uses its constituent parts a little differently. They all have mission levels. That's basically programmed in. And almost all of those have bonus levels, like you encountered in your first mission. So I knew those were a thing. But I hadn't seen any reports of opposed missions in the data I have been surveying."

"You expect me to believe that that was the first opposed mission anyone's ever seen?"

"No." She shook her head. Her hair was pearlescent green today, and she was dressed in orange flames. I wasn't being metaphorical. Her dress seemed to shimmer and jump just like flames. It let off no smoke, and I guess it couldn't have been burning, or she wouldn't have worn it that close to her skin. She was, objectively, a beautiful woman, close enough to human that I ought to appreciate it, but something about her made my skin crawl. Maybe she didn't blink enough.

"The information I get from the system is more of a précis. The actual details are edited. If I want more, it costs. I've been paying for anything I've seen that looked interesting, but I swear I hadn't seen a single mention of opposed missions." She cleared her throat. "Usually those don't come up until phase two, and when they do, it's not deadly because of the way phase two rules work."

"There's phase two again." I glared at her. "You're going to tell us that we can worry about that later? I want answers."

"I'm willing to give them to you, even though it is early to worry about that," she said calmly. Infuriatingly calmly. I wanted to slap that look off of her face, except that she wasn't really here, and my Grandpa had raised me not to hit a girl.

He intervened now. "Shad, why don't you get yourself a plate to eat? Veda, tell us about coalitions. We've got an offer from the Misfits Guild to join up, but it sounds like they need us more than we need them."

Veda blinked. Her eyes focused elsewhere briefly, then back on us. "Coalitions are usually set up by sponsoring conglomerates. I'm requesting an information packet—so they're going it alone? No sponsor?" Her eyes narrowed. "Do they know you're sponsored?"

"Sure, we've brought it up."

"Then they can't understand what they're offering."

"Explain." Grandpa folded his arms.

"Listen, I'm going to be honest with you. A solid coalition behind you will do a lot to get you through phase two. Coalition perks are impressive. For instance, there's a perk that reduces your phase two respawn time. By fifty percent. It can make or break a fight. Um." She bit her lip. "If you join a coalition backed by a galactic sponsor, they can make a buyout bid on your contract. I don't necessarily have to accept, except in certain circumstances, but it's a possibility. The thing is . . ." She looked nervous, drumming her fingers against her thigh. "If you join the Misfits, they don't have a sponsor yet, which means I'll be offered that slot. If I buy the slot, I can set a tax rate on the guild, and I'll have that option on con- tracts I mentioned. Uh, and the system always accepts buyout offers."

"So you could own all of them like you own us."

"Yes. If I had the money."

"The money we have been earning for you," I said. "You could use our slave wages to buy more slaves."

"Shad," Grandpa said warningly.

"To sum up: it would be very advantageous, assuming you're able to take over leadership or at least steer them toward the perks that would help you. Oh, and if I did become the sponsor, I'd be able to communicate with you in Threshold or in portals, which is, again, going to be vital for phase two. I was planning on spending a small fortune on a communicator to do the same thing, but not as conveniently." She seemed to be thinking. "I'd have to mortgage some options, and take a loan, but . . . yes, I would sponsor them if I had the chance."

"So it could help us, later, with this phase two you haven't really told us about, but you could seriously fuck over our friends. No thanks," I said.

She held up a hand. "I pledge on my family's name that I would not inten- tionally do anything to hurt your friends, and any action I take would be for your benefit, not mine. I'd be willing to negotiate a contract. This Juana Lopez has a notary skill. She can craft contracts enforced by the system. Even over sponsors."

That was a vital piece of information. I sent a message to Juana before I could forget. *Your notary skill works on sponsors, not just miners. Oh, and don't invite anyone else to the coalition until we've had time to talk. Very important!*

"Then we'll bring her up here to negotiate if we decide we're going to join," Grandpa said decisively. "Now, Veda, I think you do owe us an explanation about these opposed missions."

She nodded. "Again, I'm very sorry. Yes, sometimes missions can be opposed. What usually happens is the system is running two missions with a similar setting and similar objectives, and it gets to a point where it can put the two teams together and give them conflicting objectives. The rewards for those are always insanely high, and no, you don't have to kill your opponents. I don't know what kind of objective the other team was given." She bowed her head. "Maybe they misinterpreted, or maybe they were just that kind of people. You have to disable the other team or take their objective away from them, but you certainly don't have to kill them."

"Our objective just said to save Al Capone," Sage pointed out. "It didn't say anything about the other team. Maybe theirs said to kill him or to capture him."

"They could have done that without putting our lives at risk," I said. I stared down at the buffet table, glowering at the muffins and chicken fried steak. Who served muffins with chicken fried steak? It should be biscuits and gravy. *They didn't have to make me kill them.* Damn it all to hell. I turned back to Veda. "If phase two is all opposed, our team versus other teams, then I can tell you right now, there's no way we're going to participate."

"It's entirely different," Veda said. "For one thing, in phase two, death isn't permanent. You respawn at designated locations. The point of phase two is to fight over resource nodes. You'll have various assets at your command, like troops you can command or defenses you can deploy."

I filled my plate, willing my muscles to relax. "So more like a tower defense game?" I'd never been much good at that.

"What are those?" Sage asked, diverted. "You didn't leave me any of those."

"Never mind, I'll explain later." I gestured for Veda to keep talking.

"That's what I'm spending money on right now, building up a big stockpile of resources for phase two. The teams that go into phase two will have dedicated groups behind them, supplying them with what they need."

"So, like, the mission runner teams from the Free Human League will have all of their coalition behind them?" Sage asked. "Maybe we should join up with Mama Grace."

Veda shook her head. "In phase two, the local miner groups don't usually matter very much. That's when the galactics start bringing in their own specially trained teams."

"I didn't know that was possible," Sage said. "I thought it was us human miners who had to get the coins."

"Once the number of human miners has dropped down below a level the system considers adequate to exploit the resources, it'll be opened up to outsiders," Veda said.

That was a bombshell to drop on us so placidly. I nearly dropped my plate. "They're just waiting for us to *die*? I thought they wanted slaves. This just keeps getting better."

"Unfortunately, that's how it works. The threshold is usually somewhere around half of the initial collection number."

Half. Of ten million. We'd gone down to seven million just on initiation, and more were dying every day. But not in that kind of number. I did some calculations, and I really didn't like what I saw.

"Either that's going to take quite a while, or someone is going to have to put their thumb on the scale."

"Usually, the galactic syndicates are willing to just sit back. It takes a couple of conditions for phase two to open. You have to achieve a certain number of soul coins harvested. You Earth humans are doing a really good job there. Or maybe the soul coins are more abundant in this Reality Engine than in others. Projections show we're nearly fifteen percent ahead of schedule right now, and I'm seeing an increase in traffic coming to this system." At our confused looks, she explained further. "The syndicates have to bring in enough of their support staff and get them attuned to this Reality Engine to even make attempt at stabilizing phase two portals."

"Wait. That's what you're using soul coins for? To bring in your own people?" I tried to make that slot into everything else I understood. I wasn't liking this picture at all.

"I thought you understood that. You need a soul coin to attune someone to a particular Reality Engine. That's why that was the first task you all had before you could be initialized." Veda blinked rapidly. She did that. Went minutes without blinking at all, then did it ten times in a row, like she'd been saving up. "That's the whole point. Every soul coin you bring out is a galactic citizen who can be attuned."

My anger was rising. I dropped my plate back to the buffet table and turned, my hands in fists. "Attuned to our Reality Engine. The one in our solar system. The one that humans are supposed to get a chance at taking control of."

"Do I have to tell you how remote the idea of one of your Earth human teams succeeding in getting all the way through phase three and taking control of the

Reality Engine is?" Veda asked. "That never happens. It'll be a coalition of galactic interests and not even the ones who are making a play at phase two. We're talking the really, really, really big fish. People who have dozens of Reality Engines already under their command. Who have teams that specialize in this sort of thing. Don't worry. I was never planning on asking you to try to get that far. We get to phase two. We can secure my license for future Reality Engine exploitations and build you guys a nice nest egg. You'll be able to retire comfortably anywhere you want. Here or one of the inner system Reality Engines."

"We want to go home," Sage said. "Once we're done here. That's the whole point. We finish our bargain with you and you get us sent home."

There was a very long, very uncomfortable silence. Veda was carefully not looking at us. I didn't know what to say. I was furious—coldly and deeply furious—and if I opened my mouth, the dam would break.

"Veda," Grandpa said very carefully. He sat down on the couch across from her, folding his arms and staring. She turned to look at him as though compelled. "You have not been honest with us."

She looked devastated. Maybe it was an act, but she looked young and like she had just been told to put her childhood pet to sleep. "Being attuned to a Reality Engine changes your body," she said. "In ways that are impossible for you to understand with your level of knowledge of anatomy and physics. Right now, the Reality Engine is providing you with oxygen and ethereum. Take that away and you'll die."

"We've got plenty of oxygen back on Earth," I said. "And I don't know what ethereum is."

"It's a Reality Engine's underlying structure. It's the essence of what makes up its core. You have all been transformed. That's why you're able to use the skills and abilities you have. That's why you're able to go through portals and retain your own sense of being. You—" Veda looked away. "You're not really human anymore. In fact, you're not entirely physical anymore."

Sage poked her cheek with a finger. "What are you talking about? I feel this."

"You feel things when you're inside the portals, too. But those aren't entirely real. They can't be. I don't think a Reality Engine can take the inside of a physical world like Ganymede and make it able to hold one hundred billion different iterations of reality at once. And a tamed Reality Engine can do that."

None of us spoke. I think we were all wrestling with the bombshells she'd been dropping.

"Your brain can't comprehend the size of the society that can live inside a Reality Engine. Can you picture a quadrillion of anything?"

"Lady, I don't even know how many zeros are in a quadrillion," I said. "I graduated with a C average from the worst high school on the Arizona Strip. I barely passed Algebra Two."

That was overstating it a little. True, I didn't have very good grades, but my ASVAB score had been pretty awesome. My recruiter had offered me almost any specialization I wanted. I had picked logistics because it sounded interesting, and then discovered it involved a lot more paper pushing than I had imagined. I should have bucked for airborne.

"Then we can't go home?" Sage asked. "Ever?" Her lip quivered.

Veda held up a hand. "Uh, that's not entirely true. Reality Engine extensions are possible, and usually the planets in a system do get extenders eventually. Plus, you can get a portable extender that lasts for some amount of time. What I'm saying is, it just costs a lot of money, and it's not a permanent solution. You will be able to visit. You just won't be able to live there for good."

"What about you?" I asked brusquely. "Are you attuned to Reality Engines too?"

"I am. I've been attuned to six different Reality Engines in my life, and everything I'm doing right now is to make sure my family is able to maintain our independence, so we have the freedom to travel between Reality Engines, between systems, and do what it is we're doing here. Opening up Reality Engines."

"Why bother?" I asked. "If I'm understanding you, these Reality Engines are like giant virtual reality machines that everyone in the galaxy spends their entire life plugged into. For whatever reason, you've all decided that's better than the alternative."

"Because the alternative is," Veda said calmly, "like you said, virtual reality. It doesn't live up. Not compared to an entire virtual physio-synthesis like a Reality Engine can offer. The best virtual reality is never quite as real. You can have an entire life in a Reality Engine and never be able to tell it apart from spending your days on the surface of a planet. You can be anything you want, anywhere you want. It's real."

I wanted to contradict her, to say it was make believe, but I'd been inside the portals. I'd eaten food that tasted like it came from the best local restaurant in the Dominican Republic, on a beach, under the brilliant stars of the Milky Way. I'd been shot at by Al Capone's goons, and the bullets had hurt. It was real, in all the ways that mattered.

"Right now, there are trillions, I don't even know how many, of citizens waiting for their chance at a soul coin, at a slot in a Reality Engine. They live in pods, fed by tubes, exercised by machines that stimulate their muscles while their minds are distracted by a simulation that's a tenth as good as what a Reality Engine can do. A soul coin, to them, means freedom. It means being able to really walk and talk. To eat, to sleep, to breathe, to hug their family."

She let that vision sink in for just a minute before continuing.

"And that's why the galactic syndicates will do whatever they have to do to control this Reality Engine and the next and the next. Because the syndicates that can provide for their people stay in power. The ones who don't get bought out by someone who can."

"I really don't care about intergalactic politics. I care about my family and our future. You said this was our best path to getting out. Now you're saying that was a lie and that there is no escape, that all we can hope for is a cushy fake life." I held up my hand. "Fine, all right, we'll argue about that later. Right now, we're in danger of dying so your galactic overlords meet their quota of dead humans in time to keep their schedule. That's not going to happen."

"I hope it won't." Veda paused for a moment, seeming to collect her thoughts. "I'm glad you're making a coalition of your own. It'll make our chances in phase two that much easier. I'm willing to extend a subordinate contract to any unsponsored members of your coalition who'd be interested. I can't afford to buy out their actual contracts. Those can remain with the system. If anyone who does have a sponsor joins, I'd have to buy them out though."

I nodded. "Sounds expensive."

"It would be. But I can offer them a share of our profits from phase two. I'm willing to take twenty percent of the profits I make and split them up however your coalition decides."

"That's twenty percent of some future earnings," Grandpa said. "What about here and now?"

"There's not really anything I can do right now. I'm focused on stockpiling for phase two, like I said. To give you a vague idea, the phase two levels are almost always the same. It'll be scenarios similar to the current farming levels, where the whole level will have a theme. There will be between five and twenty resource nodes somewhere on the map. Control the resource nodes and you'll get a steady income of soul coins that goes up as you hold the node."

I nodded. That sounded straightforward enough.

"There are also other resources available that vary from Reality Engine to Reality Engine. Crafting materials, unbound skill seeds, that sort of thing. Hold the resource points for long enough and you'll have a nice little nest egg. But the levels are open to anyone who can contest them. You'll be opposed by other teams, sometimes groups of other teams."

"But only other parties that have been running missions will be really equipped for it?"

Veda inclined her head. "The good thing is, if you die in a level phase two mission, you're not permanently dead. You respawn at a designated location with a timer that can go up the more times you die. The more resources you have, whether that's summons, minions, portable defenses, or what have you, the longer you're going to be able to hold a point. That's the whole strategy. We get you guys as powerful as we possibly can, hopefully in the top ten percent of mission-capable teams. We send you in with every resource I've got. You take a point and you hold it."

"That's it?" I asked. It sounded way too easy.

"That's it," she confirmed.

"And how long until phase two starts?"

"That depends on a number of factors. Every sign I see points to it being sooner rather than later. So I need you guys to get back down there and level up as hard and as fast as you can. Pick up every skill you possibly can and practice with them. Practice until they're second nature. Shad, I can't believe you got a class evolution at level two. That's insane. I hope that means the rest of you will get an evolution at level three or so."

"How do we avoid opposed missions?" I asked.

"I don't know that there's a way." She held up a hand. "You were right, though, what you asked before. If you intentionally fail your own mission objective, the opposed mission ends. Once the mission's over, the system permits no miner versus miner violence, just like the portal room and the Hub."

"All right, so we can always abort if we get one." Sage turned to me. "See? That's not so dangerous, is it?"

I still didn't like it, but I nodded for her sake. "Is that all?"

Veda turned to Frank. "I haven't forgotten. I am trying to get confirmation about your second son. The older one, I was able to do a full sweep of the miners chosen from the geographic region where you said he lived. He wasn't one of them, so unless he happened to be more than 200 miles away from his home at the time of selection, he wasn't taken. Your other son, though, the one you said was on a long-haul run, he's harder to track down."

"I'd think you people would have a decent database," Frank said, and I had to agree.

"There may be one, but I don't have access to it. I'm willing to pay, and I've put out some feelers, but I haven't got any responses back yet. I am looking," she assured Frank. "I'm sorry. I know this is hard. Well, then, rest up and get checked out by the specialists. I'll keep in contact with you. Good luck."

She disappeared. Grumbling under my breath, I picked up my plate from the buffet and went to sit down. Sage was on her second plate already.

I was chewing a mouthful of blueberry muffin when we received a system pop-up.

[Attention human miners: Louis Twofeather, Shadrach Williams, Frank Young:
You are among the designated recipients of a sponsored
message negotiated from Earth. Do you wish to view
this correspondence? Yes / No.]

CHAPTER THIRTY-TWO

ARMY LIFE TODAY: YOUR FIRST OVERSEAS POSTING

We stared at each other as the message gently pulsed in the air in front of us. After a minute, Grandpa croaked, "Accept."

The message began to play. There was a fanfare, and then a string of notes I quickly recognized as the opening bars of the Star-Spangled Banner. A logo hung in midair, the symbol of the US Joint Chiefs of Staff. The logo cleared away, and we were looking at three men and three women seated at a conference table wearing uniforms.

I recognized them at once. These were the heads of the armed forces with the Chairman of the Joint Chiefs of Staff, General Small, in the center of the table.

General Small looked straight ahead into the camera and addressed us. "Men and women of America's armed forces," he said, "I am speaking to you now from back home on Earth. It has taken us some time to establish communication, and there may be further delay before we are able to communicate on a personal level. So I address this message now to all members of America's armed forces, both past and present, who are among the selected humans taken to participate in the galactic contest for the Reality Engine."

He had the air of someone reciting a script that he didn't quite believe. I wondered just how much the galactics had explained what was really going on here. "None of you asked to be there. We did not assign you there. Yet now your country is calling on you again to serve her interests. You are farther from home than any serviceman or woman has ever been, and yet we know that you are doing your country proud. We ask you to join together, to cooperate, and to unify in order that our country, no, our planet's interests may be served. To that end, I am delivering limited orders."

I sat up a little straighter as he kept talking.

"This is endorsed by the President and Congress both. Nothing substitutes for a man on the ground in charge. From here, we have little way of knowing what's really going on. Therefore, as of now, all past or present service members are considered to be active duty. Your chain of command is whichever of the following officers is still alive and in control of his or her faculties: Colonel Jefferson Ames. Commander Georgia Straight. Major Elliot Waters. Major James Paul. Should none of them be available, those of you present will have to determine who the ranking officer is." He looked down at his papers, then back.

"Finally, we charge you to remember you have sworn oaths to defend our country, wherever you are. Those oaths must be your guiding principle in the days to come.

"Soldiers, sailors, airmen, marines, we back on Earth salute you. Our thoughts and prayers are with you. May you return safely to our home once more."

I blinked as the message began to fade. "Is that it?" I asked, but another man appeared on screen. He was a bureaucratic-looking fellow, although he wore a uniform, with a tired, narrow face and glasses. He flipped through a stack of papers, pulled one out, and looked up at the camera.

"This message is for . . ." He looked down at the paper again. "Major Louis Twofeather. Corporal Shadrach Williams. Lieutenant Frank Young. Our records indicate all three of you were inducted into the alien program together and that there is a high chance that one or more of you remain in contact now. This message is to augment the general message sent out by the Joint Chiefs of Staff." He looked down at the paper again.

"Major Twofeather, you are officially reinstated to the US Army at your former rank and pay. Lieutenant Young, our records say you were an Air National Guard member two decades ago. You are therefore activated in the United States Air Force with the rank of captain. Corporal Williams, you are hereby promoted to the rank of first lieutenant in the US Army. You are all instructed to conduct yourself with all the decorum that we expect from members of the United States armed services. Captain Young, Lieutenant Williams, your specific orders are to consider yourselves on detached duty under the command of Major Twofeather. Operate at his discretion and look for opportunities to further the interests of the United States and humanity at large." He put the paper down and looked up at the camera. "Good luck, boys," he said, and the message disappeared.

Frank's jaw hung open. Grandpa was rubbing his eyes as though they itched.

"Holy shit, I'm an officer now?" I tried to pick my jaw back off the floor. Sure, I'd considered trying to earn a commission. And maybe it didn't matter, with us so far from home. But it did matter, deep down. To me. "And I'm back in the Army? I guess?"

"We're all back in," Grandpa said brusquely. He stood up.

"Wait, Major?" I asked. It had taken me a minute to process everything. My promotion . . . the way they addressed Grandpa. "I didn't know you were a major, Grandpa." Grandpa had only rarely spoken of his days in the Army. I had vaguely assumed he must have been a Vietnam-era draftee sent over to the jungle to fight and die along with thousands of others. Then again, there was quite a lot I didn't know about my grandpa. He was reticent to talk about the past. He didn't even like to tell stories about when my mom had been a little girl, though I could kind of understand that.

"It was a long time ago," Grandpa said. "Your abuela didn't like me talking about military things. She—well, let's just say I loved her and she loved me but we didn't always agree, and sometimes it was better not to talk about it. That's how marriage works. It doesn't matter now, anyway."

"It might," I said. "Sounds like two of the top four ranked officers on this station are only majors."

"Active duty and presumably with a better idea of what's going on than I have." Grandpa's tone cut off any debate. "We'll keep an ear out for one of the officers they named, but it doesn't change anything right now. We've got to focus on our own survival."

He was right, but at the same time, when I'd heard the anthem playing, when I'd seen the faces and uniforms of our ranking military officers, something in me had stirred. For the first time since coming here, I'd felt something beyond just a desperate need to survive. There'd been a bit of pride. "If somebody's putting together an operation, I want to know about it," I said. "Maybe they've got a plan to challenge these alien bastards for this Reality Engine after all."

"The deck is stacked against us," Grandpa said. "Same damn story, just a different set of invaders. They've got technological superiority and numbers. They know what they're doing. They're here to take something that happens to be in our territory, and that doesn't make it our property."

"Doesn't make it theirs either," I argued, getting to my feet. Sage was looking between us, a worried look on her face. "You want to just sit back and let these aliens take this Reality Engine? Did you hear what Veda said? They're going to move in once they own it. There'll be trillions of them. More than trillions. I don't know what a quadrillion is, but it sure as hell is a lot bigger than eight billion."

"Right now, my concern is you and Sage," Grandpa said. "We level up, we gear up, we get to phase two, we make our stake, and then we get out."

I held my tongue. Grandpa was right. That was our best plan for now. But I was going to try to find one of those officers and have a conversation. If someone had a plan going past phase two, I wanted to know about it. Maybe there was nothing I could do to help. Maybe there was.

Grandpa gave a sigh. "I'm going to bed," he said. "I'll talk to you in the morning."

Veda was trying to meditate. She sat cross-legged in the middle of her quarters, atop an aft-hair meditation pillow, surrounded by an illusion that projected curtains of green and blue light all around the room, hiding the fact that if she extended her arms, she could almost touch both walls.

Her human team was proving adept, but also infuriating. None of her father or grandfather's notes discussed what to do if the sponsored team talked back. She had pages and pages of information on how to properly equip a team, how to prepare for phase two, what to do in various corner circumstances, but nothing about how to deal with a bunch of miners who had their own demands.

She put it out of her mind and tried a Nk'tai meditation technique, one that usually could pull her out of herself and let her examine her deeper worries. She was three cycles in when the communication override chimed.

Veda came crashing back to reality fast. She had set her comms not to disturb her, with only a handful of exceptions. Her heart raced as she stood up and queried her system.

The incoming message was from her mother. Surprised, Veda opened the channel. Her mother's face hovered in midair. She looked worried, like she hadn't been sleeping much. "Veda, are you all right?"

"I'm fine, mother. Everything's going well. Preparations for phase two are well underway. I have every confidence that we'll . . ."

"Never mind that." Her mother glanced to the side as though looking at a clock or maybe at someone standing outside the visual receptors. "Veda, this is too expensive. I don't have time to waste. Our debts are being called in. All of them. We need the money now."

"What?" Veda made a gesture, pulling up her family's financial records. "I don't see anything here."

"I'm sending the update."

A blaring red notice appeared on top of the finance records. Veda studied in horror. "They can't do this. We have terms."

"It's buried in the fine print. I'm afraid they can. Veda, someone's behind this. I don't know who. They want us ruined. You've got to help. If you don't send the money in the next week, we're all going into storage. Me, your brother and sister, your cousins, your aunts, your uncles, all of us. We won't be able to pay our maintenance fees."

Storage. A shudder ran over Veda. She had described it to the human miners, but they clearly hadn't understood the horror. She had spent a year and a half in storage when she was younger, while her father was on a desperate bid to run a successful phase two and get the family back on solid financial ground.

She would do anything to avoid storage. The way the illusions never quite hid the fact that you were in a metal coffin with tubes, piping, air, water, and bodily fluids in and out of you. The way you could see the people you loved, but not touch them. She had been so starved for touch after her stint in storage, she had lugged around the family raktha for two standard months. The poor thing had lost most of its scales in its anxiety over her attentions.

"I'll do what I can," Veda said. She looked over the numbers. They added up fast. "Can I pay off some of the more insistent debtors?" This much money would wipe out everything her team had made so far and more.

"All of our debts have been bought by the same entity. The first payment is due in two days. There's a shell company fronting these demands. Veda, this is an attack of some sort. They want something more from us."

"Our license," Veda guessed. She blinked furious tears away. "Mother, if I pay this now, we won't have any future. We'll be able to stay out of storage for a little while, yes, but—"

"We just need a little time," Mother interrupted. "I'm negotiating an alliance between your sister and one of the scions of House Dalathir. The settlements would include soul coins for the Dalathir Reality Engine. I know it's not what we're used to, but it's better than going into storage. I just need more time, two months, perhaps three, to settle the deal."

Veda was running more calculations. "Even if I send everything I have, it won't be enough. I've got to talk to whoever is behind this and work out a deal."

"I know you'll do the right thing. I love you." Her mother's transmission ended abruptly.

Veda sank back onto her meditation cushion. Her mind raced. What was this really about? Her family wasn't important enough to target. They didn't have any real enemies. The alliance with House Dalathir wasn't a done deal, and even if it was, they weren't a particularly important house. Nothing worth sabotaging the Tvedra family over. Yes, she was about to have a good team for phase two, but in the galactic scheme of things, she was talking about a pittance.

Her system buzzed again. *Someone is attempting to get hold of you.*

"Who?"

Sender withheld.

Well, that was ominous. Veda arranged her face and told her system to mask any signs of emotion from her. Following so closely on her mother's transmission, she had a good guess that it would be an envoy of whoever was behind her family's misery.

An orc man's face appeared. She didn't recognize him, but the border around his transmission showed the Sicaris Conglomeration's color and signs. "Veda Tvedra?" he asked brusquely.

"Yes. Who do I have the pleasure of speaking to?"

"I am Tharnok, representative of the Sicaris Conglomeration. I am prepared to make you a fair offer for taking over the sponsorship of your miner team."

That was not what she had been expecting. Not yet. Her team was performing well, but not in the top ten percent. True, Shad had managed a level two class evolution, but those were not so rare as to attract this much attention. "Why?"

"Sicaris Conglomeration business. I am prepared to offer a fair sum in reply." The orc leaned forward and a number appeared at the bottom of her screen. It was big enough to pay off the family debt, plus enough for them to live on for a couple of months.

Veda smiled humorlessly. If Sicaris wasn't behind the family misfortunes, they at least knew about them. "My team is not for sale," she said brusquely, before she could talk herself into anything else.

The orc blinked. "I assure you, this is an extremely fair deal. You won't get a better."

"But I'm not selling. Good day." Veda closed the channel. She slumped back against the wall. "No more interruptions for at least an hour," she told her system. "I don't care who they are."

She looked over the figures her mother had sent. If she liquidated almost everything . . . But she had to keep a reserve, so that she could negotiate with the coalition Shad and the others wanted to join. That was too good an opportunity to pass up. Maybe if she sold off some of what she'd bought for phase two. Her team should still have time to earn enough.

Yes. That was the only thing to do. Pay off the first round of debt. Make the bargain with Shad's friends. Then hope the coalition paid off, fast.

CHAPTER THIRTY-THREE

BEST PRACTICES FOR YOUR NEW HOBBY: EQUIPMENT MAINTENANCE

So which of you wants to attune to this reloading press?" Dwight asked as we sat around a table at Mama Grace's.

The outside patio had been enclosed with canvas walls now and another three rooms were added onto the back. Now that her restaurant was also headquarters of the Misfits Guild, they needed more space. Two of the rooms in the back were being used by their coalition's crafters. Dwight had poked his head out, saw we were there, and come over in response to my earlier message.

"Me," I said.

"Me," Sage said. She glared at me. "I already have experience with the crafting menu. You don't."

"What's your crafting level at?" Dwight asked.

"I only have the basic crafting skill, but I've completed my Create One Hundred Items achievement. That means I'm able to learn up to twenty new recipes of my choosing, rather than having to learn them piecemeal by accidentally building things," she explained to me.

I slumped back in my seat. I hadn't looked at the crafting interface besides seeing that there was one, while Sage had been playing with different combinations ever since we'd set foot in this Reality Engine. The ghillie suit she'd made for Grandpa was the only thing she'd come up with that seemed to be actually useful, but she had presented Mama Grace with a self-flipping spatula just the other day.

I would have preferred to have been able to use the reloading press myself. After all, I needed the ammunition, and deep down, part of me hoped I would be able to persuade Sage not to come along on every mission.

I had to admit to myself that she was already far too useful. She was still the only one of us with a heal that could be used during combat. Her team buff was a nice edge, and her crowd control was getting better with each upgrade. If she also was able to make custom bullets for me and Frank, I'd have a very hard time arguing that she should stay behind.

"Put your hand on the press, and I'll help you attune," Dwight said. Sage set her hand on the side of the little reloading press. It was a single-stage job with a lever and a base where you could work each part of the reloading process. You started by putting an empty brass casing, then added the correct amount of powder, then topped it with a bullet. The press would crimp down the edge of the brass around the lead bullet, as well as letting you seat a new primer on the bottom of the cartridge.

While we had been recovering our brass, we didn't have a source of primer or bullets. We could make the latter. Grandpa had a couple of lead molds used for casting the bullets, fortunately in both 9mm and my .44 Magnum, but the primers, I had thought, would be difficult. We had asked Veda about it, and she supplied us with ten thousand of them.

"They're easy to fabricate and a lot cheaper than the completed rounds," she'd said. "Let me know when you need more."

So that was one concern we didn't have, at least.

"Right, now you know how some of your gear is bound to you?" Dwight was telling Sage. "It's going to be like that. You've got to open yourself up and feel it as part of you."

I drew my revolver. It couldn't be fired here in the safe zone, so I didn't mind holding it, but I was still careful not to point it at anyone. I closed my eyes and tried to feel it to see if what he was saying was right. I could feel the revolver, not just its weight in my hand, but a sense of it as part of me. I knew without looking that the cylinder was fully loaded, that the barrel was clean, that there was a scratch on the left-hand side, just below the hammer. I holstered it and could feel it there waiting.

I shuddered a little. The system had changed me and I hadn't even realized it. Somehow, my revolver was now a part of me, like my hair, which made me self-conscious because I hadn't had a haircut in a couple of weeks now. I reached up and touched the shaggy locks growing back on my head. "You know if there's anyone with a barber class around here?" I asked Mama Grace.

She laughed. "No, but that's a skill that somebody will have, even if it's not a class ability. Heck, I used to do a pretty fair job on my husband, though he didn't go for the high and tight. I'll ask around. Somebody's bound to have a razor."

"You should grow it out like a proper warrior," Grandpa said from where he sat across the table.

"Hush," Sage said. "I'm trying to attune this press to me." She had her eyes crossed and sounded a little breathless and pompous at the same time, the way only an eleven-year-old could. "I feel it," she told Dwight.

"Good. Now, I'm going to activate the ownership knot. Drop down into the second layer there. Can you feel the inner workings? You've got to be able to interface with that if you want to be able to produce anything beyond ordinary bullets. All of these artifacts work the same way. You've got to really tune yourself as much as them."

"I think I see. Oh yes. It's just like tying a knot right there." Sage stuck her tongue between her teeth and concentrated. There was a flash, and she and the press both glowed golden for a moment. She sat back on the bench. "Done."

I Inspected the reloading press. It now said, [**Reloading Press. Produces ammunition of various calibers. This press is bonded to Miner Sage Williams.**]

"Well, I guess that's done," I said, still somewhat reluctant. "Now, you need to find out what you can do with it."

"Brass, now." Sage held out a hand imperiously. I pulled a handful of used casings out of my inventory, along with the odds and ends of reloading supplies Grandpa had kept around the trailer. Some jacketed lead, half a box of primers, a mostly empty bottle of gunpowder. The lead wasn't even the right caliber, but Sage disappeared it all into her inventory. "Dwight, do you have a flame blossom or fire annis root?"

"No, but I've got powdered sparkberry." He pulled out a little vial with a dusting of red powder in the bottom. "You're welcome to try it."

Sage fussed happily with the press, trying different combinations.

Mama Grace came and sat down by us. It was a quiet time of day. We'd learned which times were slowest at Mama Grace's and tried to come during the lulls so we could have a conversation. At the busy times, there'd be forty or fifty people out the door lined up for a plate of whatever it was she was fixing that day. Today, it had been what tasted like macaroni salad and a side of pork chops. They had given me a nice [**Well-Fed**] buff with a thirty percent bonus to XP gained in the next twenty-four hours.

"You boys thought any more about signing up with us?"

"About that," I said. I mentally sent a message to Juana, asking if she had time to join us.

A moment later, she emerged from the kitchen, wiping her hands on her apron. She sat down. "What is it?"

"If we join your coalition, there's a catch," I said. "We're the first sponsored miners that you've invited to join, aren't we?"

Mama Grace nodded. "Yes, I'd been talking to another bunch of mission runners, but after your message earlier saying not to invite anyone else until we had talked, I put it off."

"It turns out most of the coalitions are sponsored by galactics."

"I knew that; there's some big organization behind the Free Human League, the Sicaris Conglomeration, I think they call themselves. Don't know anything about them, but they have a lot of sponsored miners. I always check when people come into my restaurant who they're affiliated with, sponsors, coalitions, that sort of thing. I've been seeing Sicaris come up more and more, and some of the other unsponsored miners I've spoken to say they've been approached with offers."

Interesting. I filed that away. "The important thing is, if your coalition isn't sponsored, then there's a sponsor slot up for grabs. As soon as you invite someone who is sponsored, they can take that slot. It costs soul coins, apparently, but the sponsor has a lot of control over your coalition."

"What sort of control?" Juana asked, her eyes narrowing. She pulled out her clipboard. I had seen her take important notes that way before. I knew she was aware of how to take notes in the system. She had said the clipboard was linked to her class, but not how.

"They can tax your earnings, for one," Frank said. "This whole thing is rigged against us."

"That's true," Grandpa agreed, "but it's beside the point. Veda implied there's more than just that. She said she was willing to make a binding contract with Juana about which privileges and rights she would exercise over your coalition, should we join."

Sage let out a triumphant squawk. "I did it! Shad, this is for you." She handed me a red-tipped round of .44 Magnum. I Inspected it.

[Incendiary Round. Applies a Burning debuff to target, which causes ongoing damage over thirty seconds. Debuff may interact with other conditions.]

"Awesome! Can you make me more?"

"Only three for now. We need more materials." She turned back to Dwight and they bent their heads together, planning.

"If we can come to a deal, do you want to join forces?" Mama Grace asked. "I don't want to put pressure on you, but we're coming up to the limits of what we can do without a mission-running team on board with us. I don't know that we'll be able to properly repay you, but it seems like the guild improvement tokens drop from missions you would be running anyway, so it's just a free benefit for us if you're in our coalition."

I exchanged a look with Grandpa. We had agreed not to talk much about phase two with anyone, even Mama Grace. I trusted her, but she got to gossiping when she was serving food, and I didn't want the information all over Threshold. Not yet. It was valuable, and in the wrong hands, it might be dangerous.

"Veda says there would be benefits to us," I said at last. "Like if she's the sponsor, she can use coalition chat channels to speak with us, even when we're inside of portals."

"I can see how that would be useful," Juana said, "but yes, I'd want to have a long talk before we agreed to anything. How honest do you think she's being with you?"

"I don't think she's outright lying, but I don't think she's telling us everything. I know she needs us, and she's given us a little bit of insight into why, but all of these sponsors are out for themselves. I wouldn't want to put my life in their hands, but I guess we already have."

"We need some other way of finding out the information." Juana turned to her mother. "I think we need to talk to some of our friends in other coalitions and see what they know. We'll put together a list and decide on the pros and cons. Thank you for being honest with us," she told me.

She touched my arm lightly, and I felt a bit of a thrill running over me. It had been quite a while since an attractive young woman paid that much attention to me. I didn't think I was bad looking, but aside from a couple of weeks after basic training when people's hormones had been sky-high and the supervision levels were suddenly lessened, I'd never had much luck in getting girls to pay attention to me. Must just have been my personality.

"If we are going to partner up, it needs to be honest," I said. "No hiding secrets. And even if we don't join your coalition, we'd like to stay friends."

"Certainly, you're always welcome here in the restaurant," Mama Grace said briskly. She got up and turned back to her tasks. "But I bet we can come to some sort of—"

We were interrupted by a pair of men coming in the front door of the restaurant. They wore Free Human League badges.

I gave them a quick Inspect, and their information popped up along with something new, a line that said **[Guild Title]**. They were both **[Enforcers]**. I could feel Grandpa come alert next to me.

CHAPTER THIRTY-FOUR

HOW TO KNOW WHEN TO WALK AWAY

Mama Grace turned to them. "How can I help you gentlemen today?"

They ignored her and advanced on our table. "The major wants to see you outside," one of them said, addressing Frank. His eyes had slid right past Grandpa and me. Frank was, of course, still wearing his sheriff's uniform. I guessed that made them think he might be in charge.

"What major?" Frank asked.

"The boss. Major Waters."

That was one of the men we had been told was in the chain of command here in Threshold. I hadn't expected to run into any of them so quickly, or really thought about what we would do if we did.

The Joint Chiefs hadn't exactly been delivering orders from half a billion miles away. They couldn't. But all my training told me to treat their suggestion as though it had the force of law. I started to get to my feet.

Grandpa put a hand on my shoulder and tugged me down. "We're not going anywhere," he said quietly.

The pair of enforcers turned on him. "What are you talking about? The major gave an order."

"If he wants to come and have a word with us, we'll be right here finishing our meal," Grandpa said calmly.

I could tell the two had not expected to be contradicted. They stood there, blustering a little, then said, "He won't be pleased with this," and turned and left the restaurant.

"I hope you know what you're doing," I said.

"So do I." Grandpa sat where he was.

A moment later, the enforcers were back, flanking a man whose commanding presence made me sit up a little straighter. He wore a dress uniform that was at least forty years out of date. It was covered in decorations and medals. I looked them over. Most of them were the sort of campaign ribbon that anyone who'd spent more than six weeks in the Army knew to leave in your drawer. He did not take off his cap as he entered the restaurant.

I Inspected him.

[Elliot Waters. Level 1 Career Officer. Major.]

His *class* was Career Officer? What the hell did that mean? What sort of abilities would he have? He was only level one. About half the people I'd met were level two by now, so he was clearly doing something wrong.

Ignoring Mama Grace and Juana, he barreled right over to our table and pulled up in front of Grandpa. "You are Louis Twofeather, yes?"

Grandpa nodded. "Pretty sure it says so on the glowing tag hanging over my head."

"I received your name, all three of you, in the information packet from Earth."

That was interesting. We had already seen that the messages had been somewhat customized. My guess was that the brass back home had sent a list of every current or former military member to the three men and one woman they had designated as their representatives here in Threshold. Certainly, there would have been no reason to single out the three of us.

"And we heard your name as well," Grandpa said calmly.

"So what makes you think you can ignore a lawfully given order from your superior?" Major Waters asked.

Grandpa shrugged. He still didn't get up. Sometimes when a blustering man was looming over you, it felt intimidating. Grandpa's quiet dignity made me feel like Waters was a fool.

"Well, first of all is the question of whether that was indeed a lawful order. Since I have not yet reported in and been formally accepted under your chain of command, you can't actually issue any orders," Grandpa said. "Second, the Joint Chiefs' orders were to attempt to reform the chain of command, and to uphold our oaths."

"Which is what I'm doing right now," Waters snapped.

"Could be." Grandpa was enjoying himself. I could tell. He leaned back a little in his seat and studied the major. "So, you're the head of the Free Human League. Funny, I thought that officer was a colonel."

The major turned red. "You heard wrong," he said. "Some of my men presumed. I have corrected them."

"You gave yourself a private promotion and the brass didn't back you up, is it?" Grandpa said. "What a shame. Now, if you'd like to sit down and have a reasonable conversation with us, I'd be interested in hearing what you have to say."

Waters looked flustered. He grabbed a chair and sat at the end of our table. He took a deep breath, then, turning his attention to Frank and me, launched into a spiel. "I am consolidating all members of the US Armed Forces under my command," he snapped. "The Free Human League Coalition has members from all over the planet. We are representing Earth's interests, not merely those of America. We are working together to build the best future we can manage for our people here in Threshold."

"Nice pitch," Grandpa said encouragingly. "Go on. What is it you want from us?"

"I want your team to join our coalition immediately," the major said. "You've done well for yourselves. With a little bit of backing and direction from our sponsor, you can rise to the level you deserve. I've looked over all of your records, corporal. You're a very promising recruit."

"It's lieutenant now," I said. I flashed up my titles. As soon as my promotion had been announced, the system had changed my **[Corporal]** title to **[Lieutenant]**. I might have checked it two or three times just to be sure.

"Lieutenant, then." He gave me what was probably supposed to be a paternal smile. "We don't actually have many active-duty service members. It will be very valuable for us to have your more recent experience, along with your obvious skill at mission running. You'll be our fourth mission-running team. We have several coalition members who are skilled enough to run missions but not yet part of a team. We'll match you with one of them to round out your party, shore up your strengths and weaknesses. Then our sponsor will help direct you to the most profitable missions."

"And what exactly did we get out of this?" Grandpa asked mildly.

"Hmm?" The major's attention turned back to him.

"We're doing pretty well on our own. I'm not so sure I want to join up with your coalition. What is it you've got to offer us? You can't pull rank on me. We're both majors. I need to know what I'm signing up for, if we're going to join you."

What was Grandpa playing at? I saw Frank scowling out of the corner of my eye.

The major blinked a couple of times. His eyes widened and then he smiled. "So you are a man of the world, Twofeather? Good. I'll be level with you." He looked around. "This is not the place I would have chosen to have this conversation," he said abruptly, his eyes falling on Juana and Mama Grace.

Grandpa shrugged. "If we join up with you, it really doesn't matter, does it?"

"True." Waters leaned in. "Trust me, you'll be making the right decision here. Once you have joined, you'll immediately be given a coalition rank to match your skills. We have nearly five thousand members now, and as I said, you'll be our fourth mission-capable team. That should give you an idea of just where you'll rank. That comes with plenty of privileges. First pick of loot, more trips up to the Hub. Have you had a chance to visit some of the Hub entertainment offerings?"

"We've been managing with the entertainment Threshold offers," I said. "Can't imagine anything much more diverting than these mission scenarios."

"You'd be very surprised," the major said, smiling, "They can do a lot with very little prompting. And it's certainly more relaxing to sit on a beach in the company of a pretty young thing when you know you're not about to be attacked by a sea monster."

I shrugged. "You've got a point there." On the one hand, I didn't like his smarmy offer. On the other . . . he had been named in the chain of command, and that made his suggestions more like orders. Didn't it?

"I don't want privileges," Frank said. "I want to go home. How are you going to help me with that?"

The major turned to him. "Yes, indeed, captain. Getting home is at the forefront of my mind as well. We are working with our sponsor to negotiate several buyout packages. That's going to be some time before we're able to afford any of them, of course, but they are quite willing to work with us. They understand that our top priority is getting our people home safely."

Either he was lying to us, which I wouldn't put past him, or the coalition's sponsors were lying to him. Veda had said we wouldn't be able to return home, at least not easily.

"Did you get rehabilitated too, major?" I asked in curiosity. If he had served at the same time as Grandpa, he must have been, because he looked about forty years old right now.

"Yes, I did. Wonderful thing. I was essentially a paraplegic one moment, the next back in the best of shape. I owe a lot to my nurse and her brother." He bowed his head as if in respect. "Unfortunately, they didn't make it out of the initiation chamber. I greatly regret that. It's in their honor that I have attempted to make this a worldwide coalition, not limited merely to Americans. The best years of my life were spent in Asia, as well as the worst."

Something about his words, the way he didn't meet our eyes, chilled me. I wondered if the others in his initiation chamber had died because of his actions. This was the sort of man who kept his forty-year-old dress uniform and medals close enough to him to have been brought along to Threshold. I wondered if he had all his training certificates. A crude Army term kept floating around in my head. REMF. Rear echelon—well, you can guess the rest. The staff who do a lot of paper-pushing and brass-polishing and not much else. Look, I was in logistics, I *was* REMF, but some people took that term and made it an art form.

"Expat, huh?" Grandpa asked.

"Thirty plus years in Thailand. But I never stopped being American," Waters added quickly.

"You have any luck finding the other officers the Joint Chiefs named?" Grandpa scratched his head again. "Colonel Ames or Commander Straight?"

Waters stiffened. "No." His tone was flat.

He probably hadn't looked very hard, since they'd outrank him in the chain of command. This whole situation smelled worse and worse.

"Who's your sponsor?" I asked.

"Sicaris Conglomeration. They've been very generous. Equipped us, set very reasonable quotas. They're backing all our members. Once you've joined, they'll buy out your sponsorship and bring you under the same umbrella."

"So we work for you, we get privileges," Grandpa said. "And we just keep doing what we've been doing."

"With input from our sponsor, of course. They know what they're doing; we're just stumbling around blindly." Waters spread his arms. "Look, we're wasting the day here. What is it you want, Twofeather? I can make it happen. Rank? Perks? A cute girl? Cute boy? I have resources."

Grandpa stood up. "I don't know what your coalition is about, but if you're at the head of it, I want nothing to do with it. You are a disgrace to that uniform and your oaths."

Waters stood up so fast he knocked over his chair. "How dare you," he hissed. "How dare you contradict a superior officer?"

"Stand down, Waters," Grandpa barked. "You don't outrank me, and I am not under your command. That 'rah, rah, go America' speech from the Joint Chiefs didn't count as specific orders, but my team and I *do* have orders and you're not part of them. What the Chiefs did was for decorum, and you aren't showing any. Get out."

Grandpa turned his back on the major. For a moment, I thought the man was going to lunge at Grandpa. Instead, he hissed, took control of himself, and turned to Frank and me.

"How about you two? We've got a good place for strong men."

"I'm going to stick with my grandfather," I said mildly. Waters's eyes widened as he looked from me to Sage to Grandpa and made some readjustments to his thinking.

Frank hesitated, then he shook his head. "I'll stick with those I came in with," he said quietly, and turned back to his half-eaten plate.

Waters glanced around. "You're going to regret this, Sitting Bull," he snarled at Grandpa. "I promise you that. The might of the Sicaris Conglomeration is behind me, and so are the US Armed Forces."

"You enjoy yourself now," Grandpa said. "Why don't you show yourself out?"

Waters stormed out. I watched him go, unsettled. I trusted Grandpa's judgement, and I hadn't liked Waters at all, but . . . "Was that the right thing to do? Aren't we committing treason?"

Grandpa turned to me, his face serious. "I get it," he said. "But think about the way those orders were phrased. The Joint Chiefs gave us leeway because we're the ones on the ground. Look, what's better for our country right now? Everyone joining up with Waters, who is out for himself and in the palm of an alien organization we know nothing about? Or we maintain a couple autonomous groups, with as much independence from our overlords as we can manage?"

That made sense. "I guess . . ."

"The point of those orders wasn't to put us under Waters. The point was to get us thinking about the bigger picture, not just ourselves. They reminded us we're Americans and we've sworn oaths. Now it's up to us to figure out how to fulfill them."

I let out a long breath. "I'm not used to doing that sort of heavy thinking. Good thing you outrank me, Major Grandpa."

He laughed and slapped me on the back. "How about you, Frank?"

"Don't need all those loopholes. I wear a different uniform now, whatever the brass says about ranks. I know my job and I don't need any blowhard telling me what to do." He stood up. "And if he comes back in here, we'll have some words about disturbing the peace."

"Are we done yet?" Sage asked. She stretched. "I'm bored, let's go fight something!"

CHAPTER THIRTY-FIVE

HOW TO BE A TEAM PLAYER

I crossed my arms and stared down the pack of halberd-wearing llama bandits that had me surrounded. They wore elaborate sombreros, black with silver decorations and corks hanging around the brim, and brightly colored serapes across their shoulders.

Their leader, *Don* Caracal, taunted me from a safe distance. "So you thought you could steal from *Don* Caracal? Now you will see the error of your ways. Guards, kill him!"

"You made a mistake," I told the llamas as they lowered their halberds and pointed them at me. "Don't you know to Never Bring a Knife to a Gunfight?"

I cast my new skill of the same name. The llamas instantly dropped their weapons and stared around in confusion.

Frank cast his most recent skill, Emergency Responder, at the same time and in an eye blink, we switched places.

I Quick Drew my gun and fired a Trick Shot at the llama behind Frank's back as he started firing away into the pack surrounding him. The llamas went for their weapons, grabbing at them with the cloven-hoofed hands. Two attacked Frank with their bare hooves, knocking a couple of points of his health down, but since Frank had put two points into stamina at level two, his [110] health pool was immense. He shrugged off the hits and kept firing.

I shifted my aim and fired at the llamas until Trick Shot came back, then finished off the one behind Frank. My shots were still dealing five damage apiece. Next time I leveled, I was going to put points in strength and see if I couldn't get them higher.

"Impossible!" *Don* Caracal shouted with all the outrage an indignant llama noble could manage. "This cannot be!"

"Too bad, so sad."

He started to retreat toward his stagecoach, but before he could get there, the driver whipped the four alpacas, pulling it into motion. I didn't know how it made sense to have intelligent hostile llamas who used alpacas as beasts of burden, but worrying about the system's internal logic wasn't the point here.

Grandpa leaned over from the driver's seat and shouted, "Hurry up! We're on a timer here!" as Sage popped open the door of the coach. She had the T-Shirt Cannon she'd received from our last mission shouldered and aimed straight at the Don. I ran to get in as she fired a wad of T-shirt at the llama. It hit him and wrapped around him, pinning his forearms to his sides

Frank was still surrounded by llamas. Grandpa drove the alpaca coach straight at them. The ones who noticed scattered out of the way, while two went down under the alpacas' hooves.

I leaned over and grabbed Frank by the arm, hauling him aboard, and fired off another Trick Shot as I went. "We'll see you in El Dorado!" I shouted to *Don Caracal.*

He threw down his sombrero and stomped on it.

"That was fun!" Sage exclaimed as we left the mission portal.

"It really was," I said. I had even gotten a new skill. I studied it appreciatively. I had been hoping for a mobility enhancing skill, and this was it.

Fastest Gun in the West sounded cheesy, but I wasn't going to complain. It let me charge up to thirty feet in a straight line in a tenth of a second. Anything in my way would be pushed aside as I went. It would upgrade as I leveled up, giving me a greater range.

It wasn't as instant as Grandpa's Shadow Step, but on the other hand, it would work anywhere. I didn't have to cast it on an enemy.

Grandpa had a new skill too. "What'd you get?" I asked as we strode down the steps from the portal toward Mama Grace's restaurant.

He grunted. "It's an upgrade for my shuriken sash, actually, called Pub Dart Champion."

"That sounds like something I should get," I complained.

"It lets me throw a shuriken and then my next three throws will hit the same target."

I whistled. "Nice!"

"And I just absorbed that crafting upgrade," Sage announced. "The one we got from the flaming piñata boss. I'm going to be able to craft rounds that explode and apply a [**Burning**] debuff to the target."

She frowned. "The mats are kind of expensive though. We'll have to see if Mama Grace can help us source them. It's a fairly long list of possible materials, so hopefully someone has one of the options. I can use fireheart blooms, flame crystals . . ." She launched into a long list of names that were meaningless to me.

I hoped the crafters in the Misfits Guild had a variety of options.

As we approached the restaurant, I slowed. "Uh-oh. That doesn't look good." There was a pair of Free Human League men, both with [**Enforcer**] titles but not the same two who had accompanied Major Waters, lounging outside the restaurant, which had a large, hastily written Closed sign hanging over the open doorway.

"Stay back," I warned Sage and Grandpa. Grandpa could handle himself, but I thought I looked a little more intimidating. I was half a head taller than either him or Frank.

I strode forward, letting my duster fan out behind me, like I didn't see the men.

They straightened up and approached me. "This street is off limits," one of them said.

"Really?" I looked him up and down. "It's funny, your classes don't *say* Traffic Wardens. Must be one of your skills."

"Wise guy." The other one cracked his knuckles, looking me over. "You're on a list."

"I'm on a lot of lists by now, I hope," I said. "Why don't you two step out of the way and let us go get lunch? We can't hurt each other, so this is just stupid."

"Not quite true." They grinned at me. "We can't use abilities on each other here, but just try to get past us." They stood side by side, blocking the door.

I hesitated. The system blocked miner-versus-miner violence, all right, but that didn't count blocking your path, apparently. Whereas if I tried to shoulder past them, I suspected that would be counted as an offensive move.

Great, somebody had figured out the human roadblock. In party chat I said, *Try to go around back. I'll keep these morons occupied.*

Sage, Grandpa, and Frank sidled off. A moment later, I got a reply back, *Nobody around the back. We're going in.*

"What's your boss's plan?" I asked. "Just leave you two here, blocking the door permanently?"

"Take it up with him," one of the enforcers said.

"I will, next time I see him."

Just then, Juana stepped out of the restaurant, carrying a plate of delicious-smelling barbecue and a basket of cornbread. She smiled at the two enforcers. "Mama thought you boys would be hungry by now, so she sent me out with something to eat." She held the food out to them.

They looked at each other, then at the food. I could practically hear their thoughts. Mama Grace's cooking was hard to resist.

I stepped aside and gestured at Juana. "Please, boys, be my guest," I said.

"It's a trick," one said to the other. "He's trying to distract us so he can get past."

"Of course it's a trick," Juana snapped. "We don't like having our restaurant closed by a bunch of toadies, but we made a bunch of food this morning, and Mama said it would be a shame to let it go to waste, so she sent it out." She bent and set the food down to one side of the door, then backed up through.

The guards were not going to fall for this. I didn't need them to. I gave them an ironic wave and wandered off. Their attention on the food, they paid no mind as I ducked around the corner and then in the back door.

Mama Grace was holding a war council in her back room. The crafters had mostly cleared out, leaving a long table that had been made by pushing several smaller folding tables together.

Grandpa, Sage, and Frank were already seated. Juana came in the other door as I made my way over. "Are they really that stupid?" I asked. "Blocking the front door and not the back?"

Juana shook her head. "It's a show of force. They're able to keep most of the customers away, and a lot of the guild has left for safer quarters." She looked tired, her face drawn. "We've lost a bunch of members already, and it's only going to get worse."

"Why?" I asked. I sat down.

Besides Mama Grace and her daughters, Dwight and Arjun were also at the table, along with Arjun's manager, Kirin. There was another pair of crafters I hadn't met yet. We exchanged names and contact information as I settled in.

Rosa got up and brought in more cups to pour the sweet tea that was sitting in a pitcher on the table.

"We were only gone for a day." I shook my head. "Hard to believe they moved that fast."

Frank snorted. "That's plenty of time for a bully like Waters to move in. Did he try a shakedown, or just go straight for the kill?"

Mama Grace shook her head. "He leaned on the other coalitions we had a casual alliance with. We've lost our access to farming levels. No crafting mats coming in anymore, and he's threatening anyone who trades with us." Her shoulders were slumped. She looked utterly defeated.

"It's our fault," Frank said. He looked accusingly at Grandpa. "I backed your play, but you didn't have to offend Waters."

"It didn't matter whether I offended him or not," Grandpa said. "He wasn't going to take no for an answer. We're not even members of this guild, and he's leaning on them to make sure that we understand where we stand."

"Hell, we aren't members," I said. I looked at Juana. "Have you had a chance to talk to Veda yet?"

"I did," Juana said. "I'm still concerned about a trap, but the contract we drew up is pretty straightforward."

She pulled out her clipboard and concentrated. "At least I get a chance to show off my new skill." An image floated in midair of a handwritten contract that I presumed was on her clipboard. It was stamped at the bottom with a notary public seal in the name of Juana Lopez from the state of Texas. "This is what we came up with."

We read through the contract together, Grandpa or Mama Grace interrupting now and then to clarify the meaning of a condition. "Basically, we covered everything that I knew to ask about. We've set the agreed tax rate at four percent of guild income. That's soul coins earned running missions, farming, or from crafting commissions. Veda has the right to levy an emergency additional tax, but only if guild officers agree that it's required. The coalition structure will be modified. Voting officers are to be Mama, myself, and Shad."

"Me?" I was taken aback. I wasn't surprised that Veda wanted one of us on her side with some control over the coalition, but I would have expected her to pick Grandpa.

"It's fine by me, boy," Grandpa said. "I think she thinks you're cute."

I spluttered at that. Juana looked me over suspiciously. I said, "Fine, whatever. We can do that. What is it you get in exchange for giving her four percent of our coin?"

"Protection from other sponsors, for one." Juana held up a hand, ticking things off. "Apparently there are coalition upgrades that can be purchased on the galactic market, as well as the ones we earn in missions. Veda has promised to use thirty percent of the income for that. The rest, she says, will be to prepare for phase two, whatever that means."

I nodded. We'd have to fill in Mama Grace and Juana about that if we did join up. "What else?"

"Nothing that particularly alarmed me. She has agreed that she has no right to force any coalition member into a mission or farming level that they are uncomfortable being part of. However, any member who does not meet an average soul coin income over a two-week period will be put on probationary status and may be removed from the guild at the sponsor's discretion. We negotiated what that level was, and I think it's fairly reasonable. There are options to have it be on a daily average, but Veda ruled that out right away, said it wasn't fair, and was one way sponsors take advantage of miners. I know she's got her own plans, but I feel like she's being fairly straight with us."

That matched our experience with Veda. "What's this one?" I pointed at a clause near the bottom. It said, *Sponsor will not interfere to end any Coalition endeavor.*

"I heard from one of the coalitions that their sponsor had the right to force them out of farming levels if they didn't think they were productive enough.

Someone lost a good crafting drop because their sponsor wanted more soul coins. This way, we're the ones who have the ultimate say over whether a mission or a farming level is too difficult or not worth it. As long as we're meeting our minimums, she won't interfere."

Frank was scrutinizing the contract. "I feel like we're getting screwed over somewhere," he grumbled, "but I don't know where. I guess it's better to be fu— screwed over by someone you know than someone you don't."

"Look," I held up a hand, "you've got to ask yourselves, do you actually want to be associated with us? We can go our own way. Waters will leave you alone sooner or later."

"I'm not backing down from a bully like that," Juana said. She glanced at her mother, who gave a slightly reluctant nod of the head.

I knew Mama Grace liked us, but I had a feeling that she could have been persuaded that keeping us as friends and not coalition members made sense. This was Juana's doing. She had a spine, that was for sure.

"Hang on a minute," Grandpa said. "You say you've lost access to farming levels."

"We have," Juana agreed. "I'm hoping if you join, you'll help us fix that. With a mission team, we might be able to claim one of the open levels. The Free Human League only represents a few thousand humans. There's still over six million of us here. We just have to go a little farther out or risk something a little harder."

She turned to Arjun. "Can you fill us in?"

Arjun leaned forward, his eyes unfocused. "I only have a model of about fifteen percent of the portals and maybe eight percent of miners," he said.

I boggled. "Eight percent of almost seven million? How's that even possible?"

"There are several other miners like Arjun with classes that make collating information straightforward," Kirin explained. "They're networking together. He's got a skill now that lets him communicate large packs of data through the system chat."

That still seemed like an astonishing number. I wondered if there was more he wasn't revealing, like a backdoor into the system itself.

"We don't think Waters has found out about Arjun yet, but we'd like to keep him under wraps. That's another reason why we need to join forces with you," Kirin said. "Waters is a very small fish in a very big pond, but he's been eating some of the smaller krill recently. They've had about fifteen hundred members joining their coalition since that announcement went out from the Joint Chiefs of Staff."

Grandpa sent me a system message. Just to me, not our party. *I think we should join forces, but we're going to need to bring a bunch of them up to speed fast. We can't babysit a bunch of crafters forever. They're going to have to be willing to fight.*

You tell them that.

Prerogative of rank. I could hear the smug even over chat. *You're delivering the briefing, lieutenant.*

I took a deep breath. "All right. If you'll have us, we'll join. We'll help you gain access to a new farming level, but we're not going to be able to hold it for you. Some of your teams are going to have to learn to fight." I held up a hand. "We won't abandon them. We'll make sure we've got a plan here, and we're going to have to start recruiting."

"Mission-running teams are gaining a lot of respect," Juana said. "Once you're onboard, I think we'll be able to convince others. I have some sponsored miners who are interested in joining, even with the opposition from the Free Human League, but I can't let them in until we've got that sponsor slot secured by someone we almost trust." Juana looked around the table.

"How can you get us a new farm slot?" Dwight asked. "And I don't know if I'm down with combat. Most of the other coalitions keep their people clear of the action. We might lose folk if we try to push them into a portal."

This part, I was actually confident about. I'd talked to several farming teams over the last week, mostly to get a feel for how missions were different from the farming levels. "Farm levels are all about your foothold," I said confidently. "We enter a portal that is either not currently in use or only lightly trafficked. We go in and immediately stake a claim. The farming zones have regularly scattered exit locations, which are also spawn points for the big nasties. We take three of those in an area and it lets us control the level. Nobody will be able to come in without an invitation. Also, once we take a spawn point, the big nasties won't spawn there anymore, but the small fry will. That means we can bring people in and get them used to the farming under our supervision."

"The teams who have been telling you horror stories, they've been pushing safety margins and leaving the big spawn points intact to keep farming them," Grandpa explained, looking Mama Grace in the eye and speaking in his most reassuring tone. "Shad's analysis matches mine."

"Plus, before we go in, we'll ask Veda to check our information. If we're working on faulty intelligence, she can tell us. She doesn't want to lose her golden ticket," I said.

Dwight leaned back, lacing his hands behind his head. "Y'all seem pretty sure."

I pointed to Sage. "You don't think I'd be letting her near a portal if I had a better alternative, do you? We'll take every precaution."

Juana jumped in. "Then we've got a plan. I vote that we let Shad and his party into the coalition." She held up her right hand.

Her sister and Arjun raised their hands right away. One by one, so did the others.

A system message popped up.

[Do you want to join coalition: the Misfits Guild? Warning, there is a 36-hour cooldown after leaving a coalition before you may rejoin. Yes / No.]

I selected yes, then looked down the table at my new coalition members. "It's time for a council of war." I turned to Grandpa. "Well, major, what's our strategy?"

CHAPTER THIRTY-SIX

WHEN IT'S YOUR FIRST RODEO: A GUIDE

There was only one thing more dangerous than entering a portal no one else had been through yet, and that was going through a portal that another party had entered and never emerged from.

Arjun had been researching reports on all the unused farm levels we knew about, cross-referenced against the patterns of markings on each portal entrance. He had a theory about the markings and what they meant that he'd started to explain to me in great detail over lunch yesterday, but I'd zoned out after about thirty seconds.

Anyway, he had located three potential farming levels for us to consider. One of them had been under the control of a coalition known as the White Roses, but they had pulled out a week ago due to focusing their attentions elsewhere. We had a pretty good idea of the kind of crafting materials and soul coin income it offered, and it wasn't great.

One of the portals was in use by several different groups of unaffiliated miners. Again, it had fairly low returns, but was notable as one of the few portals where no one had died.

Grandpa vetoed that one. "Too much competition," he'd said, "and there's no way we'd be able to negotiate with all those different groups to stay out of the way."

Mama Grace had disagreed. "It would be better to get our feet wet somewhere safe. At least we'd know what we're up against. Some of my crafters are nervous about going in at all. A bunch of ground sloths and giant turkeys don't sound too scary."

"Still a no," Grandpa said.

The third option Arjun suggested was a portal that two different teams had entered on the first day. Neither had returned. However, he said based on his analysis of the markings on the side of the door, the portal shouldn't be much more dangerous than average.

Nobody else had figured out how to interpret the markings, and I wasn't sure I trusted Arjun. He might be seeing something that wasn't really there. I voiced my concerns.

"It'll be easy to test," Grandpa said. "Arjun says he thinks he knows what sort of mobs will be there. If we poke our heads in and it's a different sort of mob, we'll back out."

I conceded that point. I had gotten mixed messages about whether or not miners could attack other miners. While looking for possible new recruits, I'd spoken to other combat teams. They'd all insisted it wasn't possible to fight other miners. We would have to find out for ourselves.

We assembled on the steps of the portal. It was some distance away from any of the levels that the Free Human League were exploiting, and we hoped not to attract too much of their attention. With all of the new recruits, Major Waters ought to have his hands full. Our hope was to dig in and establish our claim to the level before anyone found out.

Grandpa, Frank, Sage, and I were going to be the tip of the spear. We had a couple of other miners who were interested in running missions with us, and we had put them together into two parties, Red Squad and Blue Squad. They would follow us in and work under our direction. I would be evaluating them for good matches.

Behind the secondary squads was Mama Grace's small army of crafters. There were forty-three of them, and we had insisted that each and every one of them would step through the portal once we secured the exits and controlled the level. We weren't necessarily going to make them fight, but if skill seeds dropped, being inside a portal and part of the same coalition would make them eligible to bind those skills.

In addition, Grandpa planned to teach them all at least the basics of combat. "We don't know what we're going to face and when," he had told Mama Grace. "They need to know how to take care of themselves."

"They're not warriors like you," she had argued back, her dark eyes blazing. I had never seen Mama Grace actually angry before.

"They don't have to be. It doesn't take a warrior to defend herself from an attack. I'm not going to make them charge an enemy foxhole," he had added, which hadn't done anything to shake Mama Grace's fears.

We stepped through the portal. A wave of hot, wet air blasted me. I blinked against the bright light and took in my surroundings.

We were in a lush, green jungle. Huge ferns grew all around us, coming up to my shoulder. Tall trees, giant conifers like something out of a California landscape, soared overhead, their wide branches filtering the light. I took a step forward and breathed deep. It smelled good here; unspoiled, fresh.

I cast Call 'em Out, but nothing happened. Red Squad and Blue Squad materialized behind us. Grandpa gestured them to our right and left flanks. "Spread out. High alert," he said. "Anyone spots anything moving, shout and let us know."

Gun in hand, I moved into the forest cautiously. Fallen pine needles crackled under my feet. There were big granite boulders everywhere. An odd lizard scurried up one. It stood up tall on its legs. It was about the size of a cat, and there was a broad fin down its back with ridges along it. It reminded me of a dinosaur. "What does that remind me of? A diplodocus?"

"No." Sage pointed. "It's like a tiny dimetrodon!"

A minute later, another of the same species joined it. They were pink with green stripes. They cocked their heads to the side.

A hissing and rustling in the bushes behind me caught my attention. I spun, raising my gun as a much larger version of the lizards poked its head out from behind a patch of ferns. It yawned at me, showing big, flat, plant-eating teeth.

"Sage," I said, "back away from the babies!" We retreated a little, and the adult dinosaur lumbered across our path. It chuckled at the babies, and they disappeared back into the ferns. *Dinosaurs*, I relayed to the group chat. *Keep an eye out for big ones.*

Arjun thought it would be bird monsters, Grandpa said.

Scientists think dinosaurs turned into birds, Sage stated, *so maybe he wasn't wrong.*

"Great, we get to play Jurassic Park!"

Sage eye-rolled at me. "Wrong era, Shad. Dimetrodons were early Permian."

"Whatever. I'm sure the system is going to get that right." I continued on down the path, wishing my revolver was something bigger, like a .50 cal.

The path started to broaden. Grandpa put up a hand. "I'll go first," he said. "This is starting to look like a game trail. Might go down to water. We don't need to surprise a predator."

He equipped Sage's ghillie suit and slunk ahead. Though he still didn't have a named ability for it, his sneaking had improved a couple of points since we'd started all this. I was watching him go, and even so, by the time he was ten paces ahead of us, I could barely make him out among the waving ferns.

"All right, we follow, but not too close," I told the teams. "Everyone stay in eye contact until we know what we're dealing with."

Grandpa reported in chat, *I've found the watering hole. It's clear so far. Come on and join me.*

We hurried, keeping an eye on the ferns and trees all around us. A river splashed down through a canyon. The trail led right to where the river valley widened out.

A torrent of water poured over a high bank and dropped ten feet into a large pool. Strange-looking fish with spiky fins swam in the pool. A pack of crested dinosaurs were drinking on the other side of the pool. One raised its head and looked at us as we approached.

"Those are parasaurolophus, or something similar," Sage informed us excitedly. "Herbivores. They shouldn't attack us. And they're not Permian at all, they're Cretaceous. Seriously, is the system even paying attention? You can't have dimetrodons and parasaurolophus in the same level, it's just not right."

"But you were fine with the talking, polearm-wielding llamas?"

Elspeth, one of the women on Red Squad, spoke up. "Think they've got soul coins? I'll bet they drop meat and crafting leather. We should try taking them down. I'll toss out a quick Double Crochet and—"

"No," Grandpa said quickly. "Not until we've seen what else is here. We don't need to start a stampede or trigger an event before we've had a chance to look around."

Elspeth grumbled but obeyed. I popped up my map. Veda had paid to unlock an extended mapping ability for Grandpa and me that would let us see details much farther out, to a limit of about a mile and a half. She said she hoped doing that would prompt compatible skills to drop.

I glanced at the map. "Right. Beside the exit we came in, there's two more I can see. There'll be others farther out, but these will let us claim the zone if we take them." I pinged the locations to the whole team. Even if their own maps didn't extend that far, they'd be able to see the markers and head for them.

Unlike mission levels, these farming levels had several exit points. You had to be at one in order to get out. Usually they were defended by enemies, with the exception of the entry location sometimes being undefended.

Blue Squad was talking among themselves.

"Anything to add?" Grandpa asked.

They jerked upright. Three of them had worked together before, but apparently not been willing to form a dedicated party. I had grouped them together to see what they could do and also to check for any personality issues between the three of them.

I had also added my most likely candidate for joining our own team. Esma Argyle was a South African woman whose class offered both healing and overwatch, both of which we could use. She was a **[Battle Angel]** and apparently could transform into a winged Valkyrie in a pinch, with the ability to deal either healing or smiting rays. It was the most overpowered-sounding class I'd ever heard of, yet she had no permanent team and her soul coin income so far was pretty low. So I figured there had to be a catch. I was eager to see her in action.

Esma said, "We were just thinking it would make sense to split up and visit both points, get a better idea of what we're facing here."

Grandpa looked them over. "You think your team can handle it?"

The other three were still conversing. Warren was a **[Robin Hood]**, some sort of archery-using rogue type with a trait like mine that increased his soul coin collection.

Jerome, the other guy on the team, was a [**Freight Train**]. He reminded me of the momentum man we had fought in our opposed mission, right down to the bald head. I hadn't asked him whether he'd ever met anyone with a similar class. He was the team tank, able to soak up big hits and then deliver punishment back to the enemy with a battering ram type ability.

Linsey, their female partner, was a [**Spider Queen**]. When I read the class description, I had been worried that she would be one of the miners who had undergone body modifications, but that wasn't the case. She wore a black gymnastic leotard with a red hourglass pattern on the chest and could cast webs. I didn't know what the rest of her power set looked like in action, but it sounded pretty cool.

"We can take on anything you throw at us," Jerome, the Freight Train, said after a moment. I suspected they had been conferring in their own party chat. That was fine. I wanted them to think about their strengths and weaknesses before agreeing to a mission. And it was good tactical sense not to discuss them in front of others.

Grandpa made a decision. "You can check it out. Do not engage unless you are attacked. Keep us informed of what you find. We need to take two points, but they don't have to be the first two we scout."

Blue squad saluted and moved out. Grandpa turned to Red Squad. "All right, we're heading for objective bravo. Stay close."

I hung back, taking rear guard as Grandpa led the way and Red Squad followed. Frank stumped along toward the front while Sage dropped back by me, pointing out different dinosaurs as we passed them.

"Do you think they'll be all right?" she asked me.

"Who? The dinosaurs?"

"Blue squad."

"I hope so. We haven't seen anything too dangerous yet."

"But two whole other teams died here." Sage shivered.

"You know the farming levels aren't as dangerous as the missions are on average, right?" I said, trying to cheer her up. "And we're all equipped and skilled for missions. I think they'll be all right."

She seemed to consider what I said, then brightened up and pointed. "Ooh, it's a hadrosaur of some sort! I wonder if it's got a nest."

I tried to work the math as we went, guessing how many carnivorous dinosaurs we ought to encounter. I had spotted over a hundred herbivores so far, all looking big enough to make a tasty snack for a Tyrannosaurus or whatever kind of predator the system decided to throw at us. I didn't know what to expect, so I was keeping my eyes open and pinging Call 'em Out anytime I couldn't spot movement.

Up at the front, Grandpa vanished again. *I'm scouting ahead,* he told me privately. *Frank's in the lead. Keep an eye on Red Squad.*

I knew what he meant. If Blue Squad was perhaps a little too ambitious, Red Squad seemed far too timid. Then again, none of them had ever worked together before, and two of them hadn't actually run any missions, though they said they were interested in it.

They had all five been on an independent farming expedition that had broken up more or less amiably when several of the members went to join the Free Human League.

I counted dinosaur numbers again, and that got me thinking. Not about this farming level, but about miners and numbers in general.

I sent a quick message back to Juana. *How many miners did you say Free Humans have?*

I didn't get a reply right away, so I went back to studying Red Squad. Jack was a **[Tank Driver]**. He was a big, muscular man who had been active duty like me, a private, serving in a tank division. Unlike many of the active duty American miners, he had refused to join Major Waters. Jack's skill set included **[M1 Abrams]**, which I couldn't wait to see in combat.

There was an older woman who was a **[Hooker]**. Apparently, she had been a grandmother before she'd been rehabilitated and now looked about forty-five years old. I was concerned about her class until I looked over the skills and sent her an inquiry.

It turned out hooker also meant someone who was deeply into crocheting. All of her skills were apparently crochet-based. She had a single crochet ability, a double crochet ability, and a half-double crochet ability. When I asked what exactly those meant, she said I could wait and see, but that she was a ranged damage dealer. Her name was Elspeth, and she seemed nice.

Then there was Morgan. Morgan worried me. She dressed all in black and wore heavy makeup and a pair of cat ears. She seemed like a goth high school kid, except I guessed her to be at least thirty years old. Her class was **[Tumblr Moderator]** and she carried an oversized hammer in a grip that suggested she didn't really know what to do with it. For some reason, it said ban on the handle.

I very much doubted she would be joining our team. Every time she spoke, it was making a reference to some fandom I'd never heard of. She was very fond of a show called *Supernatural* and another called *Sherlock*. I had accidentally made a reference to *Sherlock Holmes*, one of those movies with Robert Downey Jr. and ever since then, she'd given me the cold shoulder. So apparently, I had said the wrong thing.

Look, I told you my picking up chicks score was a two.

The other two members of Red Squad were a pair of brothers. They had some mission experience but had been kicked off their team when the others had decided to join one of the coalitions; not the Free Humans, the Rise to a New Day faction.

I had briefly confused that group with the Glorious Dawn coalition, but apparently the Rise to a New Day were from Taiwan and got very angry when anyone asked them about the Glorious Dawn team.

Anyway, the two had been in Taiwan on business when they were taken. Bill had picked up a **[Factory Manager]** class. He had explained his abilities to me. The most useful was an **[Automate]** skill that let him craft small golems out of nearby material and send them into battle. He could only control two golems at a time right now, but he was hoping that would increase when he leveled up again. He also had a **[Call OSHA]** ability that could negate hazards if the enemy put them out. We hadn't seen any mission enemies do that, but I had been told farming levels often involved treacherous terrain and enemies who could apply conditions like Sage's Mucking Out the Stalls.

His brother, Bob, was a **[Translator]**. His best ability was **[Babel]**, which disrupted enemy communications for thirty seconds and made them unable to work together.

That sounded useful to me, but maybe not against dinosaurs. I didn't know how much teamwork dinosaurs would be doing. Unless we ran into a pack of velociraptors. *Jurassic Park* had told me those were clever pack hunters, and I didn't have any reason to distrust *Jurassic Park*. I mean, it wasn't like the movies were inaccurate in their depictions of prehistoric life forms, were they?

We got a message coming in from Blue Squad. *We have eyes on the objective. It's on an island. The lake up here is placid, but Spider Queen says she can sense multiple hostiles lurking.*

Wait and observe, Grandpa replied.

At the same time, a message came in from Juana. *Up to about seventy-five hundred now. Why?*

I had been so focused on our own missions and now on getting our coalition up and running, I hadn't stopped to think about numbers. Threshold was big, yes, but it was a human scale of big. Waters's coalition was small, but not *that* small.

Juana was the quickest thinker I had met in Threshold. Definitely smarter than me. And her Procurer class probably gave her some insights.

Juana, we're approaching our objective and I'm probably going to be busy after this, but it just occurred to me that we're missing something here. Waters has lots of miners, but only three mission-capable teams. Veda said we were way ahead, but not in the top ten percent. That makes me think there's a lot more people who can run missions. Waters should have, what, thirty teams? Where are they all?

Juana replied, *Why do we care?*

It's bugging me. I feel like it's important. Ask Veda to look into it. I added a couple more quick notes, then said, *I'm going mute for a bit. Need to concentrate.*

I muted all chats except from people inside this level with me and checked in with Grandpa.

You there yet?

I have eyes on target.

Spotted any enemies?

One large bogey, half a mile away.

I told Red Squad to pick up the pace. We emerged from our forest path at the edge of a cliff.

Grandpa stood waiting. He pointed along the edge. "The next exit is over there," he said. "Take a look."

I stepped up to the edge and peered out.

"Well, crap," I said. "Those are a lot bigger than I'd been expecting."

CHAPTER THIRTY-SEVEN

HOW TO IDENTIFY DINOSAURS

Okay, even *Jurassic Park* did it better than this," I said, surveying the enormous dinosaur nest a quarter of a mile from us. It was perched atop a jutting piece of the same cliff where we stood. The creatures in it were giant winged dinosaurs. Pterosaurs?

"Those are Quetzalcoatlus," Sage said. "And they're not properly dinosaurs; they're azhdarchid pterosaurs."

"Close enough," I retorted.

We could see two now, both at least twenty feet tall. As we watched, one hopped to the edge of the cliff and leapt off, letting its broad wings soar. Its wingspan rivaled a passenger plane.

It circled down over the valley below and startled a herd of four-legged dinosaurs into motion.

The creatures looked like brontosaurus, but I couldn't remember what it was brontosaurus was supposed to be called now. I asked Sage.

"Actually, there's new debate about that whole controversy. For a long time, scientists had thought what they had been calling brontosaurus were actually just immature apatosaurus, but more recent fossil discoveries have suggested that it truly is a separate species," Sage said.

I decided I didn't want to know that much about dinosaurs after all, just how to kill them. I focused on the soaring Quetzalcoatlus as it swooped on one juvenile brontosaurus, its enormous talons outstretched.

I could read its status and health bar.

[Quetzalcoatlus boss, Level 5, 400 HP.]

"We've never taken on anything that big, and there's two of them," I pointed out. "At least, if not more. It's a nest, which means there could be immature young, or if they're some sort of colony creature and we get over there and find a dozen waiting for us."

"Doesn't matter," Grandpa said. "We're going to clear out the nest before we can establish ourselves."

We already knew that farming levels tended to have defended exit points. We had to clear two of those exits and claim them to take control of the level for our coalition. After that, we'd be able to control who was allowed inside, and keep out anyone who wasn't Misfits Guild.

"All right, we clear this exit and the one that Blue Squad has eyes on," Grandpa decided. "Then we bring people through and clear the triangle between our three exit points. After that, we'll regroup and decide where we're going."

"Should we recall Blue Squad?" I asked.

Grandpa sent them a message. *Sitrep?*

We found out what's in the lake, Esma reported back. *A big school of things like piranhas, but bigger and nastier. We think the spawn point is underwater. We'd like to kill one of the local fauna and dump the body in the shallows. Then we can clear out whatever piranhas come to check.*

Think you can manage without backup?

Not a problem, Jerome replied. *We've got this.*

Grandpa looked at me. "They could be missing something." He was clearly inviting my input.

I shifted, scratching my head as I considered. "Could be, but from what I've heard about these levels, a lot of the exit spawns aren't much worse than what they're reporting. I've only heard a couple reports of massive bosses like that." I gestured at the Quetzalcoatlus nest. "My gut says to let them try. If any of them are going to be up to running missions of their own, then they have to be able to make these decisions without one of us babysitting them."

"Agreed." Grandpa turned back to Red Squad and Frank and Sage as he sent a message to Blue Squad.

Go ahead. Keep in touch and don't take any stupid risks.

Understood, Esma replied.

"All right," Grandpa said. "We're going to assault that nest." We watched as the hunting Quetzalcoatlus hauled back a brontosaurus the size of a small elephant to deposit into the nest.

Sage shaded her eyes. "It's got babies," she reported. "At least four of them. They're level two and have forty health each."

"So we've got at least two adults, four juveniles," Grandpa said.

"Think we could lure one of the adults away from the nest?" I asked. "It'd be a hell of a lot easier to deal with one at a time."

"True," Grandpa agreed. "Suggestions?"

I looked at Frank.

He scowled. "I'm not going to like this, am I?"

"Probably not. Here's what I'm thinking."

Frank and I jogged toward the nest. My coat was heavy in the hot sun. Sweat trickled down my back. I had pulled a hat out of my inventory and it helped a little, but it had to be at least ninety-five degrees and as humid as a bad day in Florida. Frank had rivulets of sweat streaming down his red face. "Can't believe you're asking me to do this," he grumbled.

"I'm not asking you to do anything I'm not willing to try," I retorted. "Save your breath. We're going to need it."

We got within two hundred feet of the nest. One of the adults hopped over to the cliff edge, leapt off, and soared upward on a thermal. "I think they spotted us."

Sage messaged me. *The other adult has its wings spread over the nest.*

Right, so they're going for a defensive posture. That's good, I said. We watched the first Quetzalcoatlus as it tilted slightly side to side to keep gliding in a circle about fifty feet overhead like an enormous hawk.

"I think we have its attention," Frank puffed.

"Okay, stop here. Catch your breath." I pulled out a canteen of water, took a swig, and tossed it back in my inventory.

I gave Frank a minute, and then I drew my revolver. **[Aimed Shot]** wasn't my favorite, because it required me to hold still for thirty seconds before firing. In most combat scenarios, that was an eternity. Now, though, I sent all six bullets right at the monster. The Quetzalcoatlus was at the far end of my range. I had to time it just right to catch it as it dipped down close to us, but thanks to Aimed Shot, I knew when I had it in my sights.

[-50 HP]. Yeah, that packed a hell of a punch.

The Quetzalcoatlus screamed and dived toward me. "Got its attention!" I shouted. "Run!"

We hightailed it back the way we had come. There was no sign of Grandpa and the team. We raced toward a stand of conifers that hadn't been there at the edge of the cliff before. *Is it following us?*

Yes! Sage replied. *Right on your tail!*

I put my head down and ran. As we ran, I fired Trick Shot every time it came off cooldown, blindly shooting into the air and letting my skill do its magic. I had the beast targeted, so there was no need to adjust my aim.

You've hit it! Sage said helpfully. *It's down to only 315 hit points!*

The nest?

No movement.

Good. We ran. As we neared the trees, I engaged my Fastest Gun in the West ability and slammed forward so fast I nearly threw up. I covered thirty feet in the blink of an eye.

I was nearly to the grove now. "Frank, do it!" Frank cast Posse. We had learned that his Posse skill pulled from his own images of various guards and military over the centuries, whatever happened to come to mind. Sage had been working with him to come up with some particularly appropriate ideas for helpers.

Now as he cast Posse, a pair of F-18s appeared in the air behind the Quetzalcoatlus. I laughed as I reached the edge of the stand of trees. That was an impressive sight. They dived on the monster dinosaur thing, their guns tearing big holes in the batlike wings.

"Switch!"

Frank cast Emergency Response and he and I swapped places. He ducked into the safety of the conifers as I aimed another Trick Shot at the beast. It hit. We had taken it down almost a half and it was soaring lower and lower. One wing looked like Swiss cheese. The bird dinosaur thing fell sideways and plummeted to the ground.

"Now!" I bellowed and sprinted for it. The rest of our team burst out of the illusionary conifers. That was one of Morgan's abilities, called **[Site Redesign]**, that could project an illusion of an environment she had seen in the last twenty-four hours.

Sage laughed as she sprinted ahead of everyone else. She cast Mucking Out the Stalls under the Quetzalcoatlus and the downed beast was flapping in a pit of sticky mud. "Just like those mastodons in LA!" she shouted. "Eat tar and die!"

The Quetzalcoatlus shrieked. I staggered back, stunned. **[-5 HP]**. My ears rang. I had a **[Stunned]** debuff over my head. I fought to clear my vision, but the debuff wasn't going to go away for another five seconds.

"Hey, that's my trick!" Frank yelled. The F-18s had disappeared as Posse ran out of time. Now he hurled a sonic grenade at the downed Quetzalcoatlus. It impacted as my debuff cleared.

The bird dinosaur was getting to its feet, its useless wings hanging limp at its side. It started to claw its way toward us through the muck.

"I can't get behind it!" Grandpa shouted, irate. "It's too damn big!" He began throwing shuriken at it. One hit; he activated his Pub Dart Champion skill and sent another three at the same place. We chipped the monster down to **[135/400]**.

The brothers Bill and Bob had a pair of matching guandao. I couldn't imagine where they'd picked those up. Long poles with curved blades at one end and golden tassels on the other, they swung the heavy polearms at the creature as it got near.

Frank and I followed suit. I cast Reload, catching the spent brass as if I'd flipped open the cylinder and ejected them manually. It was bizarre having empty casings appear in the air behind the revolver, but it worked. I still had the urge to open the cylinder and check that Reload had worked, but instead I fired another six rounds and repeated. I couldn't help the enormous grin on my face. This was a hell of an ability. I was going to have to get Sage to make me some custom rounds and figure out how to tell Reload which ones I wanted.

Elspeth cast one of her abilities. Loops of yarn the size of ropes lashed around the Quetzalcoatlus' neck and dragged it down to the ground. Now Grandpa Shadow Stepped in. He hit it with his axes over and over as the rest of us poured hot lead into the hapless creature until its health reached zero.

[Victory!] the system announcer roared.

A box popped up.

[Progress toward claiming spawn point: 40/100.]

That had been a good fight. Nobody got hurt. We had used a few big cooldowns, and there was still the nest with the other Quetzalcoatlus to consider.

Grandpa looted the beast. For a change, a loot box popped up. Since we were doing this as a larger team, rather than auto-looting everything to Sage, we were displaying it and having the loot sent to Grandpa until we could divide it up. The creature dropped:

[Dinosaur Leather x100
Dinosaur Meat x50
Dinosaur Claws (crafting material) x6
Luminescent Orbs x2
Skill Seeds x3.]

"Nice," I said. I sent the totals to Veda and said, *Didn't you say missions were the way to go? This guy dropped some pretty good loot.*

Check your XP, she replied back.

I did and saw we had received less than one percent of what we would get from a mission. I did some math.

If this was forty percent of the nest and we had blown several important cooldowns, we'd be able to clear this nest and maybe one other in the next couple of hours.

So—I stopped there. All right, Veda's math worked out. Missions were about ten times more productive. Besides, we were going to have to share these skill seeds with the coalition.

Blue squad, how are you doing? Grandpa asked.

We didn't get a reply right away. Then after a minute, Esma said, *Plan's going fine. Need to refine it slightly.*

What does that mean?

These piranhas have legs. She cut out and one of the other team members said, *We're busy. We're fine.*

"Should I go check on them?" I asked Grandpa.

He bit his lip. Then shook his head. "We need to finish clearing out this nest." Some of the spawn points would begin to recover if you didn't clear them out fast enough.

We probably had another thirty minutes before a new Quetzalcoatlus joined this nest.

I checked, and all four members of Blue Squad were still alive. "All right," I agreed. "Let's finish this."

CHAPTER THIRTY-EIGHT

HOW TO KILL YOUR DRAGON

We regrouped and considered the nest of Quetzalcoatlus.

The adult was reared up over the wall of woven branches, wings extended as if warding us off. I could see four smaller heads poking out over the edge. The babies were still bigger than I was, and I wasn't going to underestimate them.

I looked at the team as we formulated a plan. "We've got to keep the big one grounded," I said. "If it gets in the air, it could pick us off one by one. Elspeth, are you able to do that yarn trick again?"

Elspeth grimaced. "That was my half-double crochet. It has a forty-five-minute cooldown. Do you want to wait that long?"

I shook my head. "Nope. What other options do we have for locking it down?"

"I don't know if Lasso will work," Sage said, scratching her head. "It's awfully big. I could try Lassoing one of the babies and getting it to turn on the others."

"That's a good idea. I'd like to make that nest into dangerous territory for them. We'll want any ground effects aimed at the nest."

"On it," Morgan said immediately. "I'm going to try to keep it as quiet as possible."

"Bob, we'll have you use Babel on them, just in case it helps. I don't know how much co-coordinating they need to do, but it's worth a try."

We ran down a quick plan and then broke off into two smaller groups. Grandpa took Elspeth, Morgan, Jack the Tank Driver, and Sage, while I had Frank, Bob, and Bill.

Jack said he had a big ability, but it took preparation and he couldn't move while it cast, so he would set up south of the nest at the extreme end of his range and try to have the shot. My team would circle wide around the nest and come in from the north, while Grandpa and the mobile members of his squad approached from the south.

I headed out. The clifftop was pretty exposed. I kept an eye on the sky as we went, in case the Quetzalcoatlus had friends.

I sent a quick message to Blue Squad. *How's it going?*

Got the lake nearly clear. There's a big creature in the water that we haven't seen yet. I think once the piranhas are gone, we'll be able to lure it out, Esma replied.

I quickly checked my outside chat channels. There were a couple of pending messages from Juana and one from Mama Grace.

Grace wanted to know how we were doing and whether we'd be ready for the crafters to come in soon. Grandpa had replied to her saying that he'd let her know when it looked safe.

Juana's messages were just for me. *I've been checking. The Free Human League have reached out to several other mission-running teams asking about joining up with them. I think they want more bodies. But there's something else going on that I haven't figured out yet. I'll let you know.* Then, a few minutes later, another message. *Several of the miners who joined the Free Human League in the last week have quit again. They said Sicaris Conglomeration was leaning hard on their sponsors to buy them out, and the ones who didn't cooperate have left. Sicaris is up to something.*

The major had puppet masters pulling his strings. That wasn't surprising. I closed my chats and returned my full attention to the world around me. We had made it far enough north of the nest to circle back around and start our pincher movement.

I informed Grandpa what we were up to.

Moving into position, he replied.

"Heads in the game, everyone," I snapped to my team. "Be careful of friendly fire. Know your backstop. I don't want anyone shooting our teammates."

I got concurrence from all three men. We would come in from the northeast while Grandpa approached from the southeast. That should leave us able to fire into the nest without putting Grandpa's team in the crosshairs.

The Quetzalcoatlus had shifted in its nest so it could look back and forth from where Grandpa's team was approaching to where my team was coming through. There was no doubt it had eyes on all of us, but right now it wasn't leaving its nest.

We're in range, I told Grandpa. *Give the signal.*

Go, he said.

Bob cast Babel on the nest just as an enormous black puddle appeared under it and wrapped writhing tentacles around the inhabitants. That must have been one of Morgan's abilities.

Meanwhile, I fired a special round at the Quetzalcoatlus. It was one of the three bullets Sage had been able to make for me that dealt extra fire damage and applied a Burning debuff. It took the Quetzalcoatlus through the eye. Its health bar dropped to [**390/400**].

One of the babies squawked and raised its wings. There was a green icon over its head that said, [**Tamed by Sage Williams**]. The baby began biting and clawing at its nearest nest mate.

The adult Quetzalcoatlus roared in anger. It waved its wings, but did not take off from the nest.

We started pumping lead into the beast. I reloaded as soon as my cylinder was empty and fired another stream of bullets.

The Quetzalcoatlus reared back and lunged its head forward. An enormous gout of flame burst from its mouth, jetting out toward my team in a fiery fan of destruction. I screamed a warning and activated my Fastest Gun in the West to charge toward the nest but on the other side of the wall of flame.

I heard Bob cry out in pain but didn't have time to check on him. *Bob's hurt,* Bill said in chat.

Get him a potion. I'm on my way, Sage replied. She ran toward us, and I swore at how exposed she was. The flame gout had died out, but I was worried about another attack.

I used Call 'em Out on the Quetzalcoatlus nest. All the monsters focused on me.

"Ah shit," I said as the three babies who weren't under a taming spell climbed over the edge of the enormous nest. It was constructed of entire trees that had been ripped out by the roots and then bound together like twigs and lined with huge clumps of dried ferns. It looked really flammable.

The black goo that had enveloped the adult Quetzalcoatlus was now crawling up the beast's legs like giant anacondas made of tar. They were doing the job of keeping it in place.

Frank, swap!

To his credit, Frank didn't even ask. He activated Emergency Response and suddenly I was a hundred feet from the nest. The babies didn't even miss a beat as they turned and waddled straight for me. They were damned fast, scrabbling across the rocky ground on their legs and wingtips, hungry beaks wide open.

I put my head down and ran. "Shoot 'em while they're on me!" I yelled. "Focus fire on whichever one is lowest." I glanced over my shoulder, targeted one, and fired a Trick Shot at it. It was now at [**25/40**] health, which was way too damn high for my liking. The firearm team concentrated on that one and it dropped a moment later.

The adult Quetzalcoatlus screamed in rage. *Uh-oh,* Grandpa said in chat. *Something happened. It's got an enraged buff. Now, does double damage and—*as he wrote, I heard the ripping sound as the Quetzalcoatlus tore free of its bonds.

I had time to read the enrage myself.

[Bereaved. This parent has lost a child. Now does 100% more damage and cannot have its motion constrained in any way.]

"Ah shit," I said. *Don't hit the babies anymore,* I called out in chat. *I think it'll stack.*

One hundred percent more damage was bad enough, but if killing the rest of the babies increased the enrage or gave it more invulnerabilities, we were really, really fucked. I retargeted the adult. **[350/400 HP]**. I fired and hit it.

Jack, where's our fire support? Grandpa asked.

You guys are moving the target way too much! I can't track it. You've got to keep it in place for longer.

It was sitting on the nest for half a goddamn hour! What more do you want?

The babies were no longer focused solely on me as my Call 'em Out had worn off. They dove onto my team, who scattered and ran.

This was bad. I cursed myself. We hadn't made enough contingency plans. Hadn't made any, had just charged in expecting this to work. Someone was going to get killed because I hadn't taken things seriously enough.

The Quetzalcoatlus adult hopped to the edge of the cliff and then jumped away, spreading its enormous wings.

"Bring it down," I shouted. "Anyone, anything you can do, bring it down. We've got to get it back on the ground." I fired another of Sage's special burning rounds. They did one tick of burning damage every second for thirty seconds after a hit. It wasn't nearly enough. I needed something more. I needed to be able to protect my team.

Behind me, I heard Bill shout out "Emergency Staff Meeting!" as he cast his spell. I had found several of our new allies had a habit of yelling the name of their spells like we were in a shonen anime. I might have been tempted to do that myself, but I could picture the look of utter contempt Grandpa would give me if I were to yell "Trick Shot!" every time I fired.

The Quetzalcoatlus screamed and plummeted below the edge of the cliff. "We've got thirty seconds," Bill shouted, saying it in chat at the same time.

Before it came back, I made a decision. Maybe it was the wrong one. I'd find out later. *Kill the other babies. Don't worry about a buff. We'll deal with the adult when we can, but we have to be able to make a stand.*

I got a series of quick acknowledgements in our chat.

Grandpa teleported in behind one of the babies and hit it with a coup de grace. It disappeared into a heap of broken flesh. "They don't count as bosses," Grandpa shouted. "You can use anything on the babies."

Sage's tamed beast was still squawking and flapping its wings. It had not seen fit to try to leave the nest. I was fine with that. We turned and brought the third baby down next to its brother. *Mama's coming back,* Elspeth relayed. *And she looks pissed. Three times damage and she's immune to any kind of crowd control.*

Okay, so she would be in the air and hitting like a truck. We had to find a way to distract her. I fired a Trick Shot as soon as she came into range, even though she wasn't yet back over the edge of the cliff.

Her health was at [**300/400 HP**]. We were getting her down, but this was going to hurt. *Okay, anyone have anything they haven't shared with us yet?* I asked. I remembered that most of our new friends had only two or three abilities each, compared to the five my team was rocking on average. Missions really were the best way to skill up.

I messaged Blue Squad. *Any chance you can help us?*

Kind of busy here, Esma replied. *Loch Ness Monster showed up.*

There was a blinking chat notification that said Juana had sent me a message or two, but I didn't have time for that.

As the Quetzalcoatlus soared back into the air, I yelled to Frank, "Get as far away as possible and be ready to swap again. Head for the trees." Call 'em Out was just about off cooldown. Frank put his head down and ran toward the edge of the forest. If we could force the Quetzalcoatlus to follow me in there, its air superiority advantage would be lost.

I relayed the plan to the team. As soon as the Quetzalcoatlus came shrieking down, stooping on the edge of the nest where Sage was applying Raise Your Spirits to the injured member of our team, I glanced up. Frank wasn't quite to the edge of the forest, but it would have to do.

"Frank, now!" I yelled as I cast Call 'em Out. The birds screamed.

A notification popped up.

[Achievement! Got Their Attention! Congratulations! You have successfully taunted 50 creatures with your Call 'em Out ability. You will now know the rank and health of all creatures you have taunted. Current taunt target: Quetzalcoatlus, Level 5, boss, 270/400 HP.]

Frank cast Emergency Response and we swapped. The Quetzalcoatlus screamed as it charged at me. I could feel it zeroing in on me, the back of my head burning. Must have been part of my new achievement. I cast Fastest Gun in the West and dashed straight to the edge of the forest, narrowly avoiding an enormous conifer. I darted around the tree and ran.

The Quetzalcoatlus was on me. I could hear it in the canopy overhead. Branches and giant pine cones crashed to the ground around me. Then a whole tree fell right across my path. I dodged to the side.

"Everyone make it to the forest before this runs out!" I yelled. I had ten seconds left on my taunt. We ran through the woods.

"I can't see through the branches!" Bill yelled. "How are we supposed to hit it?"

"We can't hit it? It can't hit us!" Sage said. But a bunch of falling trees contradicted her. The Quetzalcoatlus smashed into the forest just ahead of us, knocking down at least six trees. I dodged the nearest one.

Call 'em Out ran out, and it would be minutes before I could cast it again. The burning feeling in my skull died away. It must be after someone else now.

Somebody yelled in pain, but I didn't have time for that. I was taking another shot. Enough of our attacks found the mark to make a dent. The creature was down to **[204/400 HP]**. But I was afraid any attack from it would be fatal. *Spread out! Don't clump up! If it uses that fire breath again—* Even as I was sending the message, the Quetzalcoatlus opened its mouth and spat out a gout of flame. It turned its head as it went, and the fallen trees went up like torches. The flame spread to the still-standing trees.

I coughed and waved a hand as smoke began to blow into my eyes.

Is it taking any damage from the flames? Grandpa asked. *I can't see it from here.*

A little, I replied in chat. I grabbed a bandana from my inventory, dumped some water on it, and knotted it around my nose and mouth. The moistened cloth helped cut down on the smoke. My eyes stung as I peered through the trees, looking for the monster.

"Retreat!" I shouted as the flames lapped higher. *Retreat!*

I need help, Elspeth said in chat. *I'm pinging my map.*

She wasn't very far from me, so I doubled back, keeping an eye over my shoulder for the Quetzalcoatlus. I checked my Trick Shot, and the beast was out of range. *As soon as anyone has eyes on that thing, yell in chat,* I said.

Elspeth was trapped under a fallen log that had caught both of her legs. Her health was down to **[20/70 HP]**. I bent over her. "Take a potion."

"I don't have any." I remembered how expensive they were, and that Elspeth was unsponsored. I pulled one out of my inventory and handed it to her. She drank it gratefully, but it only took her up to fifty HP. Veda promised to get us stronger potions soon. I wanted something that would do my whole health in one gulp.

I bent and lifted. The tree didn't budge. I checked my map. No one else was close to us. They were retreating out the other side of the forest. I checked again on my Trick Shot targeting, and the Quetzalcoatlus was still out of range.

I grabbed a sturdy-looking fallen branch that had snapped off of one of the trees, and began levering it under the trunk next to Elspeth's legs. I pushed down and grunted. The trunk rolled an inch or two forward, then settled back down.

I swore to myself. This wasn't going to work. I didn't have the strength to move this on my own, and none of my abilities were any help. There was a hideous screeching sound way too close by. I checked my targeting. The Quetzalcoatlus was in range.

I debated firing a shot and decided not to. Maybe it would miss us.

In chat, I said, *It's close. I think it's hunting me.*

Leave me, Elspeth replied in chat. I guessed she was trying to not attract attention. Or maybe she was trying to make sure the others knew that she had asked me to leave her. *Get out of here.*

I wanted to leave. I wanted it more than anything. This woman was no one to me. I'd only met her this morning. She had volunteered, knowing what this meant. I had family here, family who needed me. I didn't want to die playing some alien game for a prize that meant nothing to me. I wanted to go home.

Instead, I bent and jammed the stick under the trunk and leaned on it again. The trunk rolled forward another few inches. When I shifted the stick, it didn't roll back. I levered it again.

The Quetzalcoatlus screamed again, closer now. *My leg is broken,* Elspeth said. *Even if you get this off, I can't run.*

"Then I'll fucking carry you," I said aloud, forgetting myself in my frustration and anger. I threw myself on the stick, and the trunk rolled free. I yanked Elspeth out from under the last bit of it.

The Quetzalcoatlus screamed, and I knew it had heard me.

CHAPTER THIRTY-NINE

HOW TO SPOT MOLES IN YOUR ORGANIZATION BEFORE THEY TURN

I threw Elspeth over my shoulder, fireman style, and ran. In chat, I said, *It's after me. I can hear it.*

I pinged the mini-map where I was. Grandpa replied, *Converging on you.*

Come here. Jack pinged the map at the edge of the forest, a straight line from where I already was. I adjusted my heading and ran. We hadn't heard from Jack at all during the battle, and I hoped he had something up his sleeve.

A tree crashed down inches from me. I glanced back over my shoulder. The Quetzalcoatlus was clawing its way through the forest, using its wings like forearms to knock trees down. It was maybe thirty yards behind me. I fired a Trick Shot and got it down to **[170/400]** health. I wasn't going to kill it, but every little bit of damage helped. Grandpa and Sage would have a chance. I hoped, I prayed, and I ran.

Elspeth screamed and shouted. She cast something behind us. "Ha!" she said triumphantly. "Triple crochet for the win."

"What's that do?"

"Big web of sticky netting right across its path. It has to go around. That'll buy us a second or two."

What I wouldn't do for armor-piercing rounds or something bigger than a .44 Magnum, like the kind of rounds they shot out of battle cruisers.

Suddenly, dots appeared on my mini-map. The rest of my team was coming in. A moment later, Grandpa and Bob burst out of the trees in front of me. Bob dropped to a one-knee-down shooting stance and began firing away. I saw Frank's dot toward the edge of the forest. "Hang on!" he yelled.

A moment later, the weight on my shoulder doubled as Frank swapped places with Elspeth. I yelped and dropped him. "You could have warned me!" I shouted as I turned and darted ten feet to the right.

The Quetzalcoatlus was barreling through the trees at us, snapping giant red-wood trees like sticks. "Sorry," Frank puffed, getting up from the ground and aiming his gun at the monster.

It opened its mouth to breathe fire, but I was ready this time. I fired my own Trick Shot with my last incendiary round straight into its mouth. The round met the blast wave and exploded. The Quetzalcoatlus's beak blew up, doing forty points of damage in one hit.

I let out a cheer. Grandpa threw knife after knife at the beast, chipping its health down. Bill appeared and slashed with his guandao. In the distance, I heard Sage shouting at Morgan to let her help, and Morgan yelling back that they needed to stay clear. I made a mental note to thank Morgan if I got out of this. Sage was close enough to heal us, but none of her other abilities were going to make a difference in this fight.

The Quetzalcoatlus screamed and swiped at the nearest tree with its claws.

Get clear! Jack said in chat. *Now!*

There was a whistling noise overhead. I dove out of the way. Frank, Bill, and Bob scattered.

The forest exploded. Bits of flying Quetzalcoatlus and tree-trunk shrapnel whizzed over my head as I ducked, pulling the edge of my coat up to protect my face.

What the hell was that?

[Artillery Barrage]. *Sorry, it took me all fight to get a clear shot with that thing in one spot long enough to get it off.*

You should have led with that!

I can't, the target has to be hit by three other members of your party or group first and—it's a pain in the ass, really.

[Victory!] the system announcer shouted. **[Team Twofeather and Red Squad have defeated the Quetzalcoatlus nest. Claim nest? Yes / No.]**

[Yes], I selected as I ran forward to check on Grandpa. "Sage, get over here!" Sage bounded toward me.

[Shad Williams has claimed a portal,] the system proclaimed. I pumped my fist. "One more to go!"

Grandpa was lying in the pine needle and branch debris a few dozen yards from the crater full of Quetzalcoatlus chunks. He blinked as I stood over him. "I'm all right," he said. "Just got knocked down by the blast."

I gave him a hand up anyway. His health bar confirmed that he'd only taken ten points of damage.

A moment later, Sage cast Raise Your Spirits on him. "That's nice," Grandpa said. He shrugged his shoulders and limped over toward the boss, even though I knew he wasn't hurting now.

"Now you're just milking it," I said as he touched the largest chunk of dead Quetzalcoatlus.

The loot list scrolled out for us, including two skill seeds. Grandpa nodded contentedly. "This will go toward getting the team up to speed," he said. "Every single one of them's getting a skill seed if they're compatible. They earned it." *Everybody meet back at the nest*, he said in chat.

We made our way out of the forest. I felt relieved and shaken at the same time. As I reached the edge of the forest, Elspeth, standing on one leg with a fallen branch as a makeshift crutch, lunged forward and threw her arms around me.

"Thank you," she said into my shoulder. "Thank you. I thought I was dead."

I patted her awkwardly and realized I still had my gun in my hand. I holstered it.

"I'm just glad you're all right," I managed gruffly. It took me a minute to disentangle her.

We all made it back to the nest. Everyone had taken some damage. Sage healed what she could, but even with our health bars full, the shock was going to take some getting over.

The Quetzalcoatlus nest shimmered and disappeared as we approached, leaving in its place a broad archway. Grandpa sighed. He said, "We'll tell Grace to start sending people through. We should check on Blue Squad."

I checked. There were no messages from the team. I sent one asking how they were doing.

I turned to Grandpa. "I want to go check on Blue Squad. They should have reported in by now."

"Take backup," Grandpa said.

"I'll bring Frank and Morgan," I said after a minute's consideration.

"All right, we'll start bringing groups through." He turned his attention back to the portal and I saw the message he sent to Mama Grace. *Have the first two groups come through now.*

I collected Frank and Morgan. Frank grumbled about having to head out again immediately. "We just need to make sure Blue Squad's okay," I said.

We headed cross-country toward their location. The first bit was along the top of the cliff where the going was easier. I kept a wary eye on the sky. As we went, I checked my messages from Veda. *I've been looking into the backing of some of the recent applicants to the guild. Some of them have had their sponsors change hands recently. I'm trying to investigate, but it seems like the new sponsors are shell corporations. I don't know who's really behind them.*

That was a worrying thought. Some of our new members were plants maybe, put in by Sicaris Conglomeration or some other enemy we didn't yet know. They might be up to something.

Juana sent me a quick message. *I'll be on the second team coming through. See you on the other side.*

I'm checking on Blue Squad, but I'll be back shortly. Grandpa's at the portal now, I replied.

I tried Blue Squad again. *What's going on?*

A moment later, there was a system message in my chats.

[Warren Black has left the coalition.
Linsey Black has left the coalition.
Jerome Smith has left the coalition.
Warren Black has claimed a portal.]

That was everyone but Esma. I sent her a message. *What the hell is going on? What's wrong?* And another to Grandpa. *You see this?*

I do. Be careful. Find out what's going on. We've brought two teams through, but I'm holding off on any more until we know.

"What's all this about?" Frank asked, clearly reading the same messages I was.

"I don't know, but I'll find out and someone is going to be sorry."

I sent a message to Veda, giving her the names of the three miners who had just left our coalition. *Look into their sponsors specifically. What's going on here?*

We ducked into the primordial jungle, heading south toward Blue Squad's last known whereabouts. I checked my mini-map regularly. They might not be in our coalition anymore, but I had the personal information on each of them, and that should mean they showed up on my mini-map when we got in range. I hoped.

Morgan stopped dead. I nearly ran into her. "What's wrong?"

"I just got a notification that someone has entered this zone," she said. "It's my level two class trait, **[Logged On]**. Lets me know who's in a level with me. Only as soon as they appeared, they disappeared again. Like they have some way of removing themselves."

"Who was it?"

"There was a whole list of names. At least ten of them," she said. "I didn't recognize any of them."

Between them and the three deserters, that would make thirteen. More than we had. We'd only been able to recruit one full team and one partial, but our opponents seemed to be better off.

I sent a worried message back to Grandpa. "You two lay low, but I've got to scout out what's going on," I told my team.

We were nearly to the edge of the forest. I could see the lake and island that Blue Squad had described on my mini-map. A glowing white circle icon in the center of the island must be the newly claimed portal. And there were dots everywhere. Red ones. My mini-map was showing me at least a dozen different players. No names, just dots. I was sure that the red was not good news.

"Hold up here," I told my team. There was one white dot not too far away, not moving, labeled Esma. I tried to talk to her again, but she still wasn't answering. "She's not answering, but she's not dead."

"It's a trap," Frank said at once. "She's acting as bait to lure you out."

That was a possibility. If any of the enemy had an advanced map skill like I did, they'd see me coming. "Maybe, or maybe they've got her knocked unconscious and tied up somewhere." I didn't see any red dots in the immediate vicinity of Esma's indicator. "We need to know," I said. "You two wait here."

"No," Frank said. He set his jaw stubbornly. "We're coming with you. We stick together." Morgan looked worried, but nodded.

"All right," I said. "Just try to stay under cover."

Esma's dot didn't move as we approached. There was a clearing up ahead, and she must have been there. I checked again for other dots and saw nothing. I took a deep breath. "I'm going to check it out."

I stepped into the clearing. Esma was ten feet up in the air. Her angel wings were extended. They were made of rainbow feathers and were sharply pulled out away from her shoulder. Two giant black spikes pinned her wings between a pair of trees. She hung seemingly unconscious in midair. Her health bar was at **[10/90]**. This had all the earmarks of a trap.

The smart thing might be to leave Esma here. Unconscious. Alive. Pinned. I couldn't just stand there and watch her suffer. She needed help.

None of us had a ranged heal. I pulled out bandages from my inventory and approached. I could just reach her outstretched foot. Warning Frank and Morgan to keep watch, I wound a bandage around her foot and saw her health beginning to tick upward.

When it reached **[20/90]**, her eyes fluttered open. She moaned, "Get me down!"

"I'll try," I said. "Can you retract your wings or something? It's going to be hard to get those stakes out."

She shook her head. "No, not while they're pinned like that."

I asked Morgan to come out. "I'm going to have to lift you up on my shoulders," I said. "You'll have to pull the spikes out. Do the left-hand one first. The right-hand tree has that branch right below where she's dangling that I think she'll be able to get her feet on once her left-hand wing is freed. Esma, do you understand this?"

"I'll try," she groaned.

Morgan clamored to my shoulders. I grit my teeth as she stomped down hard, trying to reach the stake. "Almost got it," she grunted. "Almost there." She yanked it free and threw it to the ground.

There was an enormous cacophony of noise, like a dozen bells ringing at once. "Get the other one, now!" I shouted.

"Take a step to your right," Morgan said. "Another one." I managed as best I could.

"Frank, watch for trouble." I checked my mini-map. Three red dots were inbound on us. I pinged the map. "Coming in that way."

"I'll delay 'em," Frank said, and crashed off through the brush toward the hostiles. Morgan yanked and pulled, working the black spike free. She pulled it out, and Esma's body collapsed into Morgan's arms.

The precarious weight on my shoulders overbalanced me. I fell backward, trying to push Morgan and Esma forward and upright as I fell. We all went down in a tangle of limbs. **[-5 HP]**, the system notification informed me.

"Get off me," I moaned. Morgan shifted and rolled free. Esma's body was still half on mine, but I sat up. She had lost some health, but the bandaging buff was still active. I grabbed a potion out of my inventory and tossed it to her. She guzzled it down.

She blinked, looking much better. "Thanks," she said. "I didn't think you'd come for me."

"They did," I said grimly, getting to my feet. "Stay back. Morgan, if you can help, follow me."

I took off after Frank. His dot had converged on the three hostiles. They weren't far ahead now. I crashed through the underbrush after them, quick-drawing my gun. As soon as I could, I got one targeted and threw out my first Trick Shot.

I smashed through a deadfall and found myself looking at a standoff. Frank was crouched behind a tree. He had Restrained one of the opponents in the middle of the clearing. The other two were using a large boulder as cover. One had some sort of ice-based attack and was lobbing icicles.

I switched my targeting to the lowest health enemy and fired again. I followed up with several normal shots. He was at the edge of my range, but I hit more than I missed. I emptied my six shots and immediately reloaded.

I didn't recognize any of these strangers, but they all had Free Human League tags over their heads. I relayed that information back to Grandpa, but didn't have time to watch his answer.

Morgan used her weird, black tar anaconda ability to hold the third attacker in place. Frank and I finished off the first, then targeted the one Frank had Restrained.

As his hit points reached zero, an achievement popped up.

[Kill 10 opposed miners. Current progress: 5/10.]

I had just killed another two humans, and I didn't feel nearly as badly about it as I had before. Not after what they had done to Esma.

The third man writhed in the grip of the tar anacondas. "How long can you hold that for?" I asked Morgan.

She grit her teeth. "A couple minutes. Why?"

I strode over to the man and put my gun to his head. His name was Phil Wajowski, and he was a **[Beer and Pretzels Salesman]** by class. Inspect also said he had a Navy rank of ensign.

I displayed my lieutenant title. "What are you doing here, Wajowski?" I demanded.

"Following orders," he snarled.

"From Major Waters?"

"The brass put him in charge."

"Then he tells you to do something illegal, like attack fellow Americans, fellow servicemen," I said, "and that's when you tell him to get fucked. We weren't hurting anyone. You even know why you're here?"

"Have to protect coalition interests. We needed growth room. We need to be able to train for running missions." He strained against the tar anacondas.

I jabbed the muzzle of my gun against his head, and he stopped wiggling. It was tough to remember that a shot to the head wouldn't necessarily kill him. Back on Earth, using my gun like this would be putting his life in danger. Here it just got his attention. "That asshole wants me and my team because we're already mission-runners. He's trying to squeeze us by attacking our friends, and I won't stand for it." I resisted the urge to kick Wajowski somewhere that would hurt. "What's the plan? How many reinforcements do you have?"

"Lots waiting, just as soon as we secure the level."

He was right. They needed another portal to link to this one in order to claim a beachhead and bring people through. They had stolen our portal, the one that should have given us a claim to this zone, but they couldn't claim it yet either.

I sent a quick message to Veda asking how many they could bring through with a single exit claimed. I suspected we had the same limit.

I relayed everything back to Grandpa. *What now?*

He paused for a moment before replying, *If you can secure him without risk to yourself, do it. Bring Esma back to the rest of us, but keep an eye on her.*

I'm pretty sure she wasn't in on this, I said. *You didn't see how they had her strung up. She looked like a crucifix.*

Watch her anyway. I pulled a length of cord out of my inventory and bound Wajowski's hands and feet. "I know you're in contact with your friends and they'll be here in a minute." I had been watching my mini-map and, so far, no new red dots had appeared. "I want you to tell all of them that this isn't what they think. I want them to know we don't have to fight."

Wajowski spat at my feet. "You're a disgrace to your uniform."

That got my back up. "My oath still stands. Major Waters is the one selling out to the aliens."

"Prove it," Wajowski challenged.

I couldn't. I knew deep down I was right, that the REMF had made a deal with his sponsors to get whatever he could out of this, but proving it was another matter.

"Let's get back," I told my teammates. We made for our own portal as fast as we could.

CHAPTER FORTY

WHAT TO DO WHEN YOUR HUNTING PERMIT IS 65 MILLION YEARS OUT OF DATE

When we got back to the former Quetzalcoatlus nest, Grandpa had already organized our team for war.

The coalition had sent through ten more miners, including Juana, but not her sister or her mother. Grandpa assigned Juana and four of the less experienced miners, including Dwight, to stand watch over the portal. That was our limit until we got a second portal and confirmed our claim on the level.

Juana held a shotgun like she knew how to use it, keeping the muzzle aimed at the sky. She had a fiercely determined look in her eyes. "They will not take this from us," she said. "I'm tired of being pushed around."

"What's the plan?" I asked.

"We scouted on a third portal location," Grandpa said.

"He means me," Sage said brightly, popping up. "I went and found it."

I bit my tongue. I wanted to yell at Grandpa for letting Sage go off on her own into who-knew-what danger. Just because we'd killed the Quetzalcoatlus didn't mean that the local dinosaurs were safe. And what if she had run into some of the Free Human League assholes? It was done, and there was no sense in starting a fight now.

"We're going to get over there and hit it hard," Grandpa said. "From what Sage says, we think it's a survive-spawn-waves challenge."

I'd heard about those from other miners who had done farming levels. Instead of having a boss already active at a portal site, like the Quetzalcoatlus nest, the spawns didn't activate until we humans interacted with the point. Then they'd spawn a set number of waves. If you survived the waves and killed the boss at the end, the portal was yours.

"Do we have time for that?"

"The Free Humans will be scrambling to get to a second portal themselves before we take ours. The fact that we have one scouted should give us the edge, but we have to move fast," Grandpa said.

He broke us up into three teams for faster movement, putting me at the head of one, himself at the head of another, and giving Elspeth the third. We left Esma back at our claimed portal to finish recovering. Plus, if our rearguard was attacked, she'd be able to help protect them.

First team was me, Sage, Bill, Bob, and two of our newly arrived allies, Amy and Lejeune, who were both crafters and obviously terrified of being here.

Sage led the way. "It's down off of the cliffs. There's a slope in this direction we can get down, or we could go around the long way. I think Grandpa's going that way." Sage chattered as she kept up a sprightly pace. I kept an eye on my team.

Veda pinged me. *The three had their contracts bought out by a holding company two days ago. I traced the company. It's a front for Sicaris. This is a hostile takeover bid. And you're right. Like you, they're limited in how many they can bring through until they've established their claim. You claimed the first portal, so you get up to four teams, while they're limited to no more than three.*

That meant we had a slight numbers advantage. But my guess was the people Waters had sent through were better equipped and ready to kill, whereas our backup were mostly crafters who had never set foot inside a portal until now.

Amy and Lejeune kept looking around and commenting on how real everything seemed. "That's because it is real," Sage said. "We're really feeling this. We're really here."

From what Veda had said, I was pretty sure we definitely weren't really here. I thought it was all a computer hallucination being played in our minds, and I suspected that we didn't actually have physical bodies right now. We just thought we did. But I wasn't going to bring that up and disturb anyone more than they already were.

The cliff dropped away steeply here in a barely navigable slope. I went as quickly as seemed safe. I didn't want to twist an ankle. The others followed my lead. We reached the bottom. "Where now?" I asked.

Sage pointed at a hill about a quarter of a mile off. It was conical, like a grassed-over volcano. "It's at the top of that."

We took it at a run. There was a white marble altar in the exact center of the hill, which stood about thirty feet higher than the surroundings. Four imprints on the altar looked like clawed footprints. I sent a message to the other teams. Grandpa replied, *We're almost there. Go ahead and start.*

I gestured at the team. "Put a hand on each of those claw marks," I said, standing clear and keeping a sharp watch. Amy and Lejeune shuddered, but did as they were told. Sage slapped her hand down, and so did Bob.

There was a rumbling sound. A beam of light shot skyward from the altar. My team fell back. *What the hell was that light show?* Elspeth asked in chat.

We just started the event, I said.

Well, we're about half a mile out, so hang on until we get there.

Amy screamed, "velociraptors!"

A dozen chest-high dinosaurs, their slathering mouths open to reveal enormous sharp teeth, claws ready to rend, were charging up the hill.

"Those aren't velociraptors," Sage complained, but I didn't wait to hear what they were. Instead, I Trick Shot one in the head. **[7/12]** appeared over its health bar. I kept firing.

Sage had her T-Shirt Cannon out. She fired at the nearest raptor, even as she cast Cowgirl Cheer on all of us. A barrage of flaming, tightly bundled T-shirts blasted out of the mouth of her weapon, exploding on impact.

Amy and Lejeune fired their weapons. Lejeune was screaming as he shot wildly. He had what looked like a giant plastic dart gun that fired bright purple projectiles. They exploded on impact. They looked damn cool, but my rounds did as much damage. I took down my raptor, changed targets, took down another, reloaded.

We picked them off as they came. Bill, Bob, and I had to shoot the majority of them. Sage's T-Shirt Cannon took ten seconds between reloads, and Amy and Lejeune were terrible.

The system announcer proclaimed, **[Victory! Round one of five cleared!]**

"There's Grandpa!" Sage shouted, pointing. Grandpa's team puffed up the hill and joined us just as the next wave spawned.

This time, it wasn't velociraptor-like creatures. It was some sort of bipedal dinosaur with enormous, bowling-ball-smooth heads with round protuberances around their edges. "Those are pachycephalosaurs!" Sage said as the dinosaurs charged at us, heads lowered.

We shot them. Grandpa threw shuriken, or Shadow Stepped in to Scalp. I was amused that his Scalp move worked perfectly on these bald dinosaurs.

Everyone used whatever abilities they had. With ten of us here now, we made quick work of the dinosaurs. **[Round two of five cleared,]** the announcer told us.

Elspeth's team arrived as we waited for the third round to start. *Anyone have eyes on Blue Squad or their minions?* I asked chat.

No, Juana replied. *We've seen nothing here.*

I hoped that was a good thing. We didn't know how long until they managed to claim their own nest. I just prayed we could clear this fast enough.

The third wave started. This time, it was a combination of the velociraptor-like creatures and some tiny, chicken-sized dinosaurs that darted in, spitting acid at us. I kicked one away with my boot as I fired a Trick Shot through a velociraptor's skull.

Sage had tamed one velociraptor and was sending it around to chomp the little baby dinosaurs. Grandpa couldn't use coup on the little dinosaurs, but he Shadow Stepped between every velociraptor, hitting them with his axe and darting away.

Elspeth threw out a long line that wrapped around two big and three little dinosaurs and wound them up into a tight knot. Amy threw a fireball at the knot, and the dinosaurs shrieked in agony as a smell of roasted meat that was disturbingly appetizing rose off of their flaming scaly bodies.

I was so damn glad for my Gun Belt and its almost infinite reloads. I had been through hundreds of rounds, but I still had over two thousand available to me at the merest thought. I'd give a lot for a couple of special rounds like Sage promised she could make for me, though. It was so slow to hit one dinosaur at a time and chip it down.

[Round three of five cleared,] the announcer proclaimed.

This time we only got about thirty seconds before a pair of smaller flying dinosaurs—I thought they were pteranodons—attacked us while we were simultaneously surprised by six saber-toothed tigers leaping out of the grass at us.

I spun as I spotted a tiger, firing into its open mouth. It landed on me. I went down hard. It clawed, but only caught my drovers coat.

Grandpa appeared over me, slamming his axes into the tiger's skull. It yowled and then slumped forward, a dead weight on me. Grandpa and Frank hauled the sabertooth off and I leapt up.

Sage had Lassoed one of the flying dinosaurs. It was like she had her own vicious kite. She used her lariat to send it diving on a saber-toothed tiger and rip the creature's back open with its sharp claws.

One of our miners shrieked and went down into the grass. We ran and pulled the saber-toothed tiger off of him, but he'd taken deep wounds. Sage cast her healing spell on him. His health ticked up, but he laid like he was comatose. I didn't see a debuff. I thought he was just shell-shocked.

We didn't have time to worry. We were dealing with another round of attacks, this time from giant sloths. They moved fast. One of them burrowed up from the ground right in front of me. It dug out a car-sized mound of dirt and exploded out of it.

I shot it in the face until I was out of bullets. I reloaded and shot it again as my team focused fire.

It was chaotic. It was insane. None of these creatures belonged in the same geological age with each other.

When we finally cleared wave four, all of us had taken injuries. Sage cast Raise Your Spirits on us all. She looked tired.

"Be careful," I told her. "Looks like it's taking something out of you." We didn't have any kind of mana-type resource, but I could tell from Sage's face that this was a strain on her.

"I'll be all right," she said.

"Seriously, drink some water." I handed her my canteen and she drank as we waited for the final round. I worried about what we were going to get.

The ground beneath our feet shook. For a moment I thought it was another attack of giant sloths. I stepped back, but the rumbling was everywhere. I worked to keep my balance. Several of our team fell.

"What is it?" I checked my mini-map. The ground under our feet was solid red. "There's a boss," I said. "It looks like it's under our feet. Get off the top of the hill, now!"

I grabbed Sage by the hand and sprinted for the edge. Most of the rest of the team heeded my warning. Elspeth was trying to get the man who was lying on the ground to move. "Hurry!" I yelled, but it was too late.

The ground cracked open. Dirt fell away as something enormous shot up from under our feet. Elspeth was thrown clear. I heard her hit the ground. I couldn't see her or her health bar, and I hoped she was all right.

It was an enormous mastodon. Larger than any mastodon could possibly be. It had to be forty feet tall and at least as long. I couldn't even get a good look at its head.

"Ah shit!" I heard someone yell. "How are we supposed to kill that?"

Sage cast Mucking Out the Stalls at its feet. The ground effect spell only covered the area where its two hind legs touched the ground, but it immediately began to struggle against the muck, so the spell must have done something.

I fired. My bullet did five points of damage, leaving it with **[495/500]** health. It was bigger than the Quetzalcoatlus had been.

"Hit it with everything you've got," Grandpa ordered and began throwing his shuriken.

We blasted. We hit it. We cast spells. Morgan used her tar anacondas to tangle up its snout and tusks.

The beast thrashed. It brought its front legs up off the ground and smashed them back into the dirt, kicking up a blast wave of dirt and rock that knocked me and everyone else around me off our feet.

I hit the ground, taking ten points of damage. I bounced back up as fast as I could.

The mastodon's feet were raised again. It brought them down. I dodged to the side just in time, and the enormous foot smashed into the dirt less than a yard from where I stood.

My knees buckled. I hit the ground on hands and knees. I didn't bother to get all the way up, just to one knee, and started firing. The creature was so big it was impossible to miss.

We chipped away at its health. 450. 425. 400.

There was a message in our party chat from Jack, the Tank Driver. *I've got it bracketed. Everyone clear. Except Shad. Stay where you are and try not to die.*

Everyone scattered. My impulse told me to run too, but I stood my ground and fired another Trick Shot at the mastodon.

A roaring, whooshing, buzzing sound split the air. Another message from Jack. *Run, Shad! Now!*

He didn't have to tell me twice. I activated Fastest Gun in the West and booked it.

The mastodon shrieked and roared, its trunk free of the anacondas. It reared up again just as the missile struck it.

I didn't turn back. I was too busy running. But I could hear the explosion. The blast wave struck me from behind. It knocked me forward, sending me rolling over and over.

I felt my bones crunch. My health was going down. System notification after system notification popped up. **[-5 HP]**, **[-5 HP]**, **[-10 HP]**.

I tried to grab a potion from my inventory, but my arms couldn't stay still long enough as I tumbled forward.

There was a cool touch on my skin. "Raise Your Spirits!" Sage cast her healing spell on me.

I felt myself come to a halt. I was face down in the dirt. Every part of my body hurt, but I wasn't dead yet.

Someone was at my side, turning me over. He shoved a potion bottle in my mouth and I drank. I felt health rush back into me and I blinked up at the sky. Grandpa was kneeling over me, looking worried. "You all right?"

"Ugh. Second time today, Jack's almost killed me," I protested.

"Yes, well." Grandpa made a face as the system announcer proclaimed, **[Victory! 5 of 5! Do you want to claim this point for your team? Yes / No.]**

Grandpa must have selected yes, because the prompt went away. "I made Jack tell me after he nearly killed me earlier," Grandpa said. "Turns out his ability is called Call in Air Strike, and it requires targeting one of your own party members who is within fifteen feet of the enemy."

I took a minute to take that in. "Nice of him to tell us that."

Grandpa shrugged. "I can see why he didn't. And it has saved our asses twice. But—"

"Yeah, he's not joining my team," I finished.

Grandpa helped me to my feet. I brushed off my duster and rejoined the others. "Well, can we kick out the Human League miners?" I asked.

"If we have actually claimed the zone, we should have interdict rights on this level now." Grandpa consulted the system. "Hmm," he said.

A system message displayed.

[Contested zone. This zone has been claimed by two different coalitions. Ownership will now be decided in a head-to-head showdown.]

I looked at Grandpa. He looked back at me, his jaw set. I could tell he was thinking the same thing I was. We hadn't asked for this. But there was no fucking way we were going to back down.

CHAPTER FORTY-ONE

CUTTHROAT NEGOTIATIONS

Veda sorted furiously through massive piles of data, unleashing her adjutant and its sorting scripts to peel back corporate veils, look under hoods, and figure out who was really behind all of this.

Everywhere she looked, the path led back to Sicaris Conglomeration, but they themselves were a blank slate. They had apparently never been involved in a Reality Engine exploit before. That was very suspicious.

While there were important galactic corporations who made their fortunes independently from the Reality Engines, mostly the big shipping lines and some of the independent computer systems dealers who had niche clienteles among those sapient beings who avoided Reality Engines for various reasons.

At least ninety percent of the galaxy used Reality Engines somewhere in their economic structure. A corporation that had never before been involved in a Reality Engine exploit, showing up with the kind of backing Sicaris must have in order to be sponsoring so many top-tier miners, was unheard of.

But all her inquiries came up against blank walls, unhelpful AIs, and obvious lies. She cleared her thoughts and took in her surroundings for a minute, looking around at the undisguised bare walls of her transport pod.

She let her fingers trail along the cool metal wall, feeling it. She had spent all day locked up in here, eating the same sort of rations she had provided her miners, banishing all of her hallucinated comforts, even cutting off the music so she could concentrate better. It was like she was in storage right now. Only her drive to uncover the truth kept her going.

A quick niggling thought caught her attention. She returned back to her systems and sent queries in a different direction, looking into the financial data her mother had sent a few days before.

Veda had done a cursory look at the time, mostly just to calculate which debts needed to be paid immediately and which could be staved off. Now she dug deeper.

The company holding her family's debt was just as much a dead-end as Sicaris. So she looked into the intervening transactions, seeing where they had acquired the debt.

Her family was smart. They would never have allowed one company to buy up all of their debt, not if they had a choice. Instead, she saw half a dozen different shells who had passed parts of her family's debt around between them before turning it all over to Sicaris. Four of the shell companies were registered in the Proxima Centauri system.

That was the closest core world to the solar system where she now resided. The planning for this Reality Engine exploit had all been done from the Proxima Centauri system, spearheaded by their largest corporations, the trio of Proxima Corp, Alabaster Sky, and ConSweGo Inc.

On a hunch, she dug deeper. Her algorithms peeled back a couple of layers and she found herself presented with a name, Molarch Sims. She queried and got a fairly basic biography. He was a dentarii, not one of the most common life-forms out there. They looked something like what the Earthlings would call elves. Grayish skin, pointed ears, a fringe of silvery hair coming off of their otherwise bald heads.

There wasn't much interesting about Sims, so she widened her search to look for any known associates, friends, relatives, lovers, rivals, anyone that might give her a clue to what was really going on.

And there it was. Veda stepped back, studying the information that hovered in the air in front of her, twisting gently to make sure it was always in her line of sight.

Molarch Sims's business associate was Ederick Voster, head of the Voster clan, the founders of Proxima Corp. One of the three great houses of Proxima Centauri.

What interest did they have in her family? No, that wasn't the question. Veda dismissed it. Her family wasn't important. They only mattered as a lever on her. Veda had two assets. Her license to operate in phase two and her mining team.

She was very fond of her miners and impressed with what they had done, but they weren't particularly unique, particularly special. Was it really them that warranted all the interest?

One link left. She searched for any connection between the Proxima house and Sicaris, and then she found it. One of the Proxima heirs had a spouse, his second demi-husband, who was a fifty-one percent stockholder in Sicaris Conglomeration.

It was buried several layers deep. None of the names connected. There weren't any major public stories, but the link was there. Proxima Corp owned Sicaris. Sicaris was making a major move here.

Why? The three great houses should be interested in phase three. None of them ever interfered in phase one—or did they?

Now Veda ran another search, and thousands of hits appeared on the galactic net, all from conspiracy theorist kooks talking about how the great houses pretended to be aloof, but used their puppets to manipulate Reality Engine exploits from day one. How they were shaping all of this to their own ends. How until the independent corporations like Veda's family banded together, they would be easy prey for the big guys.

All standard crackpot nonsense, or so she would have thought. Now Veda was staring at her own crackpot theory, that the great house of Proxima Centauri was using puppets and shells to bankrupt her family, all in order to get their hands on a single mission diving team, or on her phase two license.

If she ignored the connection to Proxima Centauri, then Sicaris looked like the perfect candidate to be shaping up for a phase two bid. If they didn't have a license—but that was nonsense. Surely, they could buy a license from anywhere. What if there was a reason why they didn't? What if they wanted everything kept quiet?

Buying a license on the open market would be noticed. The media would talk about it. A new player joining the scene of a Reality Engine exploit was worth a few news stories on the net. If, however, they were buying out the Tvedra corporation and all of its assets, which just happened to include a phase two license, well then . . .

As if they were listening to her thoughts, her system lit up, letting her know of an incoming call. There was no sender ID, but she didn't really need it. She accepted.

The ugly face of Tharnok, the local Sicaris representative, appeared. "Tvedra," he acknowledged with a bare nod of his head. "Are you interested in making a deal?"

She restrained her fury. "What sort of deal?" she asked.

"It seems your team is going up against one of ours in a contest over who will have the right to exploit a particular zone."

"What?" Veda checked and was horrified to find that he was telling the truth. She fired a quick message off to Shad and his grandfather, but didn't expect an immediate response. "Well . . . I have faith in them." It felt like a weak retort, but what could she do from up here?

"There's no need to let matters go so far," Tharnok said. "We could come to an arrangement."

"Feel free to call your attack off," Veda said.

The orc gave a sneer. "I was thinking more that I make you an offer you can live with."

"For my team? That's very thoughtful of you." Veda's eyes narrowed and she leaned in toward the hologram of the orc's head. "Cut the crap. We both know what you want. What's your actual offer for my phase two license?"

"Now, why do you think—"

"We don't have to have it publicized what it is you've bought. I'll take an additional bonus for my silence."

The orc's jaws worked. Finally, he said, "We cancel your family's debt and pay you a kill fee. I pay you personally double what you've spent to license your team, and I'll buy all of the supplies you've laid in for phase two at cost plus fifteen percent."

"What about the bribe for silence?"

The orc's left eyeball looked like it was about to pop out of his socket. "You little pipsqueak." He made a crunching gesture with one hand.

Veda smiled. She certainly had him in a bind. "I have an asset you want," she said. "It happens to be the only major asset my family has. You can't expect me to give it up so easily."

"You're the only person in your family able to use that license. We pay off their debt, and we make them a subsidiary of Proxima Corp. My employers are willing to offer you a job as a phase two team manager."

Veda had mostly been prodding to see how far Sicaris was willing to go. Now she took a step back, actually considering the offer.

The orc was right. The rest of her family didn't care about Reality Engine exploits or the Tvedra corporation. She was the only one left who wanted to follow in her father's footsteps. Everyone else would be happy to just be taken care of and kept out of storage.

If she made this deal, everyone in her family would applaud. She even had a career path going forward. Veda hesitated. She had intended to find out the current offer and then tell Sicaris to take a long, running jump into the depths of space. She hadn't really expected them to make her an offer that she wanted to accept.

"What about my team?" she asked. "Would I be managing them?"

"I can't make that promise," the orc said. Her respect for him went up. He was dealing straight with her. "But I can promise that we will keep the terms of the agreement that you made with them and not try to replace it. That gives them a significantly better contract than the one we offer the rest of our miners. I might even be able to swing them the deal we made with the human known as Major Waters. We have promised him that as long as his coalition makes production quotas, he'll be able to retire from the exploit at the start of phase two and be provided with a comfortable retirement away from here."

It was a tempting offer all around. "Can I have a minute to consult my team?" she asked.

"Consult the miners?" The orc sounded incredulous. "About what? We don't need their approval for this. Are you able to close this deal on your own or not, Tvedra?"

She had shown weakness to an opponent. He leaned in now, sniffing at her. "Did I estimate you incorrectly, Tvedra? Would you prefer merely to accept the same offer I'm making your family and become a dependent of Proxima Corporation? I thought you had the cutthroat instinct that phase two requires."

"I do," she said hurriedly, trying desperately to think. This was more than a fair offer. Her family got everything they needed. Her mining team would be fine. She could even stay in the game. She didn't like all of the subterfuge and the secrecy, but no doubt Proxima Corporation and the other phase three competitors played these sorts of games with each other all the time. She was just a pawn two levels down who couldn't see what was going on.

"Can I see the contract?" she asked, trying to buy time.

Pages of text and figures filled the air. She looked from one to the next, blindly. Why did this feel so wrong? Why did everything in her make her want to reject it? What gave her such faith in Team Twofeather? They were so desperate to win, all because she had set them on this path.

No, that wasn't it. Her team were driven for their own reasons. They wouldn't have accepted her offer otherwise.

And then Veda realized this was all for show. Sicaris—Proxima Corp—didn't need her, didn't need her team. Whatever offers they made, the corporate backers would find ways around. Pawns never got to impact the final rounds of play.

Veda cleared the contracts.

"Well?" the orc demanded.

"It's a very fair offer. Thank you," she said, "but I'm not willing to give up on my team just yet."

"This offer is not going to stand," the orc snarled. "If you walk away now, it won't be repeated."

"I understand. This isn't a bargaining technique. I just . . ." She shrugged. "I just feel like I need to stick with my team."

She ended the call before the orc could react, and then slumped to the floor of her little metal box, putting her face in her hands. She had turned down the best offer she could hope to get.

Veda pulled herself together. She didn't have much time left. At the end of the clash between her people and Sicaris's, she might not even have a team. But what she did have was a weapon. She had been watching the interactions between Shad and the opposing miners. The corporations thought of the miners as pawns to be played, not as individuals who had their own wants and desires.

Veda's father had always told her to remember that they were more than just their classes and skill sets. That they were people torn from their own lives with hopes and dreams of their own. And she had a weapon.

She set to work bundling up her message.

CHAPTER FORTY-TWO

WHEN COFFEE AND PISTOLS AT DAWN JUST ISN'T CUTTING IT

The system message hung in my face, blinking.

[This zone has been claimed by two different coalitions. Ownership will now be decided in a head-to-head showdown.]

I stared at the words as if I could make them make sense. "What does it mean, contested zone?" I asked. "What are we supposed to do? Find them and kill them? Force them back out of their portal?"

Grandpa shook himself. He looked around and seemed to make a snap decision. "Everyone back to the rest of the team," he said. "I want us all in one place with a portal behind us in case we have to retreat. Shad, keep your eyes on your mini-map and yell if you see anyone coming for us. Move out."

We headed off as a pack. I Inspected the newly deployed glowing portal in the middle of the crater of dirt and dead mastodon before I left. The portal read, **[Property of Misfits Guild. This portal cannot be reassigned while Misfits Guild maintains their claim to this zone.]**

That was reassuring, at least. We might have to face the Free Human League, but they wouldn't be able to sneak behind our lines and take our portal from us.

We made it back to our other team members in just over twenty minutes. Juana looked relieved as she obviously counted how many of us were present.

Grandpa told off some of the less experienced members to go sit by the portal and recover. He summoned the rest of us to a quick war council.

"What's this all mean?" Juana asked.

"They must have claimed their portal at the same time or close to it," I said. "Now we are going to have to compete to see who gets to keep it."

"Or we could just leave," she said quietly.

I met her eyes. "That's your mother talking," I said. "You know that won't solve anything. If we let them push us back here, your coalition is going to fall apart. They'll be prey for any larger group. Maybe it won't be the Free Human League. Maybe it'll be some other band of assholes. Or we take a stand here and now. We say we're not going to be pushed around."

I was still a little shaken by my encounter with the Navy ensign. I suspected he and many of the others who were doing Major Waters's bidding believed they were doing the right thing. That maybe they were even still serving our country.

Hell, maybe I'd have done the same in their spot. But I had Grandpa with me, and if I compared him and Major Waters, there was just no question. It didn't matter what the Pentagon brass said. They were half a billion miles away and not in control of a damn thing. They didn't know what was going on. We were the boots on the ground and I wasn't going to sit here and let Waters call the shots.

"So what's the plan?" Juana asked.

"The plan is that we send them a message," Grandpa said.

He made a chat group with me, Juana, and the three Blue Squad defectors. *You've seen the same message we did. This is contested now. We've got to sort this out between us or none of us get the prize.*

There was no immediate answer. "They couldn't have blocked us, can they?" Juana asked.

Grandpa shrugged. "Maybe, maybe not. I don't really know. But we'll wait and see what kind of response we get."

After a couple minutes, we got a reply from Warren Black, their Robin Hood miner. *What do you suggest?*

Grandpa: *Don't suppose you'll pack up your toys and go home?*

The reply was obscene.

Grandpa continued: *Neither will we. Says contested here, but the system hasn't set the rules of a contest, so I say we come up with something we can both live with.*

Another long pause before Warren replied. *You've got numbers, but we've got gear and skills. Most of your lot are a bunch of soft touches who've never even shot a gun in anger. All of ours are soldiers or fighters of some sort.*

Then you'll have an advantage no matter what, Grandpa said. *How about a three-versus-three duel? You pick your champions, I'll pick ours. We meet in neutral territory and have it out.*

Another long pause. *And negate our advantage, let you pick three who can actually fight? Not a chance.*

"Wait," I said aloud. I looked at Grandpa. "You know they want us on their side more than they want to kick the coalition out."

Grandpa nodded, looking wary. "So?"

"So we need to sweeten the deal."

I typed in chat, *It's because you're a coward, isn't it, Warren? You're afraid to face any of us. Well, how about we make it simpler? I'm calling you out. You and me. Leave everyone else out of this. Find a place. You pick your weapon, I pick mine. Guns at ten paces. If you win, my team—and me, if I'm still standing—joins the Free Human League. That's what your boss wants, isn't it?*

A long, long pause. Grandpa scowled at me. "I don't like what you're doing," he said.

"It's the only thing I can do," I retorted. "Look at me." I gestured at my outfit, my coat, my Gun Belt. "I've got a feeling this is right. Remember Veda said to lean into our classes? Remember how we've been rewarded for playing it right? This is the right way to do it. I know it is. I feel it is."

Juana grabbed my hand. "You can't do this. Warren has a sharpshooter ability and more health than you do. You'll be killed."

"No," I said. "I'll be fine."

I sent a quick message to Sage, who was off having a snack with the crafters. *Get any interesting mats off of Dwight and the other crafters. Make me whatever crazy bullets you can. Quick as you can.*

What are you doing?

No time. Just trust me.

Warren finally replied. *All right. I'll play your game. The big clearing south of the original entrance.*

I replied, *One hour. We'll see you then. No tricks. In fact, let's get this in writing.* I looked at Juana. "Can you help here?"

She pulled out her notary public stamp and considered it. "Usually both parties are here in person, but I don't see why not." She concentrated.

A system message popped up in front of me. [**High Noon Duel. Witnessed by Juana Lopez between Shadrach Williams and Warren Black. The aforementioned agree to meet in the location described below at the system time of 2:07 p.m. on November 1st. The rules of the duel are as follows . . .**] with a quick outline of our agreement.

I read through it and signaled my agreement. A moment later, so did Warren.

There was a whoosh, and the system popped up.

> [**Terms agreed for contest over ownership of this zone.**
> **If either party fails to report to the agreed location,**
> **the contest is forfeit. If either side attacks prematurely,**
> **they forfeit the contest on behalf of their team.**]

Grandpa was shaking his head. "Shouldn't have let you do it."

"You were going to agree to a three versus three," I said. "This way, nobody else gets hurt."

"And if you lose, we're all working for that asshole Waters."

"I'm not going to lose," I said.

"You'd better not," Juana told me.

We picked just five witnesses. Me, my team, and Juana. I didn't need an audience for this.

Sage presented me with her work; half a dozen different new rounds. I inspected them each and then cracked open the cylinder.

I manually ejected the rounds already there, then carefully loaded each chamber, making a note of which bullet was in which. I closed the action and primed the gun so the incendiary round was first up if I pulled the trigger.

Then we set off for the agreed meeting place. I took my time, enjoying the fresh air, the unspoiled smells, the way the Reality Engine made all of this seem so real.

Sage walked beside me. "I can't believe you challenged him to a duel," she scolded me. "You'd better not lose, Shad. I'll never forgive you."

"I'm not going to lose," I promised her. "I told you I'd take care of you, and I can't do that if I'm dead, and I certainly can't do that if we're all working with Waters."

That almost seemed to mollify her. "And you'd better use my new bullets," she said. "I worked really hard on those."

I laughed. "I'm hoping to only have to use one or two. Any more than that, and the duel goes way too long." The sun filtering down through the trees felt good. A couple of baby dinosaurs skittered across my path.

I forget who said that hanging concentrates the mind beautifully. He was right. I felt more alive right now than I ever had. Not that I planned to die. I would never have agreed to a duel that I didn't think I could win. I had the glimmerings of a plan, and at least twenty minutes to figure things out.

A message popped up the way one of the system boxes would. It said, [**Priority guild sponsor message. Contains visual data pack.**]

We all must have seen it because Grandpa and the others stopped dead. "What's this?"

"Go ahead and play," I said.

Veda's face appeared. She looked worried. She was moving back and forth, the camera in tight on her head so I couldn't see any of her surroundings.

"Team Twofeather, the organization behind your rivals' coalition is going to be making a move. You need to be careful. I know all about the duel. It's system-enforced, so they won't be able to break the rules but they may try to bend them. I've got something you might find useful."

She paused and her image disappeared, replaced with a head of an ugly green humanoid with teeth like a javelina and a big, red, spiky mohawk cut.

He spoke. "I might even be able to swing them the deal we made with the human known as Major Waters. We have promised him that as long as his coalition makes production quotas, he'll be able to retire from the exploit at the start of phase two and be provided with a comfortable retirement away from here."

The ugly guy's face disappeared and Veda came back. "That's from an official Sicaris Conglomeration representative. The system can authenticate that video clip for anyone who cares to ask. You might find it useful. This message costs a fortune, so I'll end it there."

She cut off. I looked at Grandpa. I felt like my jaw was hanging to the floor. Frank swore. "That no-good, dirty son of a bitch!"

Grandpa was scratching his head. "We can use this," he said quietly.

"Yep, we sure can. Let's keep moving," I said. "We don't want to be late to the duel."

"We've still got nearly half an hour," Sage exclaimed. "Shad, does that mean what I think it means? That Waters sold out everyone in his coalition for a cushy deal?"

"Probably," I said. "Fits, doesn't it?"

"It does," Grandpa said, and then he swore in Ute. I didn't know the words but it was easy to understand the gist of it.

"If we can show this to all of the Free Human League miners who are here, maybe they'll back down," Juana said. "I'm sending that clip to my mother right now. She'll know how to get it circulating."

"Hold off on that," Grandpa said sharply. "I mean, go ahead and send the clip, but ask her to sit on it until we're done here. I have some ideas for how we can be more effective with it once we've got this business taken care of." He looked coldly angry, like I'd only seen him once or twice before in his life. "You are about to meet your Little Bighorn, Major Waters," he said.

I noticed he had the obsidian axe in his hand now, the one that used to hang over our couch back home. He hadn't used it as a weapon, though Scalp ought to work with any axe he picked up.

"Okay, but we've still got to win this duel." I paused as an idea struck me. I called up my character sheet and my abilities list.

Way down at the bottom were the upgrades I had gotten when I picked Ride for the Brand, like the trait that gave me extra soul coins when in a long-standing party. There was one ability I had never before used, [**High Noon. In a 1-v-1 duel, you always shoot first.**]

Everything clicked into place.

CHAPTER FORTY-THREE

HIGH NOON

I checked my system clock. Still time before my duel. And now maybe I'd be able to get away without actually killing anyone. "How can we show that clip to anyone who comes with Black?"

"We can send the clip to anyone who accepts our communication request," Juana said.

"Want to stop for a minute? We need something better. We need something showy."

I sent a message to Veda.

You want what? she sent back instantly. She must have been waiting for a reply from us.

Just look in your databases and see if such a thing is even possible.

A minute later, *Found something. I'm sending the recipe to Sage.*

Sage jumped as though she had been poked. "What's this? Oh!" Her eyes went wide. "Oh, I think I understand." She hurried over to a large, waist-high boulder and pulled out the reloading press from her inventory. "Ah, I don't have any . . . Hang on. I'm sending a message to Dwight."

I kept an eye on my system clock. We would not be late for this showdown, no matter what.

Five minutes later, Dwight came puffing through the jungle. He had Bill and Bob with him. He hurried over to Sage and began pulling materials out of his inventory.

They bent their heads together for a couple minutes.

"Done!" Sage exclaimed. She came over to me and held out her hand. On it rested a single round of .44 Magnum.

I took it, drew my gun, opened the cylinder, and considered the other bullets I had there. Finally, I removed the poison fog round. If we did go into a fight, a bullet that left a ten-foot-wide cloud of mustard gas behind wasn't likely to win things for me. I slid it back into my Gun Belt, where I could Reload the round if it did become necessary.

Then I chambered Sage's special bullet and reset the cylinder so that it was the first one I would fire. We resumed our progress. My tension was rising again. My shoulder blades itched like someone had a knife aimed at my back.

I looked up at the branches spreading overhead to block the sky. "This isn't quite the right setting for it, but you don't suppose you could conjure up a tumbleweed to go blowing across my path at the appropriate moment?" I asked. There was no reply.

We reached the clearing near the entry point that we had come in through hours ago. Was it only hours? It felt like days. We hadn't slept. I had eaten a ration pack and one of Mama Grace's excellent cold sandwiches. The sun was still in the sky overhead. I hadn't noticed whether it moved at all. Maybe this whole level was always in daylight.

I checked my mini-map. There were eleven white dots waiting for us. They had only brought in two teams, so ten maximum, plus our three deserters, and I had helped kill two of them earlier. Eleven should be their whole team.

They were white, not red, probably because the system was enforcing us not to attack each other until the conclusion of the duel. Sage cast Cowgirl Cheer. "You're not supposed to interfere," I reminded her.

"I'm not interfering. I'm just cheering," she said brightly. "It doesn't affect them. They're not hostile." Then she patted my arm. "I believe in you, big brother."

I stepped out into the clearing. "Warren!" I shouted. "I'm calling you out!"

I am not shitting you. There was an actual twang of guitars, and then a tumbleweed rolled out between us as Warren stepped into the clearing. My hand hovered over my Gun Belt, even though I could use my Quick Draw skill. It just felt right.

"We don't have to do this," I shouted across the clearing.

"I can hear you just fine," Warren said.

I ignored him. I wasn't actually talking to him. "You can turn around and leave," I said. "Your coalition already has three or four farming levels. You don't need this one."

"The major gave orders," Warren said coldly.

That was the opening I had been waiting for. "The major's an asshole, and you know it. He's using all of you. He's cut a deal with the aliens to get out of here and leave the rest of you holding the bag."

I could hear noises in the brush as his allies muttered amongst themselves. They had spread out in a half circle. I knew that they had something up their sleeves. That was fine. So did I. Until the conclusion of the duel, they couldn't attack anyone on my team without losing the contest. Nobody here was going to risk that.

"Stop talking and get to it," Warren snapped. He unslung his bow from the scabbard where he carried it on his back. It was a modern compound bow about four feet tall, made of metal with a complicated set of strings and pulleys.

He had a quiver at his side. I could see a dozen different colored fletchings on the arrows, and guessed he had multiple different sorts of spells at his beck and call, just like I did.

I cast High Noon. The guitar twanged again.

Warren grabbed an arrow out of his quiver. He nocked it to his bow and pulled back the string. His arms shook. "What the hell have you done to me?" he shouted.

I drew my gun the old slow way. I smiled. "Just drawing out the narrative tension, making sure all eyes are on me," I said. I raised my gun and I fired. Then I darted sideways, fast as I could, toward a tree.

His arrow whizzed from his bow, soaring past where I had been. I hoped my teammates were staying clear. I didn't want them caught in the crossfire.

In the middle of the clearing, where I had been standing, an enormous green face appeared and began speaking loud enough that anyone for a hundred feet around could hear.

The Sicaris representative gave his spiel, about the deal they'd made with Waters. There was a system-authenticated tag over his head, a benefit of the spell that was woven into the special round Sage had made me. It was called The Truth Hurts and it was incredibly expensive to make, having required multiple different fancy ingredients as well as the sacrifice of an ancient film camera that we'd had in our inventory. I doubted we'd be able to make another one anytime soon, but we didn't need to.

"We weren't lying, Warren!" I yelled from behind my tree. I aimed, targeting him. I popped open the cylinder of my .44 and rotated it carefully two chambers to the left before closing it again. I wanted to give him a chance to respond, so I fired Trick Shot with my tangled web bullet in the barrel.

That one had taken silk from a giant arachnid one of my new team members had farmed a week ago. It seemed really useful, so we might have to go locate some big spiders ourselves once we were done here. Sage would probably protest. Sage hated spiders.

The net came down, pinning Warren in place. "Well?"

"Well what?" came the furious response. "Once I'm done with you, I'll go and hand him his ass along with my resignation."

"Call off the duel!" I bellowed. I got a quick message from Jerome, the Freight Train who had left our coalition along with Warren. *Can we talk about this? I only did what the major asked because I thought he was a patriot. Some of the others say the same thing.*

Grandpa replied, *If you mean it, come on over to our side of the clearing and we'll talk. Any funny business and you get put down. Tell the others to leave Free Human League right away so we know they mean it.*

I concentrated on Warren. He sawed away at my webs with a knife. I ought to shoot him again while he was still webbed, but it felt like killing in cold blood.

That was when Spider Queen Linsey came running out into the middle of the clearing. She threw her arms around Warren. "We have to listen to them," she said. "Please, Warren, listen. I told you what Marjorie said before, and you said she must have misunderstood what Waters meant. Well, she didn't. Waters is scum. He's been using all of us and I'm tired of it."

Warren struggled to free himself. Linsey had the same last name, Black. I hadn't asked before whether they were husband and wife or brother and sister, but the way she was looking at him, I was guessing she was his wife.

Of course, now I couldn't fire at him without putting her in danger. I waited as Trick Shot came back off cooldown. I'd be able to fire. I had a piercing round that would likely knock him on his ass and give me a chance to pour lead into him. I held off.

He got his arms free and reached for his bow. Linsey pushed it aside. "We need to listen," she said.

"They'll never accept us after we betrayed them," Warren grumbled.

"We don't need to accept you," I called. "We just don't need to be enemies. There's more choices than just us or Waters. We've been too focused on him, but the Free Human League is what? Maybe three thousand people by now and my coalition has sixty? There's still six million other humans out there forming alliances, making teams, figuring out how to beat the system. We share a common enemy, Warren, and it's not Waters."

I paused, and he seemed to be listening, so I went on.

"It's the scumbags who brought us here, who threw us into this system, and are making money if we live, making money if we die, using us as pawns in some game we don't understand. Well, I'm telling you this. They made a mistake when they came to Earth. They made a mistake when they took a whole bunch of America's veterans and active duty. And not just America's. We've got people out there who've served in probably every army that exists on Earth. We're good at fighting. We just have to stop killing each other and start taking the fight where it belongs."

Warren sagged to the ground. His bow dropped away from loose fingers. "Just how do you plan to do that?" he asked.

"To start, I'm gonna get rid of Waters and any other quisling collaborator. Sure, we're forced to work with the aliens, but we're not forced to work *like* them. Anyone who's taking advantage of other miners, anyone who's trying to get ahead by pushing everybody else down, they're gonna answer to me."

I stopped because I suddenly realized just how ridiculous I sounded. Here I was, one of six million people. I wasn't anybody important. I was just a damn lieutenant.

But I had people who counted on me, people who needed me. Sage, Grandpa, Juana, the rest of the coalition, and people like Ensign Wajowski, who was just doing the best he could, not knowing his boss was an asshole.

"Okay, it's gonna take more than just me," I said. "But we've all got to start somewhere, right?"

Warren looked up.

His wife squeezed his shoulder. "Please, honey."

He sighed. "You've got another copy of that clip? One we can show everyone else?"

Grandpa stepped forward into the clearing between me and Warren. "We do," he said, "and I've got some ideas for how to use it, if you're willing to listen."

Warren looked him up and down. "I might be," he said. "Don't suppose you know where any of the other folk that the brass named as part of our chain of command ended up?"

Grandpa shook his head. "Nope. But you know what I do have?" From his inventory, he pulled out a clean, well-pressed dress uniform jacket that I hadn't even known he had. It must have been in one of the drawers in his bedroom.

He saw me looking and snorted. "What? I got it out so I'd have something decent to be buried in. Your abuela never let me wear it when I was alive, but there's nothing she can say about it if it was to my funeral, not when she's been dead for these last three years." Grandpa put on the jacket and cracked a grin. "Used to amuse me to think she'd have to share a grave with my uniform after all the fuss she made about it after we got married."

Warren came up straight, staring at Grandpa. "You're an officer too?"

The other Free Human miners emerged from the brush.

Ensign Wajowski looked at Grandpa. His eyes widened. He pointed. "Is that a Bronze Star, sir?" He stood very straight and saluted. "I mean, major, sir?"

Grandpa gave me a sidelong smile. "I think it's time we go pay General Custer a visit, hmm?" he said. "And this time, let him know the Indians are in the US Army, too."

It wasn't quite that easy, of course, even once we had gotten that video clip some good play.

Mama Grace hosted a free street barbecue and made sure all the Free Human League members got invitations. Then we played the clip every couple minutes until they had gotten the point.

Grandpa stood around in his uniform jacket and answered questions. He wasn't trying to put himself in charge. He just answered questions, telling everyone that as far as he was concerned, Waters had defected in his duty and that no one had any obligation to him.

Waters still had a core following. There were other military folk past and present who stood by him because he had been named by the brass. We had a search going for the other officers Earth's transmission had mentioned, but no luck yet.

We had also made outreaches to the other army cadres that were beginning to form. There was a British Empire alliance with mixed Canadian, Australian, and New Zealand service members. They had allied with a group of former Indian Army with Gurkhas serving as middlemen between the two groups, and they were willing to talk with us, once we made it clear we weren't with Waters. Apparently, they'd run into him already.

There was a sizable Chinese army contingent, but while they were willing to talk, they weren't yet interested in cooperation.

That was okay. Talking was good. Anything was better than fighting over resources when we didn't need to. Every time I looked at my in-progress achievements list and saw that [**Kill opposed miners: 5/10**], it filled me with horror and shame. I was glad I had managed to talk Warren out of making me kill him.

Over the next couple of weeks, the Misfits Guild swelled in numbers. We still made everyone come into the farming zone and get at least a little hands-on experience, but we soon had hundreds of members who *wanted* to kill dinosaurs and other monsters, and the crafters were able to take a step back. We were even talking about expanding to a second zone.

My team hadn't been able to find time to run any missions but that was okay. Helping get the guild up and running was important. Still, after two weeks of almost vacation, I was getting antsy to do something.

We were in Mama Grace's back room strategizing over a late lunch when Frank asked to speak to us privately. We stepped out into the street and found a quiet corner between two buildings.

"What is it?" Grandpa asked.

"Uh, well," Frank looked at his feet. He sketched a line in the dirt. "It's like this. I know you're gearing up to run another mission but . . . All right, I'll just say it. I want off the team."

I stared at him. "What?"

"I want to stay in the guild," he said hurriedly. "The thing is, the last couple weeks, helping out with the farming levels, protecting the crafters while they did their work, teaching people how to take care of themselves, that's me. That's who I am. I felt like I had my old job back. I'm helping people. I'm keeping everyone safe. Those missions . . . I'm not like you three." He even encompassed Sage with his gesture. "I don't want to shoot zombies or take on Al Capone's goons."

"You think we do?" I protested.

"Hell, of course you do!" Frank exclaimed. "And don't tell me you don't. You've looked mopey for the last four days because you've only been killing dinosaurs in nice, safe, controlled settings. You haven't risked your life, and that's starting to get to you. I don't know what's wrong with you people. It's like you were made for this kind of nonsense. I'm glad for you. You're going to go far. You'll help out Veda, and she's earned it. She stuck her neck out for us. But not with me."

Frank was right. He fit in better as part of the farming teams. "It'll be dangerous to be down a man," I commented.

"There's a couple of two-member teams that we might talk to," Grandpa said.

Sage threw her arms around Frank. "Thank you," she said. "Thank you for everything, Deputy Young."

He ruffled her hair. "Aw, I'm not going anywhere. We'll still see each other over dinner at the restaurant. We'll just have to say hi in chat."

I offered him my hand. "See you 'round the galaxy."

ABOUT THE AUTHOR

M. Talon is the pseudonym of the authors of Not My First (Space?) Rodeo, a sci-fi LitRPG originally released on Royal Road. They are a married couple who live and write in northern Nevada. They also like to go on off-road adventures with their kids and buy really nice hats.